By J. J. McAvoy

Standalone Novels
Sugar Baby Beautiful
That Thing Between Eli and Gwen
Malachi and I
Never Let Me Go

The Du Bells
Aphrodite and the Duke
Verity and the Forbidden Suitor
Hathor and the Prince

The Prince's Bride
The Prince's Bride: Part 1
The Prince's Bride: Part 2
The Prince's Bride: Beginning Forever

Ruthless People
Ruthless People
The Untouchables
American Savages
A Bloody Kingdom
Prequel: Declan + Coraline

Children of Vice
Children of Vice
Children of Ambition
Children of Redemption
Vicious Minds

Black Rainbow
Black Rainbow
Rainbows Ever After

A Vampire's Romance
My Midnight Moonlight Valentine
My Sunrise Sunset Paramour

Child Star
Child Star: Part 1
Child Star: Part 2
Child Star: Part 3

Hathor *and* the Prince

Hathor *and* the Prince

A Novel

J. J. McAvoy

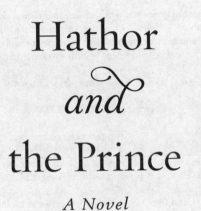

Dell | New York

Hathor and the Prince is a work of fiction. Names, characters, places, and incidents are either the products of the author's imagination or are used fictitiously. Any resemblance to actual persons, living or dead, events, or locales is entirely coincidental.

A Dell Trade Paperback Original

Copyright © 2024 by J. J. McAvoy

All rights reserved.

Published in the United States by Dell, an imprint of Random House, a division of Penguin Random House LLC, New York.

DELL and the D colophon are registered trademarks of Penguin Random House LLC.

LIBRARY OF CONGRESS CATALOGING-IN-PUBLICATION DATA
Names: McAvoy, J. J., author.
Title: Hathor and the prince / J. J. McAvoy.
Description: New York: Dell Books, 2024. | Series: The Du Bells; 3 |
Identifiers: LCCN 2023044324 (print) | LCCN 2023044325 (ebook) |
ISBN 9780593500088 (trade paperback) |
ISBN 9780593500095 (ebook)
Subjects: LCGFT: Romance fiction. | Novels.
Classification: LCC PR9199.4.M386 H38 2024 (print) |
LCC PR9199.4.M386 (ebook) | DDC 813/.6—dc23/eng/20231002
LC record available at https://lccn.loc.gov/2023044324
LC ebook record available at https://lccn.loc.gov/2023044325

Printed in the United States of America on acid-free paper

randomhousebooks.com

2 4 6 8 9 7 5 3 1

Book design by Virginia Norey
Damask art: garrykillian/stock.adobe.com

Dedicated to
the lovers of love.
May this world never
turn your heart to bitterness.

Beloved Reader,

This is a Regency romance involving nobility and high society, in which there are Black people. This is fiction, and anything is possible here. I truly hope you enjoy it.

Sincerely,
Your Author

Hathor *and* the Prince

I

Hathor

My name is Hathor Du Bell.

Not Heather, but Ha-ther. However, not a soul exists outside of my family and our servants who pronounces my name properly, so my papa instructed that I correct people each and every time, for he was quite proud of my name—Hathor, the Egyptian goddess of the sky, women, and love. As a child, I treasured nothing more than to listen to his tales of my ancient namesake. As an adult—well, as much of an adult as I was permitted to be—I felt quite goaded by the name, for my dear papa had left out one critical fact, which I realized on my own. The goddess Hathor was, and forever will be, in the shadow of the goddess Isis, and the Greek counterpart for Isis is Aphrodite—the name my papa bestowed upon my elder sister. Thus, I always found myself overflowing with a childish desire to outshine her.

It was a war I declared of my own volition.

A war my sister did not even acknowledge, yet she defeated me in every battle. My sister was supremely victorious whether it was in music, dancing, reading, languages . . . beauty. Just like her ancient namesake, Aphrodite, was the ideal, the very measure of accomplishment. It had been two years, one month, two weeks, one day, and five hours since she had become known as Her Grace, the Duchess of Everely. Her greatest triumph. And though I was truly happy for her, there existed in me a deep hurt, an unattended wound somewhere within that left me in anguish. I knew not where this wound was, but I was sure of my attacker.

It was Aphrodite.

Even now, despite the distance between us, I felt her sword striking once more.

"Pregnant!" my mama, Lady Deanna Du Bell, the Marchioness of Monthermer, all but proclaimed to us as she rushed into the study. "Aphrodite is pregnant!"

"Truly? How wonderful!" My father grinned, tossing his book onto the table in haste to see the letter my mother waved like a royal decree before us. If anyone knew anything about my father, Lord Charles Du Bell, the Marquess of Monthermer, it was that he did not toss books lightly.

"Yes, she is rather far along. She wished not to say anything until she was very well sure. Now that she is, she apologizes for not being able to make it this summer but assures us that despite persistent exhaustion and an insatiable appetite for bread-and-butter pudding, she is in good health." My mother handed the letter to him, even though she had told him all its contents.

The grin on my father's white face was so wide I could count every wrinkle. "If I remember correctly, you were similarly afflicted while pregnant with Damon. The whole estate smelled like a bakery for weeks."

"Did someone say my name?" Damon questioned as he entered the study, carrying in his arms a small girl, not yet two, with light brown skin and the curliest brown hair. Immediately upon seeing her, my mother rushed to take her into her arms.

"Mini, you are going to be a big cousin soon." My mother kissed her cheek. The girl's name was actually Minerva, Minerva Du Bell, as Damon had sought to keep Father's tradition of styling all daughters after goddesses. However, everyone had taken to calling her Mini, a nickname bestowed by none other than our youngest sister, Abena, who was most glad to have someone younger to order around now. Mini, though, had no clue what Mother rambled to her.

"Truly?" Damon smiled the same as our father as he stood next to him to see the letter. Over the years, I had noticed that while Damon looked completely like our mother, he had inherited all of our father's personality traits—except book reading. Mother's skin was a warm brown, just like Damon's, and their eyes were the same shade of dark brown. "What grand news. I will write to Evander to congratulate him. If the boy is born before Christmas, maybe we will spend the new year with them at Everely since they cannot make it this summer."

"The boy?" My father chuckled. "How are you so certain the child will be a boy?"

"Did you not say Mother was similar when pregnant with me? Odite always does everything in Mother's image. Besides, Evander has a daughter already, so I'm sure a boy will supply some comfort," Damon explained.

"Strange that you provided no such comfort with your birth, only greater concern." My father chuckled, causing Damon to roll his eyes, which then fell upon me as I sat in the corner of the room behind my easel.

"Hathor? I did not even realize you were in here," Damon said.

"Yes, I noticed. Mama did not either," I replied as I sketched the book stacks behind them to the best of my ability.

"I very well did notice you, my dear. I was merely waiting for you to offer your excitement at this joyous news. Why are you just sitting there?" my mother said as she bounced Mini in her arms. And they all looked at me, waiting.

I did not wish to come across as cruel or petty, but for some reason, I could not muster the emotions they sought from me.

"I am quite happy for Odite, Mama," I said, setting my pencil down and rising to my feet. It was the truth, though not entirely. "I was only pondering why it has taken so long for her to become pregnant. I thought all one needed was a husband to have a child. Though I am not exactly sure what the process is—"

"I should go tell Silva the news. Come, Mini, let's find your mama," Damon quickly cut in, lifting his daughter out of our mother's arms, kissing both of Minerva's cheeks, and making the little girl giggle.

"And I am expected by the men to make inspections of the grounds. Hopefully, we will have more than enough to hunt and keep our guests occupied," my father said, kissing Mother's cheek first before coming to give me a slight hug. "You must show me your work later, my dear girl. Hopefully, your depiction of me is benevolent since your mother still refuses to tell me where to find the fountain of youth she drinks from."

"Clearly, your books have given way to gross imagination," my mother replied, and he offered a wink before quickly going on his way, seeking to escape this conversation, as all men desired to do. I never understood why until last spring, when Verity—Evander's younger sister and my second mortal enemy—had offered the truth about the relations between men and women, now that she was married herself.

It was so . . . vulgar that I believed her to be playing some sort of trick on me, but I could not ask or speak of it to anyone else. And the way everyone acted when I even slightly mentioned the topic seemed to prove her words true, for if it was not as uncouth as it seemed, why shy away from speaking on the matter?

"They have fled," I said, looking at my mother.

"As you intended them to."

"I merely wished—"

"Hathor, do not think me the fool simply because I do not say what I know," she stated and stepped up, cupping my cheeks. "Whatever you think you've learned from Verity will be further explained by a husband of your very own."

"Should one ever manifest," I muttered, stepping out of her grasp, and returning to my easel. "London provided no such person . . . again. I dare say, I met the very worst men, and now we must try my luck here before the end of the season."

"By whose fault is that?" She followed after me. "You had three perfectly suitable gentlemen call upon you, all of whom you staunchly rejected. I believed you would grow up and rid yourself of this fanciful idea of becoming a duchess—"

"I have!" Mainly because there were no more dukes to be found in the land; I had checked—twice. And because it had come to my attention, by an unsightly character, that my reputation had taken a slight blow of late. Just thinking of what that horrid person said enraged me once more. To think such awful men lurked about our ton was dreadful.

"Then what was wrong with Lord Galbert?" My mother's voice pulled me from my thoughts.

"He is a known entomologist, and I can barely stand the sight of a ladybug."

"That was no reason to deny him outright. Opposites often find attraction to each other."

"I have no desire to attract anything or anyone that attracts insects, Mama. I could not even feign the slightest interest and would find myself running from him in terror if one of those creatures was still upon his person."

"What of Lord Morrison? He was a nice man—"

"He laughed when Father called me a rather proficient artist during dinner."

"It was nothing more than a nervous chuckle, Hathor."

"It felt like condescension." I did not have very many talents as it was, and he seemed completely unimpressed by me.

"And Mr. Bennett? What was his great fault, then? I noticed he took an abundance of interest in your art and complimented you profusely."

I did not wish to answer as I picked up my canvas.

"Well?"

"Mama, must I say?"

"Say what? You never explained why you all but ran him from our home."

"He was ugly!"

"Hathor!"

"What? I felt like I was going mad as you all pretended not to notice the horrid condition of his face! The only person who dared say anything was Abena, and you locked her away in her room for it."

"Hathor, will you seek to find fault in everyone? You give no one a chance, and as such, I fear for your reputation. You will not find all you want in a man."

"Aphrodite did. Why is it possible for her and not me? Why is she always the fortunate one?"

"Do you not think your sister suffered? Were you not there at her door when she wept? Do you believe these last two years have been easy for her at Everely?"

"Yet it always works out for her somehow, Mother. She always gets what she wants in the end. Meanwhile, I am told to settle for gentlemen she would never have even considered. I know I am not a famed beauty, as she is, or as beloved by the queen or by you, Father, or even Damon as she is, but at the very least, I should measure in a husband." I muttered the last part looking down at my canvas. I had drawn my father's nose too big.

"When you speak like this, Hathor, it hurts my heart deeply, for it is utter lies. You know it. You are a great beauty and very well loved by us all."

I sighed. "I do know it, Mama. I never said I was not beautiful, nor did I say you all did not love me. I—"

"You merely keep comparing yourself to your sister. And it is unfair to you, her, and the rest of us. She is living her life, and you ought to do the same. That starts by measuring suitors not by Aphrodite's standards but by yours. The most important thing is that they bring comfort to you."

"I am trying, but they are all . . . wrong. Lord Galbert, Lord Morrison, and Mr. Bennett stirred nothing in me."

"Did you even give them a chance? Love does not happen overnight. Like your art, it comes stroke by stroke and never looks perfect until completed. If you give up each time a mere line is drawn, nothing ever comes of it, my dear."

I sighed, and my shoulders dropped. "I did not think this would be so hard, Mama. I've tried so much, but it has been two years since my debut and yet—"

"One of your greatest strengths is your tenacity, so do not let it falter now. Especially when I have worked so hard planning these festivities."

The London season was almost over. My mother thought a change of scenery and fewer distractions within the city would tilt the odds in my favor. So she had selectively invited the very best of society to be hosted for a weeklong gathering upon our estate, Belclere Castle. It was rare for us to hold such gatherings, as my father believed London was for entertainment and the castle was for rest. Seldomly was anyone welcome but distant relatives and the royal family, though the latter had not been here since my birth.

Nevertheless, the queen had spoken so highly of her stay here that many often sought an invitation. Consequently, not one person had failed to send word of their attendance. Everyone would be here tomorrow. Then I would have a little more than a week to find my husband and return to London triumphantly to conclude the season at the queen's yearly finale ball, before traveling contentedly into my future on some other grand estate.

"Yes, Mama, your plans are perfect but obvious, so much so that I fear what shall be said if I do not find anyone still." Part of me was grateful she put such effort in for me, but another part felt embarrassed that the exertion was needed.

"Fears I also share since you are so reluctant to rid yourself of this pitiful disposition," Mother said as there was a knock at the door. "Enter."

Ingrid, my mother's right hand and head housekeeper—whose dark hair seemed to grow grayer with each passing day—entered. "Your Ladyship, a letter from Lady Verity for Lady Hathor has arrived."

"Oh, good. Since she and Aphrodite managed to wed in the same year, it may also be an announcement of her pregnancy. Let it rain children from on high." Just when I thought my mood could not be any more sullen. I sat back down as my mother read over the letter, waiting for my torment and carefully examining her face for any hint of what I should ready myself to hear. Her brown eyes looked over the words slowly, giving away nothing before she handed the letter to me.

"Read it for yourself and see how much others care for you since you so clearly need a reminder," she replied before leaning in and kissing my head. "I shall go check over the lists for our guests. Join me once you finish."

I nodded, waiting as she and Ingrid stepped out of the study, leaving me staring down at the letter with a date from eight days ago. Inhaling till my chest puffed and then exhaling slowly, I flipped it open and began to read.

June 16, 1815

Dearest Hathor,

I can only imagine the sulk upon you at receiving this message from me, the greatest of all traitors, as you so often proclaim. I am unsure when you shall forgive me for my treacherous act of falling in love, though I commend you on your unwavering ability to hold a grudge. I also thank you for the lovely painting you created of Theodore and me for his birthday. He and I were so incredibly moved by it that it now hangs above the fireplace in our drawing room at Glassden.

I greatly wished to have kept you company this season, but Theodore and his father have found it impossible to leave Cheshire. I will not dampen your spirits with the details, as they have done mine. Instead, I shall wish hope upon you. I hope that before the year is done, you will also find someone who makes you smile even on the hardest of days. I believe one of love's greatest powers is the courage to persevere, not for ourselves but for others. I will not speak on any of its other powers, for I know my godmother would have read this as well, and I fear another one of her stern talks with me. Besides, it is much more fun to discover them on your own.

I pray this letter finds you in good health, as I am, Hathor.

Your most unrelated sister,
Verity

"For a person who once proclaimed to know so little of love, you now speak rather confidently on the matter." I spoke to the letter as if she were able to hear my reply. Glancing over the words once more, I could not help the smallest of smiles that appeared across my lips. I could see the happiness in her words, despite whatever troubles were occurring. The revelation of her relationship with Sir—then Dr.—Darrington left me nearly too shocked to speak. I had questioned why Mother even supported the match; they were so clearly unsuited. The answer came at their wedding, for never had I seen Verity grin so wide or heard her laugh so loud.

The melancholy cloud that seemed to hover over her and her life had burst. She'd been transformed, shining like the sun was always upon her. I believed that was the moment she became my second-worst enemy. Before Verity, I had only ever been envious of my sister Aphrodite. It was the most unwelcome feeling, and I would not rest until I rid myself of it, but the only way to do so was to find a husband. And a husband I would find, even if I had to roam the countryside on horseback!

Folding the letter and leaving my painting, I marched out of the study, the butlers and maids shifting out of my path as they went on their way to prepare the rooms for our guests. I did not run, as that would have been improper, but I hastily made my way into the drawing room, where my mother stood in the center of several servants, like a general organizing their troops for battle.

"I have regained my wits and spirits, Mama!"

"Good. Do try to hold on to them, for I have just been informed the queen is coming."

"The queen? As in *the queen*?" I gasped out. "Whatever for? But all her sons are . . . are . . ."

"Do not finish that sentence!" She snapped at me and I

closed my mouth quickly. "Her Majesty is coming I presume to make an introduction of her nephew, Prince Wilhelm Augustus Karl von Edward of Malrovia."

She lifted the letter in her hand, the one with the royal seal, for me to read.

But even upon seeing it I still could not believe it. I took the paper and read it not once but twice before glancing up at her, a grin spreading across my face the way fire did across leaves.

"Mama!"

"Contain yourself—"

"Ah!" I screamed and jumped up and down, holding the letter to my chest.

"Hathor!" She hollered at me and I quickly ceased all movements but still could not rid myself of my smile.

"Mama, I very well may become a princess." That was much *much* greater than a duchess!

"Hathor, I beg of you, please do not lose your head or forget that there will be a great number of other ladies in attendance who will also seek his attentions."

"Very true, Mama, and I would worry if not for the fact that the queen is coming herself. Do you not see what that means?" I said, taking a deep breath. I read the letter for a third time. "She wishes to introduce him to us, to me, before any other suitors may have my hand. If not, she would simply wait for her end of the season ball to present him to society."

I could not believe it. This was perfect! This solved everything!

"You are losing yourself, my dear," she said, taking the letter back from my hands. "Royals are very . . . complex. We know nothing of this prince or the queen's intentions. For her to come out into society surely means there is something altogether not right. Do not, and I mean *do not*, put much faith in this. It very well could come to nothing."

"Mama, is it so much to simply allow me to hope? Must you crush my spirits so bitterly?" I sighed, heavily frowning at her. Just like that my excitement was gone. When she opened her mouth to speak I shook my head. "Never mind, I am tired, please excuse me."

I did not wait to hear her before taking my leave. I paused until the doors closed, grabbed on to the sides of my dress to lift it in order to run as fast as I could to my father's library.

Grinning wide, I couldn't wait to learn all about this kingdom I was about to marry into. I could see it written now . . .

Princess Hathor Du Bell of Malrovia!

Oh splendid! Most splendid!

Take that, Aphrodite!

2

Hathor

"What are you doing?" Abena said as she burst into my room, dressed in her nightshirt, her light brown curly hair not wrapped for bed but a tangled mess.

"Nothing. Now go away," I replied as I scanned the work on my bed. She did not go away. Instead, she rushed, and I quickly grabbed the papers before she could make a mess of them. "Abena, I am in no mood for your antics tonight as I am very busy trying to set the course of my life."

"You've been doing that forever! Maybe you need help!" she stated as she jumped onto the bed, and I fought the urge to kick her right off the edge. But as I was now the eldest sister in the house, it was my duty to be mature.

"Even if I did, which I don't, you are a child, so you are no help to me at this moment, Abena, merely an annoyance," I replied, sitting up against my pillows.

"I am not a child. I am twelve years old now," she said as she continued to jump like a child upon my bed. "I know a great many things."

"Yes, you know a great deal about food, getting Mother to call for wine, and sneaking around upon the grounds. I look to do none of those things, and as such, your help is not required. Please go away now, Abena." Still she did not listen and instead grabbed one of the pages of my notes from me so quickly that I could not stop her. "Abena!"

"Prince Wilhelm, age twenty-four—"

Taking the pillow, I smacked her so hard she nearly fell off the bed, and instead of taking it as a warning, the mad little squirrel jumped back up on her feet and grabbed my other pillow in defense, a wide grin on her face.

"Abena, no I—"

She smacked me right across my head, the papers in my hands flying everywhere. "Papa says violence brings forth further violence, so you deserve that!"

"I will show you violence, you little bug!" I hollered, scrambling to get onto my feet as she continued to hit me. Taking the pillow, I smacked her repeatedly, feathers pouring out in every direction until I hit her with such force that she slipped onto the floor with a large thud. Eyes wide, I dropped the weapon in my hands to check on her. "Abena, are you all right—"

The words were shoved back down my throat as her pillow hit my face dead on, the pain upon my nose and lips making my eyes water.

"You lose!" She stuck her tongue out at me, now back on her feet.

"What you're about to lose is your hair!" I reached for her, but she ran, so I ran after her. She'd just about made it to the doors when they were wrenched open. I feared it was our mother, but it was only Ingrid, still wearing her day clothes. She held a candle as she glared down at us, something she only ever did in our mother's stead by her permission, which meant Mother was quite aware of what was occurring but did not have the energy to come down and lecture us herself.

"My ladies, your mother has asked that I deliver this message," she said, and both Abena and I stood still, waiting. "She says if she ventures down and finds even one thing out of place in either of your rooms, she will see to it that neither of you sees the light of day till you are her age. And that would be most unfortunate for you, Lady Hathor, as all activities becoming of a lady occur during the day."

"It's not unfortunate for me—"

Quickly, I wrapped my hand over Abena's lips, pulling her back to my chest. "Thank you, Mrs. Collins. We shall tidy up before going to bed."

Ingrid nodded before turning from my door and walking down the hall as quietly as a ghost. I stuck my head out to watch when I felt a wetness on the inside of my hand. Then, releasing the wild child, I checked to see that she had indeed licked me. "Honestly, are you a dog, Abena?"

"If it gets me out of cleaning. Woof!" she said and took off running.

I gritted my teeth and stomped my foot to stop myself from yelling at her and truly bringing the ire of Mother upon myself. Turning to enter my room, I froze at the sight of the chaos before me: papers, feathers, and bedding all scattered across the floor—that little evil bug.

"Do you need help?"

I startled to see Devana behind me, wearing a dressing gown, her long, curly blonde hair in a single braid to the side of her head. In one hand she held a candle and in the other a bucket. Of all of us, she'd taken the most after Father, including his height, for despite the four years between us, she was nearly taller than me now. In fact, she had blossomed so much in the last two years that one would think we were the same age.

"Hathor?" she called, tilting her head to the side. "Come, let's start so you may rest and have energy for the morning."

"You have been rather helpful of late, Devana, when you

need not be," I said as I followed her inside, closing the door and eyeing her carefully. Devana was often in her own little world, just her and her piano. Abena and I could be tearing down the castle, and Devana would continue playing as if she had been hired by the queen for a concerto. It wasn't that she was uncaring. Instead, she preferred to mind her own business quietly. But lately, she'd been hovering about Mama and me, and now, before bed, she'd come ready to pick up pillow feathers. That was very unlike her. "What is going on with you?"

"Nothing. I merely wish to help my older sister. Why are you so suspicious of kindness?" she said, picking the white feathers one by one off the center of my bed, but in doing so, she lifted one of my papers.

"Don't look!" I rushed to her, taking the sheet from her hand, but it was too late. Sadly, she was just as fast a reader as Aphrodite.

"Are these the notes you've collected about the prince?" she asked, staring back with her bright blue eyes.

"You've heard of him?"

"The entire castle heard of him the moment you screamed in glee," she teased, and I glared at her.

"I did not scream."

"Squealed then?"

I tried not to laugh. "I might have done that slightly."

She giggled. "Mama has turned the whole castle over to make space for the queen. I still cannot believe she is coming or that you seek to marry a prince."

"You do not think it is possible for me either?" Did no one have faith in my dreams?

"I think anything is possible for you, sister," she replied, taking a seat on my bed and causing it to bounce slightly.

"Good, as you ought to." I nodded, moving to take a seat

beside her. "Now, did you come only to tease or is there something the matter?"

"I came merely to see you because I was interested."

"Interested? In what?"

"All of it. How to court, how to . . . garner attention."

"Since when do you care for anything beyond the piano?"

"I am no longer a child, Hathor, but a lady of sixteen. In two years, Mama will bring me into society as well. So, is this not the time to begin taking an interest?" she asked, and a suspicious feeling crept upon me. I did not know much about others, but I knew my sisters. Devana had only ever had one interest in her life: music. Now, all of a sudden, she wished to know about suitors. I leaned closer and closer until my face was right before hers.

"Do you like someone," I said—not asked—only to see her pink lips tucked for the briefest of seconds before she shook her head.

"What? No. Of course not! Not at all! I know no one to like—"

"You protest far too much!" I gasped, seeing the look of panic on her face. "You like someone!"

"Shh! Hathor!"

"Be honest, Devana."

She sighed and hung her head. "You must swear not to say a word, Hathor."

My eyes widened while she gripped her white hands tightly. "Have you— Who is— When did— What is happening? Does Mama know?"

"Nothing is happening, and Mama does not know, as there is nothing *to* know. It is a mere crush, that is all. The gentleman in question does not even know I exist. But please do not say anything, Hathor. Please." She grabbed my hand, and I realized then that the sister I thought I knew was gone. Just like

Verity, her personality had shifted, all from this force called love, this force that continued to skip over me as if I were invisible.

"Hathor, swear you will not say anything of it," she begged again, and the panicked look on her face was the only thing that stirred me from my rising shock.

I nodded slowly before the words finally made it out of my lips. "I swear. But, Devana, you are not—"

"Do not worry. I promise I will not do anything foolish or against the rules, not that I can anyway."

"What does that mean?"

"I told you that he does not know I exist."

"You are a Du Bell. Everyone knows you exist," I reminded her, squeezing her hands to calm her. "What is his name?"

"You are terrible at keeping secrets so I shall not risk sharing any more information. I've said too much as it is."

"I very well can keep a secret, and besides, it's best you tell me. Do you not fear I shall come upon him during his time here and steal him away?"

"With your eyes focused squarely on your prince? I doubt it." She giggled and shook her head. "Besides, he shall not be here, for he is currently employed as an officer and serving our great country."

"An officer? Is he at war? Where did you even come across such a man?"

"I will not say any more," she replied as she released my hands.

"Why did you say anything at all? Or is this your plot to torment me?" I huffed and crossed my arms as I glared at her.

She twirled the end of her blonde braid. "I told you because . . . I just felt . . . I felt as if I would combust if I did not speak the words to someone. These feelings in my chest make me feel as if I cannot breathe, and I do not know what to do, so I thought I would tell my big sister. You will not betray me, will you?"

Who is this person? I thought but instead shook my head no. "I will not betray you. Now, go on to bed. It is late."

"What of your room?"

"That is a problem for the morning," I replied gently. "Go on and speak no more of these feelings until you are out in society, or Mama will wring your neck."

"Thank you, big sister." She smiled at me before placing the bucket at the foot of my bed and walking to the door.

I waited until she was just about to leave before saying, "I love you, little sister."

"And I you. I pray all your hard work will come to fruition, *princess*," she said and closed the door behind her. I stood in my feather-infested room, unable to grasp the magnitude of what I had just learned.

My little sister had a love story brewing before me. First, it was Aphrodite, then Verity, and now Devana?

At this rate, I would not be surprised if Abena had a suitor waiting for her. There was heaviness upon my shoulders, a pressure that grew so strong I slowly sank beside the bucket and pulled my legs to my chest. Had I ever even liked someone? I mean truly liked someone so much I was aching to speak the words aloud as Devana had now? No, I could not say I had.

At the age of twenty, I had secured no great feelings for any gentleman. Was there something wrong with me? Aphrodite, too, had fallen in love with Evander at sixteen. And if I recall correctly, that was the age at which my mother had wed my father. Was that when we were meant to be in love? If so, did that mean I had missed my chance? No, Verity was eighteen when she wed. Would that mean Devana would wed immediately upon entering society as well? What if I couldn't succeed in gaining Prince Wilhelm's attentions? What if I failed this season and still had not found someone in two years' time? Devana would marry before me. No. Mama would not allow it. She would see me wed first, but that would mean I was postponing another couple's happiness, would it not? Surely that would not bring forth good karma.

I gripped the side of my head, an ache growing within. I did not wish to think any longer. I crawled onto my bed and lay down, swatting the feathers from my face before closing my eyes. Hopefully, the morning would bring me relief and renewed energy to figure out my life before it was too late. Just as I felt I had finally drifted off, my name was called as if it were a call to arms.

"By heavens, Lady Hathor!"

My eyes snapped open only for a second before I shut them again, the brightness of the light nearly blinding me. Rolling over onto my side, I tried to sleep more when I felt a slight slap on my back.

"Lady Hathor, you must wake up this moment. And why is your room in such a state!" Bernice, my maid, questioned as she fought to take the bedsheets from me.

"Abena," I grumbled, trying to hold on to the sheets and use them to cover my ears. How was it morning already? I had only just closed my eyes.

"Your mother is already awake and demands you arise at once, Lady Hathor."

How mama was always able to wake with the sun was beyond me, but it could not be healthy. I would have to write to Verity and demand that she ask her husband to warn my mother of the harm lack of sleep would cause.

"Lady Hathor, please, on your feet."

"I am so tired. Can I please stay in bed—"

"You cannot, for guests are arriving within the hour!"

I sat up as if hounds had chased me from my bed, turning over to stare at her in shock. "Arriving? Have the queen and Prince Wilhelm arrived? But I am not ready!"

"No. But this is why you must awake now, my lady," she said, reaching into my hair to pick out the feathers. Where my headscarf had gone, I did not know, nor did I have time to care. I rushed from bed as she called for assistance, and when I sat at my vanity I saw I would need every bit of it. I was quickly washed and cleared of any feathers before Bernice came to arrange my hair.

"Shall you keep all of it up, my lady?"

I thought about it for a moment before shaking my head.

"No, not yet, I wish it to be presentable but not so it looks forced. This is my home; I ought to look relaxed but not too relaxed, all the other ladies will not be so fashionable after their journey here. I wish not to look as Lady Ellen did last year." We'd all arrived at her estate dressed rather modestly, for it took us five days to reach her home, and she greeted us with four different feathers in her hair, several rows of pearls around her neck, and the newest of lace-trimmed gowns.

The other ladies were not pleased by the display, feeling as though she sought to embarrass them, and therefore snubbed her terribly for the remainder of their stay. It grew so bad that the gentlemen, who were often quite clueless, noticed and chose to distance themselves as well. To them, any lady rejected by her own sex must surely be dreadful in some manner. One simple oversight and it all came to ruin for Lady Ellen. I would not make such a blunder. I doubt any of them had gotten word that the queen was coming, and so for me to be so done up would be even more egregious.

I could not come off too strong.

"Yes, my lady, I shall twist it to the side and leave a slight curl over your shoulder," Bernice said, already at work. The unperturbed focus and dedication on her round freckled face brought calm to my nerves.

This. This was the week. It had to be . . . but what if it wasn't? What if this did not work? What if he did not like me? What if . . . what if Mama was right and there was something horribly wrong with him? What if he was mad like the king? Again, what if he did not like me and found some other lady here much better suited for him than I?

Feeling my nerves build once more, I turned back to my room as the other maids cleaned. "Quickly, hand me my papers. I must go over them once more just in case—"

"My lady, you must remain calm." Bernice placed her hands on my shoulders, forcing me to meet her gaze in the mirror. "No papers shall help now, you must simply go and show him all your greatness."

What greatness can be shown to a prince? was what I wished to ask, for he had already seen so much of this world. But I said nothing and let her continue.

"Worry not. I am certain he will be the man of your dreams and all the world will stop along with your heart at the sight of him." She giggled.

"I believe that is called the rapture, not romance," I replied, playing with the curl she placed over my shoulder, making her laugh. "But I shall be fine with either at this point in time. For if I cannot make him love me with this much effort, let the world come to a splendid end."

All the maids looked at me.

I sighed, rising to my feet. "I jest."

Though not entirely.

Hearing the voices of the footmen, I moved over to my window to see the staff making preparations. If only there were some prayer, some mystical power I could whisper to and have this all done as if it were a fairy tale.

I wanted us to smile at each other until both of our faces hurt. I wished to dance together until we both collapsed from exhaustion. I desired to hold his hand and . . . and do all Verity said we were meant to do with each other.

Flirt.

Hug.

Kiss.

And . . . make love.

Oh, how I desired it.

"Lady Hathor, we must be going. Your mother wishes for you to be there to greet the guests upon their arrival."

Please be the one, please be everything.

3

Hathor

"Hathor, why are you just standing there?" My mother, dressed in purple with two strands of pearls around her neck, called from the bottom of the stairs, a whole litter of servants behind her. "Hurry, we must greet our guests."

"Coming," I said as I rushed to her side.

"Now remember, we shall stay to greet just the first six or seven before we join everyone inside."

"When will the queen arrive, Mama?" I asked as we began to walk toward the door, though she was still overlooking the entryway for any last-minute imperfections.

"Her Majesty will have the good sense to come the very latest possible, so as to make sure no one upstages her grand entrance. Do not expect her . . . or the prince you truly inquire about, to come until the evening or tomorrow," she said to me and then stopped when she saw Ingrid, who somehow managed to look both stoic and frazzled at the same time. "Ingrid, are all the refreshments prepared?"

"Yes, your ladyship, everything is already laid out upon trays and they shall be served the moment the guests enter the grand hall."

"Perfect." Mother nodded to her and adjusted the gardenia arranged by the doors to impart a pleasant aroma as everyone entered.

When we stepped outside, I saw my brother Damon and

his wife were standing beside my father. Baby Mini must have been with her nanny or my sisters. Silva fidgeted with her yellow dress, trying to calm herself, though I did not understand why. She had long been married to my brother. She even had a child, so what did she have to fear from the ladies of society now?

Taking a step beside her, I teased, "I see you've sought to outshine me today, sister-in-law, but it is in vain, for I shall be the prettiest today like every other day."

She glanced at me, eyes wide, but it was Damon who quickly spoke to her defense.

"I beg your pardon?" he scoffed. "Where is Aphrodite when you need her? Someone has grown rather bold of late. I take it you see yourself as a princess already?"

"Laugh while you can, brother, for soon you will be bowing and I will not be able to see your face at all," I replied with my chin lifted. And of course, despite his age, he pushed me. I stumbled and stared back at him in shock.

"Forgive me, *Your Highness*." He laughed to himself.

I was prepared to resort to the same antics when my other tormentor arrived.

"Can I push her too?" Abena called now, standing alongside our brother Hector. If not for him holding her arm, she'd have already done it.

"No, you may not! Damon, as a father, do you not believe you should set a better example?" I snapped at him.

"No, not at all," he replied, making his wife giggle as she shook her head at him.

"Damon," she admonished him.

"What? It is her fault for daring to assume she could be the prettiest woman here while you stand before us," he said to her, making her smile and me wish to throw sand in my eyes.

"Thank you, my dear, but Hathor is right. She will quite

surely be the most stunning today," Silva replied back and leant over to me. "Do not fret, this is your week."

"Quite right. Try not to scare him off, Hathor, Mother's nerves might not be able to handle any more disappointment this season," Damon replied.

"If he should try to flee, big brother, I will call upon your assistance to hold him captive, since you are so concerned."

Next to me, our father and younger brother, Hector, both snickered as I lifted my head high.

"With that statement, I am more concerned for this prince and our reputation at court than I am about you," Damon said, shaking his head.

"A brother without loyalty? What a shame. I shall have to count on you then, Hector." I looked at the boy beside me. He was another person growing beyond comparison and nearly at my height now.

Hector grinned and nodded to me. "Don't worry, Hathor. I shall wrestle down whomever you wish. Merely point to the gentleman."

"Why don't we leave this to the traditional methods of introduction and not have all of society under the impression that I have raised wild ruffians," my mother said. Then, she gave us all a stern glare, forcing us to stand upright and properly once more. The only person unafraid and insensible was, of course, Abena.

"Mama, if this is all for Hathor, why must I be out here? Devana gets to stay inside and play. I want to go too." Abena sighed heavily, kicking the gravel.

The mention of Devana made me feel guilty. Devana was not outside because Mother clearly saw what I did—she looked increasingly more like a young lady than a child. As she was not yet out in society and Mother wished to see me married first, Devana was forced to stay inside. Part of me was grateful that the attention was solely upon me, but another part felt bad that Devana would be hidden away. If it were me, I would surely be sour over such things. However, Devana did not care in the least.

"Abena, you are to go where I tell you and I tell you to be here," Mother stated, and Abena sighed dramatically.

"Shall we wager how long it will take for Hathor to lose her composure and faint, as the latter has become her signature in society?" Damon asked her, making Silva giggle.

Abena nodded eagerly. Before she spoke I clasped my hand over her mouth. "Young ladies ought not wager anything. And old men . . . big brother, should not teach children such things."

"Father, if I am old, what are you?" Damon questioned and my mouth dropped open.

"Something older than old is called ancient," Hector answered him.

"You turncoat! I thought you were on my side!" I called out to my younger brother as he, as well as the rest of my family, laughed at me. "Mama, do you not hear how they all mistreat me?"

"No, my dear, for at some point, you all start to sound like squabbling chickens. What was said?"

My father chuckled the loudest and it was now Damon's turn to pretend he did not hear. He took his wife's hand and placed it on his arm. I watched as a smile spread on her lips at us all. None of us could say anything more as we saw and heard the approaching carriages in the distance. It was as if they had all planned to arrive at once. The first group, of course, was my father's friends Lord Hardinge, Lord Bolen, and Lord and Lady Fancot, along with their daughter, Lady Amity. Mother was expecting Lord Fancot and all his family, as they were still quite set that I marry their son, Henry Parwens, but they did not know he had confessed to me that he was in love with another. So I knew he would not be in attendance.

"Charles!" Lord Hardinge rushed up to us, quite excited for a man who had come on such a long journey.

"Benjamin, what is the haste? I promise not a soul has touched any of the cranberry pies yet." My father chuckled as he greeted him.

"While I do always look forward to your kitchen's pies, Charles, I must speak of something much more important. I have news of the war that arrived to me just yesterday, great battles taking place, they say at this very moment, Nap—"

"Benjamin, we shall speak more inside," my father cut in, and it was only then that Lord Hardinge paused to see the rest of us looking at him with rising concern, especially my mother.

"Yes, of course." He nodded to Father and looked at my mother, offering her a polite smile. However, the mood had soured greatly. It was not just him, but every man who arrived seemed to have news about the war, and so instead of going for refreshments in the great hall, they all moved to my father's study to speak freely amongst male company.

"You should go see to them now." My mother frowned and looked at my father. "Have your conversations but do try to coax them from the library into the hall before the queen arrives or it shall be chaos."

"I shall do my best, my love, but there is nothing men enjoy more than to become generals of wars they are not fighting in." My father sighed as he turned back to the castle. He only paused when we heard another carriage approaching. I smiled as I recognized it.

The moment it pulled to a stop, I stepped forward to see

His Grace the Duke of Imbert along with his wife and, of course, Lady Clementina Rowley. She exited last, dressed in a soft bluish lavender, with all of her very long dark hair pulled back high. She stood as tall as ever and had a bright smile on her face.

I curtsied as my parents greeted them. Clementina immediately came to me and took my arm.

"How many gentlemen have arrived thus far?" she whispered. And this was one of the reasons I liked her. We shared a clear purpose and goal—to be wed before the year end.

"Nine. However, we are expecting eight more for certain," I whispered back as I led her toward the door.

"Oh, good. I was right to wear this dress for my arrival then. You know periwinkle is my finest color," she replied

"Let us pray they notice us today, though I doubt it on account of the news."

"What news?"

"You have not heard? Well, we have only just gotten word as well. Apparently, a great many battles have been fought against Napoleon recently."

"Have we lost?"

"We better not have, especially this week of all weeks." I frowned as we entered, only to watch as my brother and Lord Covington, one of his old friends, headed toward the library. "It shall kill the spirits of everyone here, and who can find a husband under such circumstances?"

"You never know. It may hasten these gentlemen's resolve to marry, for doom is a very good motivator."

I glanced at her, and she glanced back, then together, we giggled as we entered the hall, decorated with the finest of our roses and glasses upon glasses of port piled together into a tower. A painstaking endeavor that had gone unnoticed as the women whispered amongst themselves . . . however, their conversation was not at all about the war.

"Hathor, is it true?" Lady Amity, a blur of red hair, appeared right before Clementina and me like a wall, not allowing either of us to step by, with several other ladies behind her.

"Is what true? The war? I do not know—"

"Of course not the war! The prince!" Amity snapped at me.

"Prince? What prince?" Clementina questioned, looking to me.

Right. For the briefest of seconds, I had forgotten.

"My mama has heard that the queen is coming with her nephew, a prince, to find him a wife," Amity pressed, stepping forward. "Hathor, is it true? Why have you not said anything? Did you mean to hide it from us?"

I could see their eyes slowly readying to shun me as they had poor Lady Ellen, who was also here. Despite the fact they had only arrived minutes ago and I had not had a chance to say a word. But that would not save me from them. I glanced around as though I were wary of anyone hearing us.

"It is not yet confirmed but most likely true—" Just like I had, they squealed, forcing me to lift my fingers to my lips to calm them down. "The queen wished to come as a surprise, so I was not at liberty to say anything. When she arrives, you must still act as if you did not hear any word of it . . . Truly. The last thing we wish to do is upset Her Majesty."

They nodded but were now around me as hunting dogs to pheasants.

"Do you know anything of him, his name?"

"What country is he from?"

"How old is he?"

"Is he the heir to the throne?" Lady Ellen questioned.

"Do not be ridiculous. If he was to be the next king, he

would not be here; young ladies would be sent to his palace," Amity snipped back and looked at me, waiting. "Well? What do you know, Hathor?"

"You all do know I am competition, right?" I said to them, folding my arms. "Why would I inform my rivals of anything more than I already have?"

"Hathor!" They called my name in chorus.

I sighed. "Very well, his name is Prince Wilhelm Augustus Karl von Edward of Malrovia, he is twenty-four, from what I have gathered. He's fourth in line for the throne. His elder brother already has two sons. That is all I know. Now am I free to go?"

I did not wait for a reply, and arm in arm with Clementina, I managed to escape.

"Well done on your part for quelling that uprising," she muttered to me. "Though I wonder how you shall manage when he arrives, and they all block your chance."

"What makes you think I care at all for some prince?" I replied, trying to act as if I were completely unaffected by the thought.

"Is that why you knew exactly his age and place in the line of succession?" she teased, giving me a knowing look.

"Of course not, you know I have great love of . . . family lineages."

"Especially the ones with eligible sons to marry."

"Exactly."

We both giggled, accepting the drinks the footmen offered. "You truly know nothing more about this prince?"

"Are you interested in family lineages as well?" I asked her.

"No, thank you, the last person I need to see again is the queen, just for her to ask me if I was *stretched*." She frowned and I winced recalling the words the queen said to her at her debut. It had been two years and she still had not let the word go. "A prince is a little much for me. Is it so wrong to want a quiet life in a nice house away from society?"

"Well, Verity managed it so I am sure you can as well."

"I'm awfully jealous and have sought to discover if there are any other doctors of illegitimate noble birth in society, but alas she found the only one."

"I believe there is someone for all of us . . ." My thoughts drifted as I watched all the young ladies, like hive bees around Amity, rushing across the hall to where their mamas were gathering to . . . plot.

"Mama, I am quite tired. I wish to go rest and refresh myself before the evening," Amity said.

"Me too!"

"Also me."

"Ladies, you must wait until the marchioness enters and greets us once more. We cannot rudely retire before that," Lady Fancot said to her.

"Mama, we do not know when the queen will come, we must make haste if we wish to look presentable for him—her."

Clementina did her best not to laugh. "They have all lost their wits."

I was now grateful Mama had told me yesterday, for I feared if she had not, I too would have been insensible.

"Lady Hathor"—the Dowager Lady Covington said my name incorrectly, as always—"why do you not go check on your mother." She had big green eyes and a birthmark on the side of her lip, her skin a pale white, which made the darkness of her hair stand out even more strikingly. Her daughter Lady Mary was nearly her twin, despite being a twin already, while her second daughter, Lady Emma, was rather plain-looking, with red blemished skin she tried to hide with thick white powder. If anyone would strike first at the chance to marry her daughter to a prince, it would be her.

"Of course, your ladyship, I'll go find her now. Though once again, my name is pronounced Ha-ther," I replied with a smile, curtsying to her before moving to the front doors.

Just as I was about to walk out, the doors opened, and there alongside my mother was a man who stood much taller than her, dressed in a dark blue overcoat, tan-colored breeches, and high dark boots. His dark brown hair was cut short, but curly at the top, his jaw clean shaven, chiseled as though it were carved by the Greeks, his eyes the brightest blue I had ever seen and his skin white as polished stone. It was an unforgettable, undeniably handsome face. . . . that I'd already seen.

This wretched man had stood before me once before.

"What in heaven's name are you doing here?" I whispered, shocked that such a man was allowed in my home.

"Hathor!" My mother shot me the sternest of looks and I did not understand why. She should have been throwing salt to ban him from our doorstep.

"Mama, this man is—"

"Prince Wilhelm," my mother interrupted me loudly, coming to take my arm as I stared in horror. "May I introduce my daughter Lady Hathor Du Bell."

An evil grin spread across his face that sent a chill down my spine, and just like that, all the world stopped along with my heart.

"It is a pleasure, my lady." He spoke gently, outstretching his hand for mine, though I could see laughter behind his eyes.

I did not want to take his hand or speak; I wished nothing more than to hide away in my room lamenting how foolish I was to get my hopes up.

I did the only thing I could in such a horrid situation. I closed my eyes and forced myself to crumble to the floor, pretending to faint. However, instead of the ground or my mother's soft arms, I felt the hard embrace of a man who smelled like apples and rosewood.

"Such antics might afford you a few moments, but know I shall be here all week," he whispered to mock me, despite how still and tightly closed my eyes were.

Start the rapture immediately, for the devil has escaped hell!

4

Wilhelm

One Month Ago

"Marry me." The horror of those two words was so deep-seated that I could not help but stiffen upon hearing them. They were more unbearable than being told "I love you" . . . but only slightly. "There is no need for you to become so rigid, I am merely joking."

It was only then that I was able to turn back to see Lady Vivienne Gallagher, giggling from her place upon the grass, picking the white petals off the daisy in her hands.

"It was a poor joke, Vivi," I said, hoping it truly was said in jest.

"It's much funnier than the thought of you marrying a Du Bell," she replied, amused. I wished to groan again at that word, *marrying*.

"I am not marrying a Du Bell, or anyone for that matter. I do not know how many times I must say so before someone actually listens." It felt as if I were screaming toward the sky to no avail. Was the idea that I wished to remain free of any such constraints so preposterous?

"If your aunt has her way, and she always has her way, you will be married before the end of summer. And it will most likely be a Du Bell because she is very keen on that family," she said.

"I care not," I replied, lifting my jacket from where I had tossed it in the heat of the moment. "Ahh, I do not understand what makes her favor them so, from what I heard about the girl in question, I believe her name was . . . Heather? No, it was much more complicated . . . Hether . . . oh whatever, the girl is a crude and vulgar title hunter."

"Who told you that?" She laughed outright, rising from her place on the grass. She tossed her dead flower to the ground before walking over to me. "And her name is Lady *Hathor*."

"The source is as unimportant as her name. For I will not marry her. Any silly girl running throughout society seeking a man with a title is either grossly ignorant or enormously vain and pretentious. Neither is appealing. Maybe that is why she is still unwed."

"That is hardly fair," she replied, reaching up to dust the grass off the sleeves of my coat. "All ladies in our society are expected to marry a man of equal birth or higher. You know that, August. The Du Bells are one of the greatest noble families in England. Her elder sister became a duchess just two years ago. I see nothing wrong with your aunt wishing to match you both based on status. Lady Hathor is a good, respectable young lady. And you . . ."

"And I am a notorious rake?" I smirked, placing my hands on her hips, drawing her closer to me. "I do not deny it . . . if only my aunt would accept it as well. I'm sure this *Lady Hathor* is a respectable, innocent little lamb and this is meant to subdue me. They believe she can mend my *poor judgments* and make me an honorable, *boring* man. But I like being bad, it is much more fun."

I kissed her cheek before stepping around her.

"So you wish to waste your life away seeking fun? You shall not be young forever."

"But I am young now, and it seems a waste to spend such a

grand time of life with the dull, infantile ladies of society. All of them are nonsensical, fluttering like chickens with not a clue about the world or a care beyond balls and their dresses. Their company is even worse than that of children, for a child at least has some sense of adventure and imagination."

"Marriage matures all ladies. You cannot fight this, August, and I do not see why you wish to make such a matter of it. Just marry and do as all men do after . . . whatever they like. My husband had several mistresses and lived as though he were a bachelor till the day he died. No one cared." That expression upon her face I knew very well. No one cared . . . but her.

What was the point of taking such vows if no one bothered to uphold them? Her husband carried on as though he were unmarried, and she acted wantonly in the shadows. It was all so much effort that could simply be avoided by remaining unwed.

"Besides, what of your inheritance? If you are not married by twenty-five, are you not going to lose everything?"

"Because I have so much now." My voice dripped with sarcasm. "I doubt they shall truly leave me penniless, but if they do I shall count on your kindness as always."

"This is no joke, August, you should truly be concerned—"

"Thank you for your advice, Vivi, I'll let my aunt know I heard you, for I am sure that was part of your purpose in luring me out today. But my mind remains unchanged. No, in fact, I am even more staunchly opposed. Why have mistresses when I can simply enjoy the company of the finest women in the world unburdened?"

"So you may have a home, family, and children."

"I already have home and family. As for children . . . well, there is no guarantee of that in marriage either, and so I'd rather not risk my freedoms. Truly there is nothing more liberating than going to a woman and leaving a woman with no further expectation than coin . . . or fun. So sweet Lady Hathor is going to have to find new prey to hunt. There is no threat or inheritance large enough that will change my mind." I snickered, handing her my arm for us to return. She gave me a stern look.

"You really are impossible to reason with."

"I'm glad you have surrendered. Let us never speak on this matter again. Though I do wonder what type of name *Hathor* is; it does not seem English at all," I mused as we began to walk forward. Then all of sudden, I heard an answer come from behind me.

"That is because it is not English, it is Egyptian."

I glanced back to see a light brown–skinned woman with an angelic face, honey-colored eyes, and long curly hair that hung loose down her shoulders. She wore a deep green dress with gold trim that seemed to blend into the grass field she stood upon. If not for her hands, which were clearly balled into fists, one might think she were some divine muse of nature. She glared at me with a fury I did not understand nor think warranted, as I did not know her. I would surely have remembered her face if I had seen her—or slept with her—before.

From her clothes and the maid behind her, it was clear she was not a woman I would or could have had . . . history with. Though I greatly wished to, for she was truly stunning. Breathtaking in fact. I glanced to Vivienne, thinking maybe she was an acquaintance of hers, but Vivienne stared, eyes wide, and then took a deep breath before speaking.

"Lady Hathor! How are you, my dear?"

No!

My head spun back quickly. This was her? The famed Du Bell girl? The title hunter? Once more I looked her over, having expected someone more . . . plain. Not repulsive-looking, but from the way my aunt spoke of her appearance, as if it were an afterthought or simply of no importance, I did not think she'd look so . . . beautiful. A woman with such a face should not have to hunt; I was sure her prey came happily to her.

I coughed to regain my thoughts and straightened my shoulders, waiting for Vivi to introduce me.

"Lady Hathor, this is—"

"An introduction is as *unimportant* as his name, your lady-ship," she spit back angrily and my shoulders dropped. It was clear that our entire conversation had been overheard. "Please do tell his aunt I have no interest in such an ill-bred, unscru-pulous, caper-witted man, and therefore no introduction should ever be made."

Ill-bred, unscrupulous, caper-witted? I huffed, for never had a woman called me such things . . . at least not to my face. I stepped forward attempting to flatter her. "Such harsh words for such a beautiful woman is—"

"Oh, believe me, sir, they could be much harsher," she snapped without compassion, and strangely her severity was even more enticing.

"My lady, there has been a misunderstanding—"

"I believe you were quite clear. You might not know, but it is considered common decency to avoid speaking out in the open as though it were your own private drawing room. Espe-cially if you are going to gossip about someone else. I wonder if you lack this knowledge because you are grossly ignorant or enormously vain and pretentious!"

She truly had heard every damned word. And I was grow-ing rather . . . uncomfortable with her high and mighty glare before me.

"Tell me, *my lady*, was a segment of your teaching in com-mon decency the art of eavesdropping? For even though this is not a private drawing room, it was a private conversation—"

"And it would have remained one had I not heard my name wholly slandered!" she interrupted me once more.

She was far too angry to reason with. So, to end this matter, I thought to simply apologize . . . though how I hated apologizing.

"Forgive me, I spoke out of turn—"

"I will not forgive you! For one line of apology is nothing in comparison to the several lines of insult you dealt." She huffed, moving closer to me in her rage and I stared at her in shock.

I, a prince, sought to apologize and not only did she not allow me to finish, she rejected it outright?

"You speak very highly for someone who does not know to whom she is speaking," I replied, stepping closer as well. Our faces were so close now that it was I who could physically look down upon her. However, she did not flinch or cower at my height; in fact, she seemed even more emboldened.

"I care not to whom I am speaking because I have heard enough from you to gather all that needs to be known."

"Oh, you believe so?"

"I know so!"

"And if I were a man of the highest rank and title in all of—"

"You do not look like the king, nor would I wish to marry you should you be him!" she scoffed. I had now lost count of how many times she'd interrupted me. "Despite whatever you have heard, I do not hunt for title alone. You do not meet the measure; you do not even come close!"

I laughed. "Are you sure you won't regret speaking to me this way?"

"I will not."

"And you swear never to accept my hand in marriage, no matter who asks on my behalf?"

Her eyebrow rose and she crossed her arms smugly. "Even

if the queen herself arranged for us to marry, I would refuse instantaneously."

I smiled wide and nodded. "I will hold you to that, Lady Hathor. Let us hope you are a woman of your word. What a shame though; your face shines like the sun amongst stars."

"Are you mocking me?"

"No. Quite the opposite in fact."

"I do not believe you, but it matters not. Let us hope we never cross paths again. Good day to you, sir." She spun on her heels with such a speed her curls nearly slapped me across the face . . . She smelled like vanilla, sycamore, and roses.

"Well, you have successfully managed to ruin that match; your aunt will not be pleased," Vivienne said as she once more came to my side.

"She is much more fiery than I expected," I replied as I watched the woman in question retreat with her maid. "This shall prove to be amusing."

"August . . . whatever you are thinking, stop," she warned. "There are some women you can play with and there are some you cannot . . . She is the latter."

"But aren't you curious if she will hold to her word? It's easy for her to speak so when she does not know who I am. I would like to see if she will remain so fierce when confronted with reality."

"You are not hearing a word I am saying, are you?"

I smirked, shaking my head before offering her my arm. But she just kept frowning at me. I sighed, placing her hand on my arm anyway. "Do not worry, I shall not do anything inappropriate with her . . . I merely wish to test her convictions a little. And see her apologize."

"Why, so you can reject it?"

I did not answer, leading her forward.

"So childish . . . you are lucky you are handsome."

"And royal . . . don't forget that." Because that always changed everything, though as we walked, I could not help but fight the urge to turn back. To catch a glimpse of this Hathor once more. I felt myself anxiously awaiting our next meeting and what expression or retort she would make then.

Present

She fainted.

From the moment my aunt told me I was to attend this week's festivities at the Du Bell family castle, I wondered hundreds of times what Lady Hathor would do when we were finally introduced . . . only for her to faint. No, not even truly faint. I watched her eyes stare back at me in panic and dismay, unbelieving that I, of all people, was whom she must have been expecting. She clearly forced herself to faint as a way to save face and run from me. I had not expected that. Not with such a large gathering present.

I would have laughed had I not been in public.

Either way, it did not matter, I would wait for her to return, and see how she would resolve this matter, for as I told her, I'd be here all week and she would not be able to avoid me.

"How are you, Your Highness? Still dazzling the courtiers of England?"

I glanced away from the doors, where they had escorted Lady Hathor out, to my old friend in all things ungentlemanly, Lord Lukas Howard, the Earl of Covington, with his mother and two younger sisters—one a doe-eyed, petite dark-haired girl and the other a rather white-faced young woman. Just as Lady Hathor could not avoid me, I could not avoid the mamas.

"I am well, Lukas, and you? Still boxing in places you ought not?" I grinned.

He adjusted his cuffs. "I have not a clue of what you speak."

"Is that so?" I laughed and so did he as he took my hand to shake. Before he could reply, there was a gentle cough from the ladies waiting behind him. He gave me a look and I merely nodded for him to get it over with.

"Your Highness, please allow me to introduce my mother, Lady Edith Howard, the Dowager Countess of Covington, and my younger sisters, Lady Mary and Lady Emma," he said, stepping to the side so I could see them more clearly.

"Your Highness, we are so pleased you could join us here," the dowager said as she, along with her daughters, curtsied . . . very low.

"Thank you, I am looking forward to the week," I replied as they all rose.

"When Lukas told us he had become good friends with you during his grand tour, we did not believe it." Lady Mary spoke up first, side by side with her mother. "He rarely speaks of his time in Europe, but he said you both had the greatest fun visiting ancient ruins."

I glanced to Lukas, who sheepishly drank his wine, for the places we had gone were not ancient at all. "Yes, they were magnificent. Your brother was by far the most *knowledgeable* about all the sites we visited."

He coughed into his cup and shot me a look, but I ignored it as I smiled at his sister.

"How jealous I am. You gentlemen are able to experience such wonders. I hope to travel one day."

"I am sure it shall be possible, though it is not always a great comfort, my lady."

"Has the queen arrived along with you?" her mother questioned.

"Her Majesty has been delayed, but sent me ahead first. I do believe she shall arrive later in the week," I answered. The queen would not dare spend a whole week amongst society; she preferred the comforts of her palace, and would come only to make sure I had done what she demanded.

"Well, then I must take it upon myself to make sure you are—"

"Dowager Lady Covington, I was not aware your family was so well-connected." Another older woman appeared out of thin air, her daughter alongside her, and I saw many other mamas slowly pressing forward with their daughters, like pack wolves ready to devour.

And none of them were Lady Hathor.

I looked to Lukas, all but demanding he find a way to save me from this. Understanding, he nodded and looked beyond to another darker-skinned man speaking to a group of gentlemen.

"Damon, did you not say there were cards to be played? I wish to win back my hand from last time," Lukas called out to him.

The man in question looked to him with an eyebrow raised and then noticed the gathering crowd around me. He chuckled and nodded, coming over.

"Yes, I do believe it is time for me to collect your new debts," he said. He looked to me as he nodded his head, and I did the same.

"Ah, Your Highness, allow me to introduce Lord Monthermer's first son and heir, Damon Du Bell, the Earl of Montagu. He is also my good friend, one might even say like an elder brother, and as such he does not collect debts," Lukas said.

Ah, so this was Hathor's brother.

"Do not listen to him. I very well do collect debts, family, friend, or foe. And I welcome you to Belclere Castle, Your Highness. The other gentlemen and I were about to go begin a game of cards, if you would like to join us?"

Before I could reply, Lady Mary once more spoke up.

"But you all have only just arrived. You would deprive us of your company?"

"Never, I merely wish to give you space, for I fear you all will grow sick of me before the week is done," I teased, making them giggle.

"Worry not, I shall make sure his highness is returned promptly," Damon replied to them before making space for me to go ahead as the footmen held open the doors. Only when the other gentlemen and I were through did I let out a deep sigh.

"Save your breath, my friend," Lukas patted my shoulder. "We are only at the beginning."

"I fear what will become of me by the end," I muttered.

"It depends on what you seek," Damon said as he looked me over carefully. Then he added, with a glance to Lukas, "For this is not your grand tour, Your Highness."

Apparently eavesdropping on conversations was a family trait.

"Of course not," I said with seriousness. "I have come at the queen's command, and thus must be on my very best behavior. Though in private, please simply call me August; all this *Your Highness* is rather suffocating."

"Very well, please follow me as we take our reprieve from the—"

"Damon, where are you all going?"

He turned and I looked to find . . . her. Lady Hathor, trailing behind her mother, her wits returned. Her curls had been pinned up and though her face was calm . . . she gripped her hands.

"Mother, I sought to take the men for a round of cards before they prepare for dinner," Damon said.

"Very well. I will see to it the kitchen sends you all you may need; your father and his friends are still in the library." She nodded and glanced to me. "Your Highness, should you need anything, merely say the word."

"Of course, thank you, but I hope not to trouble you too much."

She stepped aside about to walk by with Lady Hathor, who avoided all eye contact with me, her head turned as though she were watching a play in the sky.

"Lady Hathor, I do hope you are quite well?" I pressed, trying to gain her attention. She looked at me, familiar rage and heat in her eyes, but she said not a word, instead nodding once then performing the most pitiful curtsy before abruptly walking away, to the astonishment of her mother, her brother, and Lukas.

"Enjoy your games, gentlemen," Lady Monthermer said and quickly went after her. I watched them depart, a grin spreading across my lips.

Well, it seemed she was going to remain true to her word.

"Should I ask?" Damon questioned.

"There is no need." I turned back to him and looked him in the eye. "Truly, there is not."

His shoulders relaxed. "Then come, let us see if you are better at holding on to your money than Lukas."

"Don't underestimate him, Damon, he can be relentlessly competitive," Lukas said as they led me forward.

I merely followed, though I could not shake the image of her amber eyes.

Did she plan to glare at me all week? Never say a word to me? That would not do at all. I'd waited far too long to fight with her once more. I bit the inside of my cheek to keep from chuckling.

"Gentlemen, may I introduce Prince Wilhelm of Malrovia, the queen's nephew," Damon said as we entered the room, where more than eight other gentlemen were already seated at round tables, drinking with cards before them. They all moved to stand up, their shoulders squared and proud.

"Relax, gentlemen, I wish to escape the formality; I am sure the women and all their mamas shall have me preening like a peacock all week," I replied, raising my hands up in defense, making them snicker.

"Escape, Your Highness? I'm not sure we will have an hour before they riot," a tall blond man with a freckled face said.

"An hour? My mother would box my ears if we kept him for even half of that," another added, a tan-skinned man with shoulder-length black hair.

"August, this is George Holt, the Earl of Chiswick." Lukas pointed to the man with blond hair. "And beside him, Sir Arman Branham, of the Branham Trading Company. You may have noticed their sisters hovering right behind mine."

I had not. "Ah, so are you all here for your sisters or for yourselves?" I asked as I took a seat at their table along with Damon and Lukas.

"Both," all three of them answered.

"My mother's invitations were specifically sent out for that purpose," Damon replied as one footman dealt out the cards to us and another brought a drink for me.

"I will thank your mother graciously when I become your brother-in-law," Lord Chiswick joked as he accepted his glass. My eyebrow rose at that.

"Didn't my sister already reject you?" Damon shot back, making the man cough into his cup.

"That was your Lady Aphrodite." Sir Branham chuckled, taking his cards. "He's trying to play his hand again because clearly he does not know when to quit."

"You're going after both sisters?" I questioned, shocked that Damon seemed unbothered and more amused.

"They laugh but there is not a man in here that does not wish for a connection with the Du Bells," Lord Chiswick replied.

"But do we want a connection with you?" Damon mused proudly; of his family's fame I supposed.

"What is wrong with me?"

"Lady Hathor would not settle for simply an earl, George," Lukas added.

"Earl is the highest rank here outside of the Marquess of Oxmoor." Sir Branham nodded to the large-bellied man breathing and sweating heavily at the next table over. "And of course, our prince here."

"Well, it must be the Marquess then, because August has no plans to marry. Is that not right, my friend?" Lukas tossed a note into the center of the table.

They all looked to me, and I just nodded. "Sadly, I am here only for show at the behest of my aunt."

"So you mean to engage no young lady here?" Lord Chiswick smiled. "How the ladies shall weep when you tell them."

"Why bother telling them? No one ever believes men when we say we wish to remain unmarried, anyway," I said, tossing another note into the center myself.

"That's because no man actually means it," Damon replied to their jeers.

"Just because you have fallen victim to matrimony, Damon, does not mean we all shall," Lukas replied.

"Yes, you all will, because you, Lukas, are an only son who will need an heir to carry on your estates and titles. You, George, despite having a plethora of younger brothers, will do so because your ego needs the constant attention of a woman. And as for you, Arman, you have too much damn money to spend on your own; your future wife will help fund half of all the silk shops in England," Damon explained, tossing not one but several notes onto the table, causing us all to look to him.

"And me? What reason would I have to get married?" I asked, holding my cards firmly as I too placed more money in, which caused the rest of the men to fold their hands.

"You are royal; it is part of your duty," he spoke.

I shook my head. "My cousins are proving it is more of a suggestion than an obligation."

"You will need your inheritance," he shot back.

I glanced over to Lukas, who just drank. I was sure he'd spoken to Vivi as well. "I've done quite well enough without it so far. Besides, I'm sure when my brother eventually takes the throne he will relent and give it to me anyway."

"So, you truly believe you will be unwed all the rest of your days?"

"I am as certain as I am of the necessity of air."

I thought I had him on this conversation but instead he placed all his money into the center. "I'm willing to wager that not only will I beat you with this hand, but that you will be amongst the first at this table to succumb to the beast that is matrimony."

"You do not know it, but it's a fool's bet you are making." I laughed. Me fall prey to marriage. I'd watched my father nearly kill my mother repeatedly. I'd seen my mother nearly descend into madness trying to do everything to appease him. That was what she called love. It disgusted me. The idea of marriage even for the sake of my inheritance only left me with bitterness. All my life I'd watched people associate love with pain. I had no wish for anything more than pleasure from a woman, and even that I wished to keep at a distance.

I put all my money in as well. "I wager that I shall leave your castle as unattached as I entered. Marriage is not suited for me."

I would not resign myself to such suffering.

"Maybe you should not make the bet, Damon, he seems rather sure of himself," Lord Chiswick muttered to him.

"It is because of his certainty that I feel compelled to make it. After all, I too was once so certain marriage would not be in my cards," Damon replied as he placed his cards out on the table. "Well, Your Highness, who has won?"

I glanced at my cards in my hand, my jaw cracked to the side. I placed the cards down. "You have won the battle but not the war."

The men cheered him.

"Of all your father's talents, Damon, you seemed to have inherited his luck at cards most strongly," Sir Branham replied.

"His luck at everything, actually. I look forward to your wedding, *August*." Damon grinned as he collected his winnings.

"I shall disappoint you."

"We shall see at the end of the week."

These Du Bells . . . I was starting to see why everyone spoke so highly of them. Their confidence was striking, it nearly made you want to believe alongside them. Even his sister Hathor spoke with such determination and vigor. Her face suddenly came to mind, like it had done dozens of times since first meeting her a month ago.

If only she were not such a precious and innocent noble lady, we could have—no. It was best not to even think of it.

No attachments.

I would have no such attachments to women. I would not live as my parents lived.

I could not bear it.

5

Hathor

Mama had lectured me to near deafness demanding to know the reason for my behavior, and all I could tell her was that I had overheard him insulting me in the park. While that was the truth it was not the entirety of it. For how could I have told her that not only had he insulted me, but he had also boasted about being a rake, a scoundrel who saw women as nothing more than playthings for his own personal enjoyment? And if that were not already horrid enough, he had been in the arms of the Viscountess of Millchester, kissing her cheek, speaking poorly of marriage, and discussing mistresses! It was all so unspeakably vile and abhorrent. He was very clearly the worst of men, dressed up in finery, fooling all the world. Yet all the other young ladies, and even their mothers, all day long were giggling about how handsome he was and his pleasant demeanor.

It was an act. A display of mockery in fact. He was a wretch and he'd managed to ruin all hope I'd had for this week. It was as though he had drained me of my spirit and as such, I could hardly even bother to put much effort into preparing for the evening. In fact, I did not wish to go back down for dinner for fear that I would be forced to maintain pleasantries with him.

"My lady, your mother has sent these pearls for you to wear for dinner, which would you prefer?" Bernice asked, showing the two strands of white spheres upon the velvet cushion.

They were absolutely beautiful and would surely make me look even more splendid. But what was the point? There was no one worthy of seeing me in them.

"It's fine, I shall keep this necklace I have already," I replied gently.

"My lady"—Bernice bent down beside me—"even if you do not wish the attention of Prince Wilhelm, there are still many other gentlemen in attendance. You should not allow him to so affect your mood."

"He affects nothing in me! In fact, he does not exist in my eyes. Only honorable men do." I huffed before looking back at my reflection. She said nothing, instead refocusing her efforts on my hair, making sure not a single pin was showing as I sat dreading what was to come.

How could a man be so devoid of all . . . positive attributes?

"Why are you so quiet?" Abena asked as she entered my rooms unannounced.

"Because I am thinking. You ought to try it for once."

"I think!"

"Of food and how to annoy me," I shot back.

"That's true." She did not even seek to deny it. She welcomed herself to come in even farther, walking over to my bed to throw herself upon it.

"Abena, I am not in the mood, please go away," I begged.

"But I'm bored!"

I did not get to answer, as there was a knock at the door. "Enter?"

When the door opened, it was not Ingrid, my mother's right hand, but Devana. Her blonde hair was pulled into a ponytail, and she was dressed in our favorite color—green.

"What are you both doing?" she asked.

"Hathor is grumpy, and I'm bored so we are doing nothing."

I wanted to smack her. "I am preparing for dinner. Abena is bothering me—that is what we are doing."

"Abena, do you mind if Hathor and I talk for a moment?" Devana asked as she came over to us, holding the post of my bed. I looked at her strangely, not sure why she wished to speak privately, and apparently neither was Abena.

"You wish me to go? What are you speaking of that I can't hear about? That's not fair. I am your sister too."

"Yes, you are my favorite sister, and one day, I shall share all I know with you, but you must be a bit older," Devana told her. But Abena crossed her arms and refused to move, until Devana leaned in and whispered something into her ear.

"I'm going!" Quickly, Abena hopped up off the bed. "Bye, Hathor. You should give up because you are never getting married when you're always in a mood!"

"*You little—*"

Abena slammed the door behind her, cutting me off before I could finish my words. When Devana looked at Bernice, she curtsied and took her leave as well.

"What did you say to get Abena to go?"

"You remember that book Father was looking for a few days ago?"

"The one he claims disappeared off his desk."

"She snuck into the library and accidentally poured ink all over it."

I gasped, my hands going to my mouth. "Father is going to kill her."

"I think he already knows and is waiting for her to admit it." Devana giggled as she took a seat on the bed. "Abena wrote a letter to Aphrodite for help to replace it."

"Ah." Since all of our letters were read, I was sure Mama knew, and thus, so did Papa. "They are torturing her by making her live in terror of them finding out. So, eventually, she'll admit it when nothing can be done."

"Do not use it against her, Hathor."

I scoffed. "I would never."

"You would so."

"Just a reminder: I am your older sister, and I need no lecture from you," I said pointedly.

"I could never forget you are my elder sister—"

"Then you shall tell me the name of your crush at once."

"Hathor!"

"What?" I poked her side, making her giggle. "Tell me!"

"No!" She jumped back away from me. "This is your story, remember? As you wanted, we will be focusing only on you."

"Then why did you tell me at all?" I pouted. "You wished to torture me; I am sure."

She giggled. "I wish for nothing but the best for you. As I love you greatly, my dear elder sister."

"But what did you wish to talk to me about?" I asked, wondering why she had come.

"It is fine. Another time." And with that, she left.

I did not want to press the matter more. But I could see she really was in love, which made me so desperate to know.

Love.

I wanted that.

I wanted what everyone else in my family had.

"And I will not find it hiding in here," I whispered to my own reflection before slapping my cheeks. "Get yourself together, Hathor!"

I removed my necklace and lifted a strand of pearls off the cushion. Bernice was right. There were still plenty of other gentlemen here, and just as I had sought to do before ever hearing word of that awful man's arrival, I would find my match.

I twirled around once to look myself over before exiting my room.

I could hear the music already playing as I stepped down the stairs slowly. Luckily there at the bottom were Clementina and her mother.

"Your Grace." I curtsied.

"Hathor. I was telling Clementina here to go back to get her pearls as well but she is being stubborn . . . as always. Maybe you can convince her?"

"Unfortunately, I cannot, Your Grace, for she is already stunning, and I dreadfully abhor competition, even from dear friends," I said with my head raised.

"Yes, Mama, and you would not wish to drive a wedge between me and my dear friend, for seeking to upstage her in her own home," Clementina added dramatically as we linked arms.

"I would take the greatest offense and never speak to you again," I said in the same manner, trying not laugh.

"Rightly so."

"Are you both quite finished? Or am I supposed to watch the entirety of this farce?" her mother asked with a stern look.

"Quite finished. See you inside, Mama!" Clementina said quickly before dragging me off. When we were far enough away, she leaned over, whispering, "The woman wished to dress me up like a peacock for dinner. If you had seen the gown she demanded I wear, you'd think I was to be crowned."

"It is only the first night, why on earth would she wish that?" It was more customary to save your grandest gown for the final ball of the festivities.

"I believe this is why," she answered as we stepped into the hall. Every young lady was dressed in her very best gown, covered head to toe in pearls, diamonds, and feathers. The pearls I had on and the dress I wore paled in comparison to them all.

Even their faces were more made up than normal . . . All because of him . . . Prince Wilhelm. "Imagine what they'd wear if he was the heir to the throne."

"They are all being rather silly," I said, leading her inside, walking toward the windows.

"Why, because you mean to take his attention?"

"I have not the slightest interest and I mean it. In fact, it is better they all focus on him so I may pay attention to other gentlemen."

"Truly?" She raised an eyebrow.

"Yes, truly."

"Then—"

"I am surprised, Hathor," Mary said. She was dressed in yellow, standing alongside Lady Amity, who came forward in white to meet us. "I didn't expect you to dress so simply."

"Yes, well, as a natural beauty it occurred to me I did not need to put in much effort at all," I replied with a smile. "Both your gowns are quite . . . grand. I'm sure Prince Wilhelm shall notice."

"If you do not faint upon him *again*," Amity added with a frown. "Do you not tire of such tricks to gain attention?"

At least they believed it was a ploy to gain attention rather than the truth of me having already known him.

"Are you upset that I did it first or that I did it at all?" I asked.

"Hathor," Mary said with her head raised. "Do know that the rest of us will not simply roll over and allow you to have your way. We all know why we are here, and so we are free to compete for his attentions . . . fairly."

I pulled out my handkerchief and lifted it before her. "I hereby surrender and leave him completely to your mercies, ladies."

The doors opened just as I finished, and then he walked in

dressed again in dark blue. Immediately, it was as though all the air in the room had been taken out. Each lady curtsied toward him. Even Clementina. His eyes glanced over the room before he landed on me. Not allowed to be rude, I grimaced and bowed my head, barely. One would have thought he would understand and go away. But instead, the criminal came toward us.

"Ladies, you all look so beautiful this evening," he said to our group, with the most deceptive of smiles on his lips. I felt the urge to roll my eyes.

"Thank you, Your Highness, I thought it best to start the week off in grand fashion." Mary's voice had now become very soft and gentle.

"And your coat is quite marvelous, Your Highness," Amity added, making sure she stood right beside Mary.

He nodded to her and then looked to me. "Lady Hathor, good evening."

Hearing him utter my name turned my face sour. All I could do was force a smile and mutter back as if tortured, "It was a good evening, if only briefly . . . Your Highness."

For some reason the man smirked!

"Was? Only briefly? Whatever has ruined your night, my lady?" he pressed, and I could tell he was toying with me. It was not as if I could speak the truth before everyone.

"Hunger."

Before he could say more, my mother and father motioned for the butler to announce dinner and I was able to quickly make my escape. I headed toward the dining room, thinking I would be free of him there. After all, I had told my mother he'd insulted me and therefore I wished not to be near him, so I expected the table settings to be changed. However, there in the center was the card with my name, next to . . .

"Here I am," he said, glancing at his card beside mine.

Normally the tables were set by rank. Since he was a prince, he would have had to sit higher than my father but that would not allow him to sit beside any ladies. So the next option would be the daughter of the host . . . me. But I had hoped that Mother would have switched me with Clementina, the daughter of a duke. Why she had not, I did not know, but now I was forced to be in his company during the entire meal.

"Shall you not be sitting, *my lady*?" He raised his dark eyebrow and nodded to the footman who was waiting to pull out the chair I was blocking. I exhaled through my nose and stepped aside, allowing my chair to be brought out. I sat down and chose to just stare straight ahead.

"You are aware that you only draw more attention by trying to ignore me, Lady Hathor?" he mused.

I could not take it any longer. Immediately, I turned to him. "Then how about you ignore me?"

"That would make me rude, for you are the daughter of our host, are you not?"

"Your Highness—"

"Please cause me August, it is a nickname all my—"

"I shall not."

"Why?"

"Firstly, because it is against the rules of decorum for a man and a woman who are unrelated to be so familiar with each other."

"You have heard one of my most private conversations, does that not make us familiar?"

"Absolutely not. Not ever."

He chuckled and nodded. "And your second reason?"

"What?"

"You said 'firstly,' so that means there is a second reason, correct?"

I paused, for the second reason was that it made me remember Lady Vivienne Gallagher and how she called out to him in the park. Clearly she was one of his many women . . . associates. However, I did not wish to say that aloud . . . especially considering that the people beside us could still hear us though we whispered.

"As I was saying before you distracted me, *Your Highness*," I once more tried to speak through a stressful smile, "we need not make an effort to be in each other's company, or converse, or have any dealings whatsoever together."

"I—"

"I can see now why you asked me if I would regret my words. You knew we'd meet and be introduced no matter what. Now you wish to lord your great title over me. But do not fret, for I regret nothing, and I meant everything. If I have to, I will even write to the queen and repeat my words. You may be a prince, but you are also a villain and I have no interest in villains. I will only marry a hero. So . . . do enjoy your soup." I nodded to the first course as it was brought and set before him first.

Once more I turned and faced forward, waiting in silence for my plate to be set. I was feeling rather satisfied with myself when he broke out into a laugh that caused everyone to look in our direction, to my absolute horror. I looked to see if he'd gone mad, but he merely leaned closer to whisper.

"Since you have cast me as the villain, I shall play my part to the very end and make sure everyone thinks we are the *closest* of acquaintances. Let us see which *hero* comes to your rescue."

He was a monster!

I glanced around the table only to find everyone now either pretending not to notice us or staring in jealousy. And I could not say a word because I was sure they all assumed it was as it appeared . . . two young people flirting.

No!

"You said you were hungry, Lady Hathor, please eat, the soup is delicious," he added sweetly before he took a spoonful himself.

I would not be taken for a fool in this manner. Lifting my spoon, I began to plot my countermeasures, for I was going to war.

6

Wilhelm

I am the villain?

She had one poor encounter with me and thus I was to be so labeled and disregarded? Yes, my words had been rather . . . unbecoming, but they were honest. If she should take issue, it should have been with how she garnered the reputation of a title hunter. I was merely judging her person based on what I had been told. If it was an incorrect assessment, she need only say so. Instead, throughout dinner, she did her best to engage the gentleman to her left, seeking to forget I existed at all, and so I spoke to the lady to my right. By accident, my foot had touched hers and she kicked my leg so hard, my mouth nearly dropped open. For someone who spoke so highly of decorum and courtesy, she seemed to have none.

Who in their right mind kicks a prince!

After dinner, we returned to the hall for dancing. I watched her laughing alongside her company now. Again, she was avoiding eye contact. What tenacious stubbornness!

"You are staring quite hard, my friend," Lukas said as he came to my side, holding his glass of wine. "Lady Hathor is . . ."

"Your thoughts are mistaken, and I have no interest in Lady Hathor, nor was I looking at her," I replied a little sharply, and made sure to add, "or at any young lady here. I am merely being polite, as my aunt demanded."

"If only I could be the same," he said with his eyes still upon the ladies like a wolf's on sheep. "Damon is right. I am the only son. As such my mother is insisting I choose a wife and continue our line as soon as possible."

"And you believe you are ready for marriage?"

"What's there not to be ready for? Is it not a few words in church and an adjustment in rooms? My life would not change much," he mused. He finished off his glass as he prepared to approach his prey. "Wish me luck."

I watched him go forward for a moment, and just as I moved to follow, the sheep turned and came toward us. Looking me directly in the eye, Lady Hathor smiled as she walked up to me, arm in arm with none other than Lady Emma. Lukas paused, taking a step back, and my eyebrow rose, as I was unsure what had caused her sudden smirk. It felt devious.

"Your Highness," she said very sweetly, and now I was certain she was plotting something. "I thought much on what you said over dinner, and I feel for your predicament tremendously."

Predicament? What I said over dinner? I had not a clue what she was speaking of and it made me wary.

"I—"

"I often get homesick as well!" Lady Emma cut in, a smile on her pink lips. "Everyone thinks it silly, but I much prefer to stay home and read by the seaside."

I could only stare at her because I was still at a loss as to what she was saying. It was a grave mistake—my silence allowed for Lady Hathor to speak up.

"Emma says the best remedy for homesickness is to do things that remind one of home. And I thought, given how much you said you enjoyed dancing—"

"I said I enjoyed dancing?" I interrupted her onslaught of lies. Unflinchingly she nodded. "Yes, Your Highness, you did, you spoke of the Malrovian Waltz. I do not know the step, but Emma says she does, and I believe it shall be a sight to behold. I have already asked the orchestra to play."

It was only then that I noticed the dance floor was empty, and all eyes were upon us. Even the musicians were awaiting me . . . She'd laid out a trap and put live bait before me. For how could I now reject the poor girl before everyone, including her brother beside me, without being considered the very scoundrel she proclaimed me to be. I glared at her, and she glared right back . . . This was terribly unjust.

With no way out, I outstretched my hand toward Lady Emma and smiled. "Lady Emma, would you do me the honor of this dance?"

She took it with the greatest glee, and I led us forward . . . all the while thinking of how I would repay the horrid little prevaricator that was Lady Hathor for her transgressions. Not only had she lied about our conversation, but she'd also orchestrated these events, with little care for the implication it would have for my very first dance to be with this young girl . . . who did not know the steps as well as she claimed.

"Ah," I hissed, stopping as she stepped on my foot for the third time.

"Forgive me, Your High—"

"It's quite all right," I lied through a forced smile and lifted my hand up again for us to begin.

As we spun, from the corner of my eye, I watched as Lady Hathor giggled with Lukas. I had misjudged her greatly. She was not an innocent little lamb; she was a conniving fox. The rumors were true—she was exactly as they said, she was a hunter. She wished to remove any idea that she was attached to me by immediately pushing me off to another young lady while she conversed freely with the gentleman of her choosing . . . her *hero*.

The more I thought of how she'd entrapped me with ease, the more annoyed I grew. Did she really believe she could brush me aside so easily? I stayed calm throughout the dance and several more missteps upon my toes before finally the piece concluded. Bowing to Emma, I turned toward where I had last seen her, but she was no longer beside Lukas . . . in fact, I could not see her in the room at all.

Where had she run off to?

"I'm sure every girl will be looking to learn that dance by the morning," Lukas said as I approached him.

"I will not be dancing again so there is no need."

"Then you will have danced only with my sister and that will prove to be . . . a conversation." He smirked and I frowned.

I had forgotten, once a dance had been accepted, several others had to follow or else all of society would believe she was the one I sought to give my sole attention. This mess was all because of her! I wanted to ask him where she had gone but did not wish to expose myself to his queries on my interest in her.

"Why did your sister even learn the Malrovian Waltz?" I asked, changing the subject.

"How would I know? She must have seen it in one of her papers. She likes to dance." He took another drink. "Did she do well? I did not catch much of it."

"Yes, your attention seemed otherwise occupied."

He smirked, taking a sip before answering. "Lady Hathor and I were speaking of art."

"Art?" I repeated, confused.

"She is quite the artist. She was either completely smitten by my knowledge . . . or by the idea of becoming a countess."

"Is that so? Then why did she depart from your side so quickly?"

"She excused herself for a moment. But I'm sure she wished

to keep me on my toes, as they say, and not seem too eager, after all it is only the first night," he mused happily while his gaze shifted to the next lady who passed us. "Have you thought of whom you shall dance with next? For a great many seem to be passing by us solely for your attention."

It was then that I noticed the ladies who seemed to be walking past us slowly back and forth like ducks in a pond.

I was beginning to regret coming here at all. "I need some air."

Hathor

I ran away to avoid being reprimanded by him or worse, falling victim to whatever he deemed would make us seem like the *closest of acquaintances*. The only problem was there was no place in the hall to hide, and so I had chosen to step outside and feel the warm evening breeze upon my face. Walking out onto the balcony, I leaned over the railing, resting my body against it as I looked up at the moon. It was so beautiful and felt so calm, I almost wished I could grab my brushes and paint.

"What an absolute failure this all was." All this effort to create the perfect week for my love story ruined. Mama had taken care to plan everything to work in my favor and yet because of one man . . . "One despicable prince. Truly, Hathor, your luck is impeccable. Of all the princes you could have accidently come across, you met him. Aphrodite meets a passionate romantic who has desired her for years, Verity meets a charming thinker with a heart, who tends to the sick. Me? I meet an obnoxious impudent rake in a blue coat."

I laughed because it truly was not fair! I looked up to the stars. "Whatever did I do to deserve such a fate?"

"Hypocrisy might be my guess."

I glanced back to see the man in question glaring at me again with those eyes of his. "For I believe you went on viciously lecturing about common decency, only to slander my name in the same manner."

I moved off the railing, turning to him. "I beg your pardon, sir, but when was your name spoken?"

"My name was not clearly stated, but it was implied, for how many other *despicable princes* do you know?"

"I need not tell you, and if you cannot prove for certain you are the only prince I know, then there is no way for it to be inferred." I huffed and lifted my head high. He cracked his jaw to the side and smirked. "Now, please excuse me, Your—"

"Another reason you might be punished is your cruelty," he stated before I could walk away.

"I beg your pardon? Cruelty? And what malice have you suffered?"

"Not I, but Lady Emma," he replied, frowning at me. "In order to rid yourself of me, you gave no thought to that girl's feelings. You crafted a lie, forcing me to dance with her, even though I have no interest in her whatsoever."

"You make it seem as though I forced you to propose to her; it was merely a dance—"

"Nothing is *merely* anything for a prince. Having been the only girl I danced with thus far, she will have the ire of all the other young ladies for the rest of the evening, especially considering I will not dance with anyone else."

"That is you being cruel, not I!"

"You forced my hand!"

"You have come to weeklong festivities, part of which includes dancing. So surely you knew you were going to dance with ladies one way or another."

"If you cannot prove that for certain, then there is no way

for it to be known." He twisted my words and threw them back in my face with a smirk upon his lips. He stepped forward. "I believe the way to solve Lady Emma's problem is for you to be my next dance."

"I would rather break my feet!"

"Break them then," he snapped, stepping far too close, and when I stepped back, he stepped forward. So I took another step back and he another forward until my back was pressed against the railing and his body stood like a wall before me. For some reason my heart began to quicken. "Well, jump and break your feet, Lady Hathor, or do you need my assistance?"

His voice was softer and closer. I could strangely feel . . . feel something from him.

"You are a horrible man."

"You are a horrible lady."

"Am not!"

"You are so!"

"I dislike you greatly!"

He leaned in. "Likewise."

Angrily I pushed his chest with all my strength, but as I tried to escape him, I rolled my ankle on a damn stone, making me fall into his chest rather than away from him. His arms were around me tightly, and I was so startled I froze. Before I could say anything, he lifted me up, his hands on either side of my waist, and sat me upon the railing as though I were a child.

"Are you all right?" He moved to check my ankle. "Does it hurt?"

I just stared at him.

"Lady Hathor?"

Blinking, I shook the clouds from my mind. "I am fine. You ought not to touch me."

"Fine, I shall call for a doctor—"

"I do not need a doctor, do not be so dramatic," I muttered, tucking my ankle behind my leg, embarrassed by it. "Do you always touch women so impertinently?"

He glanced up from my feet to meet my eyes. "And if the answer is yes? What shall you do?"

I did not have an answer, and I was not sure why I could not speak. I felt somewhat stuck. Stuck on the ledge, stuck in his gaze. Stuck . . . in this moment.

"Well, Lady Hathor, do you have no more curses to scream at me?" Once more he moved closer.

"Is this your method for ruining women?" I asked calmly.

"I beg your pardon?"

"Do you speak softly, lean closely, touching them freely, confusing their thoughts before you strike?"

"You truly believe me to be so villainous?"

"Yes."

"Then as I said at dinner, a villain I shall be," he replied. And before I could ask him what he meant, his lips were on mine.

My eyes widened and I . . . my mind was blank. It was as if I were watching myself from another self as his tongue entered my mouth and rolled over mine. It sent a shiver down my spine. Maybe that was what drew my senses back. Pushing him away, I slapped him across the face as hard as I could.

"Have you gone mad?" I gasped, hopping down, touching my own lips in shock.

"Maybe," he muttered softly, not looking at me.

"Hathor?"

I jumped to see Silva staring at me. She bowed her head to the fiend beside me before looking back to me. "You've been gone for quite some time, how about we return together."

"Yes! I should return! The air is rather thin out here," I huffed, linking arms with her and without saying another word to him.

Why had he done that?

He was teasing me but even still. Was he seeking to ruin me? Such harsh revenge for such a small slight? He was horrid. Truly evil.

"Hathor, you are dragging me."

"How much did you see?"

"See of what? What happened?" she questioned, confused. I was relieved, glancing around to make sure no one else had seen.

"Nothing," I replied, adjusting my grip upon her.

"It does not look like nothing, so I suggest you take a breath . . . In fact, several might be in order."

I paused in the hall and inhaled once, then again. When it didn't work, I turned back to where he was outside; however, he wasn't following us. Instead, he was walking down the steps leading down the side of the balcony toward the gardens. "I have never met a man so discourteous in my life."

"Hathor, tell me! Did something happen?"

"He . . . He . . ." I did not even know how to explain it. "I just do not like him."

"Very well, but you must keep such feelings to yourself. He is the queen's nephew, and we ought not bring trouble on ourselves over anything trivial," she said gently.

I slapped my cheeks gently to gather my wits. I took another deep breath and nodded to her. "You are right, I shall just keep my distance. Come, let us see who shall win the honor of my first dance this evening."

She giggled and nodded as we reentered the hall. I had hoped to keep a cheerful disposition, but it faded when I noticed the sharp gaze Emma was receiving from her sister . . . along with the other girls. It seemed like they were all ready to descend into a mob around her . . . All this because of a simple dance?

"Hathor?" Clementina came up to us.

"I shall go find your brother," Silva said as she released my arm and left.

"Thank goodness you've returned. I am not sure Emma can handle the attention much longer," Clementina whispered to me as we began walking past a pair of mamas whom I heard muttering to each other.

"Mary, I could understand, but Emma . . . she does not have the look of a princess, now does she."

"I am sure nothing will come of it."

"A great many matches have been formed with a lot less. Don't let her looks fool you, those who lack beauty often must employ other methods."

I gasped in shock, whispering to Clementina, "What is the matter with them? It was just a dance."

"It is jealousy. You should have heard what they were saying about you over dinner."

My eyes widened. "They were speaking about me?"

"Viciously. They said your mama was cunning in sitting you both together."

"That was just proper etiquette, no?"

"Well, they have forgotten all about it and chosen a new target," she answered, and we looked back at Emma, about whom Mary was muttering something . . . harsh, I was sure. Emma looked as though she wished to sink into the ground and hide.

Had I really caused this?

It was not my intention.

I did not wish to be cruel.

Emma often talked about how she enjoyed dancing and wished to show us all the other dances she'd learned. When I asked if she knew of any dances from Malrovia, I realized I could distance myself from the rude prince by making every-

one think he was merely being friendly to *all* of the young ladies. I did not think it would turn into an attack on her person.

"Now what?" I muttered.

"What do you mean? Nothing can be done, can it?"

It was then that the rogue in question reentered the hall.
Quickly all the ladies readjusted their expressions, smiling
tenderly in his direction. He glanced to me and I looked away.

"Lady Hathor, if I may have the honor?" Lord Covington
said with his hand outstretched . . . all but saving me.

"Of course," I said, taking it brightly.

"Do not mind Prince Wilhelm, he is a bit temperamental
when it comes to young ladies," Lord Covington said as we
reached the center of the dance floor.

"I do not mind him in the least," I replied.

"I see August is proving himself uncharming." He replied.

"August?" I repeated, pretending not to know of whom he
spoke.

"Ah, I mean Prince Wilhelm."

"You call him by a nickname? I did not realize you were so
close."

"Yes, I met him while on tour years ago. He's a good man . . .
just . . . complicated. But then again, what do you expect from
a royal?"

"Decency, righteousness, and honor, is that not what we are
all meant to expect?"

"Expectations are heavy. I know and I'm only an earl," he
replied and then seemed to remember something. "Though
I'm glad to say my estates are properly run and healthy . . . all
they need is a good mistress."

Right . . . I kept forgetting that other men were here for
matches as well. "And what makes a good mistress in Covington?"

He shared his thoughts with enthusiasm that sadly I could not match. Not because I did not wish to but because I was keenly aware of the blue eyes that were staring intensely at the side of my face. I did not wish to think of him or even be aware of his presence.

But I was.

My lips still burned from his actions.

No matter where I spun and danced throughout the hall . . . I could sense him.

7

Hathor

I had collapsed onto my bed the moment I returned, without bothering to change. Never had I felt so tired, and what was worse . . . it felt like I had gotten only thirty minutes of sleep before it was daybreak and I was expected to be up once again.

"How much longer do you plan on lying about?"

I groaned, rolling onto my side. "Mama, I'm so tired. I believe I might even have a fever."

"One does not get fevers in June. Now get up, you must prepare," she ordered while Bernice helped me sit up straight.

I sighed and slid off my bed, marching to my vanity only to see my own reflection and scream. "Who is this?"

"It is you, dear," Mama said as she came beside me, brushing my tangled puffy hair away from my face where all the rouge had smeared. "Apparently you decided to make your outside as messy as your inside."

"What does that mean?" I asked quickly, hoping no one had seen or spoken of what had transpired last night.

"You tell me, as I am very curious about what made you act as though you'd lost your senses before Prince Wilhelm last night. You were glaring at him and avoiding him as though he were carrying the plague."

I panicked.

"I already told you; he insulted me most viciously."

"So why were you both flirting during dinner?"

I looked at her in horror. She always saw the truth in everything; how did she not see it here? "Nothing of the sort was happening. In fact, it was very much the opposite. I was trying to tell him we ought to maintain our distance from each other and then—"

"And you just muttered his name in your sleep. That is not distance, Hathor."

"Mama!" My mouth dropped open . . . How . . . was I supposed to explain this?

"Close your mouth, that is not ladylike," she snapped at me. I immediately shut my mouth, though my cheeks puffed up like a chipmunk's in frustration. Why was no one else seeing the truth here? I was being tormented by an evil prince. "Hathor, you must be very careful with your actions around Prince Wilhelm. I know you wish to be a princess—"

"Mama, I promise you I no longer have any such desire. Not with him anyway. I swear it is not at all what it looks like." She let out a sigh and looked over my face as if she did not believe me. I took her hand. "Mama, Lord Covington showed interest in me. Today I will go riding with him and I will even bring some of my art to show him. He was very keen on it yesterday."

"Very well, I'll tell the stable hands to prepare your horses. Bernice, make sure she is ready on time," she said, brushing my cheek before moving to leave me.

I waited until she left before I spun around and looked directly into the freckled face of Bernice. "What is everyone saying about me?"

"My lady—"

"Do not seek to spare my feelings. The servants hear everything and know everything—what is being said?"

"It is nothing but a mess of gossip right now, my lady. Some people are saying the prince likes you keenly, others are saying he snubbed you terribly last night."

"That is what they are saying about him, what are they saying about *me*? Did I do anything wrong?"

"Wrong, my lady?" she asked, not understanding, and it was only then that I could calm down. "Do you like him, my lady?"

"Ah!" I groaned, turning around and placing my head on the vanity top. "I do not like him. Why does no one see that?"

"I see it, my lady, though others might not because they know how much you wished to be a princess."

"Oh, so they just believe me to be a title hunter." I frowned. I still felt bitter at how that had become my reputation . . . as if I were the only noblewoman in England looking for a man with a title.

"Worry not over what they say, for you are Lady Hathor Du Bell, an honest, upright young lady from one of the greatest families," she reminded me and smiled. I looked at her in the mirror only to be met with the sight of myself again.

"Thank you, Bernice, can you repeat that again when I do not look horrendous?"

She laughed as she began to work on my hair. "Of course, my lady."

Knock. Knock.

"Enter."

When the doors opened, I saw the blonde curls of . . . Devana.

"I am merely checking on you," she said.

"Bernice, can you give us a moment—"

"No, it is all right, Mama will be upset if you are late. We will talk later, yes?" she said gently.

"I promise," I said back to her as she left.

I truly was a mess. My insides and my outsides were just . . . chaos, no matter how I sought to better myself or my situation. I could feel myself growing dejected and truly did not wish to spend any more time being so.

"I must look stunning today, Bernice, let us spare nothing." I would regain control of the situation I was in, firstly by making it abundantly clear to everyone that I was not going to be that horrid man's princess, and secondly by securing the attentions of other suitors. We'd spend most of the morning and afternoon entertaining upon the castle grounds; I'd surely have the upper hand.

Seventy-two minutes and three outfit changes later, I had finally managed to make it outside. Though it was my fastest time yet . . . it still was not fast enough to compete with all of the other young ladies who were already out bright and early, clearly awaiting an ill-mannered prince. I glanced down at my bag, making sure I had brought my art supplies with me, when I heard someone call out.

"Good morning, Hathor, I must say we were not expecting you to be out so early," Mary said as she approached me from the right side, dressed in soft pink with a matching parasol. Beside her was of course Amity, who stood in a deep green dress, also with a parasol.

"And why is that?" I asked.

"Well, if I had been so utterly rejected as you were last night, I do not think I would show my face for days," Amity said. It looked like she desperately wished to laugh at me.

"Amity, when you possess a face as fine as mine, I believe it is rather insulting not to showcase it," I said with a smile.

"Hm," Mary scoffed. "Is it fine or is it duplicitous? One moment you are claiming you do not wish for Prince Wilhelm's attentions *at all* and the next you two are sharing glances. I saw how you both looked at each other last night."

I wished to scream to the sky, but since everyone was now coming out for the morning, all I could say was "You are free to believe whatever you wish about my face, Mary, but do know I shall not think of yours at all. Now, if you will excuse me, I am expected at the stables."

I did not wait for another word before turning from her and walking as fast as I could without looking as though I were running away.

"Stay calm, Hathor. Stay calm," I muttered to myself the whole way to the stables. I took deep breaths, and tried to think of positive things, like how I'd make a magnificent countess. I'd be able to host a great many balls, like Mama, go to court, and paint whatever and whenever I pleased. I'd have a peaceful and happy life. The more I thought of it, the more my mood improved.

"Lady Hathor, good morning." Mr. Johnathon, the stableman, bowed his head to me. "I have your horse here."

"Good morning, Mr. Johnathon," I said as I walked up to my horse just outside the stable and tapped the white patch on her nose twice, making her brush up against my face—a trick I had taught her. "Good morning to you, too, Sofonisba."

"She's in good spirits this morning, my lady. I'm sure she is excited for the exercise," he said, petting the side of her neck cheerfully.

"No exercise from me today, as it is only a stroll," I replied, noticing that he'd given her a normal saddle instead of a side one. "The saddle will need to be changed."

"Forgive me, my lady, I will go fetch the correct one. I was not told which you preferred today," he said and called out to one of the other hands to get the sidesaddle.

I glanced around the stables to see if anyone else had arrived. "Has no one else called for their horse to be prepared?"

"Yes, just one, he's inside now—"

"Really?" I said, moving into the stable, expecting to see Lord Covington. However, holding on to the reins of a white horse with black legs was . . . Prince Wilhelm. I stared at him and he stared back. When he opened his mouth to speak, I turned around and went back to my horse. I placed my sketchbook into my saddlebag.

"Never mind getting a different saddle, I think some exercise is in order," I said as I mounted up, though with my dress it took a bit of extra effort.

"Lady Hathor, I do not mean to interrupt—"

I was off as fast as I could be, without a second thought. I galloped forward with every desire to put as much earth between us as possible.

"Lady Hathor!" I heard the stablemen yell out behind me.

As I traveled farther and faster down the path from the stables, the wind whipped past me fiercely. My lungs filled with air and my heart pounded vigorously within my chest.

Just when I was sure I'd gotten far enough away, I saw a blur of white appear beside me.

"Slow down!" he yelled at me, now beside me, racing along with me. Why? Why was he following me?

Faster, I thought, and somehow Sofonisba heard me. My heart nearly rose into my throat as we burst forward, and I grinned as I thought I'd lost him. However, within a matter of moments, he was back riding right beside me. I glanced over only to see him staring at me, his eyes wide in utter shock or maybe horror. I was not sure which, but I did not stop, racing past him and farther down the path as fast as I could. Again, a third time, he was beside me keeping pace.

"Hathor!" he yelled at me, pulling in front of me, forcing me to slow down.

"What on earth are you doing?" I yelled back as Sofonisba

came to a stop, leaving me a few paces in front of him. I turned to see him clearly. His hair was tousled in every direction by the wind, and his white face was rather striking while breathless, actually.

"I could ask the same of you! Are you all right?" he snapped at me with a strange tone, given the question.

"Yes, why?" I said, taking another deep breath.

"Because you were riding as if you planned to save the king!"

"I do believe one of my ancestors actually did, so it may very well be possible," I replied, brushing my hair from my face. "However, my ride today was solely to rid myself of your company. Clearly, I did not go fast enough. So, if you'll excuse me—"

"Is my company so horrid that you would risk your neck? What would have happened if you were thrown?"

"I would fly, then land."

He huffed, or was that a chuckle? I was not sure, but either way he then let a sigh go and shook his head. "Do you not believe your disdain of me is a bit excessive?"

"No, I believe it is rather proportional, thank you. Or did you forget what you did last night?"

"I did not forget. And I wished to apologize—"

"I do not want your apology!"

"When do you ever!"

"Are you mocking me?"

"I am trying to apologize here!"

"Why?"

"What?"

"Why did you . . . why did you do what you did?" I questioned.

He frowned before letting out a sigh. "I do not know."

"That is a horrible answer."

"I am aware, but I cannot explain. All I can do is beg forgiveness for my actions. It shall not happen again."

"And you can never speak of it!" I hollered at him. "Not to me. Not to anyone. I shall wipe it from my mind utterly, and should you speak of it I shall deny—"

"Lady Hathor, fear not. I would not do such a thing against you or anyone. I swear upon all that is holy, I will never speak of it again."

"I do not know that I can trust you."

"Lady Hathor . . ."

"You have broken the rules of propriety and you have no reason as to why. Now you demand forgiveness, and I am supposed to give it based on what? Your word? What good is that when you act . . . as you act. Do you believe me a fool?"

He chuffed. "The way I acted? I was willing to take the blame, as it was I who caused the ordeal, but do not forget you returned the kiss."

"I did not!"

"You very much did so!"

I gasped back. "No—"

"Yes, Lady Hathor, you did."

Once more I stared at him and held my head high. "I know nothing of what you speak and I will not talk of it again. It is your word against mine and I say I did not."

"And I say you did—"

"You swore upon all that is holy you would never speak of it again. Therefore, I will hold you to that, Your Highness, or do you not fear God either?" I continued on my ride, and I wanted to believe the thundering in my heart was from the exercise, but I could not say for certain.

Wilhelm

Hopping down from my horse, I ripped off my gloves. I was damn well ready to rid myself of my coat as well; all of my body was boiling over. I could feel my jaw clenching tighter and tighter.

Why the bloody hell had I kissed her? I'd been asking myself that every moment since it happened. What was wrong with me? And she, she was so . . . unforgiving of me. But then again, I could not blame her. She was the one who was proper. Then at the same time would it not have been easier for her to use it against me? I knew many ladies who'd trapped men into marriage in such a way.

My mind was an utter mess.

"August?" Lukas called as he approached the stables . . . with none other than her brother. I marched toward them, compelled to ask . . .

"I must ask you, Damon, is your sister a lawyer?" I spit the words out, gripping tightly to my gloves.

"No, I do not believe so."

"Then has she ever spoken of her desire to be a lecturer? No? For even professors do not have such pride, so I must assume she wishes to be a preacher?"

"No, Your Highness, for if my sister were so unfortunate as to pick an occupation, I'm sure it would be that of an artist."

I scoffed, shaking my head. "That does not seem to fit her personality in the slightest."

"Hathor's personality is rather . . . varied depending on the day." He laughed to himself.

"Well, she seemed rather taken on the subject of art when I spoke to her."

Lukas forced a laugh and then gave me a look, trying to

remind me that I was in fact speaking to her brother and to control myself.

"Your Highness, I must ask, has my sister offended you in some manner?" Damon questioned. He too looked me over carefully. I was unsure what he saw. I just felt annoyed and now exhausted from my annoyance.

"No" was all I could say to him. "Excuse me, I wish to change."

I did not wait for either of them, instead heading back into the castle toward my rooms. How this had all become such an utter ordeal was beyond my understanding. I had come here thinking very little of the reasons as to why, beyond obeying my aunt and wishing to test Hathor's conviction. To my surprise she was more steadfast and stubborn than any other woman I had ever encountered. Normally whenever a lady such as herself made my acquaintance and discovered I was a prince, they spoke gently, sought to show themselves in the most amiable light. They ran toward me and devoted all their efforts to gaining my attentions. Even in situations where I was less than gentlemanly, they still sought to be agreeable . . . until now.

Now I was insulted or mocked every time I spoke to her. She was unforgiving and severe in her words with me. Yes, I had teased her last night at dinner, and she paid me back for it. I thought I'd ended it there by offering her a dance, and to my face she laughed, saying she would rather break her own feet!

It was clear she'd meant it and she only changed her mind when she saw the condition of the conversation around Lady Emma. . . . Today, once more I thought to end our feud and she threw words in my face!

"Psss."

I paused, turning to find the source of the noise when it . . . she . . . spoke from above me. "Up here."

There was a small girl with light brown skin and messy curly hair peeking down over the railing of the stairs.

"Are you the prince?"

"I am a prince," I answered. "Who are you?"

"Abena Du Bell."

Ah . . . one of her sisters. "Hello."

"I've come to warn you."

"Of?"

"Hathor. She is a horrid monster and will drive you insane."

For some reason hearing someone else say this of her made me laugh. "Is that so? Where were you to warn me weeks ago?"

"How could I have warned you weeks ago? I only heard of you just days ago," she questioned.

Logical. "Yes, well, true. Thank you for letting me know; however, I feel as though I have learned this lesson on my own."

"So, you won't marry her?" she said with a glee that was rather strange.

"Why are you speaking so poorly of your sister?"

"That is my concern," she said, and for a moment I saw a familiar stubbornness. "All I need to know is that you will not marry her."

"Who I marry is my concern and so I need not answer to you."

Her smile dropped drastically and now her hands were on her hips. She came down the stairs just so I could see her small frame on the landing. "You're being difficult."

I laughed again. "Am I? Forgive me."

"I will if you promise not to marry Hathor."

"May I ask why you are against me marrying her?"

"I told you. She is terrible, she snores . . . very loudly. She takes forever to get ready every day, she's absolutely horrified by all bugs—even butterflies, and she's always telling me to go away because she's in a mood!" She huffed and I bit my lip to keep from snorting.

"Yes, this sounds very ghastly indeed."

"I—"

"Abena!" She jumped at the sound of another girl's voice. This girl, with blonde hair and bright eyes, rushed down to grab her arm. "What did Mama tell you about disturbing the guests!"

"Devana, let go! I'm not done talking to him—" Devana clasped her other hand over Abena's mouth.

"Forgive her, Your Highness, and please excuse us," she said, already taking the girl back up the stairs. Because they were both struggling, she nearly slipped but quickly recovered. She rushed her back up and I just stood there, thoroughly confused but greatly amused as well.

What an odd bunch this family was . . . these Du Bells.

Maybe the secret to understanding Hathor was to . . . wait, why did I wish to understand her? And why was this woman consistently plaguing my thoughts?

Damn me for kissing her!

And damn me twice for wanting to do it again.

8

Wilhelm

When I arrived downstairs, the first person I saw was another Du Bell. This time her brother was speaking to an older maid. Upon seeing me, he dismissed her and moved to gain my attention.

"Is everything all right?" I questioned first.

"I've been informed that one of my sisters may have disturbed you," he said with concern. My first thought went to Lady Hathor, as she was the cause for my true disturbance. But he added, "I apologize on Abena's behalf; she has a tendency to be riotous."

"I assure you she did not say anything that I found disturbing or worth invoking a riot," I replied as I followed in step with him.

"Believe me, that would not be the case should Hathor find out." He sighed and then stopped at one of the doors. "Would you care for a drink?"

"Certainly," I said as we entered the library, and he moved to pull wine from some secret compartment within the oak desk.

"My father often stores his best here for moments when we seek to hide from the girls, my mother included," he said as he removed glasses from the sideboard.

"I can only imagine how often that has happened . . . though I am not surprised that even a great lord must take refuge somewhere from the monotonous demands of being a husband and father," I said as he handed me a glass.

"Monotonous would not be the word either my father or I would use." He chuckled as he lifted the glass. "In fact, it is rather the opposite. The women of this family take us on countless adventures. In here is the only time we are free to be dull in peace."

"Surely you jest, for what adventure could a woman take you on?"

He stared at me for a moment and then shook his head. "You shall see when you are wed."

"This again? If I did not know better, I would think you were my aunt's spy."

He smirked. "I do not make a habit of losing bets. I am more concerned about what Abena may have said to you."

"What she said?" I asked, noticing a covered canvas in a corner of the room.

"Yes, I heard it was something horrible about Hathor?"

"It was hardly horrible, more amusing."

He frowned and shook his head. "That girl. Pay her no mind. She is just . . . reluctant to see any of her sisters married off."

"Why on earth would she not wish her sisters to get married?"

"Because they'll leave," Damon said with a hint of sadness on his face for the briefest of moments. "I've caught her three times now trying to scare off Hathor's suitors with horrid stories of her. I have not told my mother or Hathor, as I fear they will string up Abena by her toes should they find out. My other sister, Devana, immediately sent one of the maids to find me after uncovering Abena's latest attempt with you."

"How quickly you act over something so small."

"The reputation of my sisters is not a small matter to me."

"I mean . . ."

"I understand what you mean, but nevertheless, for Hathor's sake, I thought it important to speak to you and clarify the situation immediately."

It was abnormal to me, these siblings who rallied for one another at the slightest risk. "You Du Bell siblings are very close it seems."

"Aren't all siblings close?"

What a life he must have lived to ask such a question with true perplexity upon his face. Not wishing to destroy the illusions in his head, I pointed to the canvas in the corner to change the subject. "What is that?"

"Ah, one of Hathor's pending masterpieces—"

"Damon?" The door opened to reveal a simple-faced woman with blonde hair who was dressed in a light blue gown. Upon seeing me, her eyes widened and she curtsied. "Hello, Your Highness, forgive me, I was not told you were here as well."

"It is fine," I said, remembering her to be his wife. "If you need the room, I can return outside—"

"No, not at all. Please stay and relax," she said quickly and then looked to her husband. "My dear, when you have a moment, Mini—"

"Is she all right?" he asked, already putting his glass down and walking toward her.

I did not wish to pry and so I turned to face the stacks of books before me, lifting one to casually read, only to find it was written in Arabic . . . In fact all the books seemed to have come from the east. It was a massive collection, all in a variety of foreign languages, though there were bookmarks and notes in English in the margins of many of them.

"Your Highness."

I turned back to Damon, who was partially out the door

already. "I must tend to a matter momentarily. If you need anything—"

"I'm quite fine, thank you."

He nodded before stepping out. When the doors closed, I placed my drink down and moved to the canvas. I lifted the sheet up gently. It was clearly unfinished—she'd begun painting some spots while the vast majority were still sketched . . . even still, I could see a wondrous talent. It was not just the image of her father that was striking but the whole cast of characters within the library. By their heights and number I could only assume the others were family as well. I noticed even the books upon the shelves were copied exactly as they appeared before my eyes. I stepped back to see the vantage from which she was creating, backing up so far I knocked into the one of the shelves and caused a few volumes to nearly fall.

Catching them, luckily, I started to put them back when I spotted a familiar book. Earlier this morning, I'd noticed Lady Hathor holding a book that looked not just like this but like several on the shelf. I should have left it be, but curiosity, maybe boredom, got the best of me.

On the first page, in the most delicate handwriting, was *To my future love, know I do not speak well with words but with art*.

I flipped to the next page to see drawings of herself, but that was not what was unusual. It was the partial figure beside her at a picnic. Everything, from the lace of her dress to the blades of grass, was drawn as if captured from real life, but next to her was only the start of a sketch of a person. Page after page showed her walking through London, at a dinner table, on a boat upon the river, and in every image, there were the faintest of lines drawn of another person meant to be there.

"What are you doing!"

I jumped at the rage within that voice. Turning toward the

door, I found, staring at me in her familiar fashion of horror, none other than Lady Hathor.

Shit.

Hathor

I felt utterly bizarre trying to speak with any other gentlemen.

It was as if every conversation were nothing but dull flattery and repetitious observations on the weather. The longer I sought to engage with them the greater my frustration. It was odd, they were acting normally, properly, and yet—it displeased me. Desiring not to show that I was put out, I slowly withdrew from their company and excused myself to change out of my riding clothes. I came to the library seeking a new reference book only to find him . . . Prince Wilhelm . . . flipping through the pages of my previous work as though they were his own personal letters.

"I did not mean to pry," he said as he snapped the book closed and hid it behind his back.

"Whether you meant to or not does not change the fact that you are prying," I said as I rushed over to him, trying to get the book back.

He stepped out of my way, still holding the book. "So you admit they are yours?"

"Clearly they are not yours, so return it at once!"

He did not.

Instead, he still held the book away from me, grinning. "Is this what you believe love to be? Forcing a gentleman to accompany you on picnics and boat rides? You already have the image of your whole life set, you wish only to insert his face into your fantasy, it seems."

"Fantasy? You believe picnics and boat rides to be things of fantasy?"

"I think them to be trivial attempts to appease women." He chuckled and opened my book for me to see one page. "No man finds enjoyment in this and would only do it upon being forced."

"Just because you are not a man who finds enjoyment in doing such things does not mean all men will not find enjoyment in them." I tried once more to reach my sketchbook, this time jumping to take it from him. He jumped back . . . too far back, and knocked over my canvas, which fell back onto one of the chairs, the arm ripping a hole right through the center.

My mouth dropped open to make way for a scream that would not come. I could only stare in disbelief.

"Forgive me, it was an accident!" he said, quickly going to lift it up. I saw no point; the piece was dead. He'd killed it. "I shall replace—"

"You cannot replace art, you imbecile!" I snatched the canvas from him and hugged it to my chest.

"Imbecile? You are calling me a—"

"Yes!" I snapped. I marched up to him and stuck my finger into his chest, trying to poke a hole into him as he'd done to my art. "Yes, I am calling you that, for you continuously injure me! Why? What did I do to you? Nothing. I am sure of it. And yet each time we cross paths you commit some act of harm against me."

"Lady Hathor, I did not mean to—"

"I do not care!"

"What is going on?"

I turned to see my brother now at the door, staring between us both worriedly. It was only then that I realized . . . we were a man and woman alone, with no chaperone, standing far too close to each other. Immediately I took several steps back and opened my mouth to explain, when the villain spoke first.

"I have accidently ruined Lady Hathor's art, and she is rightly cross with me over it." I inhaled through my nose as he walked toward my brother. "I shall seek to apologize when she has calmed."

"I will not be calmed!" I hollered. My brother's eyes snapped to me with a fury similar to our mother's. I looked away, breathing again through my nose. I could hear them muttering to each other, but I refused to give him another look.

"Must you be so uncompromising?" Damon asked me once Prince Wilhelm had left the room.

I lifted up my painting for him to see. "Can you not see that it is *he* who is uncompromising? He ruined my—"

"Hathor, this is not the first time one of your pieces has been ruined. You've never looked ready to kill someone over it, nor have you ever insulted them with such vulgarity," he said in return.

"I was barely vulgar," I muttered, setting the ruined work back down.

"Barely is still inappropriate. This may be our home, but they are our guests . . . and he the most important guest of all."

"So because he is a prince, he is allowed to destroy whatever he pleases? And I must accept it? Is that compromise?"

"Hathor . . . my dear sister"—he put his hands on my shoulders—"please breathe. You've always been dramatic, but you've never been stupid."

"What does that mean?"

"They are royals. They do not compromise; we do. That is what it means to be a loyal member of society. That is what it means to be a great lady, or have you forgotten?"

"Well—"

"Think of what will happen if you make an enemy of this prince," he said, looking me in the eye. "If the queen hears you have offended her nephew. Even if he is wrong, we must ignore it. If he greatly upsets you, stay away from him. Find me if you need to, and I shall stand as your shield, but do not act recklessly. If not for your sake, then for Devana's and Abena's, who still need to debut into society."

I frowned but nodded.

"Good. Now should I call your maid to join you here as you sulk? Or will you go outside and socialize, since Mother put in a lot of effort for you?"

"I guess I must socialize, though all the gentlemen have been greatly disappointing thus far. And please, do not tell Mama I was in here alone with someone. I do not wish to be lectured right now." I moved to put the ruins of my work to the side when I noticed my sketchbook, the one he'd looked through, laid carefully on the table. I lifted it up and flipped through the pages. "Do men truly not enjoy picnics and boat rides?"

"What?"

I looked back to him, hugging the book to my chest. I actually didn't want to know the answer, so I just shook my head. "Never mind—"

"That is your second 'never mind' this afternoon. If there is a third, I may have to call a doctor."

"Must you pick on me?"

"Yes, for you are being odd . . . more so than normal."

"I am starting to think I dislike all men in general," I huffed at him before marching out. Where were the romantics? The men who rode out into storms and wrote epic poetry? Why was everyone so . . . so . . . unlike what I wanted?

Was I truly just waiting on a fantasy?

If so . . . were my grand expectations of love the real cause of my distress?

Could no man live up to the one I had sought to create in my book?

9

Hathor

I t did not matter if the prince was in the room or not; every single conversation was about him and what he might fancy.

Strangely enough, after the incident in the library, he did not show his face for the rest of the day. He even sent word that he was unwell and would have dinner in his rooms. That caused Mama, and everyone else, to panic. She immediately thought to call a doctor, and all the other mamas were gossiping about what the nature of his ailment could be. I suspected he was not truly ill. He merely wished to avoid everyone's company . . . my company in particular, for good reason. I could not believe I'd called him an imbecile and yelled at him as though he were a servant. Damon was right: It was wholly improper, even if I felt justified in my rage. Though I would not apologize, I still saw the harm that could be caused if the queen heard I was insulting royals like a madwoman.

Lying back on my bed, I felt the stress of the day weigh on me until sleep began to take me away. I was just about to roll over when I heard a gentle knock on my door.

Who could be coming so late?

"Enter," I called out with a yawn, sitting up to look at the door. But it didn't open. "Hello?"

Still nothing.

Confused, I got up and walked to the door. Upon opening

it, I saw no one. I did, however, feel a pat on my knees. I looked down and saw a canvas . . . and a letter. I lifted it up to see . . . my art. No, it wasn't my art, but it was *very* similar to the painting the prince had ruined in the library. The whole layout was the same as well, except a few corrections to the proportions and . . . my father's nose, drawn better. It was even completed to the same place I had stopped. Taking it along with the letter, I closed the door and moved back to my bed, carefully putting the canvas beside me before reading.

> *Dear Lady Hathor,*
>
> *You are correct: Art, lost or destroyed, can never be replaced. It is more than simply strokes of paint on paper. It is an artist's feelings, time, and effort. I know this very well, which is why guilt has compelled me to make amends in any way possible. Forgive my lack of talent; it has been some time since I last painted. However, I did my best to salvage what I could from memory. Do accept it as my most sincere apology.*
>
> *From*
> *A Villainous Imbecile*

I stared in shock, first at the letter, then at the painting. He did this from memory . . . and he called it a lack of talent? All within a day? Was he joking? He had to be, for he was far more accomplished than I was. I lifted the canvas again, inspecting every line in utter amazement. He'd truly forfeited all company just to work on it. Never had anyone done something like this for me. Guilt filled me for insulting him as I did. But that wasn't the only thing I felt. Magically, all my exhaustion had left me. I was invigorated—no, I was *inspired*—and slightly sour that he had such talent. I moved to my dresser trunk, pulling out my paints and tools, setting them up on the floor around me.

It was as though something had taken over me. I would not be able to rest until I finished this. I started first on my father, working around where the prince had left off, using the browns to bring out the oaks of the desk . . . my hands could not stop moving. I found myself humming gently as I planned out the colors of Mama's dress. It would be purple, of course. She loved that color.

I was so engulfed that I did not notice how long I'd painted. I did not see the sun rise, nor hear any birds or maids. It was as if everything else vanished. I could have sat there for several more hours, happily unbothered, when I heard my name yelled.

"Hathor? What in all the heavens are you doing?" I looked to the door to see Mama, alongside Bernice, staring back at me with wide eyes. Both of them gasped at the sight of me. "My dear, please tell me you have not spent all night painting!"

"I have not spent all night painting," I lied, as she wished.

"Hathor!"

"Mama, I have to finish this."

"No, you do not. Bernice, help her up at once," she ordered. Bernice was already at my side, her hands under my arms.

"Mama—"

"We have several guests here and activities you must attend. Your art can wait. Oh . . . you've paint in your hair! Look at you!" I looked in the mirror, and sure enough, there were smudges of paint all over my face, arms, and clothing. Not to mention the slight dark circles around my eyes from lack of sleep. "Have a hot bath drawn quickly, and then have ice brought up. We will need to make her eyes less puffy as quickly as possible."

"Mama—"

"What has happened to your enthusiastic quest to find a husband, my dear?" she questioned, cupping my face.

"I met the men, and saw they were not similarly enthusiastic about finding a wife," I huffed, trying to wipe the paint off my hand.

"Of course not. To many men, a wife is a symbol of further responsibility and death to youth."

I gasped. "That is not what you have always told me. You always said a good marriage is a blessing. And a man who loves you will give up all the world for you, and—"

"And all of that is true." She brushed strands of hair from my face. "But it applies directly to the man who loves *you*. Surely, you remember how your brother was before he met Silva. Your father and I could not even hold a single conversation on the subject of marriage without him rolling his eyes and desperately seeking to escape. Then, one day, he was in love and ready to run off to the nearest church. Men fear marriage, and yet crave a woman to love."

"Mama, that makes no sense at all!"

She laughed at me. "I know, but it is the reality we are working with. As I told you before, it does not happen overnight. It takes constant presence and perseverance. So long as you stay close, your special gentleman will realize he wants you to remain close to him. But none of that can happen if you are locked away in your room painting, so gather your wits!"

"I assure you, they are gathered. In fact, I fear I have too much."

"No more snark. Your behavior with Prince Wilhelm is plenty."

I groaned, wondering how much she knew, but then thought better of asking. She was Mama; I was sure she knew everything. Glancing back down at my painting, which Bernice and the rest of the maids who now entered were carefully setting to the side, I couldn't help but smile. It seemed Prince Wilhelm wasn't all bad.

I actually wanted to talk to him.

But solely for artistic purposes.

Wilhelm

I was exhausted and, in all honesty, wished for nothing more than to return to bed. However, I could not be absent for two days, or else all the guests would think me either dying or horribly discourteous. Though fighting back the urge to yawn in everyone's presence was equally rude. On top of that, my wrist and fingers ached. I could not believe my own foolishness. I truly had spent nearly a day working to re-create her painting by any means necessary. I did not understand the overwhelming guilt that possessed me, that forced me to pick up a paintbrush again after so long.

Each time I thought to take a break or to abandon the work altogether, I saw her face in my mind staring at me in horror . . . and pain. Immediately, I was painting again. Before I knew it, I'd finished late into the evening and pleaded with the same maid who'd brought me the art supplies to deliver the piece to Hathor's room. I could not even inquire as to her reaction; I'd collapsed in utter exhaustion, only to be woken up early this morning and forced out by Lukas.

Did she like it? Well, it was her work, so that might not have been the best question. I was a bit out of practice; with her character, she may very well have been insulted. Either way, I was sure she'd speak her mind . . . if she ever came down.

"Your Highness? *Your Highness?*"

"Yes?" I looked back to Lady Mary, whose company I'd

completely forgotten I was in. Not just her, but all the other ladies who were now also staring at me. "Forgive me. What were you discussing?"

"Whatever has ensnared your thoughts away from us, Your Highness, and how are we to recapture your attention?" She giggled as she fanned her neck. I'd learned young ladies were taught these tactics in order to trick men into staring at their breasts. Hers looked rather high and tight.

"Are you thinking of the war?" another girl, I believed her to be Lady Amity, said, stepping up beside Mary as though she wished to push her out of the way. She, too, fanned herself. Though we were outside, it was not so warm that one needed their own wind.

Normally I would play along and joke about something or other to amuse them, but I was exhausted, and I could feel my annoyance rise as they encircled me.

"I—"

"Papa says it is best not to think of such dreary things," Lady Mary cut in, once more trying to bring herself center stage. "I recommend riding, as it clears one's thoughts."

"Oh, wonderful! We should make it a point of duty to go for a ride," Lady Amity said, with a larger smile, if that were possible. "I am very fond of horses."

I was just about to lose my temper when, all of a sudden, I heard a familiar voice behind me.

"While you may be fond of horses, Amity, I do not believe they are very fond of you."

I turned around to see Lady Hathor wearing a scarlet red dress, holding a parasol in one hand and a book in the other. Beside her stood a very tall Lady Clementina, dressed in purple. "You were nearly thrown the last three times you rode, and your father forbade you to ride unaccompanied, is that not so?"

"I—"

"Yes, I believe it is so!" Lady Mary added. "You ought to be careful, my dear; one can never be too careful."

"Agreed. It is a lady's duty to always be mindful of her condition. As such, Mary, my maid can help you with your dress. It looks rather tight," Hathor said to her.

"It's quite fine, thank you, Hathor," Mary huffed.

"Oh. Well, if you believe so despite the ripped seam, then by all means continue on with your ride," she said, linking arms with Lady Clementina and continuing their walk. I truly believed she planned to pass by without saying a word to me. However, she paused before me and curtsied . . . correctly. "Good morning, Your Highness. Do forgive my friends. Normally, they are much more courteous, and would not crowd around someone freshly recovered or demand they partake in excess exertions of energy, but they are not accustomed to royalty. That is why they behave as a gaggle of geese."

She looked over the ladies one by one, with a cheerful amber eye, and said not another word before taking her friend and walking off toward the lake. I watched her go, somewhat . . . disappointed? Confused? I was not sure, exactly. She laughed and walked on disinterestedly, never turning back.

Not even a single word of thanks for all my efforts? No acknowledgment, not even abhorrence? Just nothing?

What on earth was wrong with this woman?

"By heavens, what did she say?"

I glanced over to Lukas, who had magically appeared at my side, as the position was only now open. All the other young ladies had vanished, his sister included.

"One moment I was worried I'd have to save you from an ambush of noble ladies, the next they were all fleeing as if under fire." He chuckled, his gaze on Hathor's distant figure.

"Was it not you who told me she was a title hunter, Lukas?"

I said, forcing him to look at me. "That she cared for nothing else, and only desired to be a lady of great standing and influence? Why does that now not seem to be an accurate picture of her character?"

He laughed, shaking his head. "My dear friend, have you forgotten all you know of women? If anyone should understand the games they play, it should be you, shouldn't it?" he said, hinting once more at my sordid past.

He was not wrong. I'd spent a great deal of my time seeking to seduce lonely noble widows . . . when I was not lost in a brothel. I wondered what Hathor would say of my background. Actually, I did not need to ponder that, she'd made her feelings well known to me. If she knew the depths of it, she very well may have convulsed in disgust at the sight of me. That thought . . . brought me displeasure. I did not wish for her to know. I did not wish for her to hate me.

"August?" Lukas called out to me.

"Games?" I said, as if I had not been lost in my thoughts. "You believe her to be playing games?"

"Yes, of course. Is she not playing hard to get? Clearly, she is plotting something. If not, why did she force all the other girls from your side?" he questioned.

Was that it? Was she only pretending to keep her distance? Pretending not to be interested in me? I frowned. That did not feel like the case, but then again, women did have a tendency to plot.

"Do not think too hard on it. Come, let's find the rest of the gentlemen and see if they have any word on the war."

I followed, and found myself once more surrounded, this time by men. To be honest, their company was not that much better than the ladies'. Though I did not have to fend against advances, I found myself observing as they all sought to prove their knowledge and expertise in battle strategy and maneuvering.

"My second cousin, poor fellow is fighting in Lisbon, I believe . . . he writes of the horrid conditions and nonstop cannon fire," the man to my left added to his story of his heroic family, which was odd; there had not been any battles in Lisbon for some time now.

"Your Highness, I heard your elder brother is leading a campaign against the French in the east. Is that so? What says he of how we are faring thus far? I heard there were a few disgruntled soldiers who were abandoning posts?"

They all turned to me. Instantly, I preferred the ladies' company. This day was already tiresome.

"I fear the greatest issue in war is information. By the time a letter is sent and returned, the conditions may have altogether changed, gentlemen. However, I trust that any news of discontented soldiers may be lies disseminated by Napoleon to harm the morale of our army. Other than that, I know no more of the state of things than any of you; nor did I come to Belclere to dwell on it. I am sure the ladies do not appreciate us neglecting them over it, either." I nodded to the group of young ladies waiting not so far off, their attention upon us. The men all stood up a bit straighter. "Men at war should be at war. Men at home . . . should be among ladies."

"I do believe I am meant to go for a walk with Lady Elizabeth," Lord Chiswick said, causing me to nod proudly at him and the rest of them to snicker. I took my chance to leave their company.

My only goal was to seek refuge somewhere, to sit and rest. I swear it. Yet, somehow, my feet led me far from everyone else, and directly to her. She sat upon a blanket, her back against a large tree, an open book in one hand and a pencil in another . . . sleeping! Her head back and her mouth open, snoring just as loudly as her younger sister had attested. Never had I seen such a thing. A lady, so finely dressed and put together, passed out as though she were drunk!

I could not help it. I laughed. If only I had a brush to paint her. When she stirred, I bit my lips closed, sneaking up to her quietly. I only sought to take the pencil and book from her hands to set them beside her. But as soon as I touched them, her eyes snapped open, and there I was: hunched over, my face far too close to hers. I could see every eyelash, every strand of hair upon her eyebrows, all the different shades of brown in her eyes . . . eyes that widened in terror.

Oh no.

"Do not scream," I said calmly.

"Ordering someone not to scream means there is a reason why one ought to scream!" She quickly stood up and stepped away from me, holding her pencil as a dagger and her book as a shield.

"You are being ridiculous. Do you truly believe I am the type of man who would attack someone?" I said, dusting my hands as I stood up straighter.

"You are the type of man to kiss someone!" she snapped.

Touché. "I thought we were not speaking of it?"

She huffed, but thankfully relaxed. "Why are you here?"

"I was invited to a weeklong—"

"Not here as in Belclere," she interrupted and then motioned to the space around the tree. "I mean *here*, as in under my tree?"

"Do you own the tree? Is no one else allowed to venture toward it?"

She sighed. "Were you not promising the ladies you'd go riding?"

"Did you not scatter all the young ladies around me, thus

ending all conversation of a ride? As such, I am free to go where I please."

"Must you argue with me?"

"Must *you* argue with *me*?" I replied. "Especially after the great pains I took to re-create your painting, for which you have not thanked me."

"Why would I thank you when it was an act of contrition?"

"Because it is common courtesy, in which you claimed to be well versed."

"When someone does something wrong and makes amends, you are to say, 'I forgive you,' not 'thank you.'"

"You have yet to say that, either."

"I have not had time to speak with you on the matter until now!" She groaned, and then took a deep breath to compose herself . . . which was amusing. "Your Highness, I received the painting. I *thank you*, and I forgive your folly in destroying it in the first place. Is this matter now settled?"

"That sounds so forced and spurious."

Again she breathed in through her nose slowly, and I waited for her retort. Instead, she just got up to go. "I promised my brother I would not argue with you, so I am leaving. Good day."

"Wait!" I called after her.

"Why? So you can find another reason to pick at me?"

"Is it I who seeks to fight, or you?" When she made a face again, I quickly added, "I truly did not mean to come across you here. I meant to leave you be after putting your things away, so you would not injure yourself. Then you woke, and I wished to inquire about how you liked the painting . . . but apparently we cannot have a conversation without conflict. So, I will continue on my way."

"You are greatly talented," she said suddenly, stopping me leaving. When I turned back to her, she was smiling. "When I saw your painting, I was in awe. Inspired. I stayed up well into the morning to continue working on it."

"You mean to tell me you did not sleep? You stayed up painting?" Was that why she was sleeping under the tree?

"Yes. I know I ought not to have, but truly, that is how moved I was."

I grinned. "I'm glad. You are very talented as well. I could tell from what I saw in the library that you have a level of mastery that surpasses many men."

Her grin widened and she nodded. "Yes, I know."

I laughed at the look of pride on her face. "You do not even feign humility?"

"In art, absolutely not. I'm quite horrid at a whole host of things, which serves to humble me. The one thing I am good at, I shall declare proudly."

Such a strange woman. "Do you always speak your thoughts so candidly?"

"No. That would be improper for a lady to do in the company of men."

"So you are being improper with me?" I should not have asked.

"You started it."

I chuckled. "You truly know how to hold a grudge."

"Thank you."

"That is not a compliment."

"I'm free to take the words any way I wish."

"You just enjoy arguing with me, don't you?"

She smirked and then shrugged. "It's fun besting you in conversation."

"Besting me? Hardly. You merely get the last word and leave before I can reply."

"Exactly. That is how you win."

Now I laughed.

"I have just realized we are alone! I must go. But see? We were able to have a conversation without conflict!" She smiled, picking up her skirt with her right hand to hurry back.

Why was the one conversation I was actually enjoying forced to come to an end so abruptly?

If she was playing hard to get . . . she was definitely winning.

Wait . . . was I trying to get her?

The more I tried to think, the worse my headache became. Sighing, I sat back in the same spot she'd risen from and closed my eyes. But the very first images that came to mind were of her eyelashes . . . and her eyes, right when she woke up. I tried to push the thought from my head, but all it did was remind me of how wide she smiled.

She truly is quite stunning.

Immediately my eyes opened at that thought . . . all my thoughts lately, which seemed to be centered on her. A sudden panic came over me . . . I was not immature or misguided enough to pretend not to be attracted to someone. On the contrary, I was rather purposeful about whom I did show attentions to, for I was steadfast in my position against marriage. Widows, light skirts, and, of course, courtesans, were the standard women of pleasure . . . not high-born innocent ladies with a propensity for decorum and courtesy.

Not women like her. No, I avoided her type for a reason. Once you gave them your attention, they and all of society would demand marriage. And I would not be moved on the subject.

Even if my aunt wished me to marry for the sake of securing my inheritance and future, I did not wish to be trapped. Being attracted to a woman was one thing. Being utterly responsible for her future and well-being was another. I was not a reliable person. I acted impulsively, despite my best intentions. I'd ruined my own life with my actions back in my own country.

I'd only succeed in destroying hers as well. And for what? A momentary attraction.

I was flying too close to the sun.

I needed to distance myself from her before it was truly too late and I went too far.

10

Hathor

"Men are very odd creatures," I said to Clementina as I scooped the jelly from my glass into my mouth from a table on a patio overlooking the rest of the ladies playing nine pins in the center of the yard. I watched as Prince Wilhelm somehow managed to be engaged in the company of Lady Mary, but at the same time kept her distant enough that one could not confidently say she'd captured his interest. One moment he was speaking to her, the next he was calling out to a friend and ignoring all others, before speaking to another lady and then again with Mary.

"Are you speaking of all men, or just one prince?" Clementina asked. When I looked at her, she was grinning with her spoon in her lips.

"Prince is a title. At the end of the day, he is just a man."

"So you *are* speaking of him."

"I am speaking of all of them," I assured her, looking back over all the guests. "For truly, they make no sense to me. One moment it seems as though they seek your attention, the next they act as if you have vanished from the face of the earth."

He had seemed to wish to speak with me today, and so I spoke to him, before realizing we were alone, which could cause foul gossip. I expected us to talk more when a chaperone was present, but instead the man had been avoiding me since this morning. Why?

And that damned kiss. I could not forget about it, despite my best efforts.

Why had he kissed me if he did not have interest? Was this some sort of game he played with all the ladies?

"Well, I have never attracted a gentleman's interest. Consequently, I have no way to answer that question," she replied, watching as Lady Emma rolled her ball down the path, knocking over only two pins. When I did not say a word, Clementina refocused her eyes upon me. "Oh, I beg of you do not give me a look of pity, you know how I detest these sorts of events. I'm very confident I shall be married, if only for my dowry, and as such, I know that games and ploys like this will be of no use to me. Besides, I do not have your talent for fainting. It is a rather high fall for me."

Their "use" was fun, and I was sure she wished to experience it, which is why she stared so pointedly. However, her pride would not allow her to admit it.

"Hathor . . ."

"I am not looking at you in pity, but in jealousy!" I scoffed, taking another bite.

"What reason do you have to be envious? You have everything I possess and more."

"I certainly do not have your composure, though I desperately try. You and many foolish others do not see you beyond your height. But I do. You move calmly, patiently, unfaltering, even in the face of the ill-mannered." In truth, she was the perfect young lady, everything we were taught to be. Yet simply because she was tall, she was ignored. "On top of all this, you are kind and practical. Pity you? Never. If you were any more fitting a lady, I'd have to loathe you as I do Aphrodite, and I quite like your company, so do not speak willfully against yourself; I shall take it as an affront."

She giggled. "You do not loathe your sister. You love her

dearly; you just loathe being compared to her. I know this, as I also have a dearly beloved, perfect sister."

"Yes, how is Domenica? Oh, forgive me, *the Countess* of Casterbridge? Living splendidly in Roseburg House I presume?"

She tensed, but smiled, gripping her glass tightly. But before she could speak another word, Lord Covington stepped up to us.

"Ladies, whyever are you both sitting? Do you not care for a game?"

"Forgive me, my lord, maybe another time. My mother seeks my attention," Clementina said, quickly rising from her seat beside me. She looked to me, knowing all too well her mother did not need her. She gave me a slight wink before making her escape.

"Lady Hathor?"

I looked back at him. All my interest for him had faded; however I could not waste the opportunity.

"I care not for nine pins, sir. I merely thought to be a spectator."

"May I spectate with you?" he asked, moving to sit, but I rose to my feet. For us to be sitting and conversing privately would be far too . . . intimate.

"I would much prefer a turn about the gardens. Would you care to join me?"

"Of course. After you." He outstretched his hand for me to go first, and when I did, the very first person I noticed, scowling at me from a distance, was Prince Wilhelm. It was the first time he'd looked at me since this morning, and he did so as if I'd somehow insulted him. His lips were tight, his gaze sharp.

"I do not understand him in the least," I muttered softly.

"Who?" Lord Covington asked, looking to where Prince Wilhelm was, but he'd turned back to the game before him.

"Ah, I would not put much thought or effort into trying to understand royals, Lady Hathor."

"You sound like my mama."

"Does she wish for you to become a princess as well?"

"She has not said anything of the sort, but in all honesty, I gather she feels rather relieved I am not interested in that prospect."

At least, not with *him*.

Lord Covington paused and looked at me with a smile. "Are you truly not?"

"Why do you sound so surprised?" I frowned, and then my shoulders slumped as I gathered the reason. "Let me guess. You believe me to be a title hunter as well?"

"No," he said too quickly, stepping beside me, "I'm merely glad. Truthfully, I would hate to see a young lady such as yourself get hurt."

"Hurt? How so?"

He frowned and glanced back over to Prince Wilhelm and his ever-growing crowd of admirers. "Let me just say that August is not the marrying type. I've tried saying so to Mother and my sisters, but they do not believe me. Mary thinks she shall be the special one to win his hand in marriage."

"Yes, I know about his loathing of marriage very well," I said, remembering his conversation in the park again.

"He told you?"

"No, I overheard . . . that and his true opinion of ladies." Just thinking of it upset me all over again. "He's very good at hiding his real nature. I do not blame Mary in the least, for how could she know his character?"

"I can only imagine what you heard, though it is well known that his unfortunate life has made him a bit insensitive."

"Unfortunate? He's a prince."

"He's not the heir," he said with a frown. "I do not share this to gossip, but for you to understand why it is better that he abstains from marriage. His father, the king, is quite famous for his many mistresses, whom he flaunts openly; he is even more notorious for his vile temper. It is rumored he nearly beat a man blind once."

"By God, truly?" I gasped in horror.

"Yes, they call him King of Fists. No one, not even his own family, is spared from his hands. As such, August's mother spends half her days drunk on wine, weeping, desperately seeking to deter his wrath by any means necessary."

"That is awful."

"Yes, it is. August has not been home in over five years, and do you know why?"

"He wishes to escape his family."

"He was all but banished."

"What?" I had heard no mention of that.

"August apparently inherited his father's propensity for conflict and tried to fight back."

"Fight whom back? No, you could not possibly mean . . ."

"Yes . . . I do." He chuckled. "He attacked the king."

My mouth dropped open. "But . . . but that is treason."

"And I'm sure if he were not the king's son, he would have been tried for it and hung. Instead, he's quietly banished, and makes it seem as though he is merely roaming freely throughout the world. The truth of the matter is: He is a prince without a kingdom, and no lady in his own country would marry such a man, considering his time with . . . unsavory women. Thus, our good and great queen is looking to have him settled here, among the nobility. August will at least receive his inheritance once married, banished or not, and will be able to start afresh. It is kind of her to apply her talents to his case, if not I'm sure no nobleman would wish to give over his daughter."

My shoulders dropped. Suddenly, my anger toward him morphed into deep sorrow. How could family, a father, be so horrid to his own son? I did not understand it.

"Lady Hathor, I do not divulge this information lightly or without thought. I have not even told my own mother and sisters. I speak to you only out of concern, since I see that you and August share . . . *conversation*, quite a bit. The man you associate yourself with should be filled with joy and laughter, not sorrow and suffering." I thought he'd only picked up a rock when he bent down. I had not noticed the yellow wildflower in his hand, which he now outstretched to me. He smiled gently and said, "You are deserving of only the happiest of happily ever afters."

I smirked, taking the flower from him and lifting it to my nose. "Thank you, Lord Covington, for being so candid with me. I truly appreciate it."

"Anything for you."

I smiled. Maybe I should have been focusing my interest on him. "Enough of everyone else, Lord Covington. Tell me of yourself."

"What would you like to know?"

"Surprise me."

"I enjoy gardening."

"Truly?" I grinned. Yes, Lord Covington was a better match for me.

Wilhelm

Damn Lukas to hell! How could he be so shameless and sly? I was the one who'd shown him the rock and flower maneuver.

In fact, I was the one who'd taught him how to talk to women in the first place. When I'd first met him, he was shy, awkward, and only knew how to get a woman by throwing coin onto the table like a damn pirate.

"Hathor very well may become your sister," Lady Amity giggled to Lady Mary, as they gazed over at her and Lukas.

"Not again . . . I thought he was rightly over her," Mary muttered back.

What? "Over her?" I said, looking between them. "What does that mean?"

"Oh, nothing, Your Highness!" She quickly clamped her lips shut. Clearly, it was not at all nothing, and I could not help but wonder if I had been had. Had Lukas, all this time, had feelings for Hathor? Was that why he'd spoken so poorly of her to me? So I would not have any interest? I felt my jaw tighten, then my fist, as I watched her laugh while she spoke with him. Apparently, she was easily amused by any gentleman who gave her attention.

"Your Highness, it is your turn," Lady Mary said to me.

"Ladies and gentlemen, if you could join us inside for a small production before dinner," the marchioness called to the guests, as the footmen moved to relay the information to the rest of the party in the garden. I watched as Lady Hathor and Lukas began to return. Once more, he met my gaze and then quickly looked away. He was no longer hiding his interest in her at all, it seemed.

"Are you coming, Your Highness?" Lady Mary asked.

Nodding, I followed the rest of them inside. At the doors were footmen, handing each guest a drink and light snack. I had been told that the Du Bell family was one of the wealthiest in England, and each day the marchioness seemed dedicated to reminding us. Every day so far, the décor and splendor of their castle had been transformed in a new theme or array of flowers, with the most luscious of food spreads. Today seemed to be the grandest so far: They had arranged for a theater troupe to be our entertainment in their ballroom. A large stage had been constructed right under our noses, and actors were performing every manner of tricks and comedy, surrounded by a sea of red roses. This sort of thing was meant to be the grand finale to a week's visit.

"Hathor!"

Hearing her name, I turned to see her moving toward her tall friend, grinning with excitement for the spectacle of the day. Her eyes were like amber, and her brown skin shimmered under the light of the fire. Lukas was called by his mother, and I took the chance to follow Hathor as she made her way to the seats. After several hellos and other men asking for dances, which would come later in the evening apparently, Lady Hathor finally reached a seat in the front row. I noticed Lukas moving to sit with her. Sadly for him, I had longer legs.

"Is this seat taken?" I asked, causing her to turn and look up at me. Her brow furrowed, confused as to why I was here, but before she could reply, I sat down.

"What are you doing? You cannot sit there," she whispered to me.

"Why? Is that not the purpose of chairs?"

"Yes, and whom one sits next to is very critical. The person who sits here should be a gentleman who is interested—"

"Shh . . . it is beginning," I whispered to her, as actors, mostly women—that was strange—began to appear onstage. I was not familiar with their attire.

"What shall they be performing?" I whispered to her.

"Papa chose *Lysistrata*."

"*Lysistrata*? From the Greek?"

"Where else could it be from?" she whispered back, her eyes glued to the women onstage.

I asked because I was shocked at how a father would allow his daughter to watch a play such as this—after all, it was about women denying their husbands sex to end a war. However, as I watched, I noticed some alterations had been made. Instead of saying they were denying the men sex, they claimed they were denied the presence of women altogether. Since they wished to fight a war, they could have the world all to themselves to do so. It was a small adjustment for decorum, but it was humorous to me, and, I was sure, every other gentleman who knew the play. Why the men were in such agony without women was not discussed. Instead, it was implied the men could not withstand never seeing their beauty or hearing their laughter.

When I glanced over at her . . . she was spellbound in joyful awe, a closed-lipped smile on her face. She even clenched her hands together in excitement. I did not know she enjoyed watching plays so much. I found myself staring more at her than I did the stage, and before long, Lysistrata proclaimed:

> Let each man stand beside his wife,
> each wife beside her man,
> and then, to celebrate good times,
> let's dance in honor of God.
> And for all future time,
> let's never make the same mistake again.
> The end.

Hathor's applause was thunderous. The play had been significantly shortened and distorted but had left all the young ladies enraptured.

"Were they not excellent?" Hathor exclaimed to me as she clapped.

The expression on her face was . . . "Most exquisite," I muttered.

"If only we could do the same with the French," Lady Clementina suddenly spoke behind us.

Hathor turned back to her, enthusiastically asking, "Shall we write to the French ladies?"

"Are there any French ladies left?" Lady Clementina replied.

"The commoners then. They fight, too. All ladies of all backgrounds shall come together and make the men miss us terribly," Hathor replied.

They both laughed, but stopped when Lady Clementina leaned forward to whisper, "Look who misses your company now."

It was Lukas, who was walking over to where we sat. Hathor sat up straighter, adjusting her dress.

"I cannot believe you, of all ladies, fall so easily for such tricks," I muttered.

"What do you mean?" Lady Hathor asked.

"Do you know how many ladies he's given a pathetic little flower to? Said some gentle words of endearment to? Let me guess: He said you are 'deserving of only the happiest of happily ever afters'?" When her eyes widened in shock, proving I was right that the man was just repurposing all my lines, I shook my head. "You were so insulted when I called you nothing but an innocent little lamb . . . yet, here you are, proving me correct. How very disappointing and foolish of you, *my lady*."

When her lips trembled, her nosed bunched, and her eyes narrowed at me as though I were the most bastardly bastard in all of England, I realized I had gone too far.

"I—"

She stood up immediately and glared down at me. "Excuse me, Your Highness. As always, I seem to find your company *astonishingly* intolerable."

Fuck, I thought, rising to my feet as she marched off.

No, truly, *fuck*! What was I saying? Why was I acting like this?

"That was harsh." I looked at Lady Clementina, who was now the only lady near me amongst the chairs. "And you did not mean it."

"Then why did I say it?" I grumbled, more at myself than at her.

"Is it not obvious?"

"Is what not obvious?"

"You're jealous," she remarked with a soft smile.

"What? Jealous? Why would I be jealous of her?"

She laughed at me, shaking her head. "You are not jealous of her. You are jealous of Lord Covington for taking her attention. I do not know much about courting, Your Highness, but I do believe such feelings only arise when you're smitten with someone."

I did not say anything. Instead, I watched as Lady Hathor smiled and talked to some other gentlemen next to her brother, my expression grim. Lady Clementina was right. But had I not, just this morning in fact, resolved myself *not* to like Hathor? Did I not tell myself to stay away from her, to draw a line? I failed, and it had not even been a day's worth of effort.

"Normally, I would say don't worry. Hathor only pretends to hold grudges. However," said Lady Clementina as she walked by me, "she seems quite determined to despise you, so I do hope you find a way to apologize quickly."

Was I meant to spend all of my days apologizing to this one woman?

Still silent, I took the offered wine that came around with the footmen. I could do nothing but stare at Hathor and drink. Clearly, I'd lost my mind over the course of my time here. I was adamant about not wanting to marry her, and now I was jealous of those who did want to!

What kind of torment was this, and why the hell was I the only one suffering?

11

Hathor

I had been too shocked and angered by his insults to offer any sort of rebuttal yesterday, so all the words I had wanted to say swirled in my mind throughout the night. I tossed and turned, kicking my feet out in frustration. How dare he slight me so? Not just him, but Lord Covington as well. All that conversation we shared was nothing but a game he played on women? It made me wonder if what he said about Prince Wilhelm was true. Was that part of the ruse? Making ladies believe they are looking after our best interests?

Were we ladies nothing but fools to them? They shared lines amongst themselves to deploy on women without care, respect, or true emotion. And while I loathed Lord Covington for using me in such a manner, I despised that damned prince more. It felt as though he were laughing at me, mocking me for being foolish and not knowing men could be so dishonest. But in what world was it justified for those who were undeservingly fooled to be taunted? To make it worse, he did not even apologize. Instead, he insulted me on what was meant to be a jubilant evening, then proceeded to just drink and glare at me from afar. I could not even converse with the gentlemen before me, because I could feel his eyes upon me all evening, including at dinner.

When it was over, I was so incensed that all I wished to do was march to his door and give him a piece of my mind. Several pieces, in fact—the rude and pompous brute! But alas, I could not. However, I did learn from Bernice that he'd called for his horse to be prepared for him in the morning. So I resolved myself to wait.

I barely slept, nor did I care what I wore that morning. I had one singular mission, and that was to make him take back his words immediately. I marched to the stables, pulling on my gloves hard. I'd show him who was a foolish little lamb!

"My lady, you are walking so fast," Bernice called from behind me.

"Yes, for murder must happen quickly!" I huffed, mostly to myself. When I reached the stables, I saw my horse being tended to by the stableman.

"Where is he?" I questioned immediately upon arriving.

"Who, my lady—"

"Prince Wilhelm, has he not come down for a ride yet?"

"He's already gone ahead, my lady. He did not seem to wish to wait for anyone," he replied, as he helped me onto my horse.

"I care not for what he wishes. Which direction did he go?" I asked, taking the reins.

"My lady, maybe it is best to speak to him later? When you have calmed down perhaps?" Bernice asked as the stableman brought out a horse for her as well.

"Oh, believe me, I have never been calmer," I said, looking back to the man assisting her. "Which direction?"

"Southeast, my lady, he was going toward the pavilion."

I did not need to hear anything else before I kicked off.

"My lady, wait for me!" Bernice called out, but I did not, pressing Sofonisba to go as fast as she could down the path. The trees became nothing but a blur of green before me, and the wind slapped across my face, whipping my hair. Just as I expected, I had to ride deep into the woods of our estate in order to catch up with him. When I did, I noticed his horse under a tree, grazing. Tossed beside it was his coat and in his hands . . . was a sketchbook. He was so lost in his work that he did not notice when I hopped down from my horse and came over to him. Only when I accidently blocked out the sunlight did he look up. His eyes widened, and he quickly shut his book.

"What on earth are you doing here?" he snapped, frowning at me.

"What were you drawing?"

"What I was doing is no concern of yours. So, you may continue on your way, Lady Hathor," he replied, rising to his feet.

"Unfortunately, my way takes me directly to you this morning, and for good reason. I believe I deserve an apology from you."

"I have none to offer."

I clamped my teeth together and gripped Sofonisba's reins tighter, not wishing to yell like a madwoman. He packed up his things and walked past me toward his horse, not giving me another glance. A familiar anger entered me. Before I could stop myself, I picked up an acorn from the ground and threw it at the back of his head. He froze, and so did I. Slowly, he turned back to me, eyes wide.

"Did you just throw an acorn at me?"

I hid my hands behind my back and shook my head. "Of course not! Why would a lady do such a thing to *you* of all people, Your Highness? It must have been a squirrel."

"And where is this squirrel?"

"It scurried away after its attack."

"How convenient."

"Truly."

He glared at me, and I glared back. When he turned around once more, I threw a second one at the center of his back, trying not to laugh.

Again, he paused, and when he turned to me I pointed up to the sky. "That time it was a bird. Apparently, the wildlife here does not like you, Your Highness!"

He just nodded to himself, slowly sinking down to pick up a few acorns himself. When he looked back at me, I immediately stepped back.

"You wouldn't."

"Oh, I shall," he said, and threw one right at me. I tried to dodge, but he was unrelenting, chasing me around the tree.

"This is ungentlemanly behavior!" I yelled as I tried to hide from him.

"It shall match your unladylike behavior," he retorted, coming around and forcing me to run again.

"It was not me."

"You are clearly lying!"

I tried to make a run for the horses, but he caught my arm and held on to me. I closed my eyes, preparing to be hit by an acorn, but one never came. When I peeked, he was staring at me with an expression I did not understand. His blue eyes looked over my face; he was breathing heavily, as was I. So I just stood there in his arms taking in the air as we stared at each other.

"You are so very beautiful, it is unfair," he whispered, the corners of his lips turned up. "How is anyone to argue with you?"

"You make do just fine."

"Not fine at all . . . for I do not intend to argue but you confuse my thoughts." I could not take my eyes off his lips as they came closer to mine. All of me felt as if I were growing warmer, and it did not help that he had not released me from his embrace. His fingers traced up and down my back.

"What do you intend to do then?"

He bit his lip and shook his head, his face strained . . . "Very bad things. Things much worse than a kiss."

"Make love?"

"We ought not speak of this." He suddenly let go of me.

"Isn't—"

"There is a spider on your arm," he blurted.

I screamed and jumped back, smacking my arms in horror as I tried to get it off me. "Is it gone?"

"Is what gone?"

"The spider!"

"Sorry, I meant squirrel. Or was it a bird?" he smiled slightly.

My nostrils flared. I dropped my hands as I glared back at him. "You were teasing me? All of that was just a—"

"Oh, I see the spider now—it's in your hair!" I couldn't help but jump again, moving to taking it out, when he laughed at me. "Your little sister is right. You truly *are* terrified of bugs."

"Wilhelm!" I yelled at him, not at all liking this game. And apparently, Abena was to blame for it. I'd deal with her later. First, him.

"Wilhelm? Are we so close now, *Hathor*?" he asked, and I realized I had no idea how to deal with a man such as him. This was not at all how this morning was supposed to go.

"Can you not just apologize, and let me be on my way?"

"I see no point, since you will not accept it."

"That is my choice!"

"As is mine to apologize."

"Ugh!" I groaned, throwing up my hands. "You are . . . you are . . ."

I could not get the words out, because a sudden bolt of lightning ripped through the sky . . . only to be followed by an even more sudden downpour.

"Come!" he said, taking my hand and pulling me toward

the stone pavilion. Only when I was under the dome did I look back and notice that Bernice still hadn't reached us.

"Hopefully this will clear up quickly," I muttered, mostly to myself.

"You fear for your reputation should you be found in my company?" he asked, brushing the rain off his hair.

"Any man's company without a chaperone, but yes," I said, wiping my eyes with my hand. He handed me his handkerchief. I looked at it for a moment, and then took out my own. "I'm fine, thank you. Who knows if it has another spider?"

He chuckled, drying his chin instead. "So far, your younger sister is quite accurate in her description of you."

"When exactly did you speak to Abena?"

The amusement on his face did not bode well. "I believe she said, 'Hathor is a ghastly monster, who snores like a wild boar.'"

"What? That is untrue."

"You are aware that I myself have come upon you snoring?"

"It was normal snoring, not the boarish kind!"

He laughed at me. "How would you know?"

"What else did that little bug say?"

"That you were horrified of insects . . . even butterflies. Clearly, that is true as well. So, I wonder, was she also correct in saying that you are moody, and incapable of dressing in a timely manner every morning?"

"I am going to kill her!"

"As your brother feared."

"My brother knows of this as well? Have you spoken to everyone in my family?"

"No, for I have yet to meet your oldest sister—"

"*Those traitors!*" I huffed as I moved to take a seat on the stone bench in the center of the pavilion. "My own blood, my own family, a den of ravenous wolves conversing behind my back with my enemy?"

"Oh, but it's all right for you to converse behind mine?"

"What?"

"You and Lukas yesterday. Were you not speaking of me?"

I froze and stared at him. How did he know? "All right. Fine, you win that round. So we shall call it even. Nevertheless, you owe me an apology."

"Again with this need for an apology. If left to you, I'd be forced to atone daily."

"Because you insult me daily!"

"I do not mean to insult you," he said, turning to face me. "Somehow, it just always ends up that way."

"What do you mean it just—"

"This! Here! Your manner of speaking is combative and unforgiving, which leads us to argue, because you will not show grace."

"Why must I be the one to show grace?"

"You are a lady!"

"You are a gentleman! In fact, a *prince*. It is you who must show grace first. But you only pretend to, and so everyone else is pretending along around you. I refuse to do the same."

"Is it not part of the common courtesy you hold so dear, to pretend? All the men here are pretending they are not lustful beasts in order to secure a wife. All the ladies are pretending to be the perfect embodiment of refinement in order to gain a husband. Even you, as I have seen with any gentleman but me, speak gently and walk gracefully, smiling at jokes you do not find the least bit amusing. If not for having met me earlier, you, too, would be giggling at my side as everyone else does."

I hated to admit it, but he was right.

"Even still, was I truly deserving of your words yesterday?"

I said gently. "How am I, or any young lady, to know a gentleman is deceiving us with pitiful lines?"

He sighed and shook his head. "Forgive me. I apologize."

"I shall accept that and call a truce—but only if you show me your art."

I pointed to the bag in his hand, the one with his sketchbook. He seemed surprised at himself for still holding it.

"I would, but . . . the art is not acceptable for a young lady."

"The only thing that would be deemed unacceptable would be a drawing of the nude human figure, and I have already seen those, so worry not," I replied, stretching out my hand for it.

"Even still, it would not be—"

"Would you like a truce or not?"

He inhaled and then handed me the bag. "Should you scream or shudder, know you only have your own stubbornness to blame."

"Yes, yes, the silly girl would scream at . . ." My voice trailed off as I saw the drawing of nude human figures . . . not just standing or posed as I had seen in other books but engaged in the act of lovemaking. A man kissing a woman's neck and his naked chest pressed against her breast. . . . and then another man kissing her . . . Was such a thing done?

Dear God.

12

Wilhelm

I did not know what to make of her. Nor of myself for that matter, because whyever would I show her such works? I was sure she'd already heard far too much about me from Lukas. I did not want to show her any more of my dishonorable side. But at the same time, was this not better? If she found me horrid and kept her distance, it would be perfect. Then I could lay all the blame at her feet should my aunt wonder why her matchmaking once again failed.

But instead of looking appalled, she turned her head to the side to examine further . . . never did I dream that seeing a lady intently study art could be so lust-inducing. However, the more she looked, the more I found myself desiring to be closer to her. When she bit her lip, her brow furrowed, I swallowed the saliva pooling in my mouth and turned around.

"How did you create this type of texture for the bedding?" she questioned, clearly not human, as I was, to remain so unaffected.

"Lady Hathor, your reputation could be ruined simply from looking at that, let alone if I should go into detail . . . as would mine," I said, not at all turning toward her. I could feel myself growing rather . . . hard, and I did not wish to push my already low limit of tolerance.

"You are right, forgive me, I often lose myself when I see such beautiful work."

"Beautiful or vulgar?" I asked, looking out at the rain.

She was quiet for a moment before speaking. "If husbands and wives are truly involved in such ways . . . I do not think it is anything but beautiful."

"And if they are not husband and wife?"

"The vulgarity would come from the lack of love, not the action."

I could not help myself, I turned back to her, but she was not looking at me.

"And if the man and wife were not in love?"

"Then it would be neither beautiful nor vulgar, but a tragedy," she replied. When her honey-colored eyes met mine, it was as though the lightning in the sky had somehow struck my heart. "Do you not think so?"

"I am a villainous rake, remember?" I muttered, trying to shake my head free of the thoughts rising. "I do not think of beauty, vulgarity, or tragedy."

"Liar." She giggled, glancing back down. "There is not an artist alive who does not think of any of those things. And you, Your Highness, are a very talented artist. Were you taught much by masters? My father had a few teach me when I was younger, but they were always women, and oftentimes they lacked knowledge, or withheld it."

"I was actually self-taught."

"What?" She seemed shocked. "But . . . but you are a man. You are free to learn whatever you wish."

"My father did not approve of my time being wasted on the arts. He much preferred I join the military and gain honors. So most of my lessons were of guns, swords, horses, and strategy. Whenever he found me painting, he had the work destroyed. He forbade anyone from teaching me . . . ah, 'distracting me,' he called it." I was nearly overcome by those memories when I heard her curse.

"The bastard," she muttered and then her eyes widened. "I mean . . . he . . . how awful!"

I laughed as she stumbled over her words. "No, you were right the first time. He is a bastard."

"Is that why you attacked him?"

My teeth gritted together and my fists clenched . . . damn Lukas.

"I am sorry, you do not have to speak of it if you do not wish to."

"The first time you apologize to me, it has nothing do with your own faults? How on the mark for you."

"You do not have to talk about it, but you do not have to pick a fight to deflect, either," she said and looked back down at the page.

I exhaled, releasing my hands. "Yes, my father is a bastard of a man, which is why I fought him, which is why I left my country. Is there anything else you would like to know, or would you prefer Lukas—"

"You were doing so well before you grew defensive and tried again to pick a fight. I am not judging, Your Highness, truly. I do not think ill of your situation. It actually makes me think I've been rather ignorant."

"Ignorant? Of what?"

"The concerns of men." She frowned. "It did not even cross my mind that a father could restrict his own son from learning something as worthy as art. I always believed you men were free to do whatever you pleased."

"Maybe some are. I just have not been so fortunate," I said as I took a seat beside her. "Though I must admit, I've enjoyed far more freedom than I ever thought possible."

"Is that how you had time to draw these?" She flipped to the next page, where a sleeping woman lay curled up on the bed.

"This is nothing but a figment of my own imagination," I lied.

She giggled. "Sure. I believe you."

"You clearly do not and that is enough perusing for now," I said, trying to take the book from her, but she held it away. Her eyes narrowed on me and mine back on her. We glowered at each other, effectively having a staring contest like children, when she sneezed.

"I win, give me the book."

"Were we playing a game?" she prevaricated, now that she had lost.

"Lady Hathor."

"Do not rush me, I am still looking. There is no point taking it back now. It is not as if the situation becomes more scandalous with each page turned." Her nose flared, as I had to agree once more. I never thought I'd find such silliness to be so amusing.

"Did it ever occur to you I may not be comfortable with my art being viewed?"

"You have two options: We can sit and talk about your melancholy existence or I can look at your naked lady friends in this book. Which do you prefer?"

"Neither!"

"Unfortunately, that is not one of the choices."

"Has anyone told you that you are a bit odd?"

"Yes." She frowned. "Why are you trying to start a fight with me again?"

"I honestly don't know. Though I must say your boldness and self-confidence are extraordinary. You speak your mind without trepidation." It made talking to her so easy, as if we'd long known each other and she did not care about any of my faults.

She let out a deep sigh. "I am not all that confident. I am merely dedicated to doing things right."

"What is the difference?"

"Fear," she said very softly, the conviction in her face fading. "My elder sister, Aphrodite, is as divine as her name; there is nothing beyond her capabilities. On top of that she's the most beautiful of us Du Bell girls. If she were the youngest, it would not matter as much, but because she was the first girl, she set the standard. So, when I fail at my walk or curtsy, if I am unsuccessful in my attempts to hold charming conversation, it looks even worse next to her. Everything comes naturally to her . . . while I, not wishing to be mocked or ridiculed in her shadow, had to practice. Over and over and over again I practiced everything to be the very best lady. And when I mastered something and I rushed out to show society or my own family—everyone shrugged. Days, weeks, years of practice, and in the end they all looked at me and said, *good*. That was it. That was all. Because Aphrodite had long since accomplished it already. I was just *good*."

She wasn't looking at me any longer, her eyes transfixed in sorrowful thought.

"My father believes strength and fear are the only ways to rule a nation and family. My eldest brother, Frederick, the heir, was born premature, and thus has been sickly all his life. Growing up, my cousin Edmund and I were told by my mother to never overshadow him. We were instructed to always lose to him and make sure he'd be seen in a good light by our father. This caused Edmund to resent him. He purposely made Frederick look worse by outshining him any chance he could. One day he took it too far, and during the annual hunt, Frederick fell from his horse before all the lords and ministers. My father was enraged and considered it an embarrassment."

Her eyes widened in concern. "Did he hit him?"

"Father never hit us; yelled at and berated us, yes, but he did not strike us . . . however, our mother was a different story. He blamed *her* for Frederick's weak condition. I'd watched him strike her all my life, always feeling far too small to do anything about it. But I was not small any longer, and this time when he raised his hand to her . . . I . . . I lost my composure. I struck him *hard*. Not just once either. It was as if my entire mind were painted black. I could not see anything. When they pulled me off of him, his face was covered in blood. And they all looked at me as if *I* were the monster. They knew what he was like, yet I was the monster because he was the king."

"They banished you for that? You were just trying to protect your mother."

I laughed bitterly, because she truly did not get it. "Who do you think forced me to leave while his face recovered? My mother privately gave the order."

"But why? Surely—"

"He is the king and she is his queen. Nothing and no one else is above that except God."

The frown on her face was so strong, I would not have been surprised if her mouth got forever stuck that way.

"What an awful mess."

"Yes, so be grateful that your family at least sees your efforts as good. Be satisfied that you have a family that is so deeply concerned for your well-being. Not even royals are guaranteed to get that."

"What have you been doing since you left your home?" she asked, her eyes peering into mine, not at all listening to my advice for her.

"Do not look so concerned. I've been having a grand time. I went on tour, then visited other relatives. I have quite a few of them, and very few know of what transpired, so I am still treated honorably and well. Lukas only found out after I said too much over drinks. On top of which I have newfound freedom to indulge in all my most passionate interests."

"Such as women." She held the next page up for me to see. "This one must be a favorite, she comes up a lot."

My eyebrow rose as I glanced over to her. She was clearly teasing me but for some reason I felt she also wished to lift the mood. "Lady Hathor, do not be so bold. We are not friends, remember?"

"Yes, of course. We are enemies divulging our vulnerabilities after declaring a truce, as is custom nowhere."

"Exactly."

She giggled and I grinned.

"So, what do you believe the ending of your sad story will be, Prince Wilhelm?"

I was taken aback by the question. No one had ever asked that before.

"I do not know. What do you believe yours shall be?"

"I shall be much beloved by my husband, have many children, and grow old on a grand estate."

"How precise and boring. Do you not wish to do something else? See the world perhaps?"

"All of that can happen. I can travel with my husband, then return home, where I will still have many children and a grand estate. No matter where you travel in the world, you must have a home to return to. If yours is no longer Malrovia, you must create one somewhere else . . . you cannot wander forever."

"Now you are starting to sound like my aunt."

She grinned. "I shall take that as a compliment, because the queen is wise."

I stared at her . . . never did I believe I would have such a conversation with a woman.

"There is no discouraging you, is there?"

"There is, but I recover quickly. Now, if you do not mind, will you please go over there?" she said and pointed to the columns at the pavilion's entrance.

"What?"

"You are too close for me to draw sitting here."

"You wish to draw me?"

"Yes, I feel inspired, and you are the only thing before me, so I shall draw you."

"After all I have said, you wish to draw?"

"What do you wish me to do? Cry? What has happened has happened. I see no reason to dwell on it any further, and so I shall draw."

I smiled . . . She was such a strange woman. Most others would feel uncomfortable and distant in this situation. How could they not? I'd confessed about my dysfunctional family and past, and she sat, barely fazed, holding my erotic art.

I never spoke of these things. Yet, with her, everything came spilling out—and she treated me no differently.

"Well, are you going to move into place or not?"

"Why do I fear you will draw me as some ghastly beast?" I said as I rose to my feet.

"That shall only be the outcome if you should call my work lacking."

"You do not think that a rather harsh punishment for such a small criticism?"

"No, I do not, for I greatly abhor criticism of any degree," she muttered, adjusting the page. "Now, go stand by the entrance."

I did as she asked, moving to the columns that marked the entrance.

"Stop," she ordered, and I did. "Look toward the rain, then

turn your head slightly to the left and lean on the column to your right."

"Like this?"

"Yes . . . sort of," she replied.

Again I listened to her without argument, looking out at the scenery before me. I often liked the quiet but her silence as she began drawing was rather unnerving. I wanted to hear her speak.

"You are a very good artist," I said, watching the rain. "I'm glad your father allowed you to become so well trained."

"Are you saying that now only because you fear I shall draw you as a beast?"

I smiled. "No, I am confident you will render a fair likeness."

"You have far too much faith in me, Your Highness, for I am drawing horns as we speak," she shot back.

"Lady Abena is right. You *are* truly horrid, then!"

"Hey! Truce, remember?"

I turned my head back to see her face, and just as I expected, she was glaring at me. "I jest! Draw on, da Vinci."

She huffed. "Turn around."

I moved back into position, and once more silence came upon us as she worked. As I watched the rain, I found myself reflecting on this strange moment in my life . . . and the woman I could not have. I could not marry her, and yet each time we met, I found myself wishing to stay in her company. The very reason I was even here this week was to see her. Had I liked her even before I arrived? Surely not.

Feeling a hand upon my arm, I jumped slightly and glanced back at her. "What are—"

"One moment. This will look better," she said, not at all fazed that her hands were upon my person. She moved from beside me to stand directly in front of me, just barely in the rain. My eyes widened as I felt her palms clasp the sides of my face and tilt my head to her desired position.

Her touch took me utterly by surprise, and left me unable to move of my own accord.

"Why are you looking at me like that?" She paused, staring at me.

"Do you often grab men so . . . uninhibitedly?"

"Ah." She drew her hands back and smiled. "Forgive me. I was thinking only of positioning."

"It is all right," I lied, still feeling the lingering touch of her fingers on my face. "But how long am I meant to hold the position?"

"Until the rain stops, of course," she ordered before moving from me back to the bench.

"And what if the rain never stops?"

"You must become immortal."

I grinned. "That will most definitely not sit well with the church."

"Then we shall create our own religion." Just then, lightning flashed in the sky, and the earth trembled with thunder. Behind me, I heard her yell, "Father in heaven, I was only joking!"

"Who shall get horns now?"

"Hey!"

I laughed, truly laughed, until the sky thundered once more and forced my silence. In the distance, I saw even darker clouds approaching, and I stood up straighter.

"You are moving again," she called out behind me.

"As I think we ought to be, for the storm looks to be getting worse, not better," I said, glancing at our horses agitated by the sudden rainfall. "We must be getting back. I'll fetch the horses."

"You wish for us to ride back in this weather?" she said, stopping me.

"We have no choice. Hold this," I replied, putting my coat over her shoulders before dashing out into the rain.

The water beat down, soaking into my shirt as I pulled the reins of her horse. Mine, upon seeing me, followed.

I brought them as close to the pavilion as possible before rushing to get her.

"We shall ride together; my horse knows to follow me."

"I can ride my own horse."

"Lady Hathor, it is—"

"Yes, yes, dangerous. I know, and I shall not ride so fast—"

"Now is not the time for your stubbornness. Come on!" I all but carried her over to her horse. I helped her up before hopping onto its back.

"Stay close to me," I said, grabbing the reins.

She shifted, resting her back against my torso. I kicked my heels only once before we were off, and did my best not to focus on how good she smelled and fit beside me. We reached the castle even faster than I thought possible—only for me to wish to head right back into the woods the moment I saw whose carriages stood before the entrance.

I tried to head toward the stables, but it was too late. All the footmen at the doors had already noticed us. Bringing Hathor back in this manner was bad enough; seeking to avoid coming through the front entrance altogether would only inspire more rumors.

There was no other choice.

"Lady Hathor!" one of the servants called.

"Lady Hathor, wait!" I called out, trying to warn her, but she was quickly off the horse, seeking shelter from the rain—not at all realizing that she was running right into the queen's arrival!

Shit!

13

Hathor

It was so strange how I was so much more aware of him than I was of the rain. I tried not to think of it, but I could not help but notice how his body was like a shield around me. By the time we had made it back to the castle, there was no part of me that was not wet and cold, which made me wonder how freezing he must have been. But I had no time to ask, as our footmen along with many other people I did not recognize were at the entrance. The footmen were already rushing to take us inside.

"Lady Hathor!" our butler yelled from the doors. As the other footmen rushed forward, I tried to put distance between myself and Prince Wilhelm, as well as get out of the rain. "Are you all right, Lady Hathor?" All I could do was nod as I hugged myself and tried to keep warm. "Quickly, take her to her rooms and have a warm bath drawn. I shall tell his lordship she has returned."

"Hathor!" came the voice of Mother, who rushed out of the hall alongside my father, with every other lord and lady who'd come to visit trailing close behind. I was not sure why they all stared at me as if they'd never seen someone soaked from rain before. But I was rather embarrassed enough and wished for nothing more than a warm bath.

"Finally, I am graced with your presence, nephew. Here I thought you'd vanished."

I stood in greatest horror. For it could not be, *surely* not now of all times. But it very much was so. They all parted, even my mother, allowing Her Majesty The Queen to step forward. Now I understood who those strange people were at the entrance . . . they were her retinue. She wore a bright gold dress with several bows and strings of pearls. In her white hair was a feather, and her brown eyes watched us the way eagles did their prey. Immediately I curtsied, dripping wet before her.

"Your Majesty, welcome to Belclere Castle."

"And what a memorable welcome it is, Lady Hathor," she replied sternly. "Tell me, my dear, do you often go riding in the midst of a storm?"

"It wasn't storming when we began our ride, Aunt," Wilhelm said from beside me. "We had thought to wait it out with her maid, but when we realized the weather was worsening, I judged it best to return quickly."

"Oh, is that so?" she replied. They shared a pointed look. All I knew was that I was growing colder by the minute. I looked at my mother, pleading for her to save me from this. Luckily, she understood, coming to my side.

"Your Highness, I believe they should change quickly before they catch a chill, don't you agree?" my mother said, placing her hand on my shoulder.

"Very well." She spun around, her dress whooshing as she did, and everyone quickly parted for her. "Do hurry, nephew. I long to hear your thoughts on Belclere."

"Quickly, move. Now," my mother said, forcing me to go.

I glanced over at Wilhelm and saw the water that dripped from his face and his brown hair, his clothes so drenched that they stuck to his body. I wanted to say thank you; only a few minutes into our ride, I was sure I would not have been able to return in that storm on my own. But there were so many people now surrounding us, and I, for some reason, could not find my voice. It was odd, for I always found my voice.

"We need to get you warmed up," my mother said as she hugged me and led me to the stairs. "And you must tell me everything that occurred."

"Nothing occurred beyond what he said." Other than the fact that Bernice had not been with us.

"And the reason you are wearing his coat and holding his bag?"

I glanced at my shoulders and then remembered what was in this bag . . . his art. Which would ruin me, should anyone see. "I must return it—"

"Later, my dear . . . later. I'm sure this has caused a big enough scene for the morning."

My eyes widened as I looked at her. "How big a scene do you suppose it shall be?"

She did not answer, which only made me wary. How? How had things gotten here? Why had I even gone out this morning?

I wished to curse my own foolishness, but there was no time for that. The queen was here. By the time we entered my room, Ingrid was already there with several other maids, pulling out dresses and seeing to getting me bathed, dry, and dressed for a proper audience.

"Drink this. It shall warm you up," my mother said, as she gave me a bowl of soup. I took it, standing by the fire as I drank. "And where is Bernice? Why did she not return with you?"

I did not answer. Ingrid did.

"She just returned to the stables now, your ladyship. Apparently, she followed Lady Hathor but lost sight of her and went in the wrong direction. Then the storm came."

"Why were you going so fast your chaperone lost sight of you?"

I licked my lips. "I did not notice . . ."

"Hathor!"

I jumped at her groan.

"Forgive me, Mama, but I promise nothing occurred that ought not to have. We spoke, we waited for the rain to end, and we returned."

She crossed her arms and shook her head at me. "Very well, but should anyone ask, insist Bernice was keeping watch. Ingrid, Bernice must say the same. The queen has already questioned Prince Wilhelm and he laid cover, so I believe the matter to be finished. Even still, I wish there to be no gossip. Warn the stablemen."

"Yes, your ladyship." Ingrid nodded, taking the bowl from my hands and moving to make way for my mother to stand before me.

"Hathor, tell me honestly: Do you wish to marry Prince Wilhelm?"

I froze, somehow shocked by the question. Marry him? *No, of course not*, I thought, but for some strange reason, our time at the pavilion came to mind. Talking to him like that, it was bizarre . . . no, *I* was bizarre. One moment, my body felt very hot, and the next I felt like I was struggling to breathe as he leaned closer to me. Maybe it was the smell of him that distorted my senses . . . but he did not smell bad. On the contrary, he smelled rather nice. And though he teased me, he often spoke kindly, too. I found myself looking at his lips a lot. But that was not liking someone. I did not like him. We were merely forced to make conversation due to the weather. Yes, that was it. And the weather was gloomy, therefore our conversation was a bit forlorn—but I did not feel sad after it. I actually felt . . . a bit better. But why? He had not solved anything.

"Hathor . . . Hathor!"

"Hmm?" My eyes snapped back to her. "Yes, Mama?"

"My girl, where is your mind? Or am I supposed to take your silence as an answer? Do you wish to marry Prince Wilhelm?"

I paused a moment, gathering my wits. "No, Mama, of course not."

"Hathor, that did not sound very certain. Have you come to like him?"

"Of course not! I told you before, he is not truly a gentleman. I mean, he was a gentleman to me, at no point was he improper, I—I— He loathes marriage, and his family is . . . well. I could not marry into such a family."

"You spoke of his family?"

"Yes—but only casually. Nothing of consequence," I lied. She eyed me with a heavy frown, like she knew I was lying. "Mama, all we do is argue when we are near each other."

"If you say so, then act so, Hathor. Do not be seen alone in his company again. It will cause misunderstandings such as today. And we cannot have misunderstandings, especially not with the queen now here."

"Of course."

"When you go back down and stand before the queen again, you are to be calm and collected. No dramatics whatsoever, do you understand me?"

I nodded. "Yes, Mama."

Only then did she take a deep breath, nodding to herself. She reached up and brushed the wet strands of my curls off my face. "You worry me greatly sometimes, child."

"I am twenty, you need not worry so."

"If you were one hundred and twenty, I would worry even still."

I wanted to ask how old that would make her but feared what she'd do to me, so I just smiled. "Go, Mama. I shall be down shortly. We cannot leave Papa to handle all the guests and the queen alone. He's probably ready to run to his library as we speak. And who knows what the other mamas are saying?"

She chuckled and nodded. "Very well. Wear the green dress, with my pearls. You will look most stunning."

"Thank you, Mama," I said as she moved toward the door. She paused, looking at Wilhelm's coat and bag, left on my bed.

"Someone must have these returned to Prince Wilhelm's rooms immediately," she added. I did not trust any other person to return it without looking inside. Luckily, it was then that Bernice entered, her hair soaked, but her clothes changed.

"Bernice, how have you returned so soon?" I said, moving from the fireplace and toward the bed to gather the prince's things, making sure to wrap his coat over the bag. "Please drop this with Prince Wilhelm, and then go rest."

I gave her a pleading look and she nodded.

"Yes, my lady," she said, taking them from me and leaving quickly.

My mother gave me a strange look but was luckily distracted as Abena stormed into my room.

"Is the queen really here?"

"Yes, which means should I hear even the slightest bit of noise out of you, I will send you to the moon," Mama said, pulling her cheeks before leaving. "Do not disturb your sister. Come on."

"This is the worst week ever. I cannot do anything!" She huffed and turned back around to leave with her.

With both Mama and the sketchbook gone, I threw myself onto the bed and took a deep breath. I did not blame Abena. This truly was an unforgiving week, and I felt powerless to do anything about it.

But I was sure I did not like him.

"My lady, we must get you prepared at once, we cannot keep the queen waiting."

"Coming."

Dear God, please . . . help me any way possible. I am at a loss for what is happening.

Wilhelm

"Well?" the queen asked as she watched the gathered guests dance from her chair, me standing newly changed beside her.

"Well what, Aunt?"

"Spare your feigned ignorance for someone who *is* ignorant, Wilhelm, and tell me directly. What do you think of her?" Straight and sharp, of course, for that was her personality to the letter. My mother called her the unwavering arrow. "And before you waste my time and foolishly ask me *who*, I mean Lady Hathor."

"I am sorry to disappoint you, Aunt, but I do not think anything of her."

"Is that why you gave her your coat and personally escorted her through the rain on horseback?"

"I would hardly be deemed a gentleman if I allowed our host's daughter to walk back in a storm, now would I?"

"Oh, is that your excuse? Strange, for I've seen you leave ladies nearly drowning in ponds to assure no connection could be made between you."

Before I could reply, the doors opened and she entered: Lady Hathor, as though she were a princess draped in green silk, the trim laced with glistening fabric. Her sweet face shimmered under the light. She walked slowly and gracefully, pearls around her neck and a few in her curly brown hair. All of which was pinned up, with the exception of one long curl over her shoulder. Not one person, gentleman or lady, was able to look away from her . . . except for the queen, whose eyes seemed to be on me.

"That is not at all the look of a man who has not thought of a lady," she said. I could not reply, as Lady Hathor made her way to us.

Hathor curtsied low before us . . . and I was quite stunned at how refined all her movements were. It was so unlike the woman I was used to. That woman was ready to curse and throw acorns at me without a single thought to my position or hers. The lady I was used to was a fierce, thundering force of confrontational energy. This woman before us . . . looked to be the very definition of a polished young lady of high society.

"Lady Hathor, you are dry and here at last."

"Forgive me for coming before you so uncouthly earlier, Your Majesty. I pray you are in good health and that your journey was fine." Her voice was barely above a whisper, and I realized that this gentle lady before me was the formation of all her practice.

"My journey was quite dull. Why don't you stand near me and tell me all that has occurred in my absence?"

"Aunt, I shall go—"

"Remain where you are, August. Come, Lady Hathor, what has been the nature of this gathering so far?"

She kept her hands clasped before herself as she spoke, still in such a delicate manner.

"I fear there has not been much to tell, Your Majesty. Everyone does their best to hold conversation, but many think of the war . . ."

"Ah, how I tire of hearing of that. August, I have not seen you dance in quite some time. Escort Lady Hathor to the dance floor."

"Aunt—"

"Now."

I could not defy her, and so I stepped around her chair and outstretched my hand to Lady Hathor. She stared at me for a long minute, causing the queen to look at her. Only then did she take my hand. I led her into the center of the room, and only when her back was turned from the queen did her face change. *There* was the lady I knew.

"It is hard to believe it is you, under such refined speech and mannerisms," I teased.

"I told you, it takes practice."

"Well done. I have yet to see any other lady do better before her thus far," I said. With the smile that spread across her face, you'd think I'd given her a rare diamond. It made me wish to smile in return, but I was very aware of the eyes on us, and how that would translate to the queen. "As you can see, my aunt is very set on matching us."

"So I have noticed. But why is she so keen on me? She never showed any interest in me in the slightest before. Aphrodite was her favorite."

"A monarch's favor changes as seasons do. Your sister is not here, and you are the most incomparable of ladies, so now you are her favorite. Is that not what any woman would wish for?"

"Am I her new favorite? Or am I just a tool to tame you?"

"It could be both, but I lean toward the latter," I whispered.

"Exactly. So why me, of all ladies? Can you not tell her you are interested in Lady Mary?"

"But I am not."

She gave me a look but could not hold it as we broke apart to make space in this section of the dance.

"Can you not tell her you are in love with some other lady, maybe one from your drawings, and that you will not marry anyone else but her?" she asked when we were together again.

"I cannot, because I am not in love with a lady from my drawings."

"So, they are real ladies you are acquainted with?"

I bit my lip, for I had forgotten with whom I was dealing. She let nothing get past her.

"What can I do to make you forget that book altogether?"

"Absolutely nothing."

I sighed. "You are—"

"Choose your words carefully, Your Highness, or I will not converse with you any longer."

I stepped closer to her, my face lowering toward hers. "Would you rather converse with the queen again? She looks to be speaking intently with your mother."

Her eyes whipped back and she looked toward them. "What if she truly seeks to marry us, no matter what we think?"

Suddenly, the idea did not seem as horrid as it once did.

"My aunt is determined, but she is not so cruel as to force a marriage. She believes greatly in love."

"What? Really?" Her gaze was back on me, and she did not look away. Or was it me who did not?

"Surely you know her match with the king was one of love?"

"Yes, I'd heard that, but . . ."

"His condition," I whispered low, and she nodded.

"Yes, his condition, and with him being away from society

for so long that . . . that . . ." Her voice trailed off, so I finished for her.

"You forgot he was once her most beloved husband."

She nodded. "We usually think of him as the king . . . not a husband."

"As is the case with most royals. People see us not as individuals, but as institutions. However, I have spoken to many at the palace, including my cousins. It is *because* she loves him so deeply that she hurts so greatly . . . and thus, she distracts herself with society and matchmaking."

"And what is her matchmaking record?"

"She says she is *perfect*, with everyone *but* her own children," I teased. "I think it is because she loves them that she is not so firm with them. She is soft at heart, I promise."

"The queen, soft?" She giggled. Once more, the sight of her smile was wondrous to me.

"The very softest in society. You merely have to look beyond her icy glare."

"I do not have such courage, and so I shall leave it up to you to dissuade her from choosing me as your tamer."

"She only just arrived. I believe she has the energy to withstand any such persuasions. Why don't you tell her *you* are in love with someone else?"

"But I am not, and lying to the queen is treasonous. She may forgive *you*, you are family, but I cannot risk it. I like my head on my shoulders."

"They would not dare behead such a beautiful woman in England," I said without thought.

"Obviously no one has taught you English history yet," she replied without missing a beat, and at that, I did laugh. "Do not laugh! She will think you are courting me in earnest."

"Do not be funny, and I will not laugh."

"That is quite hard. I am very witty."

I bit my lip. She truly was amusing. "You are also very good at complimenting yourself. Is this how you survived your sister's shadow? Paying yourself compliments you wished to hear?"

Her eyes widened in shock, and I realized I was right. That was why she was so good at it—she'd been doing it all her life.

"Do not pretend that you know me so well, sir," she shot back.

"I think I've finally figured you out, *Hathor*," I whispered as the space between us closed. I inhaled the smell of her, wishing to pull her closer to me. She stared up at me, and for a moment, the briefest of seconds, I was sure she wished for me to hold her, too. But it was at that moment that the music came to an end. We both stood there, and   and I wanted to dance with her again.

"I shall try to make my escape now, before she calls me. Goodbye," she said quickly, curtsying to me before leaving the dance floor.

I turned back to my aunt, whose eyebrow was raised. The look on her face . . . I would not hear the end of this dance should I return to her side. Not wishing to, I bowed my head to her and withdrew into the company of the other gentlemen. Lukas came up to me with a glass in hand, staring at me sternly.

"What a lovely dance, Your Highness," he said. "I would ask her for my own, but she has been ignoring me since you spoke to her at the play yesterday."

"Is there a question you wish to ask me, Lukas?"

"Will you be honest with the answer, *Your Highness*?" He spat out the words *Your Highness* as though they were a curse.

"Honesty?" I repeated with a chuckle. "Pray tell, did you offer me such honesty, or were you working in your own self-interest?"

"I do not know what you mean—"

"If you liked her, Lukas, you simply could have said so, and not sought to slander her to me or me to her," I said slowly, seeking to walk away from his company when he stepped back in my path, looking me directly in the eyes as he spoke.

"I like her, and I shall seek her hand in marriage before the week is out."

Without realizing my fist was clenched, I mustered out a simple "Good luck to you, then," before walking away. I did not get very far before the queen's first lady-in-waiting was before me. She was a woman of nearly sixty, and yet possessed the energy of a woman of twenty. Her white hair was pulled into a simple bun with two white curls in the front, framing her furrowed brow.

"Lady Crane—"

"Her Majesty is asking for you, Your Highness," she said abruptly, and then turned for me to follow.

I bit the inside of my cheek as I noticed who was also being brought to the queen's side by another of the queen's ladies. Hathor and I gave each other a look of utter exasperation . . . for this was madness.

"Good. You've both returned," the queen said as we stood before her and the marchioness, whose brown face let not a single emotion slip. "Lady Monthermer was just telling me of the hunt planned for tomorrow. August, you shall be joining."

It was not a question, and so all I could say was "Of course. I look forward to it."

"I look forward to seeing your talents tomorrow as well, Lady Hathor."

Still no room for question.

"Of course, Your Majesty, I have quite the reputation as a *hunter*," she stressed and shot me a grimace. "Do I not, Your Highness?"

This again? I gritted my teeth at her. She truly could hold a grudge like none other. "Is that so, Lady Hathor? Here I thought you a *peacemaker*."

I stressed the word to remind her of our truce, and she shrugged like she could not recall or be bothered by it.

"Your Majesty, we ought not keep them; young people are meant to socialize," Lady Monthermer said at her side.

"Ah . . . well, you both may go then."

For the second time, I sought to make my escape, but Hathor moved past me and whispered, "Tomorrow I will explain my plan to dissuade her."

"You have a plan?" I whispered back.

"I will think of one tonight and let you know tomorrow . . . now stop talking to me." She huffed and walked off.

I could only pause and stand there baffled. Between Lukas, Hathor, and the queen, I was going to lose my bloody mind before the week was done.

14

Hathor

"Are you sure I shouldn't hold the gun?" Wilhelm asked for the third time as we walked through the forest.

"As I said the last two times you asked, I am very capable of holding it myself," I replied.

"The hole you put in that last tree suggests otherwise."

I stopped and turned to glare at him. "Forgive me for not being the king's finest marksman, but at least I hit something, unlike someone else!"

"It's a little hard to focus on firing when you're worried your hunting partner will accidentally shoot herself or, worse, you," he fired back, and, once again, he looked like he was about to laugh at me. "Lady Hathor, surely you know you are terrible at this sport."

"No, I do not know that in the slightest!" I huffed and turned back down the path when I thought I saw something that looked like a snake slithering past. Screaming, I aimed the gun and pulled the trigger to fire, but nothing came out. I stared at the gun in my hand, confused. "Is it broken?"

"You have not reloaded from the last shot," he said, now coming over and snatching the gun from me before giving it to one of our loaders. "Lady Hathor is done for the day."

"No, I am not. Reload it. I am not leaving until I catch something."

"You were about to shoot a stick."

"It moved!"

"Yes, I believe there was a squirrel on the stick," he smirked.

"You are holding a grudge. It is unbecoming of a man."

"Oh, so only you are allowed to hold grudges, because you are a woman? Who, may I ask, wrote such a law?"

"I believe it is in the Bible somewhere," I said seriously and he stared at me for a moment before simply laughing. I had to bite my cheek to keep from laughing along with him; he looked so gleeful.

"You are honestly the most outlandish woman I have ever met, and I have met queens!"

"Why is it the more time I spend with you, the less amiable you become?" I replied, marching over to Mr. Dawson to retrieve my gun. I was thinking of taking a shot at him before turning back to the bushes.

"I can assure you the feeling is mutual," he replied.

"I am ignoring you now, as I am preparing to hunt something for the queen," I said, nearly dropping the gun as a tiny creature ran past my foot . . . it really was a bloody squirrel. When I looked back at him, he gave me a smug, knowing look. "Say not a word!"

"Lady Hathor, I beg of you, truly beg, leave the weapon in the care of Mr. Dawson. If not for my sake, then for your poor maid's, for her heart has nearly given out twice now watching after you."

I glanced over at Bernice, who was standing beside old Mr. Dawson, her face grave and her eyes pleading.

"It is a hunting party. I cannot be out here and not hunt," I said to both her and Wilhelm. "I'd look ridiculously out of place."

"I believe your outfit already accomplishes that," he muttered once more, taking the gun from me and giving it back to Mr. Dawson.

I glanced down at my bright red-and-gold riding habit with its close-fitting bodice, gold buttons, and double collar before adjusting my red hat. "What is wrong with my ensemble?"

"Nothing, Colonel Du Bell. Now come on. The sooner we find something to hunt, the sooner we are free of each other's company. Unless you wish to share your grand plan to dissuade the queen with me now?" he asked, looking at me and waiting. I frowned, because . . . "Let me guess. You could not think of one?"

"I could think of plenty," I called back.

"And?"

"And . . . it only ever works against me."

"What do you mean?"

"I thought maybe we could have a large argument before her, and vow never to cross paths, but then it would look like I am disagreeable and uncultured. Then I thought I could reject you before society, but that would be greatly insulting to you, rumors would spread that a *prince* was callously rejected by a mere marquess's daughter. That would be the talk of the ton for . . . far too long."

"That sounds as if you are worried for me, not you." His eyebrow rose as did the corner of his mouth. "Have you come to like a villain such as myself?"

"Do not be absurd," I muttered, brushing my curl way from my face. "Ask anyone: My greatest priority is always myself. If everyone is speaking about how you were rejected, they would wonder about the lady who rejected you, and that would be me. Then I would be judged as someone who considered herself above royalty. This would put me under greater scrutiny, and what gentlemen would seek my hand then?"

"That sounds like nothing more than well-reasoned nonsense. You and I both know people would merely say there is something greatly deficient with me. The longer I stay in one place, the more the rumors grow. Soon, someone else will find out about my past and spread it. Thus, no one will fault you, and you need not worry."

I did not like the look on his face. It was not fair.

"Royalty is royalty, and I will not be seen as turning up my nose at a prince, no matter the circumstance. It is unbecoming of a fine lady such as myself, and you waste your breath trying to convince me otherwise."

He chuckled. "Those are a lot of words to mask your kindness. I've noticed you do this often. Why do you wish people to think you are self-important and ostentatious?"

"Again, you are pretending as if you know me so very well."

"Didn't I tell you I have you figured out now?" He grinned. "You are soft-hearted, but sharp-tongued. Prideful, and yet humble."

"You have no idea what you are saying. I am not in the least bit humble—"

"You only boast about yourself when provoked by the other ladies or to brighten the mood with humor. All other times, you credit yourself only with being a good artist. Despite how you look, you . . . you don't go around . . ."

His voice drifted off, and then he just stopped midsentence.

"Despite how I look— What? How do I look?" I thought he meant to make fun of my outfit again, yet the look in his eyes did not seem teasing but serious . . . too serious. "Well?"

"You've proved my point."

"What point? I do not understand."

"Never mind. Come on, we should keep going," he said, walking forward.

"You cannot just say 'never mind' midconversation," I called after him.

"I can, and I do."

I wished to kick the back of his legs like a child. Truthfully, I'd noticed that despite our truce I found myself behaving rather freely. He was not a gentleman related to me. As a lady, I was always supposed to watch my speech, behavior, and expression; I was to be faultless. But with him, I was the very opposite.

"Do not worry too much about coming up with a plan for the queen. Eventually she will grow bored and move on to something or someone new," he replied, still not looking at me, but instead around the shrubbery. "How do you think I have survived her meddling all this time?"

"True. But I must say, we would not be in this predicament with the queen had you not come here to unnerve me."

He paused at that and looked at me. "You think I came here just for you?"

"What other reason could there be? You have been in London since the beginning of the year, which means you were also there for the opening of the season, but no one has seen you or made your acquaintance apart from a few gentlemen. Which means you've been hiding from society, and the queen surely would not have allowed that, so you were ignoring her orders . . . until after meeting me."

He made an odd face as he looked me over, his mouth practically open. He then took in air before speaking. "I take it back. You are not humble in the slightest."

I giggled. "See, I told you that you do not know me. How could you, when even I am unsure of myself most days?"

"And you proudly admit that?"

"Yes."

"Do you ever let a person win an argument against you?"

"No."

"God help the man who marries you, he will require either the patience of a saint or—"

"What makes you think I will argue with my husband?"

"I have yet to see you *not* argue, even when being complimented."

"Only because I am speaking with you. But with my husband, I shall be the most demure of ladies, and he shall do all I ask to make me happy."

He laughed so loud the birds above us scattered. "Once more, we have entered your fantasy world of marriage. Do you truly believe it will be as perfect as you say? So much so that you would not even argue?"

"You laugh, but some people *do* have perfect marriages. My mama and papa are such people. I don't recall them ever really arguing. Papa teases her often, but in the end, he always does what she wishes."

"Always?"

"Yes."

"That is impossible. Are you sure they are not just putting up a façade?"

"For twenty years of my life? That would be rather trying, would it not?" I tried to imagine it and shook my head. "Papa honestly does not like upsetting Mama, and she does not like troubling him, either. But even if she does something to annoy him, Papa merely goes into his library or busies himself inspecting the grounds. He does not even raise his voice to her . . . so it's hard to know he's upset. Mama still figures it out, and then they will go on a walk together. Everything is settled after that."

"You people are so strange," he muttered. I realized we'd walked farther along the trees. He was silent, and for some reason, the grimace on his face made it hard for me to continue. "When my father is upset, everyone is aware. The whole palace runs in fear. When my mother is upset, things go shattering across the room."

Ah . . . right, his family was much different. "Forgive me, I didn't mean to—"

"It's fine. Not everyone is so blessed in family and marriage, which is why you should not have such high expectations. Life will not go as you wish."

"Are not high expectations better than low ones?"

"Low ones protect you from getting hurt."

"But living in fear of being hurt is cowardly," I said, when in the corner of my eye I saw a giant stag with only one full antler, the other broken, grazing between the trees before me. Without thinking, I reached over and grabbed him. "Look!"

"Gun," he called softly, and Mr. Dawson handed it to him, only for Wilhelm to place it in my hands and whisper in my ear. "Keep your hands up and steady your feet. Do you have it in sight?"

I nodded, but was more aware of his closeness to me.

"Brace yourself."

I wanted to ask what I had to brace myself against, but he answered with his body. I felt it directly behind me. Why did he feel so much bigger all of a sudden? Like he was a massive warm rock . . . and again I found myself taken with the smell of him. So much so that part of me wished to lean against him.

"Focus," he whispered again, and because he was so close, his breath tickled my face when he spoke. I tried to ignore him by staring at the creature before us, but I couldn't. I could feel his heart beating.

"On three, you will pull the trigger." His hand came on top of mine. "One, two . . . three."

Bang.

I thought I would miss because he'd squeezed my waist on three, but sure enough, I hit the stag.

"Well done," he whispered again. My voice caught in my throat. All I could do was nod until he stepped away, taking my gun and moving to talk to Mr. Dawson. I turned back to look at him, not sure why my entire body was warm all of a sudden.

"My lady, are you all right?" Bernice asked me, moving closer.

"Huh? Yes, why?"

"You look . . . flushed. Are you tired from the walking?" she asked.

"Yes, that is it." I touched the back of my neck; it was hot. "The walking has tired me."

"Why don't we go back and rest? The gamekeepers can take care of everything else—"

"Hathor!" The sudden call of my name interrupted her. I turned to see Mary, Amity, and Lord Covington, as well as another, rounder gentleman named Lord Barrow beside Emma, all coming over to us.

"Fine catch, Your Highness!" Mary said, immediately getting closer to him.

"It was not I, but Lady Hathor," he clarified. They all looked at me, unbelieving.

"You?" Amity questioned with an expression of scornful disbelief.

"Yes, me. I do not know why you are surprised. I am quite the fine marksman," I lied with pride, and Wilhelm merely snickered, shaking his head.

"Well done," Lord Covington said to me as he stepped closer. It sounded strangely . . . empty, in comparison to when Wilhelm said the same words. "We shall eat well tonight, thanks to you."

Ever since Wilhelm told me Lord Covington used the same words over and over again with other young ladies, I had found myself avoiding his pleasantries and attention. All I could do was give him a polite smile. "I'm glad. Please excuse me."

"Lady Hathor." He stepped into my path again, whispering, though with all the other ladies focused only on their beloved prince I doubted anyone noticed either of us. "It is clear the queen wishes to see you and August together, but you need not force yourself to be with him. If you desire someone else's company, know that I am here for you, in anything you need."

In that moment I realized two things: I did not wish to need Lord Covington, and not once while I was with Wilhelm had I ever wished to be in another person's company. I glanced over to the small group gathered around him, and when I did, I saw his eyes were trained on us. On me.

Thump.

. . . For the first time ever, my heart went thump.

"Excuse me," I said to him, grabbing on to the skirt of my dress so I could run.

"My lady!" Bernice yelled after me, but I ran faster, so fast I had to reach up and hold my hat with one hand. I was sure I looked mad, running through the grounds as though I were being chased by a wild beast. But I did not care. I ran until I was finally back in the castle, and then up the stairs, bursting into Devana's room, who sat startled with her music sheets.

"Hathor?"

I could not breathe. My chest ached and burned, and my lungs were on fire. All I could do was slowly sink to the floor just inside the door and just sit there, breathing heavily.

"Hathor, are you all right?" She rushed over to me. "I'll call for—"

"The gentleman you fancy . . ." I managed to say when I looked at her. "When you looked at him, what sound did your heart make?"

"What?"

"Your heart . . . did it feel like it suddenly thumped against your chest?"

"Yes . . ."

"Oh, no . . ." I groaned and slid farther down. I'd waited years, dreamed and begged God for this feeling . . . and now it was here, for someone who'd vowed never to marry.

It could not be him.

I was mistaken . . . yes, it was just a flutter, not a thump.

It would go away, surely.

"How long do you plan on staying like this?" Devana asked me as I had come to lie on her lap to sulk.

"As long as it takes for me to make sense of my thoughts." I rolled over and glanced up at her. "So, a few years should do."

"My legs will surely fall off; you are very heavy."

"Hey!" I sat up, poking at her sides and causing her to giggle . . . and then there was a hammering at the door.

"Devana? Is Hathor there?" Abena called.

"No, she is not," I yelled back, only for her to wiggle the door handle. With us up against the door, it would not open.

"No fair! You both are leaving me out again!"

I sighed, rolling my eyes and getting up. The door swung open as she entered, wearing . . . Hector's breeches.

"Why are you dressed in Hector's old clothes?" I asked her.

"It's a disguise." She grinned and came in, closing the door. "When you dress up as a boy you can do so much more outside. No one even notices it is me, and I can join the other kids on adventures."

I opened my mouth to speak, but threw up my hands. I was far too tired for this. I moved to the bed, taking off my coat. "That is for you and Mama to figure out, Abena."

"What is wrong with her?" Abena asked Devana, who'd gone back to her desk.

"I believe she likes someone."

"I do not!" I yelled at her, lying back on the bed. "I merely had a slight excitement of the heart after shooting a stag."

"You shot a stag?" Abena ran up onto the bed. "Really? *You?*"

"Yes, me! Why is everyone surprised by that?"

"Because you are a horrible marksman," Devana said.

"You lack balance," Abena stated at the same time.

I looked them both over. "With little sisters like you, who needs enemies?"

They laughed at me as I sulked.

"What else has happened?" Abena sat up, waiting for me. "What is the queen like? Is she still mean?"

I pinched her cheek. "You are not allowed to call her mean. And I have not spoken to her much today."

"I'm more interested in who made your heart go—"

I took the pillow and threw it over at Devana, who caught it quickly. "Those in glass castles ought not throw stones."

"What does that mean? Our castle is made of stone, so shouldn't you say not to throw glass?" Abena questioned, and I laughed, pulling her cheeks.

"Do not worry, little bug. One day you'll grow up and understand everything."

"I do not want to grow any older." She smacked my hands away. "Can we not all just stay as we are?"

"No, Abena, we all have to grow up one day," Devana said to her.

"Or spend the rest of our lives with Mama," I said.

"Mama has been busy. Papa is busy. Everyone has been busy . . . except Mini and Hector. But Mini is a baby and Hector only wants to read." She huffed, kicking her foot.

"What of me?" Devana asked.

"You're boring too—all you care about is music," Abena replied, making me laugh.

"That is not true. She also cares about—" Devana threw the pillow at me as hard as she could.

"What?" Abena questioned.

"Nothing!" Devana snapped, glaring at her.

Abena sighed. "See? I do not know about anything going on. I can't go anywhere unless I disguise myself. I cannot wait for it to be over. Thank goodness there are only two more days left."

"Are there only two more days?" I paused, trying to recall where all the time had gone. "How can it be almost over, and my love story hasn't happened yet?"

"What have you been doing all this time?" Devana asked. It was a very good question. What on earth *was* I doing? Quickly, I got back on my feet and grabbed my coat.

"I must go back out there."

"I just got here! Are we not going to play?" Abena called out.

"Later, little bug, later! I must figure things out quickly. I do not have much time."

And the very first thing I had to figure out was whether or not I had somehow come to like Prince Wilhelm.

I rushed down the stairs, only to run directly into . . . his body.

"Why do you keep doing this to me?"

Wilhelm

"What did you say to her?" I snapped to Lukas, when Hathor left so hastily.

"It is not any of your concern—"

I stepped very close to him. "If you upset her in the slightest, you will learn very quickly how vast the difference is in our stations."

"Are you threatening me, *Your Highness*?"

I gritted my teeth. "Do I need to?"

He inhaled deeply before speaking. "You have said numerous times that not only would you not marry, but you have no interest in her. Yet here you stand before me, applying pressure, as though I were your rival. Be a man and be clear. I told you where I stood on this matter yesterday. What of you?"

My hands and mouth tensed. I had no words with which to reply.

"You cannot even answer. So what right do you have to say anything? If anyone was going to upset her, it would be you. You take nothing and no one seriously. You have toyed with and broken every woman you've ever encountered . . . just like your father."

"Watch your tongue, it speaks recklessly. I have never hurt any woman—"

"Just because you do not physically strike them and you vanish before they can show you their tears does not mean they are not hurt. You may be a prince, but Lady Hathor deserves better than you and your family. You know it. So, I must ask you to pull back, before you destroy her." He brushed past me on the way back to his sister.

And I could only stand there, rage building inside me.

"Prince Wilhelm, will you—"

Ignoring them, I began to walk off on my own. I did not know what to make of myself. Truly, I did not. He was right. I said I did not wish to get married; I said I did not like her. Yet here I was, laughing on hunts with her. I told myself I had to go this morning because the queen commanded it. But did I? Since when did I listen to every order given to me? I could have done as I always do, and gone off wherever I pleased. I was free now. A prince with no home. I could live as I wished. But without a second thought, I had woken up early and awaited her this morning. I hung on every word she said. I took the opportunity to be closer and hold on to her when she lifted that gun. I knew what I was doing when I whispered in her ear, when I placed my hand upon her waist . . .

I needed to stop. I needed to leave before I found myself growing any more attached to her.

That was it.

I had to leave.

I'd done it before, simply lied about an emergency and with that I was gone. The queen would be annoyed, but so be it. In time she'd move on from it. Nodding to myself, I made my way back to the castle.

This would be the best solution for everyone. I would not hurt her like this. She already thought me ill-mannered. She'd most likely just curse me and move on to . . . to someone else. I pushed the thought from my head. No, I would not be distracted.

"Your Highness. Welcome back," their butler said to me.

"Thank you. I have just received word that I must leave. Have the stablemen prepare my carriage and footmen sent to my rooms to take my things," I said.

"Of course, I shall see to it at once," he said, moving from me to a footman.

Yes, leaving was correct. Pulling the ties at my neck uncomfortably, I headed toward the steps. Just as I made my way up them, the very last person I wished to see ran right into my arms, her body coming so fast we both slipped. Quickly I wrapped my hands around her and held her tightly to me, to soften her fall . . . which left me on top of her, my hand behind her head and her face far too close to mine. She stared up at me, and never had I seen a face so fiercely beautiful, so utterly stunning. And just like that, there was no other place I wished to be, but on top of her.

"Why do you keep doing this to me?" Why did she keep making me forget myself?

"Doing what?" she asked.

I could not answer her because instead, behind us, I heard the maids say, "Your Highness, my lady, are you all right?"

Quickly I let go and rose to my feet before helping her up as well.

"Yes, I am fine, forgive me. I did not see you," she said, taking my hand as she got up and looked over herself. All the while, our hands were still touching.

Damn me . . . let go.

"It's fine," I lied, releasing her hand and placing mine behind my back. "Excuse me. I must go."

"Your Highness, would you like the maids to come assist you in packing?" the butler said. I wished to curse, because of course, she turned to me and said:

"Packing? Packing what?"

"I need no assistance. I shall pack on my own," I said to him. He nodded, walking off.

"Why are you packing? Are you leaving?"

"Yes," I said, walking up the stairs.

"Why?" She followed.

"Something important has come up," I lied.

"What?"

"I do not have to tell you."

"Wait!" She rushed up, stepping right in front of me. "You cannot leave!"

"I can if you move."

"I do not wish to move."

"Lady Hathor—"

"You cannot leave now. How am I going to figure out if I like you?"

I had to take a step back and stare at her. "What?"

Her honey eyes widened as her mind caught up to the words that had left her lips. And just like that, she moved away and tried to rush down the stairs. "Nothing!"

"No." I followed her, trying to stop her leaving—and once more, she slipped.

"Damn this dress!" she cursed as I caught her.

"If you slip a third time, I'll have to assume you are doing it on purpose . . . or God has made us his personal comedy," I teased, but she was eager to get away from me. I had no choice now but to block her at the bottom of the stairs. "Running away is not going to change what I heard you say."

"You are the one leaving. I'm not going anywhere but outside." She would not meet my eyes.

"Hathor," I whispered gently, wanting badly to turn her face to me. "Misunderstandings happen frequently between men and women because no one speaks openly about what they mean or feel. I need you to tell me plainly: What do you mean by 'like'?"

"I do not know. That is what I am trying to figure out, but you are leaving—so it is not important any longer."

"Then I won't leave." What was I doing? What was I saying? Why was I acting like this? What she felt did not matter . . . and then she looked at me and smiled.

"Good. Excuse me." She quickly ran off.

I stood there on the bottom step, frozen. This was the beginning of madness, I was sure.

15

Hathor

*G**ood. Excuse me* . . . All I could say was "Good. Excuse me!" What was the matter with me? Why? Why did I have to run into him like that? I'd barely begun thinking about what all of this meant. What was supposed to happen now? Was I supposed to stay at the staircase? Were we supposed to go for a walk? I needed help figuring this out, but as I looked out across the grounds, I wasn't exactly sure to whom I should speak. I definitely could not speak to the other ladies about this. My mama was too preoccupied with the queen, who sat under a rather large canopy surrounded by a few of her dogs and the other mamas, discussing heaven knew what. My father was still hunting with the men. My brother was most likely doing the same. There was no place for me to go . . . as always.

"How long do you plan to stand here?"

I jumped, turning to see . . . Wilhelm. Standing beside me, looking over the grounds.

"Why are you here?"

His eyebrow rose when he looked at me. "Did you forget our discussion from two minutes ago? You said—"

"Shh!" I exclaimed loudly. "Do not repeat what I said, I know what I said."

"You asked—"

"I meant: Why are you outside? Here? Standing next to me."

He let out a chuckle—or maybe a sigh. "You don't wish for me to leave, but you don't wish for me to be standing beside you. So where would you like me to be, *my lady*?"

"I don't know." I frowned, my shoulders drooping. "I do not know what I am supposed to do right now. Am I supposed to go for a walk with you?"

"Do you wish to?"

"I do not know!"

He laughed at me.

"Don't laugh!"

"It is hard not to, considering you always seem to know what to say or do. Now you look like a lost puppy."

"Compare me to a puppy again, and I shall call you a wild boar."

"I consider that an improvement from all the other names you've called me thus far."

I glared at him, and he glared back. "I've decided. I do not like you."

"I see. Then I shall take my leave, as originally planned." He turned from me.

"Wait— You . . ." I scoffed when I saw the grin on his lips, turning my head from him and crossing my arms. "Fine. Goodbye!"

He was so infuriating! What was I thinking? I did not like him in the least. Not at all, in fact.

"Lady Hathor." He was still beside me, but I refused to look at him. He stepped in front of me. "Would you care to accompany me on the water?"

My eyebrow rose. "Did you not tell me before that men do not enjoy boat rides?"

"Will you seek to argue with me, even now?"

I clamped my mouth shut and just nodded, motioning for him to go toward the lake. He shook his head at me and motioned for me to go first. Rolling my eyes, I did so.

I noticed I did not hear the distant laughter and conversations from the queen's canopy any longer. When I glanced over, I saw that all of their eyes were now on the both of us as we reached the dock at the lake's edge where a few boats had been brought out for any couple who wished to use them instead of hunt. Of course, no man chose to forgo the hunt but him.

"If a group of geese is called a gaggle, what do you call a court of gossiping women?" he asked as he stepped inside.

"A conspiracy?" I answered.

"No, a Medusa," he whispered, his hands on my waist as he helped me down into the boat. He smiled softly. "Avoid eye contact, or surely you will turn to stone."

I laughed. "They will be the ones to have your head on a shield if they hear you say that."

"Then it shall be a secret between you and me," he replied, untying the rope from the dock before he sat down across from me and took hold of the oars.

"Do you have many secrets?" I asked him.

"Yes. Doesn't everyone?"

"I don't."

"Everyone has a secret."

I tried to think, and then shook my head. "I know other people's secrets, but I have none of my own. Does that make me boring?"

"I believe that makes you . . . a lady of good standing."

"To you, ladies of good standing are boring."

"Normally. But you are . . ."

"I am what?" I waited for him to finish, but he just looked

at the water. "You are aware that no matter how fast you row, you will not be able to avoid answering, correct? I am in the boat with you."

"This is why you are not boring. Other ladies would understand not to push further, but you are unrelenting." He shook his head at me. "You are different, Lady Hathor. It is both infuriating and refreshing, which is why I am here, rowing. So spare me, if only slightly. This is . . . new for me as well."

"What, you've never rowed before?" I teased. "I applaud you, you are doing quite well."

He gave me a stern look as he understood my humor. Looking away from him, I focused on the water, reaching out and spreading my fingers to touch it. The water was cool, and the breeze tickled my face. I could not help but grin.

This was nice and calming. And the more I looked out across the water and over the landscape, the more I wished I'd brought my sketchbooks.

"It would be so lovely to paint this. I've never thought of viewing the estate from this angle before," I said.

"Yes, I am starting to see the appeal of boats more clearly," he said in a strange voice. When I looked back to him, I noticed he'd stopped rowing and was now staring at me. For some reason, the intensity of his gaze was too much for me; I had to look away. After a few more moments, he was rowing again in silence.

I hoped he could not hear how fast my heart was beating all of a sudden.

Who knew a man's eyes could make you feel so . . . warm?

Wishing to distract myself from the pounding of my heart, I thought quickly of something to say.

"I know your name is Wilhelm Augustus. But why do you go by the nickname August and not Will?"

"I was born in the month of August," he replied.

"That's it? Well, that's anticlimactic." There went my effort to make conversation.

"My father is King Wilhelm II. He wanted to name his heir after himself, but believed my brother would not live past infancy as he was so weak. Thus, the name was given to me. My mother called me August so as to not remind my brother, and I preferred it because I dislike my father. Climactic enough?"

Well, damn. My shoulders dropped. "Must all your stories be sad? It ruins the mood, utterly."

He laughed. "My apologies. What great and joyous story exists behind *your* nickname?"

"I have no nickname. Everyone just calls me Hathor. Well, they *try*; many people mispronounce it as Heather. My family is not very big on nicknames. The only person who has one is Aphrodite, whom we call Odite or Dite, because she disliked always being compared to Aphrodite the goddess. I call Abena little bug, because she's a terror. Oh, and Abena gave Damon's daughter the nickname Mini. But that is it." I considered for a moment if any of my extended family had nicknames, but none of them did.

"Ah" was all he said, catching my attention. I watched him row onward quietly, and I could not help but feel as if he were rather miserable, considering the fact that he'd said he did not enjoy this activity. Yet here I was, rambling.

"If you would like to go back to shore, I would not mind."

He frowned, his brow furrowing in confusion. "Do you wish to go back?"

"No, but . . . you look rather uncomfortable."

"More so out of practice . . . and out of shape." He took a deep breath, pausing for a moment. "This is actually much harder than it looks."

I giggled. "Would you like me to take over?"

"With those delicate arms of yours, how could you manage?"

"You have a poor sense of a woman's capabilities," I replied, snatching the oars from him. He leaned back and watched as I continued us on our way. "See? Easy."

He looked me over for a moment. "The wind is doing most of the work. It is blowing in your favor now."

"That sounds like the pitiful excuse of an out-of-shape man to me." I huffed and continued rowing with ease. The wind really *was* helping me, though. He reached for the oars, but I held them to my chest and shook my head. "No, please, Your Most *Gracious* Highness. Allow me."

"You will never pass on a chance to fight with me, will you?"

"Ladies never fight; we merely engage in witty banter. I read somewhere that the power of a woman is in her tongue."

"That is a universal truth," he said, reaching to place his hands over mine on the oars. His body leaned forward, his face closer to mine. Once more, there was that thumping in my chest. "But I promise: Banter is not the only thing that makes a woman's tongue powerful."

Without thought, my own tongue curled back in my mouth. He glanced down at my lips for a moment, and I swore by all the trees in the land that he was going to kiss me right there. Instead, he took the oars from my hands and sat back. I just sat there, dazed.

"Are you flustered, Lady Hathor?"

"Of course not," I lied, adjusting my dress. "Why would I be? Be well assured, your villainous tricks have no effect on me."

He smirked. "Is that why you think you *might* like me?"

My mouth dropped open. "I will push you into the lake!"

He laughed at me again.

"You laugh, but the truth is you have come to have some affection for me as well," I snapped, not at all liking this topic of conversation.

"And you came to this conclusion how?"

"You did not leave. When I said what I said, you asked me for clarification. If you did not care, if you had no interest, you would have ignored me and left as you wished. So, do not pretend it is only me." I did not realize my voice had gotten softer. I could not bring myself to look at him, so I watched the rest of the hunting party as they all walked back toward the castle.

Suddenly, I felt cold water splash across my face. Jumping, I turned to see that he had purposely wet his hand to flick it at me, an evil grin on his face.

"Forgive me. Your face was rather serious, and your cheeks were flushed. I thought some water—"

Reaching down into the water, I scooped as much as I could and flung it at his face, wetting the whole top half of him.

"You were saying?" I grinned.

He wiped his eyes. "This is significantly more water than I sprinkled on you."

"Forgive me, I often do not know the strength of my *delicate arms*."

He nodded and pulled the oar to his right up so he could also scoop water at me. I quickly rushed to the left to prepare my own ammunition. When he flung his hand, I did so as well, and just like that we were throwing water at each other without care for decorum or reputation or even common manners.

It was as if we were children . . . and all I could do was laugh.

This was never how I expected a boat ride with a man to be, but I dare say, it was altogether the greatest of fun.

That was, until we nearly tipped the boat. He rushed to grab on to me. My body pressed against his chest, and instantly my mind went blank and my heart truly went mad.

"Are you all right?" he asked gently down to me.

I nodded, quickly shifting from his arms back to my seat.

Yes, I thought I did like him, very much.

But he was so smug and irksome! How was this going to work?

Wilhelm

This did not happen to me.

Many had tried, many had come close, but no woman had ever made me enjoy rowing a damn boat. And it was not just that I enjoyed rowing it, it was that I now had no wish to stop. I'd carry her out to sea, to new continents, if she wanted. All for a chance to continue seeing her like this: the carefree way she laughed so hard that she snorted, the fierceness of her nature as she chastised me, the scent of her hair carried in the breeze.

Shit.

I could feel it . . . that quiver in my heart.

But this did not happen to me.

I did not become enamored by women's smiles and giggles . . . their breasts, yes. The sensuality of their beauty, of course, but it was always because I desired to see them in my bed. A woman was merely for personal pleasure. Yet here I was, more content than I ever thought possible . . . due to her silly, loud laugh.

Was this what other men were thinking when they brought women out onto the water, or shared a picnic in the park? If so I finally understood them, but I understood myself less. It was unsettling how fast these feelings came without warning. She was right. I would have left if I did not like her.

But I liked her. I liked how she showed me no pity; it made me more comfortable by her side. I had not a clue what I was supposed to do now.

By the time we finally reached the dock, a servant was already waiting to assist us. When he reached out for her, I quickly stood to help her first. Again, she looked at me. Those amber eyes of hers were worse than Medusa's, for I did not turn to stone, but water.

"Thank you," she said gently, and I wanted to hold on to her longer . . . closer.

I wanted her not just for a night or a season, but for— forever? Was that truly it? Forever? So, marriage? But marriage was so . . . permanent. How did I know these feelings would not pass? What if one day, years from now, I woke up and realized I did not wish to be married to her any longer? Or worse . . . what if she realized her whole life had been ruined because she was married to me? What if all I could ever give her were sad stories?

I did not desire that, and I did not wish her to suffer it.

"Are you coming?" she called back to me, waiting.

"Yes," I said, stepping out myself, feeling the need to stretch my arms. But since she watched me, unflinching, I could not bring myself to do so. I placed my hands behind my back.

She looked me over carefully and grinned. "Your arms hurt, don't they?"

"No, why would they?" I lied. She just shook her head at me. "They really do not hurt. I am fine."

"Thou doth protest too much, methinks," she chuckled as we walked back.

"*O, but she'll keep her word.*"

She looked at me strangely. "What?"

"I thought we were reciting *Hamlet* now. That is the next line, is it not?"

"You've memorized all the lines of *Hamlet*?"

"You've memorized only one line? Is it not normal to know plays?"

"You know all the plays?"

"Not all of them, but a good many of the popular ones. Why?"

She paused and looked me in the eye. "*I was born to join in love, not hate—that is my nature.*"

I thought for a moment, then recited the next words. "*Then go down to the dead. If you must love, love them. No woman's going to govern me. Antigone,* yes?"

She grinned. "You shall come in handy . . . *August.*"

"Don't." I shook my head. "I've gotten used to you calling me Wilhelm. Changing that now will make you seem— like everyone else."

"And I am not like everyone else?" she asked gently.

I inhaled and quickly thought past that. "Why will my knowledge of plays come in handy?"

"Fine, I'll let you change the subject this time." She smiled. "You will come in handy as my shield."

"A shield from what?"

"All my family teases me because I am not very good at remembering plays or books. I only ever recall my favorite lines. So they always best me in recitation."

"And you mean to use me to beat your family in petty arguments?"

"Precisely," she said without shame.

"Is that not juvenile?"

"Yes, it is, but silliness is what makes a family happy. When my aunt, my mother's older sister, would come to visit us, she and my mother would sneak into the kitchen cellar to take wine and a few cakes after we had all gone to bed. They'd get so drunk they'd start singing, and because they are both very competitive, they would argue about who was to sing the melody." She spoke loudly and quickly, waving her hands frantically before herself as she tried to explain. "Their efforts to be discreet failed terribly, as all the castle could hear them. Can you imagine, the great Marchioness of Monthermer and the Viscountess of Armmore, screeching like madwomen? Papa said all mothers need a moment to be childish, so we were all ordered to pretend as if we knew nothing about their antics. He was right, like always, and Mama was much happier afterward."

Just as she opened her mouth to add something more, she stopped abruptly, as if some revelation had come to her. She looked at me and clamped her lips shut.

"What is the matter?"

"Nothing." Her voice now low and gentle, her hands drifting back down to her sides. "What of you? I am very interested in . . ."

"In what?"

"In anything you have to say." Again, her voice was sickly sweet, unlike herself. "I've been rambling, it's unladylike."

"Yes, you were rambling, but I enjoy it. It is oddly soothing." And amusing; her whole spirit seemed to shine in her liveliness.

"That is the first time I've ever heard that," she replied, and then stopped, noticing the eyes on us as we lingered by the lakeside. "I think we should part here. Any more time together and—"

"They would usher us into a chapel to be wed. I understand. Good day to you, *Hathor*."

"And you, Wilhelm. Thank you for rowing," she said, before walking off on her own. I stood there, watching her figure retreat from me.

"I have done quite well in matching you both, have I not?"

I turned to see the queen walking up on my left with her ladies-in-waiting a few paces behind her . . . along with her dogs.

"Aunt—"

"Oh, spare me, for it is far too late to pretend you are not smitten with her, August," she replied as she came up beside me. "You made your choice the moment you decided to stay."

"You know?"

"I am the queen. I know everything. That is what queens do: They know things." She walked on, and I had no choice but to follow. "I shall write to your mother and let her know I will see to your wedding and Lady Hathor's training, though I doubt she shall need much."

"Wedding? Aunt, I am not—"

"You're not getting married, yes, that seems to be the silly mantra of you princes all over the world these days. As if marriage were solely for your benefit, and not that of a nation." She huffed at me angrily. "In my day, you were considered fortunate if you were given a person's portrait before seeing them on your wedding day."

"Yes, Aunt, we thank God for the progressive nature of today's society. You've created such a splendid kingdom that the youth of today believe in—"

"You must be under the impression that I am made of bread, with all that butter slipping from your lips. I must assure you that I am not," she said sternly. I closed my mouth, merely nodding. "You like her, correct?"

"Aunt."

"Am I correct? That is a direct question."

I sucked on my cheek. "Just because I like her does not mean—"

"It means everything. All the eyes of society are on you both. There will be expectations, you will rise to those expectations. Therefore, you will marry Lady Hathor. The end."

"Not the end!" I snapped angrily, causing her eyebrow to rise. I did my best to calm down. "I do not know how to be married. I do not know how to love someone. No one in my family knows how to love anyone. That emotion was not given to us. She will be miserable, I will be miserable, we will sit in a castle or a house in the countryside miserably regretting agreeing to a marriage simply because the Queen of England wanted it."

She stared at me for a moment before calling out, "Lady Crane?"

"Yes, Your Majesty?" The slender woman stepped forward with the queen's puppy in hand.

"Find me a doctor who can cut out my nephew's heart. I'm quite interested to see if it's black, since it is apparently incapable of loving."

I rolled my eyes. "Are my words but a joke to you, Aunt?"

"Jokes are for jesters. Orders are for queens. Find me the doctor, Lady Crane," she said, and turned from me to continue on her way.

"If you are serious, then it seems you mean to murder me!" I called after her.

"It is not as if you are doing anything worthwhile with that life of yours!" she called back, and I watched the parade of people follow behind her.

Apparently, I could not win an argument with any woman in England.

16

Hathor

"Well, when is your wedding?" Clementina asked, pretending to read when I came to sit beside her in the gardens.

"Please do not tease me. My mind is rather spent beyond its limits as is." I sighed and lifted the drink I had brought with me to my lips.

"I do not have to wonder who your mind was spent on; we all watched you and Prince Wilhelm in the boat. Mary almost fired a shot in your direction." She giggled, closing her book before shifting closer to me. "So—what happened?"

"I do not know." I was saying that a lot today. But it was truly how I felt. "One moment we are fighting, the next we are . . ."

"Flirting," she finished for me. "Well, they say love and hate are opposite sides of the same coin."

"*Love* is a bit drastic of a word. I have only just gotten to *like*." I frowned and drank the rest of the contents of my glass, pouting.

"Hathor!"

We both jumped, looking to where Mary and Amity were now marching toward me. I let out a groan, because I did not have energy for this. I turned to Clementina, but she shifted farther away from me. I gave her a look; she just shrugged.

"I knew you were lying, Hathor."

"Well, hello, Mary. How was your hunt?" I asked, my head held high. "Catch anything worth noting?"

"You said you were not interested in Prince Wilhelm." Amity crossed her arms. "We asked you over and over again, and you were lying to our faces."

"I was not lying. I wasn't interested, *then*. *Now* I am."

"What changed?" Mary questioned.

Good question. I wished I had the answer. "I need not explain myself to you, and so I will not. Though I am rather confused as to why you are *both* so upset. Were you planning on sharing him between you? What would the church say?"

They gasped at the hint of indecency, and Clementina tried not to laugh, opening her book once more.

"Very well." Mary held her head up high. "My mama says nothing is over until the church bells ring."

"Good luck." My indifference only angered them more. They both spun away just as quickly as they had come.

"This has been the most entertaining of weeks," Clementina said.

"I'm glad you're having fun, at least. I—"

"Lady Hathor?"

My name was apparently going to be called all day. I turned back to see . . . the queen's lady-in-waiting. My shoulders dropped.

"Her Majesty has sent for you. Please follow me."

I sucked in as much air as I could before rising from my seat, nodding goodbye to Clementina before following the tall, slender woman. And of course, everyone watched as I was led back into the castle by the queen's lady. The other mamas whispered among themselves, looking me up and down. It was quite obvious that the queen would only need to speak to me privately for one thing, and so my heart began to race with each step and turn we took, until we stood outside the double doors of the most opulent of the castle's drawing rooms. It was never to be used for anything or anyone other than the most noble of guests. So, essentially, it was only opened when a royal or archbishop visited us. We called it the chapel room because, in either case, we'd need a prayer in order to enter.

I took a deep breath, relaxed my shoulders, and lifted my head, saying the first small prayer that entered my mind.

The queen's lady-in-waiting opened the doors and stepped in first. "Your Majesty, Lady Hathor Du Bell."

Immediately, I curtsied low and kept my head down. "Your Majesty."

I did not hear her say anything, and thus I did not move to rise. But I was aware that her attendant had now left the room.

"Do you know what I find most perplexing in the world, Lady Hathor?" she finally spoke. Only then did I rise to see her standing at the gilded window, looking out at the guests who stalked about the garden maze below.

"No, ma'am."

"Men," she answered.

"Men?"

"Yes, those infernal creatures. They own all the world, all of this, even us, and yet they still have the audacity to rage, whine, bicker, and complain. When they are not doing that, they are fighting a war to own more things or places they do not know what to do with." She turned to me, her face stern, a furrow in her brow. "Perplexing, is it not?"

"Yes, ma'am."

"Why do you believe they do that?"

"If it perplexes you, ma'am, I doubt I would know," I answered softly.

"Smart. You know how to answer without answering, and how not to seem foolish in doing so," she said, moving to sit in the bright red chair with gold-embroidered arms closest to the fireplace, waving for me to sit down before her. There was hot tea already waiting. "Your elder sister was quite skilled in that."

Again, I took in air and forced myself to smile. "Yes, Aphrodite is quite good at a lot of things."

"Her demeanor makes her a perfect duchess. Yours makes you perfect to be a princess," she stated, lifting her tea cup.

"What? I mean . . . I do not understand. You believe me to be better than my sister?"

"Do not put your words in my mouth," she sternly stated, giving me a harsh look. "You are suited for something. That does not make you better or worse than anyone."

"But why do you believe I am suited to being a princess?"

"Because you have just the right amount of boldness and *rashness* to argue, as well as to question a queen. Had your sister been sitting before me now, she would merely nod and thank me."

"Oh."

"Yes, *oh*. Despite what many others may think, women in a royal house are not meant to be merely pretty and able to produce children. They must also be quick in wit, stubborn, and persevering. Why? Because men are perplexing, and left to their own devices they are prone to self-destruction, taking everything they own, us included, down with them. As women, we cannot allow that."

"You make it seem as if we are the ones who control them." I chuckled, and then quickly moved to lift the teacup to my lips.

"We do. Despite the fact that they have armies full of guns and swords, we are in control, so long as we persevere. That becomes so much easier when we conquer their hearts."

"Aren't gentlemen supposed to conquer ours?"

"Kings and princes are not just gentlemen, my dear. Their

hearts are like their palaces: heavily guarded. They do not allow themselves to love easily. In fact, they actively avoid it . . . to their detriment. It is rather exhausting, so we must *what?*"

"Persevere?" I answered slowly.

"Good. You are keeping up. Now, tell me, has August told you anything of his family?"

"Yes, a bit."

"Be specific. How much is a bit?" She lifted her cup to take a drink.

"I know he attacked his father to protect his mother after a hunting trip. His mother then forced him to leave the country, and he has been wandering throughout Europe ever since."

"Good. The fact that he's shared such intimate details is good. It means he is comfortable with you."

"To be honest, Your Majesty, he did not tell me first. I found out, and then he clarified—"

"Was he drunk when he shared the details of his life with you?"

"I do not believe so."

"Then like I said, he is comfortable with you. Comfort breeds love. Thus, we are in an excellent position to begin speaking on a proposal."

"A proposal? Your Majesty, I do not believe—"

"Do you like my nephew?"

"Yes, but I only came to that realization today . . . ma'am." *Keep calm. Keep calm, Hathor.*

"And now that you have had that revelation, you will need to get closer. How do you plan on doing so when the week comes to an end, and everyone returns to London?"

I paused, for I had not had time to think that far.

"Exactly. As you may have noticed, far too many people are

observing and interfering. This proposal is to give you both space for *like* to turn into *love*. It is a favor, from me to you. So, thank me dearly."

"Does Wilhelm—His Highness—desire this favor?"

"You are no longer keeping up," she replied, placing her cup back down. "Who is in control?"

"We are—so long as we persevere."

"If you wish for it, he will follow. So, thank me and take your leave."

"Yes, Your Majesty. Thank you," I said, curtsying to her.

She rose to her feet and returned to the window. When I stepped back out into the hall, my mother was waiting. I did not want to be lectured, or to explain; I walked up to her and hugged her tightly.

"Mama."

"You do not need to complicate your life if you do not wish to." She placed her hand on my head, leading me from the door. "You can say no, especially when you have another option."

"What?"

"Lord Covington has asked your father for your hand in marriage. And he did so quite boldly, proclaiming his enduring love for you."

"His what?" I gasped, standing on my own. "I—I— This is a lot, Mama. So much has happened in such a short amount of time. I feel as if the ground beneath my feet is spinning, and I do not like it."

"Then focus on what you desire more than anything else. Not just the title it can bring you, or how it elevates you above your sister. The most important person here is *you*; this is your future. You must decide what will bring you joy, not just for today, but forever. Your father and I support you unfailingly, even against the queen if we have to. You are our daughter, and more than anything we wish for you to be happy." She cupped my cheeks tightly.

My heart beat heavily with joy, and a bit of sadness. Not for me, but for Wilhelm. Here my parents were, willing to go against the wishes of the Queen of England for me, while his . . . his were not the same.

He was not a villain. I was wrong.

"Hathor, my sweet girl." She brushed my hair gently. "Please think carefully before you agree to anything."

It felt like I'd already agreed to the queen's proposal, but I merely nodded, as I knew no true engagement could be made until Papa gave his blessing.

"Thank you, Mama. I should go rest and prepare for the evening."

"Your ladyship!" Ingrid rushed to us, her eyes wide, which was never a good sign—nothing ever surprised her.

"What is it?" My mother was already walking. "Has some-one been injured?"

"Prince Wilhelm." At his name, I stepped forward, causing her to turn to me. "He and Lord Covington have come to blows."

"They are fighting? With their fists?" I exclaimed in shock.

"Stay here," my mother ordered me.

"But, Mama, it is clearly—"

"Stay here. I will not say it again."

What was the matter with everyone today, myself included?

Wilhelm

"Have you gone mad, Lukas?" Lord Chiswick chuckled along with the other gentlemen inside the parlor room, pouring glasses amongst themselves as Lukas moved to sit.

"He must be, who asks a man for his daughter's hand in marriage while he's holding a rifle . . ." Their eyes shifted to me for a moment as I took a seat in a chair opposite him. "The woman very well may be spoken for."

"Lady Hathor is engaged? I've heard nothing of the sort. To whom?" he asked, smirking when none of them answered. "As I thought. Fortunately, she is unpromised, and so it is within my right to offer my hand if I so choose. Is that not right, August?"

"Clearly," I answered, bringing my drink to my lips, though my jaw felt unreasonably tight. "Just as it is her right to reject you, if she pleases."

"I do not see why she would. Her father seemed rather pleased with the proposal—"

I chuckled. "She might reject you because she's barely spoken with you but a few times."

"You might not be aware, but that is customary here."

"Ah, I am sure Lady Hathor will be overjoyed at your unromantic approach."

"Romance is for poets and playwrights, not husbands," he replied sternly. "Women need the stability of a proper estate, the comforts of high society, and . . ."

"Many children to keep them preoccupied," the man to my right added.

"Exactly. Such things a *husband* provides. Where is your estate, again, August?" Lukas questioned, with a sneer on his face.

"What is your estate like, back in your country, Your Highness? You've never spoken of it," the other man pressed, and I had the distinct feeling he spoke to aid Lukas in leveling veiled taunts at me.

"I doubt a prince has only one estate. Does it matter?" another asked.

"It matters greatly. What father would not want to know where his daughter is to live?" Lukas replied, lifting his glass to his lips before looking to me. "Well, August?"

"When I speak to my future father-in-law, I will let you know. Or better yet, I'll let him choose. After all, where besides France can a prince not live?" I snapped back, growing very tired of seeing his face before me.

"But do you not loathe high society?"

"How well you think you know me, Lord Covington. I look forward to proving that to be one of your many mistakes."

"You would know about mistakes, would you not, my friend?"

"*Friend?*" I repeated the word and shook my head. "I do not count the gutless among my friends."

"Gutless?" He sat up. "And to whom do you refer?"

"Gentlemen, let us all remain civil," one man called out, trying to intervene, but civility did not exist here.

"I refer to you, sir." I leaned back in my chair. "I refer to your whole charade. For it shocks me in its desperation. You could not gain the lady's affections or attentions through your own efforts, and now you wish to push the matter before all of society in a pitiful attempt to win her hand. And you call that customary? It is, as I said, *gutless*."

"Oh, I nearly forgot: We are before a man who knows all about gaining ladies' affections and attentions for no other purpose than to ruin them! Young, old, married, unmarried . . . it matters not to you, right? A family trait, I suppose? How I pity your long-suffering mother!" he sneered.

I placed my glass down and rose to my feet, making them all rise but him. When I took a step closer, a man grabbed my arm, but I yanked it back.

"I don't believe I heard you clearly, Lukas. To whom were you trying to refer with that comment?"

He finished the drink in his glass before rising and looking me in the eye. "I wonder to whom I was referring, as well. You would know better than anyone else whom you take after. Is that not why you have chosen to forgo marriage?"

"Whom I propose to is none of your business!"

"And to whom and how I propose is none of yours! You may be the queen's nephew, but that does not mean this land or the women in it belong to you. I will not be dissuaded or insulted by a criminal—"

My fist connected with his jaw before he could finish the insult. I felt all the annoyance he'd brought me since we had met again rushing back to me, and nothing brought me greater joy than to feel the bone in his face beneath my knuckles.

"Enough! Have you all gone mad?" the marquess hollered. When he had arrived, I was not sure. I was not even sure how long I'd been held back for.

"I have not, but any man who allows this beast near his daughter truly is!" Lukas hollered as he, too, was restrained, his mouth and nose bleeding furiously. "This is his true nature. He does not even fear attacking his own father—"

"Keep speaking and I will cut out your tongue myself!" I hollered at him.

"I—"

"Did I not say enough!" the marquess roared once more. "Should this continue, prince or not, lord or not, I shall throw you both out of my home. Take them away!"

"Come on, quickly." I had not realized it was Hathor's brother holding me until I felt him push me from the room. Outside there were servants, and the marchioness, all staring at me with a look I was far too familiar with: The look most of the servants in my palace wore whenever my father had one of his outbursts. The stare of revulsion and trepidation.

I said nothing, walking toward the stairs quickly, hoping I

would not come across her, too—that she would not look upon me like this, either. However, I was not so lucky: She was at the end of the hall.

Fuck!

I hung my head and just kept walking.

"It's all right!" I heard her call out. Pausing, I turned back to her, thinking surely she was speaking to someone else. Instead, she stared at me with those eyes, and with a small smile on her face. "It's all right."

"You do not even know what happened," I replied, and she just shrugged as she walked to where I stood.

"It doesn't matter what happened, it's still all right." I was not sure why her words made me feel better. It was clearly not all right. This would be a scandal, and it would further tarnish my already tarnished name. Her family had put so much effort into this week, and all anyone would recall was that I punched the man who sought her hand in marriage. "Everything is going to be all right."

"And if it's not?"

She pretended to think. "Dying is always an option, but if that is too drastic, you can also go to America. I am not sure if that is a better or worse fate."

I laughed. I could not help it. She was ridiculous, and—wonderful.

"Hathor!" She jumped at the sound of her name. Her shoulders tensed, and slowly we both looked to find her mother glaring at her. The marchioness inhaled through her nose before glancing toward me. "Your Highness, forgive her for intruding. I am sure you wish to go clean up."

I wished to say she very much was not intruding, but I had disgraced myself more than enough for the afternoon. I nodded to them and continued on my way, but not before whispering to her.

"Even if I've ruined my chance—do not accept that man. You deserve better."

I meant those words, but I also truly hoped I had not ruined my chance. Because the idea of marrying her was no longer just an idea: It was now my greatest aspiration.

17

Wilhelm

"Is it your desire to be run out of all of Europe entirely?" The queen hollered at me as I sat before her, my hands being tended to by the doctor who was fetched to cut out my heart for observation.

"I—"

"No, no, no. Do not speak. Fools do not get to speak," she replied, standing in the middle of the drawing room. The walls were colored white and gold, while the ceiling itself was painted with heavenly beings. It felt as though I were being judged from on high. "Fools stay silent as all the world mocks them for their foolishness."

"Aunt—"

"You are a prince. You are not supposed to be foolish!" she snapped again. "You are born to be a leader of men, August. A leader, not a beater—I cannot even say the word properly, for I feel foolish!"

"I think you've run the word *fool* into the ground, Aunt," I replied as she took a breath, finally letting me get a word in.

"Better a word than a lord. Look at your hand. Surely not even a boxer has such wounds."

"Have you ever seen a boxer?" I questioned, trying to imagine the sight of the queen at a match of that sort, dressed in her layers of laces and pearls.

"No, because I find the pounding of another man's face for any reason to be most vile and— What is the word I am looking for, nephew?"

"Foolish—ah." I gritted my teeth as the gray old doctor pressed around my knuckles, examining them through a monocle as though my hand came from the other side of the world.

"Tell me you shall need to cut off his hands," she demanded.

"No—no—Your Majesty, it is nothing more than minor cuts and bruising, which will heal in a few days' time," he answered.

"The same thing I said—"

"I said *silence* from you," she warned me, once more focusing on the doctor. "Do whatever you must for his hands, while I try to sort out the course of his life. Lady Crane!"

"Yes, Your Majesty?" The woman stepped forward.

"The marquess and marchioness: Have you gathered their position on this matter?"

"Lord Monthermer was rather calm and unbothered after breaking up the fight; however, her ladyship seems most displeased. I believe she is against a match between them."

My aunt looked back to me. "Are you quite proud of yourself?"

"Am I allowed to speak now, Your Majesty?" I asked her as the doctor wrapped my hand.

"Will you say anything of sense or substance?"

"Only you can judge that." I groaned, for I was more than tired of this. It had been nearly half an hour already. "I apologize, truly. I did not mean, or desire, to cause such a disturbance. I lost my temper—"

"Because another man had the good sense to propose to the woman you are in love with?"

"Love?" I laughed. "You've said much today, but that is most outlandish—"

"Press his hand firmly, Doctor."

"Ah! Bloody— Aunt!" I hissed, yanking my palm away from her mad doctor.

"You know what is outlandish? Two people who clearly like each other wasting all of our time pretending they do *not* like each other."

"We are not pretending anything," I said, taking the roll of cloth to wrap my hand myself. "We are merely not rushing to an altar."

"Do you believe you shall be young forever? That all the world shall move at your leisure? It is relatively simple. You like a lady of noble birth and respectable status, you marry said lady, you have children, and then try to die of old age— *not* a person's fist."

I let out a deep breath. "If I propose to her, will you spare me this lecture? I am at my limit."

"Yes. Now go propose."

I rolled my eyes and ignored her. Why I had bothered to speak at all, I did not even know.

"Ahh, you now choose silence. No matter, I have already proposed for you."

The cloth dropped from my hand. "I beg your pardon? You've done what?"

She finally took her seat, one of her maids entering to offer her a cup of tea. "Moments before you lost your sanity, I informed Lady Hathor that there will be an engagement between you both, and she thanked me for my efforts."

I could only stare at her blankly. "Hathor— You spoke with Lady Hathor, and she thanked you?"

"That is what I said," she replied, now far too calm as she drank.

I did not understand. "Lady Hathor says she wishes to marry me?"

"The week is coming to an end. The only way you may remain in each other's company is if you are engaged to be wed."

How did I get to this point? It had only been a week. How could all my desires, intentions, and world change within a week?

"Or do you wish her to be in the company of Lord Covington instead?"

My jaw cracked to the side, and almost immediately my fist clenched, which caused pain to spread up my arm.

"Your Highness, allow me to—"

"I am fine. You may go, unless Your Majesty is still pondering the color of my heart," I interrupted the doctor. The queen nodded for him to go. Not just him, but also the rest of the servants who stood by silently. When it was just the two of us, alone, she spoke again.

"If you cannot stand even the thought of her being with another, you must claim her as yours, or lose her."

"It is not that simple."

"It is. Or at least it *was*, until you showed Lord and Lady Monthermer this side of you."

"Which side? My father's—"

"No. No. I will not have this conversation overlooked for your self-pity. I have told Lady Hathor to expect a proposal. You will either have to go to her and explain why that shall not be, or you will go to Lord Monthermer and ask for his daughter's hand."

"You expect me to go to him looking like this?" I questioned, lifting up my poorly bandaged hand. "I am sure all the world outside this room gossips upon my head now."

I was sure Lukas and his allies had disclosed the true nature of my circumstances to all of society, and I would have little to defend myself with, considering I had once more used my fists.

"Again with the self-pity. Do you know why it is unbecoming?" She placed her teacup down. "Because no matter how dire your circumstances in life are, your position is still greater than the majority of the world. No matter what you have done, no one can strip you of your title as prince. You are royal, it is in your blood. Society gossips and mutters behind our backs, but before us they smile. Do you think I am unaccustomed to this? Do you think me naïve enough to believe that all the people here have not gossiped of my own circumstances in life?"

"Who dares? Call the executioner for us to behead them immediately," I replied jokingly, but her face remained stern.

"You speak in jest, but that is the attitude you are required to have among them. You must look them in the eye and say, *Who dares*? It is the only way we can survive until a new scandal or story takes their attention."

I inhaled slowly, nodding, for she was not wrong. "That might work with the rest of society, but what do I do about her parents? These Du Bells, their family is among the closest I've ever seen. They will not be pleased with me, prince or not."

"They will come to like you in time, so long as you behave yourself and show sincerity to their daughter. The more you love Lady Hathor, the more they will come to love you."

So, that was it?

It was settled.

Hathor and I were to be engaged.

The thought stirred a feeling in me I did not wish to dwell on. And so my thoughts went to Hathor. I was sure she would not desire to be engaged so . . . formally. She yearned for romance, and I'd offered nothing but a boat ride.

If I was going to do this, I needed to do something for her, something so magnificent that not even poets or playwrights could muster it. Something she'd want to draw in her book. But I did not have the slightest idea of what to do. I had no past experience in such matters.

God, what a very long day this was.

Hathor

"Apparently, he is a prince in name only. He was banished for his wild nature and predisposition to violence. As we have all seen," Amity said to the group of ladies gathered around her as though she were the most knowledgeable person in the world, instead of the most ignorant.

I took a step toward them when an arm wrapped around mine and held me still. When I turned to look, it was Silva, my brother beside her.

"You and I both know no good will come of you confronting them," she said, forcing me to keep my back turned on the gossiping ladies. "It is better to simply ignore it."

I could not help but frown. "They are slandering him unjustly."

"And what is it to you? Did you not tell me you disliked him? That he was horrid?" Damon whispered back to me. "Clearly, you were correct in your assessment, and no one would fault you for not marrying him now."

"You, brother, of all people, should recall how easily one's reputation can be tarnished. I believe they used to call you much worse. And it speaks poorly of you to join them in their gossip now. You know nothing of him!"

He gasped. "What in heaven's name has gotten into you? I have barely said anything to anyone, and yet you snap at me? It was you who was—"

"My dear," Silva gently interrupted him, giving him a look. He huffed and shook his head as he walked away from us.

I clamped my mouth shut and just glanced around the room, ignoring him. Watching as all the ladies and gentlemen fluttered about from one group to another, discussing what had transpired this afternoon.

"Hathor?"

"Hmm?"

"Come, why don't we step out into the gardens and take in the air?" Silva said, leading me away from my brother and everyone else in the hall. We walked from the double doors out onto the balcony. Detaching myself from her, I moved to the very edge and rested my hands on the ledge, taking a deep breath.

"So. When did you realize you liked Prince Wilhelm?" Silva asked as she came up beside me.

"Would you think me mad if I said this morning?"

She giggled, shaking her head. "No, I myself was in a similar position with your brother, if you recall."

Yes, I did. They'd hated each other when they first met. Damon said she was dull and pesky, while she'd called him an overindulgent man-child. I believed she was quite correct, but apparently love was blinding.

"One moment, I was throwing a book at his head; the next, we were married." She laughed at that. "I soon came to the realization that some couples fall lovingly into each other's arms, and others battle until they collapse into each other."

"I would have preferred the first option." My parents, my sister, Verity, it was like they were all immediately drawn to their other halves.

"No, you would not have, for you crave a good sparring partner."

"I do not!"

"Why do you think Abena taunts you so? It is because you are the only one who bothers to truly tease her back. Everyone else brushes her off for the child she is. But you chase after her, throw pillows and shoes as if she were your friend, or better yet, as if *you* were *hers*. And you let no one, not your parents, siblings, friends, or even the most esteemed ladies of society, go unrebuked for any slight."

"Of course I don't; to keep silent would be to allow them to continue."

"It is that attitude that requires your husband to be just as forceful, or else you would all but eat him alive with your words," she mused. "And you'd be very bored. Though, I am biased; I must say, I believe the other type of couples have much more fun than us."

"Us? I rarely see you argue, with my brother or anyone."

"Well, I cannot be constantly arguing with him before your mother and father. Besides, we agreed that all of our arguments would be saved for our bedroom. It's much more convenient." She muttered that last part under her breath, but before I could ask her why, she placed her hand on mine. "Do not dwell too much on the timing and enjoy it. This is what you always wanted, is it not? You are to be a princess, a wife, someone's beloved."

I pinched my hand to remind myself to stay calm and not let those words sink in too deep. "He has not really expressed his feelings for me—"

"He broke a man's nose over you; I assume his feelings are quite deep."

"Lord Covington's nose is broken?" I gasped in shock. I had not even thought to ask about his condition. Neither he nor his sisters and mother had come down for the evening. I presumed it was to avoid the queen and Wilhelm, both of whom were also absent. "I cannot believe this truly happened."

"Well, you must believe it, as well as prepare yourself for what happens next."

My gazed whipped to hers. "What happens next?"

"You choose a husband."

"Right." My mouth was agape.

"Luckily, I doubt either of them will show their faces tonight, so you may think on it for a while yet," she said, taking my arm again. "Come. Let us return inside, before they begin to gossip about you. Please, do your best not to give in to confrontation."

I allowed her to take me back into the hall. As if timed by God exactly, the doors at the front of the hall opened, and there entered the queen —beside her, Wilhelm. Just like that, there was not a whisper, not even a breath. Even the music stopped as everyone curtsied to them. I kept my head down. Because for some strange reason, my heart was beating far too fast, my hands felt shaky, and for the first time ever, I wished to run away.

What was wrong with me?

"Lady Hathor?"

My head snapped up, and there was my answer. *He* was what was wrong with me. That smooth, smug face and those blue eyes of his were unnerving.

"Prince Wilhelm," I replied, seeking to calm myself down.

He leaned forward, making my eyes widen, as I was sure everyone was watching. Nevertheless, his face was far too close to my own. And he had the audacity to smile at me, as if he did not know or care how this looked.

"I seem to have given a rather poor impression of myself today, so if I may, could I inconvenience you by asking you to be my partner for the evening? Or maybe the rest of my life?"

I heard the girls to my left and right gasp.

My eyes became even wider.

"Are you mad?" I spat out without thinking, which only caused more gasping. "I mean— Are you proposing to me here? Right now? Like this?"

He bit back a laugh. "I am asking, first, for a dance. To propose, I must first speak to your father, but I fear he might not look fondly on the prospect right now. I mean to convince him otherwise by showcasing how happy we are dancing."

He lifted his hand to me. I noticed it was his left, as his right was bandaged. I had so many things I wanted to ask him, but now was not the time. Everyone was waiting to see my choice. I had already made my mind up throughout the day, and with each passing second it was more and more obvious.

Reaching up, I placed my hand on top of his, and he kissed the back of it.

I think my heart nearly exploded.

18

Wilhelm

It was well past midnight—nearly one in the morning, in fact—when I entered the library. To say I was anxious would be an understatement. I think this was far worse than that. I felt a raw fear that I had not felt since leaving my home, years ago. However, I did my best not to let it show as I now stood before him: Hathor's father. He'd kept his distance from me throughout the week. I had barely spoken to him, but I knew for sure that despite his calm and bookish demeanor, he was not one to be trifled with. I did not think any man who'd raised such a family had done so by accident, or with simple luck.

"Welcome, Your Highness," he said from where he stood near the shelves of books on my right.

"Thank you, sir. Please call me August or Wilhelm, if you prefer."

"If I prefer?" he repeated, pulling a book from the row above him. "Her Majesty did not make it seem as if our preferences mattered."

"Please excuse my aunt; she is rather determined."

"That is the problem. I cannot excuse her, for she is the queen," he said as he went back to his desk with his book. "If she were not the queen, I would be compelled to tell you not to bother with the words you seek to say now. I could not bear the thought of my beloved girl marrying a man who throws fists at other men in his anger, instead of words. I prefer her to marry a nobleman of England, with land *in England*, so should she ever need me, I could go to her. I prefer my children to fall in love with people I can respect. And while I believe myself a tolerant person, I do not think I can respect a man who spent years traveling from brothel to brothel."

I hung my head, because I knew this would be the case. And he was not wrong. Outside of being a prince and nephew to the queen, what could I truly offer?

"I can commend you, at least, for not making excuses for your behavior," he added.

"I know that no excuses can be made. I am well aware of my failings."

"Yet you still stand here? Is this by your own volition, or the queen's command?"

"It is my choice."

"Is that so? I hear the queen has been seeking to convince you to marry my daughter for quite some time now, and you have sternly rejected it. Once, even to my daughter's face."

Fuck.

"That is true."

"Then how is this of your own volition?" he questioned, sitting down. I still stood.

"Because while she is the queen to you, she is my aunt." I would not back down now. "You may not be able to do what you prefer, but I can, and have. For years, I have done what I preferred. I did not care for the consequences. Why would I? I had already lost everything. I lived for my own gratification only."

"But now you are miraculously a changed man?"

"No." I shook my head. "I believe I am still much the same. But now, all I want is Hathor. I can think of nothing else."

"And when you decide to want someone else? When your thoughts move on to some other woman—"

"They will not."

"How can you be sure? Your past does not give much confidence."

"It is because of my past that I know she is different for me, sir. You said I traveled from brothel to brothel: Yes, it is true. Countless women have passed by me, and none have ever made me so sick with worry and doubt. Not one had the power to infuriate me one moment and charm me the next. Not one ever made me feel so lacking, or made me yearn to be better, to be different. When I do not see her, I am agitated. When another man dares get too close to her, I am colored green inside. When she is beside me, there is a rippling joy that goes through me, and I seek her smile or frown or gaze by any means possible. I know I am not worthy of her, and I desperately wish for her anyway."

"And if I say, 'how nice,' but the only way I would accept this is with a written command from the king?"

"Then I will go to the king and get that command." I truly would. "But I would much prefer to prove myself to you and your family."

"And how will you do that?"

"By being the type of man you can respect."

"Such men are not built in a day."

"Then I will use as many days as needed."

"Prince Wilhelm, even in your circumstances, you could have anyone else."

"Are you not hearing me, sir? I desire no one else. I can love no one else."

He frowned, and for a moment his eyes looked as if they were begging me not to say the words. But I could not avoid it, not after the display I carried on with her this evening, not with the way my heart was screaming inside of my own chest. "Lord Monthermer, I seek your permission to marry your daughter, Lady Hathor Du Bell."

Hathor

I had not slept. At least, not *well*. It was hard to sleep, when your dreams were happening in reality. I could not help but feel as if, maybe, this was not really happening. That maybe he did not want me, but was compelled to seek my hand due to yesterday's chaos. I tossed left, right, and nearly off the end of my bed, trying to come to grips with what was happening. Just when I had decided he truly did not like me as much I had come to like him, Bernice placed a letter in front of me.

"From His Highness," she said gently, before stepping behind me to fix my hair.

Quickly, I took the letter and opened it. Instead of a letter, there was a picture. It was a sketch of the stone pavilion where we'd waited out the storm.

That was it? I needed more than that! Was I to ride there? What were we to do? What was I supposed to wear?

Dropping the paper on the desk, I slouched. "Why does this stress me so?"

"I believe you are anxious, miss, not stressed. It is normal to feel so." Bernice giggled as she pinned my curls back.

"I would normally have some witty rejoinder to that, Bernice, but today I have nothing. My mind is so full of . . . anxiety. I cannot think. How can I go to him when I cannot think?"

"You *feel* when you cannot think. I promise that will help you just as much," she stated, putting the last curl in place.

I thought *feelings* were what had gotten me into this.

I didn't bother changing my dresses over and over again, as I feared he'd grow tired of waiting. I did not utter a word to any other maid in the hall. In fact, I actively tried to avoid meeting anyone. It was still so early that many were not awake yet.

To my surprise, Sofonisba was already prepared and waiting for me when I stepped out of the castle . . . and beside her, Wilhelm. He was dressed rather simply, with only a dark blue riding jacket, white blouse, and trousers, along with dark boots. He stood between his horse and mine, stroking them both gently.

"Good morning, my lady." The stableman nodded to me, and it was then that Wilhelm turned.

Keep calm! I hollered at myself, and kept my head held high. "Good morning to you, as well, and you, Your Highness. I hope you slept well."

"I slept not a wink. I hope you fared better."

"Of course I did. Why wouldn't I?" I lied, going up and stroking Sofonisba's nose. "Good morning to you, too, Sofonisba."

"Well, for one, I'd hoped your mind was rather preoccupied with thoughts of me, as mine was with you," he said, stepping up beside me. I jumped.

"Do not do that."

"Do what?"

"Say nice things, so close to me—it's distracting."

"No."

"No? What do you mean, no?"

"I mean that I wish to keep distracting you. So, I shall get closer, and say many more nice things."

Stay calm! I once again begged myself.

"Your horse is beautiful." He swiftly changed the subject, running his hands over her neck. "Sofonisba: a noblewoman turned painter during the Italian Renaissance."

"Yes, she was the first woman painter I'd ever learned about," I whispered, trying to gather my wits. "And yours? What is its name?"

"Augustus."

I laughed. "You named him after yourself? Is that not a bit conceited?"

"No, he was named after the first Roman emperor. My mother has a dog named Caesar."

"Your mother's dog is named Caesar. As in Caesar, the father of Augustus, which makes me think your mother's dog is your horse's parent."

He grinned and nodded. "My brother named them specifically for that reason. It was a running joke with all the animals at the palace. Whenever he bought a new one, he made them related by name somehow."

"Are they all Roman?"

He shook my head. "No, we have a swan named Cleopatra."

"Is there a Mark Antony?"

"Yes, he is the duck that shares the same pond."

I chuckled. "A duck . . . as in, an easy target? Your brother's humor is apparent."

"I was not aware you knew so much about ancient history," he said, moving to help me up onto Sofonisba. Though I did not need it, I did not fight it, either.

"Have you not met my father? There are a great many arbitrary facts my siblings and I have been obliged to learn throughout our lives," I replied, only now noticing that Bernice had not moved to follow me. "Are you not coming, Bernice? Where is your horse?"

"No, miss, I need not come," she said.

"Why is that?"

"You shall see when we arrive," Wilhelm said to me, now upon his horse.

This was not dispelling my anxiety at all. And to make it worse, he did not speak, which made it hard for me to speak. So we rode at a gentle pace away from the castle. It grew so agonizing, I could not take it for another second.

"I—"

"This—"

We both had tried to speak at the same time, causing us to look at each other. There was a slight twinge of amusement on his face.

"We've become so self-conscious with each other already."

"It's your fault!"

"Why is it my fault?"

"Because you are you, and you are not saying anything, when so much needs to be said!"

"You say something, then."

"What am I supposed to say?"

"Whatever comes to your mind, like always."

"My mind is currently a mess because of you!"

"As is mine, because of you!"

"Ah! Talking to you is still frustrating." I huffed and rode on ahead to get away from him, but of course, he caught up immediately. Once more, I tried to move farther ahead, only for him to come right up beside me. I turned to glare, and he smiled. It was a stupid smile. And it was surely infectious, for I could feel myself wishing to smile as well. "Stop it!"

"Stop what? Riding?" His eyebrow rose. "After I put so much planning into this morning? Never."

"What planning?"

"You'll see when we get there," he said, and took hold of the reins. "But at this pace, it might take us all morning. Do you believe you can keep up?"

"I believe I can beat you with ease," I said, not waiting for a reply before taking off, as fast as I could muster, down the path. I could not call it a race, for I noticed he never once moved to overtake me. Instead, he either matched my pace or stayed just slightly behind. There was part of me, the part Silva was talking about last night, that actually wished to race him, to beat him. I was so used to being in competition with someone that I expected it, no matter what, and despised anyone who did not compete back in earnest. It made me feel as though they were pitying me. That was often the source of all my arguments with Aphrodite. It always felt as if she pitied my efforts.

But it was different with him. His effort to purposely stay close, allowing me to stay ahead of him, did not feel like pity. Instead, it felt like care. Like he was watching over me so as to not lose sight of me, to make sure I was all right.

Before much longer, the stone pavilion came into sight, and I slowed. The closer I got, the more shock I felt. There, upon the floor of the pavilion, was a blanket, a great number of pillows, food, flowers—a setting for a picnic. Not only that: Just off to the left side were a few of the musicians from last night's orchestra, and to the right there were two maids with baskets, one holding sherry, another holding tea all on trays. There was even a footman standing in wait.

Slowly, my gaze shifted from the sight before me to him, only to see that he was already off his horse and at my side. Just as he had last night, he offered his hand to me. Silently, I took it, gently reaching the ground right before him, Sofonisba at my back. The space between us closed. He did not release my hand. Instead, he kissed the back of it again, then kept it firmly in his own and drew me forward.

My mind was now blank. All I could do was follow as he led me across the grass and up the stairs, allowing me to see it all up close. And I noticed all my favorites were laid there. My favorite flowers, pink peonies, along with my favorite buttered scones with red jelly, favorite macaroni made with bacon, several cuts of chicken, more bacon, fresh toasted bread with strawberries, heirloom tomato salad, green grapes, fresh lemon loaves, and every other fruit I had ever once mentioned enjoying.

"I know picnics are usually done on grass, but considering your aversion to bugs and clear love of everything sweet, I figured the pavilion would be better suited to host us," he said, trying to bring me in. I quickly let go of his hand and moved to take off my shoes. "What are you doing?"

"I do not wish to track in dirt and ruin its beauty."

"I believe you being here is what makes it beautiful, but if you wish to go barefoot, then so shall I," he whispered, bent beside me. "Though you are aware that undressing even your shoes will be considered scandalous."

I smirked as I undid the laces and took the first shoe off. "We've already caused enough scandal. What is this little bit more going to do?"

"A little bit more always leads to a little bit more," he said gently, allowing me to lean on him as I took off the other shoe, before he took off his boots.

Stepping inside, I slowly took a seat across from where I expected him to sit. Instead, he sat directly next to me. I stared at him, but he glanced over the food before picking up a flower. "Never in a thousand years would I have thought I'd do something like this."

"Why have you then?" I wanted to mention how he adamantly criticized the idea of this just days ago. But I did not wish to ruin this.

"Why else but you?" he replied, his gaze shifting to me as he held out the flower to give it to me. "I believe I—no—I *am* captivated, *enamored* with your very being, Hathor. All night, I wondered how that came to be in such a short time. I'm sure it was not just this week, but beginning when I saw you all those weeks prior. I could not rid you from my mind, nor would I want to."

"You said you never wished to marry," I whispered, taking the flower.

"I never did until you, and to be honest, I am still rather fearful."

"Fearful?"

"I know not the first thing about being a husband." He shifted so we were looking at each other. "You take my hand, and you've clearly seen all the worst parts of me, all my flaws, but nevertheless, I must still say plainly that I am not a fairy tale, Hathor. I am just a man with a high title, but zero future prospects. I have no land here, and where I do have land, I cannot return. My family is an utter disaster, and because of that, I've always acted immaturely, even when I mean well."

I smirked, lifting the flower to my nose to smell. "Are you seeking to scare me off?"

"No, I merely wish to be honest."

"Then I shall be honest in return." I inhaled deeply before letting the words out. "I am . . . perfect."

He stared at me for a moment before breaking out laughing, and so did I.

"Your parents were entirely correct in naming you after a goddess, for you think so highly of yourself, and have no compassion for men."

"I am only joking!"

"Are you? It felt rather sincere."

"I do that sometimes—well, a lot of the time," I replied,

now actually honest. "When I am nervous or unsure of myself, I say and do whatever I can to display confidence. It normally serves to make everyone leave me alone, or to shift conversation."

"And no one ever teases you?"

"They do but I merely double my efforts, and they quickly grow exhausted." I giggled.

"I shall keep that in mind for the future," he said, his hand on mine again. "I cannot promise to always make you happy, nor do I believe I will listen to you as well as your papa does your mama. I think we shall fight a great deal, in fact."

"But?" I waited, squeezing his hand back.

"But, I swear, there will be no person of greater importance, no person I will ever live for or give myself to other than you, Hathor. I swear to devote myself to giving as much as I humanly can to you, for as long as I may live. I will love you unendingly. Will you marry me?"

I nodded first, before finding my voice to speak. "Yes. I will marry you, Prince Wilhelm."

There were no more words in my mind, but sensations of joy.

After all the years of searching, crying, waiting, dreaming— the man who would be my husband was finally here.

Finally.

19

Hathor

We spent most of the morning talking about our-selves . . . it was the only thing we could do under the eyes of so many servants. Which I was sure was the only way my parents allowed for us to be away from the castle so long. I also noticed how his fingers twitched closer to mine through-out the conversation, though never touching me.

I tried to focus on his words; the things he liked. This in-cluded art, of course; we'd clearly established that. Riding and fishing, natural for a man, were not so unexpected as his love of books and plays. He said he much preferred to read while in a hot bath in the evening, which he tried to have once a night. However, the thing that took me most by surprise was that he apparently loved to sing. Never had he mentioned or showcased such an ability, and he refused to allow me to hear. The more I pressed, the more sheepishly he shook his head. He looked dashing when he did, very young and innocent.

"What are you thinking about?" he asked as we walked closer to the castle, leading our horses. We chose to walk be-cause riding would return us far too quickly.

"You, singing."

He let out a sigh, again shy. "I should not have told you."

"You very well should have, and I demand to hear your voice one day. It does not have to be today. I shall wear you down eventually." I shrugged, petting Sofonisba's neck.

"How do I always end up giving you my weaknesses without getting yours? First my drawings, and now my voice. What great spell are you casting on me, Lady Hathor?" he asked, bumping his shoulder into mine.

I tried to shove back but he was so much . . . sturdier. "I cast no spells. You are merely weak against my great beauty."

"Is this your nerve speaking again, to bolster yourself?" His eyebrow rose as he peered over me.

"What a horrid reply. You are supposed to say yes, I am a great beauty, and it affects you most acutely."

He snickered, still watching me but not saying the words. Huffing, I tried to walk faster and away from him, but those long arms of his caught my hand and pulled me back to him with so much force that I let go of Sofonisba, landing against his chest.

"Wilhelm—"

"Complimenting your beauty with only the word *great* is far too modest, and comparing you to a goddess seems disingenuous, considering your name. No, your face is like a star plucked from the heavens," he whispered down to me, and again, I could not help but grin. Heat was rising to my face and ears.

"That was a much better response." Quickly, I broke out of his arms and reached back to grab Sofonisba's reins.

"Anything to please you, *my dear*." I nearly tripped from how he said that. He laughed at me. "What? Is that not how husbands address their wives?"

"We are not married—yet! I still need to speak to my mama and papa about all of this." I couldn't even say the words in seriousness, as my smile was wide.

"Yes, I know." His voice trailed off, a small frown upon his lips. However, before I could ask him why, the castle came into view—and the carriage in front of it. It wasn't arriving, but leaving. Lord Covington and his family were speaking to my parents at the entrance, and when my mother's eyes shifted to me—us—so did all their eyes.

"I shall take the horses in while you speak to them," Wilhelm said to me gently, taking the reins from me.

I did not want to, but I knew I had to, now that they had all spotted me. Inhaling through my nose, I lifted my head high and began to walk toward what would no doubt be a very awkward encounter.

"Good day to you both," I heard Lord Covington say when I reached them. He tried to pass me quickly, but I could still see the bruising around his nose and eye, which had turned purple and yellow in color. It looked utterly horrid and painful.

"Lord Covington, I—"

"Spare me, truly, Lady Hathor," he scoffed, exhaling as he allowed me to look upon his face clearly. The kindness he'd shown me before was gone, and now it seemed as if he wished to spit in my face. "Nothing can be said. Your choice is clear. Do not pity me; it is I who pity you, for you have no idea what you have brought upon yourself. I could have afforded you a much more peaceful and uncomplicated life. My face will heal; your future, however—"

"Is my own to decide," I snapped, not at all liking his tone. Was this what he was truly like? That he assumed he could determine what my future would be or could have been was preposterous. "We appreciated your company this week. Good day, sir."

"Mhh," he muttered, nodding to me before entering the carriage.

"Your ladyship, my lord. Thank you for this week," Mary and Emma said, both of them curtsying to my parents. Mary spun quickly toward the carriage with her chin turned up, avoiding all eye contact with me.

"They will get over it in time," Emma whispered to me.

I gave her a doubtful look. "Will they really?"

"No, never. But you'll be a princess, and they will not be able to be inhospitable. Congratulations, Hathor," Emma replied.

"Thank you. Return safely," I said. She nodded before entering the carriage as well.

"We thank you again for your wonderful hospitality, Lady Monthermer, and look forward to the coming—celebrations, Lord Monthermer," the Dowager Lady Covington said to my parents, giving them a tight smile. When she walked past me, she paused, her big green eyes peering over me. "Lady Hathor."

"Your ladyship." I curtsied before her.

She took my hand, petting it as she led me over to her carriage. With my back turned to my parents, she said, "My children have lost, this week, but that is no matter. Their lives will go on, truly unaffected. But you, sweet child—you shall never be the same. So I shall give you this small piece of advice, to show we harbor no hard feelings." She smiled, but it did not feel warm. "Be very mindful of your steps from now on, for all the eyes of England are on you, my dear. And with eyes, come mouths."

She gave my hand another tight squeeze before letting go and joining her children inside. I waited for the footman to close the door and the driver to pull off before I turned back to my parents. I was not sure what expression I was expecting, but the one they gave me was not it. They looked at me so sadly.

"What is the matter?"

"Come, my girl. We shall speak." My mama offered her hand to me, and I took it, allowing her to lead me inside.

I looked past her as my father muttered something to the footmen and kept pace behind me. The other guests were only just arising and moving about the grounds. It was still a bit early, and I was sure today was the day everyone was preparing for their return to London. Clementina came down the stairs. She waved when she saw me, but paused, clearly noticing the seriousness of my parents' demeanor as well. She gave me a look that meant, *What is happening?* I just smiled and entered the piano room behind my parents.

"Am I overly excited, or do you both just seem more grim than expected?" I asked, moving to sit down.

"Hathor," my mother said, sitting down across from me, my father stepping behind her chair. "What was your answer to Prince Wilhelm this morning?"

I smiled. "What else could I say but yes, Mama? It was splendid, truly. He said that he went to the kitchen and begged for them to create my favorite dishes. Then he had to press Damon to find out my favorite flower—"

"Did you not tell me before that he was villainous and horrid?" Mama questioned.

"I did, but—I think he's not very well understood and—"

"And you believe to understand him, in only a week?" Papa frowned. "Hathor, sweetheart, you have desperately wished to marry a duke or a prince for so long. Are you sure you are not closing your eyes to his character just to accomplish it?"

My shoulders dropped. "Papa, you believe me to be so vain?"

"No, my dear, we worry that you might be . . . as you said, overly excited?" Mama said. "And we do not blame you. I know the idea of being royal is very exciting, but I fear it is not actually for you."

I looked between them both, confused and—angry. "You believe I am not fit to marry Prince Wilhelm?"

"No, sweetheart, we do not believe he is fit to marry you," my father explained.

"The queen believes so!"

"The queen is looking to pin her nephew down," Mama retorted with displeasure. "My dear, one of your greatest attributes is your keen observation of the people of society. Princes marry princesses, and many abound. Yet none wished to marry him. Why? Because they did not wish to make an enemy of his father . . . a king. A notoriously harsh, brutal, and unforgiving king."

"So, because of his father, he is not allowed to marry?"

"He may marry whomever he likes, just not you!" my father snapped. "Whatever animosity his father has toward him will fall on his wife and children as well. And no one can stop a king!"

"Have you met the French?"

Mother sighed. "Hathor, this is not a joke, this is your life—"

"And yet it is *you* determining how it should be lived!"

"We are your parents! It is our duty to see to your future and safety!" Father's voice had never risen to me like this, ever. I'd never seen them like this.

"Why are you doing this to me?" I did not want to cry, but I felt so—so hurt. "Damon was a rake who married well below his station, and you said not a word to him. Aphrodite was in love with Evander and you, Mama, moved heaven and earth to see them together, despite the fact that there were horrid rumors about him. Even though he'd abandoned her for four years and his father was a menace to them and society, still you were willing to give her to their family. Verity is not even your daughter, and you both labored for weeks to make her future husband a respectable member of society. You even went to the queen to get him a knighthood! And now you stand before me, and you tell me this?" The tears came down my face despite my effort.

"Hathor, sweetheart." My mother tried to reach for me, but

I just stood up and moved away from them, wiping my eyes quickly.

"Neither of you has even asked me what my feelings are! You do not think I could even *have* feelings. You believe me to be so senseless and gluttonous for a title that I would choose to marry solely for that reason. My own parents truly think I am a title hunter!"

"Hathor, please hear—"

"No, Papa!" I shook my head. "He asked for my hand; I gave it. And since he is a prince, and the queen's nephew, you cannot stop this. I will be marrying Prince Wilhelm, and if you do not like it, I will not be here much longer to remind you of it!"

I ran out of the room and closed the door before they could say anything else, holding on to the doorknob tightly behind me. I tried to breathe, but my chest felt as if it were on fire.

"Hathor?" Clementina rushed up to me, quickly blocking my body from anyone else who might see.

Hanging my head, I whispered, "Please help me get out of here without causing a scene."

"Of course, but you are going to have to put more effort into your face. Everyone is watching you," she said as she linked arms with me.

The Dowager Lady Covington's words from just moments ago came back to me. I did not really understand what she had meant until Clementina and I began walking together, and I forced a smile as she laughed and spoke quickly about nothing important, to make it seem as if we were having the most humorous conversation. So humorous, in fact, it would explain my teary eyes and odd expression.

This was supposed to be the happiest of days for me. How could they ruin it like this?

Wilhelm

"Where is Lady Hathor? She should be beside you when I make this announcement," the queen said as we stood in the gardens, which she had demanded be splendidly decorated, despite the fact that this was not her home, in order to create the best atmosphere for the announcement of this engagement. Everyone was arriving—everyone with the exception of Hathor, whom I had not seen since she'd seen Lukas and his family off.

"I am not sure. I shall go look for her," I said, scanning the gathering crowd of people. However, I could not spot her anywhere outside.

"Your Highness."

To my left appeared Lady Clementina, curtsying beside me. "I believe you should go to the far west end of the castle, where you will see some old stairs that lead down to a private garden by a fountain."

"Is something the matter?"

"Lady Hathor—"

I did not even wait for her to finish before I went. It took all my effort not to run, which was odd, because I was sure if there was something serious, if she was ill or hurt, we would have gotten word of it. Nevertheless, my legs took me as swiftly into the castle as my feet would allow. I had not gone far within the castle before I was sure I had gotten lost. But I kept going west until I did at last come upon a spiral staircase that did not seem to be in use any longer. I would have missed it, if it were not for the muttering.

Carefully heading down, I entered what appeared to be a small courtyard, with a swing and a fountain that held no water. There, sitting on the ground, her white-stockinged legs sticking out from under her riding dress as she sketched angrily, was none other than Hathor.

"They always think I am nothing but a joke," she grumbled. "If it were Aphrodite, I'm sure they would have—"

"Should we have a doctor testify to your sanity before this engagement is announced?"

Her head snapped up, her eyes wide, and she moved her sketchbook behind her. "What are you doing here?"

"I am looking for my betrothed. What are *you* doing?" I asked, stepping forward. She brought her sketchbook back into her lap, but closed it.

"I am—taking in air."

"This is a very remote place to go for air, do you not think?"

She gave me a glare. "I am quite distraught at the moment. Your sarcasm is not needed."

"My sarcasm is the only response to your lie." I bent down in front of her. "Why are you so distraught?"

Her shoulders slumped, and her glare melted into a pitiful frown. "It does not matter—"

"It matters greatly. In fact, it is everything to me—you are to be my wife. So, tell me, what is wrong?"

She stared at me for a long time. I was not sure what was on her mind, but finally, she said, "They don't want me to be your wife."

"Who? Your parents?"

She hung her head, but nodded.

Reaching out, I lifted her chin up, forcing her to keep looking at me. "Do you wish to be my wife?"

"Yes, hence I am distraught. Are you not understanding?"

"I am, but I do not think you are."

"What—"

Bringing her face toward me, I kissed her. And I shivered all over with pleasure at the feeling of her soft lips finally on mine. My tongue entered her mouth, and the back of my throat burned with the desire to do more, to push her back onto the ground and take her. The thought came so easily, so quickly, and the way she kissed me back . . . did not help matters. With the strength of God, I pulled back only slightly, our lips still so close I could feel her breath.

"I've been aching to do that once more," I whispered, stroking her face. "It has taken all my strength to keep from touching you so these last few days."

She stared at me for a moment and the corner of her mouth turned upward. "Do it again please."

"Happily," I replied. And just like before, a gentle, innocent kiss turned sinister. Pulling her body toward mine, I felt her breast pressed up against my chest as our tongues battled. I could not stop the rising lust within me.

God I wanted more of her. I wanted to rip the lace from her and feel her skin. I did not know how or when, but I found myself already on top of her. Her legs on either side of my waist.

I was so close.

I was so . . . desperate.

I wanted her.

I needed her.

My cock tightened, begging for freedom. The meager layers of fabric barring it from entering her did not help. I knew if I did not stop, I'd take her now.

Fuck!

It was almost painful to separate our lips but I managed, only to be blessed with the sight of her under me. Her breast rising and falling, her beautiful lips parted as she tried to breathe evenly, the curls of her hair a halo around her head.

"Wilhelm?"

Oh, how I wanted her to moan my name.

"This is why they do not want you to marry me. I am not at all a true gentleman. I am very comfortable breaking rules. That makes me reckless. No good parent wants a reckless man for their daughter."

"You agree with them," she whispered.

"I understand them. And if I were a better man, I'd listen to them. I'd stay away from you, and let you marry some unbelievably boring lord. But I am selfish, and I want you as my wife, too." I did not think I could be happy married to anyone else but her. "So I am going to take you as mine . . . just not here, I am not that senseless. I do hope, for the sake of your feelings, that they will come to terms with us eventually."

"What if they don't?" she asked as I helped her lower the skirt of her dress.

"If they love you, and I know they do, they will. And I will do my best to win them over."

She smiled. "If my father sees us like this, if he knew what we had just done, I do not believe it would help your cause."

"Do you even know what we just did?" I mused.

"We kissed?"

"We went very close to going far beyond a simple kiss," I replied, lifting her palm to my lips. I already missed the feeling of her body. "And it is your fault for tempting me so, with such great beauty."

"Is that sarcasm?" She glared at me and I found the expression humorous.

"It's truth with a hint of teasing."

"Do not tease me!" she said.

"I fear I will not be able to comply with that order in the slightest. I greatly enjoy teasing you." I kissed her cheek before reaching down and lifting her forgotten sketchbook.

"Wait, no—"

"I am sure it is no worse than what I drew," I said, flipping through the pages to see that she had drawn caricatures of all her family. Her little sister Abena she'd drawn as a real squirrel. Then her mother, a giant marching around small people; her sister Aphrodite, sitting big-headed in front of a broken mirror; several other people as well. And when I flipped to the end, there was me with horns, hunched over a woman begging in the woods, the words *The Prince of Rakes* above us in Latin. I just glanced up at her.

"In my defense," she snatched the sketchbook back, looking away, "I drew that before I met you again."

"You wish me not to tease you, yet you mock me?"

"I never said I was not slightly hypocritical."

I laughed, shaking my head. "This is one of the reasons I desire to marry you. You are a very bad lady as well."

"I am not bad! You are not allowed to call your future wife bad!"

"What am I to call you when you draw me like this then?"

"I do not know. I will come up with something, though."

"Very well. Take your time on that while you hurry and change. My aunt is waiting for us."

"Why?" she asked as she held on to my hand while I helped her up from the ground.

"Why else but to announce our successful engagement . . . should you still want it?"

"Yes! Give me a moment, I will be right out." She ran from me back toward the stairs. Part of me wondered . . . would she have objected to me taking her here of all places? She seemed—unbothered by it. Or maybe I was just insanely desperate for her to want me as much as I wanted her.

There was so much to learn between us, and I was excited for it. Which was why I had to ignore her parents' feelings on this. But part of me worried they would find a way to force her from me, or worse, she would grow despondent from their lack of care.

Once again, for her sake only, I truly regretted my past. I even regretted striking my father, because had I not done those things, had I been honorable and gentlemanly, they would never have objected to me.

Then again, if I were honorable and gentlemanly, I would never have been here, or met her.

So maybe all of this was fate.

Hathor

My heart was drumming again, and my lips were now buzzing. It was just like before. When his lips were on mine, it burned in a sweet way. Like ice cream that didn't melt, but tasted delicious on the way down your throat. That didn't make sense, but I could not describe it otherwise, and truthfully, I was more interested in experiencing it again. The way he held me tightly to him as if all the world could fall away but he'd never release me. I missed his arms. I missed his lips. I—I wanted to do more. I wish we had done more.

I rushed to change, to Bernice's surprise, and ran downstairs, nearly tripping. It did not matter; all I wished to do was go to him.

I was so excited I nearly leapt into the garden. However, I took a moment to collect myself in front of the doors before *gracefully* stepping out, as I expected all eyes to be on me. But when I made my entrance, everyone was bunched into groups, whispering amongst themselves and moving frantically from one party to the next.

I saw Wilhelm speaking sternly with Damon and not one person noticed me as I walked up.

"What is going on?" I asked him. Wilhelm jumped slightly. Again, his eyes were not where they were supposed to be: on me.

"You are here." He smiled, nodding to me.

"Yes, I am here. Where is the queen? Mama and Papa are not here?" The realization of that made me panic. "Please tell me they did not say something ill-advised to the queen."

"As if Mother and Father would ever do such a thing," Damon said to me. "Relax, little sister, and remember the world does not revolve around you."

"But today specifically is supposed to be about me—and him." I pointed to Wilhelm, who handed me a glass from one of the footmen. "But for some reason, this is not going as it is supposed to."

"Take it up with the writer of your story," Damon teased, patting Wilhelm's shoulder before going to where his wife was being held hostage by the other ladies.

"Your brother is amusing." Wilhelm chuckled.

"That is one word for him, I guess." I smiled, glad that at least *he* did not seem against us. "Anyway, where is the queen? I thought you said she wished to announce our engagement."

"She did. However, I arrived at the same time as a messenger from the palace. The queen went back into the castle quickly."

"A messenger from the palace?" I gasped and moved closer to him, whispering, "Is it the king?"

He frowned, looking back at the doors. "I have no idea. I hope not. That would crush her spirit, and mine."

"Are you close to our king?"

"What?"

"If something was wrong, you would be greatly upset, would you not? I truly hope he is well." I really was concerned, but he smirked at me. "What?"

"I've never met King George," he chuckled. "I said it would crush my spirit because if something has happened, our engagement would have to be held off. After all the effort I put in today, that feels rather—unfair."

It was not right to chuckle. It was horrible. That was his uncle, and the queen's love. "You are selfish."

"I'll work on it." He smiled at me. But almost immediately his face fell, as the doors opened and out stepped the queen. And behind her, my parents.

My heart twisted with fear again.

"Do not worry. Whatever comes, we will be all right," he whispered behind me, and it relaxed me.

The queen's face was stern, and everyone gathered waited nervously as well as very quietly. Her eyes shifted over the crowd.

"My beloved people," she spoke softly. Her pause was agonizingly long. It was as if she were torturing us. When she finally opened her mouth once more, we all leaned forward to hear clearly. "It is my responsibility, and great honor, to announce . . . that the war is over, and we have won!"

The cheers that broke out made me jump in shock. The gentlemen all around shook hands, congratulating one another as if they had planned it themselves. The ladies laughed, hugging each other.

"Such joyous news is only buttressed by my nephew Prince Wilhelm's engagement to the Lady Hathor Du Bell. May this all be a sign of a brand-new era!"

Wilhelm offered me his arm and I took it, turning to all the guests who clapped for us. In the corner of my eye, however, I could not help but notice that my parents were not clapping—just watching.

It hurt. But I just focused on Wilhelm.

And then it hurt a lot less.

20

Wilhelm

It had been two weeks since our engagement, and I had not seen her since. The very next morning, I was forced to leave with the queen back to London, due to the news of the war. The queen had made it known that the moment Hathor returned to London, she was to come visit *her* at the palace daily, to go over etiquette and training for royalty. It was pretense, of course; there was no one the queen wished to see daily. And if there was any *etiquette* Hathor had not already learned and needed to be taught, it would be done by Lady Crane. Whenever she was not doing that, she'd be free to . . . wander into my company.

For some reason, I was both apprehensive and eager. Apprehensive about how she would handle being at the palace, being in the company of my—my company. But I was eager to—to see her. Since leaving, I could not help but wonder about her constantly. What was she doing at this hour? Was she painting? Going for a walk? Fighting with her sisters? Thinking of me?

How utterly embarrassing this was! I felt like a fool, a lovesick fool. I had to avoid most of my former acquaintances, because I was sure they would not recognize me, as I did not recognize myself. Nor could I explain how I'd come to be so afflicted. So, since my return, I'd spent my time looking for property. What kind of a man marries a lady without an estate of his own? I could not expect her to join me and live in my aunt's palace. Unfortunately, with my banishment came much less money than I had assumed.

It was brilliant. One more title to add my name: Wilhelm, the banished, near-poverty-stricken prince. Just one more thing to make her family despise me.

Truly, I was a fool.

I had not the situation or means to marry. Yet here I was at the door of their London estate, to take her with me.

"Welcome, Your Highness, please follow me." The footman bowed his head to me when I entered.

I nodded a short thank-you to him, and ignored the maid peering into the hall as I was led into a large, light-blue draw-ing room. There waited almost all of the Du Bells.

The marquess and his son Damon stood by the fireplace, speaking. They immediately became quiet when the footman announced me and stepped in. Not just them, either. There was also Damon's wife, Silva, their daughter in her arms, along with Hathor's younger siblings: Devana, who sat at the piano; Hector, who sat by the window reading; and Abena, lying on the floor, eating cookies. They were all silent, staring directly at me, as if to ask who this most unwelcome intruder into their perfect family could be.

"I object to this union!" the little girl on the ground sud-denly shouted.

"Abena!" Silva hushed her.

"What? Whenever people get married in church, they al-ways ask if people object. I object!" She huffed, tossing her cookie on the plate as she moved to rise.

"You can only say you object during the actual ceremony, Abena." Hector snickered, shaking his head at her. "It's useless now."

"Then how do we stop it? I've been waiting for all of you. And none of you are any help!"

"Abena!" Damon snapped at her. "Do not be rude."

Though the small smirk on her father's face was not unnoticed by me.

"And what reason do you give for your premature objection to our union, Lady Abena?" I finally spoke, getting all of their attention again.

The girl turned to me, her face bunched up as if her cookies were sour, and with all the seriousness in the world she crossed her arms and said, "You're not handsome enough to be my brother-in-law."

All her siblings snorted with laughter, along with their father, though they tried to hide it quickly. Apparently, this was a vicious bunch, and she was their leader. Even I could not help but grin. I knelt down to her level in order to look her in the eye.

"Unfortunately, I cannot change my face to fit your *high* standards, my lady. Can you be persuaded to compromise?"

She shook her head no. "I dislike compromises. They never work in my favor."

"I see. Then can you be bribed?"

Her head tilted to the side. "Bribe? That's when you give someone something, and they do what you want?"

"Exactly." I nodded, smiling.

"What will you give me?"

"Your sister told me you like pastries. I will buy you any treat you want, once a month, forever."

Her eyes widened and she gasped. "*Forever*? As in, the rest of my life? Even when I grow up?"

I nodded. "Yes, even when you grow up."

She was thinking. "How many pastries?"

"A box." I grinned.

"That's a lot! And I can pick from anywhere?"

"You'd trade your sister for a box of pastries?" Hector asked her. "Have you not learned what a fair trade is?"

She turned back to him. "Ladies have to get married, because you all say ladies have to get married. I do not want him to take Hathor, but no matter what, she'll get married. No one else has offered me anything whenever someone gets married. So far, this is in my favor. Right?"

She posed that question to her father, who stared at her with a very calm expression that made her shoulders drop. She turned back to me, shaking her head no. "Du Bells do not accept bribes."

"I see. Then, you leave me with no other choice." I sighed, rising to stand.

"What does that mean?"

Before I could reply, the door opened and Hathor walked in dressed in light green, a string of diamonds around her neck, her hair pinned up in curls, a single long curl over her right shoulder. Her cheeks were a bit pink in color, but it was truly those eyes of hers that caught me. They were as dazzling as ever. A small smile appeared on her lips as we looked at each other, and I was all of a sudden much more relaxed.

"Your Highness." She curtsied to me.

"Lady Hathor. It is good you have come; I am in need of your assistance," I replied.

"What?"

"Lady Abena has informed me she will be objecting to our union, both now and in church."

Immediately her eyes snapped to her little sister. "Is that so? After all the secrets I've kept for her, she seeks to hurt me so? Mama, did you know that Abena has been sneaking off to play disguised in Hector's clothes?"

"What?" Her mother gasped in horror, and it was only then that I noticed the older woman dressed in purple behind her.

"Hathor!" Abena grumbled angrily.

"You've been doing what, young lady?" Her mother stepped forward.

"My dear," the marquess said, clearly seeking to save his daughter. "We have guests."

"Abena, go wait for me in your room, please." The marchioness spoke calmly, though her eyes were still raging. "Now."

Her whole face fell. She glared at Hathor angrily, and Hathor only made a face back at her.

"I can't believe I gave up pastries for you," she snapped, grumbling as she went out of the room, and faintly I could hear her still complaining. "I knew it, but *no*, everyone is always picking on me, now that prince is too, *tattletale*."

"Pastries?" Hathor repeated in confusion, looking to me. All I could do was smile, shaking my head to tell her not to worry about it.

"Prince Wilhelm, you are a bit earlier than we expected," the marchioness said to me.

"Forgive me, your ladyship. In all honesty, I was not paying attention to the time." I was just pleased that she was finally back.

"We must ask you to do better in the future, Your Highness, as it is very important she returns *on time*," the marquess spoke, as he stepped to where we were by the door. He looked directly at Hathor. "You are there to be taught by the queen. That is an honor. Do not become *distracted* from those lessons."

He spoke to her, but it was very clear from his tone and the look he gave me out of the corner of his eye that he was warning *me*, the *distraction*, not to cross any lines.

"Yes, Papa. I know," Hathor said, unaware, smiling at him.

"You both should go. Bernice will attend you until you are met by Lady Crane," her mother said, leading Hathor out of the room first.

As I followed her, the marquess walked with me, speaking sternly and low. "Yes, she is betrothed to you, and yes, I am sure you will spend time together, but do remember she is a lady. A very sweet, young, and *naïve* lady. Do not expose her to anything *beneath* her."

Fathers and their daughters. Hathor was sweet, in her own unique way. She was young, though not so much younger than myself. However, naïve? The woman who looked upon drawings of sex with interest and astuteness? The woman who kissed me back so passionately whenever I kissed her? That was not a *naïve* woman, just an inexperienced one. But I could not tell him that. He did not want to hear that. He just wanted to know his daughter would be safe, and not left in ruins.

"She will be my wife, and just like you, I wish her never to be harmed or ridiculed in any manner, sir. I shall look out for her. I swear it."

"Make sure you do."

I just nodded, stepping toward the carriage, where she and her maid were waiting. I allowed them to enter before me.

"I shall return her before supper," I said to the marchioness before I also climbed inside.

It was only when we finally pulled away from her home that I could let go of the breath I'd been holding, my shoulders relaxing fully.

"I am sorry."

I looked to Hathor, confused. "You are sorry for what?"

"The very many . . . guards around me," she snickered, looking over to her maid, who pretended to be most interested in the scenery of the city outside the window. "One would think I was the princess."

"A lady is a jewel that must be protected at all costs, I'm told. Your parents are correct in their precautions."

"A lady is a jewel?" Her eyes narrowed on me. "You are only saying that because we have a spy."

I grinned. I'd missed her directness.

"What shall I say instead? How I wish we were married already, so that your family would no longer be the ones to guard you? So, you'd be left under my care to . . . enjoy?" My foot touched hers, and she pinched her own fingers.

"I must tell you; I am quite tired of guardians—though I am curious about what your definition of *care* is. Can you elaborate?" Her foot tapped mine back. What a painfully long ride this was.

"Unfortunately, I cannot now; your maid is already blushing," I replied, looking out the window, also hoping to focus elsewhere.

It was a cool day, since it had rained in the early hours of the morning, but there was this burning ache in me to touch her. To do exactly what her father was worried I'd do to her.

When her foot tapped mine again, not on purpose but due to a bump in the road, I glanced over to see her staring unwaveringly at me. I watched her chest bounce slightly as the carriage swayed.

Fuck.

I wanted to fuck her.

I wanted to see her bounce on me.

I had to tell the driver to turn around and send her back, because I was not going to withstand this lust, not for long. Not if she kept staring at me like that.

Thank God my aunt wanted to have this wedding next week.

Thank God.

21

Hathor

"You have to be careful, my lady," Bernice whispered when we reached the palace gates.

She could not follow me: She did not have permission to enter the palace. Mama and Papa only insisted she come to escort me because they did not wish me to be alone in a carriage with a man. Even if that man was meant to be my husband.

"Careful of what? The palace is the safest place for a lady," I whispered back.

"Of yourself, and his . . . emotions. Your wedding is next week. You need only hold out until then," she replied gently, as the carriage pulled to the front.

Wilhelm stepped out first, then turned back and offered his hand to me. The moment we touched, there was that burning feeling in me again. The way he stared at me as if I were the only woman in the world also did not help.

"Thank you for accompanying us. Sir, take her back safely," he said to the driver, not allowing Bernice to say another word . . . and he did not let go of my hand. He held it as he led me up the stairs. There were a few guards in the front, but they seemed completely oblivious to us. I stared into the grand foyer. How massive it was; how empty it was. I'd only ever come to the palace twice: the days of my sister's and my own debuts to the queen. Both times, there were so many people anxiously trying to prepare that I never really *saw* the palace.

It was beautiful, of course, but so very quiet.

"Wilhelm, where are we going? Do I not need to see the queen? Present myself?"

"The queen is sleeping. She does not get out of bed until at least noon, and she does not see anyone until half past one. So, there is no one to present yourself to."

"What? Then what are we supposed to do until then?" I asked as we entered a long hallway with portraits of the royal family to the right and windows to the left.

He paused midstep and turned back to me. He came close . . . far too close, staring down at me, holding on to my hands.

"We will do whatever you wish to do. We will be left to our own devices here whenever the queen does not require you. So, pray tell, what do you desire to see first?"

When I woke up this morning, I felt a flurry of nerves. I was so anxious to see him. What if his feelings had changed?

What if he'd met someone else?

What if—what if— I'd felt as if my mind were going to implode, and when I tried to stop thinking, I'd find my heart racing painfully with each passing hour.

I thought seeing him would help ease that. Instead, I was even more desperate to know what he was thinking or feeling. What I desired was to be near him.

"What do you do when you are here?"

"Go to look at the royal collection of art, in order to study the work of men I can hardly compare to."

"Then let us do that."

"What? I am merely joking. I do not spend much time in the palace. It is rather boring but—?"

"If it is boring, I will make you sing. Until then, show me the art."

"Ugh," he groaned, stepping away from me, but only at arm's length; he still had not let go of my hand. "Why must you bring that up once more?"

"Because I am still very curious. I've never heard a man sing before, outside of an opera."

"For good reason. It is embarrassing and childish."

"Nevertheless, you enjoy it, so I must come to accept and encourage your interests. That is what makes a good wife."

"Is that so? What if I were to have an awful voice, waking you each and every morning with it. You would still accept and encourage me?"

"I would wake up even earlier the next day and screech back in your ear, calling it singing. We shall do this until we are both so exhausted and near madness that we come to a compromise. Or kill each other."

He laughed when we stopped at a white-and-gold door. "Why am I so certain being married to you will be both grueling and hilarious?"

I shrugged. "Because you like to fight with me."

"It is you who likes to fight with me," he said, opening the door for me. When I stepped inside I froze, utterly stunned. For some silly reason, I had assumed it would be one room. However, it was an entrance into a wing of the palace that went on farther than my eyes could see. On every wall there was a painting that stood four men high and at least ten men across. I stepped in humbly, walking past a statue of a veiled maiden, who kneeled, holding out before herself . . . a heart.

"In ancient Rome, young virgins were chosen to be consecrated to the Roman goddess Vesta as a priestess. Their duty was to tend the sacred fire perpetually kept burning on an altar," he explained from behind me. "They were depicted with veils over themselves as a sign of their purity. Artists from all over Europe created these in honor of the girls. This one is about Pomona, the girl who cut out her own heart."

"What?" I gasped, reaching up to put my hand over my chest to feel my heart beating inside. "Why would she do that?"

"She fell in love: the greatest of all sins for a priestess. She never wished to serve Vesta, and tried to escape with her lover. They were caught, and he was charged with kidnapping a priestess and she was returned to her watch at the altar. In anger and sorrow, she cut out her heart and threw it into the flames, but it was so full of blood and life that it extinguished the fire. And no Vesta priestess could ever bring it back."

I frowned, not at all enjoying that story. "When I was younger, I used to love myths and legends, until I realized they always ended so bitterly. As if it were a crime for anyone to live and love happily for the rest of their life."

"In the defense of the storytellers, most people's lives are bitter," he replied.

"Isn't that more of a reason to give people hope?" I turned to him, not realizing he'd been standing directly behind me, so I came to face his chest.

"Sometimes hoping is equally bitter, and it is much more comforting to be cynical," he said, reaching up and cupping my cheek. "If you don't hope, you won't be disappointed."

"If you do not hope, you cannot dream, and if you cannot dream, you cannot live." The words came out of me with little thought, as I was very aware of every time his thumb brushed my cheek.

He leaned forward, bringing his face closer to mine. "Are you a philosopher, Lady Hathor?"

"No, I just have moments of wisdom, Prince Wilhelm," I whispered in the small space between our lips. I so badly wished to kiss him once more. "Though I must say, the moment must have come and gone, because it is not wise for us to talk this closely."

"Wisdom is nothing without foolishness. And I would love nothing more than to be a fool with you, but I promised your father—"

I couldn't take it anymore. I pressed my lips against his. He was still for a moment, and just when I thought of pulling back, his arms wrapped around me and he pulled me to him. His tongue entered my mouth just like before, but this was different. I could feel his hands upon my body squeezing my waist and thighs. In the blink of an eye, I was no longer standing but lifted for a moment, and a second later my back was against the wall. He pinned me, and without realizing it, my legs were open and on either side of him. He kissed from my lips down to my neck, and my voice caught in my throat—I could not even describe the sound.

"Hathor," he whispered in my ear. I shivered, not just because of that, but because his hand somehow found its way underneath my dress, allowing him to caress my thigh. "I am trying so very hard to be a gentleman for you, not to revert back to my instinct—which is this. When I pull back or stop, you must stop, too, or I will have you up against the wall, or on a table, or the floor. Anywhere, to do the most despicable of things."

All of me was burning. "Define *despicable*?"

"Hathor!" He squeezed my thigh.

"If you wish to warn me, you must make it clear for me. What is despicable about this?"

"It leads to this," he replied. My mouth dropped open and

my eyes widened as his fingers stroked the most intimate part of me, the very core of my womanhood. And to my surprise, it felt amazing. My breath caught in my throat. He stared me in the eye, rubbing and pressing between the folds of me.

"Ahh . . . please," I whimpered, and he cursed before, once more, his lips were on mine. His fingers continued, going faster.

And then he just stopped.

"No—"

"Shh . . . don't worry, it gets better. Just trust me."

I did not understand what he meant. But he dropped to his knees before me and lifted up my skirts . . . exposing me to his gaze. Embarrassed, I tried to stop him but he just looked up at me and said again:

"Trust me."

Swallowing hard I nodded, allowing him to do as he wished. Which was to lean forward and begin licking me. I moaned at the sudden wetness of his tongue.

"Wilhelm—"

"Lift this leg onto my shoulder." He helped move my right leg over his shoulder and, as soon as I was situated, his tongue licked deep in me again as if I were his dessert. My mouth remained open as a jolt sprang through me. Soon I could not even think—it was as if every part of my body were now being set ablaze. He started slowly and then I felt him spread those . . . lips, and he sucked. I moaned heavily, gripping on to his hair, as I feared I could no longer hold myself upright. I felt myself rocking into his mouth. That was when he became . . . hungry.

"Ah. Ah! Oh! Oh!"

He paused, squeezing my other thigh. "Quiet, my dear, or someone will hear."

All I could do was use my other hand, the one not holding on to him, to cover my mouth as wave after wave of . . . pleasure hit me. My eyes became heavy and teary. I wanted to scream out when I felt him suck on me.

Again, all of me shook, and the tightness in my stomach grew worse and worse until . . . until I burst, collapsing back against the wall when he released me.

"Forgive me, I could not control—"

"I do not want to forgive you, I want more," I said breathlessly, still shaking as I stared at his figure before me.

He licked his lips and breathed through his nose. "Hathor, I cannot stand any more temptation."

"And I cannot stand this feeling in me. I know not what it is, but it feels as if I am burning." I gripped my chest, for it ached unbearably. "What am I to do?"

"Fuck." He cursed and grabbed my hand, leading me out of the room.

I was not sure where we were going, I could barely think straight as it was, and so I simply followed him. We went up the stairs and then down one hall and another before finally he pulled me into . . . a bedroom.

The doors closed and he leaned his head against them.

"Wilhelm—"

"I promised your father not even half an hour ago to behave. Yet here I am misbehaving," he muttered, finally turning to me. The look in his eyes . . . it excited me. He took off his coat and tossed it aside, just anywhere. "Hathor, only you can stop me right now."

"But I do not wish to."

"But you must," he said, though he took off his waistcoat and began undoing his necktie. "If you do not, on that bed behind you I will make love to you and there will be no going back."

I turned around to look at the bed for a moment before walking up to it and taking a seat.

"Should I take off my shoes?"

"Yes, my love, you should."

Wilhelm

I could not describe how hard my cock was. How excited I was. I was bloody trembling . . . and so was she. She was the innocent one here and yet she was the one pushing . . . pleading. And I had not the strength to deny her. Quietly I helped her remove the layers of her clothing until she was naked before me. She looked away, of all times to show modesty, she chose now. Reaching up, I cupped her breast, pinching her brown nipple, causing her to jump and meet my gaze.

"Your body is beyond beautiful but still it cannot compare with your face, so allow me to look upon that as well," I whispered. She said nothing, merely nodding. "See me as well."

Standing before her, I stripped down slowly. Her eyes watched every piece come off until finally I was just as bare as she was. Immediately I saw her shock at my . . . manhood standing up and strong for her.

"Are you always like this?" she asked softly.

"No. Only when . . . in the heat of desire does it rise so. The rest of the time it just hangs."

She giggled. "Is that not . . . inconvenient?"

"Sometimes."

"May I—I touch it?"

"Please."

She bit her lip and reached out as if it were a pet she was not quite sure of, touching with just the tips of her fingers. Yet that slight touch made me twitch. Her eyes widened.

"It moves?"

I tried not to laugh at her. "Yes, especially when touched or . . . when inside a woman."

"Inside me? How?"

"I believe we are well on our way to finding out, are we not?"

Again she stared at me; it made my heart flutter. She had no idea how much control she had over me in this moment.

"If you want to stop—"

"We have gone too far for that now." She smiled and shifted back on the bed. "Make love to me, Wilhelm."

It was all I needed her to say.

I climbed onto the bed toward her, and pulled her legs to me and then apart. "This may hurt a bit. I'll be gentle. But then it will feel much better, I promise, merely relax and trust me."

She nodded and lay back, though she was still quite tense. Crawling on top of her, I pressed my lips to hers once more. The longer we kissed, the more comfortable I could feel her becoming. Her hands gripping my shoulders, her legs around my waist. I kissed down her neck, making my way down to her nipples. Taking them into my mouth, I ran my tongue around them before biting softly.

"Ah," she moaned.

Reaching down between her thighs, I rubbed inside of her once more, making sure she was wet enough for me, and she was . . . pouring out onto my fingers. Sitting up, I held my cock with one hand and began guiding it into her.

She grimaced and so I moved even slower, giving her time to accept me. I kissed her face to distract from the pain, feeling her hands grip me.

"It's all right, my love," I whispered, meeting her lips with mine as the rest of me entered her. Her back arched but all I could do was kiss her and slow myself. "Tell me when the pain passes."

We stayed like that, embracing, with me kissing her face, my cock in her hard and painful as I so badly wished to move. But I did not want to hurt her.

Finally, after what felt like years, she spoke.

"I am all right."

I bit my lip, pulling out before thrusting back in.

"Ah."

I waited.

And when she nodded, once more I moved. When she no longer whimpered but moaned, I knew she was ready.

I pulled out again, and this time slammed in harder.

"Oh!"

Again, I did it, my hands rising to hold on to her waist.

It was like a dream. My fantasy unfolding before my eyes. I'd seen and taken many women in pleasure . . . but none had ever brought me this much joy. I relished the way her body bounced as I took her. She bit onto her own knuckle to keep from crying out in pleasure, but even still her moans were music to my ears.

I did not want it to end.

If this was a dream I would not mind sleeping forever. She was perfect; everything about her was perfection. I lifted her body up. We clung to each other, me holding on to her thighs, her holding on to my shoulders. Both of us looking into each other's eyes. When I saw that she was close, I kissed her lips quickly before saying:

"I love you."

Her response was to call out my name. And like it was a command, I came for her.

22

Hathor

I was too stunned to speak. It was as if I were floating in his arms above the sky, just like Verity had described. When she had first told me about relations between a man and his wife, I was so confused and terribly concerned. I badly wished to experience it but at the same time I worried I would not be able to have the same feelings she did. But I was sure now—this was the best feeling in the world. I laid my head on his chest as he gently stroked my back, humming softly for me.

"I love you too," I finally managed to say now that my mind was slowly coming down from the clouds.

He kissed the top of my head. "I will speak to the queen about moving up our wedding."

"I do not believe it can be moved up. Not without causing suspicion."

"I care not about such suspicions. I merely know I will not be content with having you only this one time before the week is done."

"How many times until you are content?" I glanced up at him and he smirked down at me.

"A thousand doubled a thousand more times before being doubled another ten thousand."

"Surely our bodies would break." I laughed.

"Then happily we will lie in bed immobile the rest of our days." He kissed my knuckles as he tried to sit up. "However, we cannot stay in bed any longer now, my love. We are not husband and wife yet."

It was as if I only then remembered all the rules of society I had dedicated my life to maintaining. One man had shattered everything in a matter of weeks. But in return, I felt as if I had gained a new sense of freedom. He was like air to me now. How I was not sure, but I was greatly pleased by it. So much so that I did not want to get out of bed.

"Can we not stay a few more minutes?"

He shook his head. "Sadly, we cannot risk it. When we are married, I promise you we shall stay in bed for however long you wish."

I nodded, trying to get up. But for some reason the moment I tried to lift my legs to get out of bed they fell right back onto it. When I glanced down, I saw the small amount of blood that stained the sheets and my inner thighs. Quickly I moved to take the sheets to cover myself but he grabbed my wrist. When I glanced up at him, he cupped my cheek and stroked it.

"Do not be embarrassed or hide from me. Nothing here is wrong," he whispered. "I'll get water to clean up and take care of the bed."

"Someone will see—"

"They won't. And even if they did, I'll protect you. I do not want you to fear anything when I am here."

When he spoke to me like this, looked at me like this, I could not speak. All of him was tender. I reached up and touched his cheek as he did mine. He leaned into my palm, closing his eyes and breathing in gently.

"I shall leave myself in your care then."

He smiled, kissing my hand. "Wait here just a moment."

I was not sure what he wanted, so I did as he asked. I watched as he quickly put his clothes back on before stepping outside. Only when he was gone did I lie back on the bed. I was not sure what I was feeling, but I could not stop smiling. I rolled over in the sheets, burying my face in the pillows, when I heard the doors open again. Panic filled me as I sat back up, holding the sheets to my chest. But it was him, holding a small basin, a towel, and a bottle of wine.

"You're back already?"

"We do not have the luxury of time," he replied, coming over to me. "This is for you to clean with."

My eyes narrowed at him. "You are truly an expert."

"Retired expert, for I exist for you alone now. Which is why I shall be your humble servant and help you wash," he said sweetly, reaching for my legs again, but I pulled them back.

"I fear your help will lead to . . . further distraction. I shall do it," I replied, reaching for the basin myself.

He pouted when I took it from his hands. "Very well, may I at the very least watch?"

His eyes made me warm and that warmth made me . . . desire his hands again. I shook my head. "You may not. Turn around."

He sighed dramatically but did as I asked, and I quickly tried to clean myself up. Even having him in the room as I did so left me speechless. I could not believe I had acted so impulsively, and yet at the same time I wanted nothing more than to act out more. Finished, I rose from the bed, my legs finally strong enough, or maybe it was my will. Either way I collected my clothes and began to dress. I could do almost all of it without help, but the corset. But before I could ask for help his hands were already at my laces.

"How did you—"

"I could see you in the mirror," he whispered into my ear.

I glanced to the left of the room and sure enough he'd had a clear view of me the whole time. "You—"

"Villain? Yes, I know." He chuckled, tying the strings together. He bent over, kissing the tops of my shoulders. "And you knew I was too, yet you fell for me anyway."

"I think it's more appropriate to say I tripped," I muttered, annoyed yet giddy.

He chuckled again and said nothing as I donned the rest of my clothing and he tended to the bed, stripping it bare. He took up the wine, but he poured it on top of the sheets and dropped the bottle to the side before coming to me. He looked me over and adjusted the sleeves on my dress.

"No one will be any the wiser," he said, taking my hand and leading me from the room. His grip on my hand was tight, or was it my grip on his? Either way, we held on to each other, another breach of decorum but I noticed no one was posted down this wing of the hallway.

"Do no servants come here?" I asked, glancing around.

"Not at this hour, the servants work the palace in shifts."

"Ah." His knowledge was truly . . . detailed.

We had just reached the main stairs when we came face-to-face with the stern countenance of Lady Crane, the queen's most loyal lady-in-waiting. She was dressed in the lightest of blues, and her sharp-angled face was tilted as she looked between us . . . especially at our hands. Immediately I released him and took a side step away, curtsying to her.

"The queen is awake and has called for Lady Hathor," she stated.

"What?" I gasped in horror.

"I shall bring her in a moment," he said to her.

"Now is preferred, not in a moment, and I shall take her," she replied and looked to me.

I nodded.

For the first time coming here I felt . . . fearful.

Wilhelm

I stayed for a moment as Lady Crane took her. I desperately tried to collect myself, begging the blood to rush away from my cock and back to my damn brain! What in the bloody hell was wrong with me? Actually, it was a stupid question to ask. I knew exactly what was wrong with me: It was her. Hathor was wrong with me. I had, barely an hour ago, sworn to her father that I would not cross the line. Well, I hadn't said it in so many words, but the meaning was clear: Be a gentleman, and protect her innocence.

And I, savage that I was, took it the moment she was out of his sight. And I could not stop thinking of it. I could still feel her wetness on my fingertips. I could still hear the moans coming out of her lips, from deep in her chest. The taste of her in my mouth . . . how utterly sensual her face was.

Fuck.

"Calm the fuck down," I ordered myself. I wanted her so badly again. I couldn't think of anything else. I had just had her and I still wanted her as if I had never touched her before. Just knowing what I could do to her . . . what more I could teach her. I wanted to lick every inch of her beautiful brown skin.

Fuck.

I needed her like the earth needed the sun; daily, hourly . . . forever.

Like a man who needed air.

All I could do was tell myself to be patient. To relax. It took a few minutes, but finally I managed to move from my spot in the hall.

I walked to where I knew my aunt and Hathor would be. Sure enough, there they were, in the center of the blue room. To my surprise, they were surrounded by dozens of other court ladies. Not a soul noticed me; they were far too busy speaking of the wedding. And of course, Hathor listened as if all their words were bread and water. There was a look of fierce concentration in her hazel eyes as Lady Crane pressed down on her shoulder with a cane, forcing her to kneel very slowly before the queen, whose lips were puckered, eyes sharp, ready to critique any mistake.

"The queen called us in very early to begin preparing her, but you could not be found," Lady Vivienne Gallagher whispered as she stepped up beside me, dressed in white, her long blonde hair pinned only partially behind her ears. Her pink lips formed a sly smile. "It's been far too long. I'd ask how you've been, but I can see quite clearly, you've been busy getting a wife."

"Hello, Lady Millchester."

"*Lady Millchester?*" Her head turned to me as she stepped closer, as if we were not already far too close. "Please do not tell me you are reverting to such pleasantries for your soon-to-be wife already?"

"It is not as though it would be correct for me to go around calling you Vivi, now, would it?"

"If you don't tell, I won't—"

"Don't," I said, pulling my hands behind my back when she tried to brush her fingers against mine. "Let's talk outside."

I stepped into the hallway first, moving away from the door as far as I could, over to the windows.

"What is the matter with you?" She laughed as she came to join me.

"Lady Hathor and I are to be married, Vivienne."

"Yes, I know, I am the one who tried to convince you to marry her in the first place." She stepped closer to me, this time bringing her face closer to mine. "That doesn't mean you and I—"

"That's exactly what it means." I turned my face from her attempted kiss, glancing down the hall to make sure no one else was near.

"August?"

"You are to call me Prince Wilhelm, Your Highness, or sir from now on, as well."

"August, you cannot be serious!"

"But I am." I exhaled. I never wanted to have this conversation, but I had to. I was already lacking in so many things, I could not be an adulterer also. I did not want to hurt Hathor with Vivienne, or any other woman from my past. The mere thought of what her face would look like made me sick.

"August, it is very sweet and honorable that you wish to be faithful to that girl, but you and I both know you need—*more*." Again, she tried to touch me, and again I stopped her.

"I will be satisfied with whatever Hathor offers me. Do not call her *that girl*. She is Lady Hathor, the future Princess Consort of Malrovia."

"Are you—are you in love with her? As in, truly? You did not give in merely for your aunt?"

"Yes. I am in love with her. I am marrying her because I wish to. And I know it is . . . laughable, considering all I told you about how I felt about the subject before." I paused and looked her in the eye. Her smile was gone, confusion on her face. "I also know that you were not joking when you asked me to marry you all those weeks ago. You said it in earnest, because you are earnestly in love with me."

Her eyes widened, and she stood frozen. She opened her mouth to deny it, but the words didn't come out. "How— You are— That is silly."

"No, it was silly of me, *cruel of me*, to continue pretending as if I did not notice. I think part of me was hoping that you'd give up on me, or I'd come to find some real companionship with you, too. But the truth is I do not love you, Vivienne."

"Please stop," she whispered, hanging her head.

"I cannot. Forgive me, I must say this. You are a good person who deserves to be loved. But being someone's mistress is not love, it is greed."

She shook her head. "How has she changed you so much, in such a short period of time? I do not understand."

"Neither do I, so I've stopped bothering to try." I chuckled for a moment before becoming serious. "I merely wish to be with her, and I do not wish to do anything that will ruin that. I am, in this moment, begging you to simply let me go. Insult me if you must, but let me go as a faint memory of foolishness. And leave her out of it."

"You believe me to be so petty?" She huffed, stepping away from me and turning her head as she took a deep breath, staring out the window. "What do you think? I will go claw her eyes out, or plot some menacing trick to tear you both apart like some cruel witch? Do not think so highly of yourself."

I nodded. "Of course not."

"You should go now, *Your Highness*. The queen can often be a lot to handle on one's own, and you would not wish for anything to scare your precious Lady Hathor."

"Thank you, Lady Millchester, for your care all this time. Truly, I am grateful." I nodded to her before walking back toward the doors. When I entered this time, a few of the ladies, along with the queen, shot me quick glances. However, Hathor was still focused, now on her knees, reading from some book. I wanted to go save her, but I had the feeling she did not at all mind.

So instead, I nodded for one of the footmen to come over.

"Yes, Your Highness?"

"I wish to draw as I wait. Have someone bring me a fresh sketchbook and pencils."

"Yes, Your Highness." He nodded to me.

Moving to the corner of the room, I took a seat and watched over her. I had a feeling this would be a regular occurrence.

And I did not mind.

I merely needed patience.

The sight of her gave me that.

Hathor

"Whatever have you done to leave him so besotted?" Lady Eleanor, the queen's fifth lady-in-waiting, whispered to me while the queen was distracted by the menu for my wedding. The *him* she was referring to was Wilhelm, who sat by a window in the corner of the room, which was colored blue top to bottom, sketching quietly. "He normally despises spending any more time than he needs to in our company."

"That's because he much prefers a different type of female company," Lady Scarlet, the queen's seventh lady-in-waiting, stated. She'd been giving me glances of dissatisfaction and perturbed interest since I entered. With a smug look upon her face, she said, "Men such as him are often enthralled for a moment, then taken away the next. You shall have to stay on your toes, Lady Hathor."

"Why? Do you seek to be next, Lady Scarlet?" I asked her calmly, and she nearly tripped, making me smile. "That would explain why you keep glancing in his direction."

"You—"

"Please excuse me. I must go stay on my toes," I replied to her, before finally getting up from my position and walking over to where he was sitting. A cooling cup of tea was beside him, as he had not looked up from his work since he began. It was only when I bent over to see, blocking his source of light, that he raised his head. Realizing it was me, a smile spread across his lips, and he placed his sketchbook down.

"Has she finally released you?"

"Only for a moment, while she decides whether or not to have oysters and lobster at this wedding," I said, taking the book from his hands.

He rose, standing beside me. "You are not interested in knowing? Don't most women fantasize about their weddings?"

"It's strange. I've thought about my wedding for years—since I was a little girl, in fact. I was often picking ribbons and lace I knew I would just *have* to have." I grinned, noticing the inaccuracy of his sketch. He'd failed to draw any woman but myself and the queen. It looked as if we were in the room alone, and she was teaching me privately. There was no Lady Scarlet or any of the others. "Yet now with it set to take place, it does not feel real. None of this feels real."

"Maybe happiness has made you delirious," he whispered. When I looked back into his eyes, I could feel myself melting. Yes, this was strange; all I felt I needed was to hang on to him.

"Are you happy, Wilhelm? I'm sure you would have much preferred not to sit here for hours, listening to us. You do not have to stay—"

"Do you desire that I go?"

"No," I said immediately. "I quite enjoy you staring at and drawing me. But I am seeking to be considerate of you. Apparently, it is what wives are meant to do."

He chuckled. "I think I've become accustomed to you not being considerate of my feelings."

"Don't say that—" I said, nearly too loudly, glancing over to make sure the queen was not annoyed with me. Seeing her still speaking about the menu, I faced him again, but he had leaned in so close that it startled me.

"Never stop being yourself, Hathor."

"And you remain yourself. Without, of course, all your female companions," I said sternly. "You have not yet seen me jealous, but I promise you it is not an enjoyable experience for anyone involved. You very well may end up poisoned."

"Lady Hathor, are you threatening me with murder?" He laughed outright, his grin wide.

"Shh! Do not laugh so much, they are watching everything," I grumbled. He took my hand, holding it. "Wilhelm."

"What are they going to do? Tell the world we are in love? I thank them for their efforts."

I held my head high. "Just because you have me in your hands for the moment does not mean you will have me for a lifetime. I must be given a healthy profusion of love regularly, or I shall lose interest."

"Should it not be women who worry about losing their husbands' interest?" He leaned closer.

"I am not *women*. I am Hathor."

"How much longer do you two plan to make us witness this little display?" the queen called out from behind me, making us separate quickly. I turned around to face her, noticing that she was now sitting while tea was presented to her. "I terribly hate wasting my time. Should I simply call for the archbishop and have the matter resolved this evening?"

"Is it truly possible? If so, I would be much obliged," Wilhelm answered.

"It is not possible. And we are very grateful for your time, Your Majesty," I cut in, giving him a glare before quickly walking back to their circle. "In fact, we are very grateful for all you have done—"

"Do not overflatter, my dear, it is an act of the peasantry."

She waved me off, and just like that, Lady Crane—who should have been called Lady Stone, as she seemed unshakeable and unwavering—stepped forward once more, new books in her hands.

"You walk decently for a lady. However, it must be refined for the wedding. Place these on your head and walk about the room," she said, handing me three books.

I did as she asked and began to walk slowly. I was sure I could do this well—I had practiced thousands of times before. But just as I was about to complete my first turn about the room, I noticed his eyes on me once more. All he had to do was wink and I tripped, making him snicker.

"Your Highness, are you sure you are not needed elsewhere?" Lady Crane asked him.

"Yes, quite sure. Why?"

"Because you are becoming a distraction," the queen answered.

"On the contrary, I believe I am helping. Will she not be walking toward me? What if she sees my handsome face and trips then? It's better she becomes accustomed to it now, if possible."

I scoffed. "Your Majesty, if overflattery is an act of the peasantry, what is self-flattery considered to be?"

"I believe the church brands it as vain. Though I must admit, he is handsome; of course, it comes from my side of the family," she replied.

I looked at her, realizing that was not the only thing he seemed to get from her side of the family.

"The books, Lady Hathor," Lady Crane reminded me.

Sighing, I lifted the books and placed them back on my head.

I could not wait for this wedding to come and go as quickly as possible.

23

Hathor

"Lady Hathor—"

"I know, I know! I am late!" I said, rising from the vanity and rushing toward the door, where Ingrid awaited me, surely to tell me Wilhelm was here. "I cannot believe I overslept!"

"It is only natural, my lady. You have been working so hard," Bernice replied as she followed me out of the room with my hat in her hands. I paused, looking at her.

"Why does it sound like sarcasm when you say it like that?"

"It is not. Truly, my lady, it cannot be easy going to and fro every day with the queen. Everyone is speaking of her lessons with you," she replied, placing my hat on my hair. "They say she is quite strict."

"I do not think her that much stricter than Mama; in fact, she is rather amusing," I said, allowing her to fix the pin that held the hat to my curls. "During the last few days I've realized that once you get over her being queen, her company is rather normal."

"Normal? Or, maybe, you are becoming more royal." She smiled at me.

"That is a proper compliment." I giggled, rushing down the stairs to meet Wilhelm before he and Abena got into another row. She now saw him as her greatest nemesis and Wilhelm seemed to enjoy sparring with her. He said she made him feel as though he had a little sister—like he had a real sibling, for the first time.

"I am so happy to see you, my dear," said my mama to the people entering the doorway.

"Who is here?" I looked at Bernice, knowing Mama would not be saying that to Wilhelm.

"I was trying to tell you; Lady Verity and her husband, Sir Darrington, are here, my lady," Ingrid said from the top of the stairs.

"Yes, Hathor, we are here. Have you missed me?" Verity stepped forward, dressed in purple, her hair much longer than I remembered, and smiled as bright as the day she was wed. "It is hard to determine, since you have not written me a single letter or told me you were engaged! And to a prince, no less!"

"Hello, Verity, how are you? I am engaged to a prince," I said with a grin, causing her to roll her eyes as she walked up to me and gave me a tight hug.

"You really are the most frustrating of friends," she replied when we let go.

"Oh, I am sorry. Were you expecting a detailed account of my life? Strange, for I was not given as much with you. You disappeared one day and came back engaged to him." I turned my head to Sir Darrington, who stood off to the side and watched us both, his hair cut shorter on the sides and left longer on the top. "Hello again, Sir Darrington."

"Hello again, Lady Hathor. I see you're still as healthy and lively as ever." He nodded to me.

"Well?" Verity questioned, looking at me.

"Well, what?"

"Where is your prince? Rumors of you two are all over the ton. Everyone says that you are inseparable and madly in love. So much so that the queen keeps a good eye on you both. I wish to witness it myself," she stated.

It could not have been a *very* good eye, considering all Wilhelm and I had done over the past few days. But I could not say that so instead I looked toward her husband. "Why is she so nosy? What have you done to her? The Verity I know cares not the length of a cat's tongue for society."

"Do not change the subject," she replied. "I came all this way to hear firsthand about you and your prince."

I walked around her, spinning away. "There is nothing to tell. I am quite magnificent, and since he is not blind, he noticed, becoming undeniably, unreasonably besotted with me."

"Is that so?"

I knew that voice. I had spun right into the arms of Wilhelm. He stared down, eyebrow raised.

"You're here," I replied.

"Yes, I am. And, apparently, *undeniably, unreasonably* besotted," he mocked me.

Before I could reply, Verity and Sir Darrington curtsied and bowed to him.

"Your Highness," they said, and it startled me. I had gotten used to no longer curtsying before him. On top of that, he was always here waiting when I came down, so I never saw my family do it either.

"These people are?" Wilhelm whispered to me, waiting for me to introduce them. Right. Immediately, I stepped to the side and stood properly.

"Prince Wilhelm, may I introduce Sir Theodore Darrington and Lady Verity Darrington. Lady Verity is the younger sister of the Duke of Everely."

"Ah, so they are family of sorts," he replied, relaxing slightly as he outstretched his hand to Sir Darrington. "It is a pleasure."

"No, it is ours, Your Highness," Sir Darrington said quickly, stepping back to allow Verity to step forward a bit more.

"Are you visiting Hathor, Lady Verity?" he asked her.

"Yes, Your Highness, we got word of your engagement and I thought it would be nice to visit. But it looks as though we are intruding. Were you both on your way out?"

"We are expected at the palace. However, I think a break is in order." Wilhelm nodded to himself and then looked at me. "I shall tell the queen you've family visiting, and we can re-schedule for tomorrow."

"You will tell her? That means you will go? I'd rather you stay and join us," I said gently back. "Can you not send a messenger instead?"

"I do not wish to intrude—"

"How can you be intruding, when the reason she is here is because of you?" I replied, stepping away from him to look to where Bernice was speaking to my mother. "Mama, can a footman notify the palace that Prince Wilhelm and I will be spending the day with friends?"

"The queen will not like that. I planned on going with you today, so I shall tell her myself," my mother replied, and now I was nervous about what else Her Majesty would say to her. It must have been on my face, because she let out a sigh and gave a small smile. "Do not worry. She merely wishes to share some details of the wedding with me, of course."

"Thank you, Mama," I said. She nodded before moving into the drawing room with Bernice.

"Then it is settled," Wilhelm replied before looking to Sir Darrington. "The house is rather full. Would you be all right with a trip to the park? It is a lovely day outside."

"Of course, Your Highness," he said, without even thinking on it. He was rather stiff, too. Not just him, but Verity as well. They stood together, staring at us oddly.

"We shall see that the maids pack some food as well," Verity stated, her voice also strained.

"Thank you," Wilhelm said to her, before offering me his arm to lead me out.

"I apologize. I do not know why they are acting so strangely," I whispered as he led me to the doors.

"They are acting so because they know nothing of me other than my title. It is normal," he whispered back as we stepped outside.

"Must you come here every day?" Abena suddenly appeared at the gates, her arms crossed as she glared at us both, but mostly him. "Hathor is not so bad at directions that she can't find her way to the palace without you."

"I am not bad at all," I snapped at her.

"No matter how poor your sister is at directions, it is still a gentleman's duty to escort a lady," Wilhelm stated, not at all listening to me.

Abena made a face at him. "But Papa says you're not really a gentleman."

"Abena!" I gasped at her.

"Hathor says you're not really a lady. More like a bug," Wilhelm teased back.

Abena's cheeks puffed up. "You cannot call me a bug! Only she can call me that! Hathor, tell him!"

"Why bother? Neither of you are listening to me." I huffed, though I was amused with the faces they were now making at each other.

"Hathor, you cannot marry him. I dislike him." Abena crossed her arms.

"She used to say that, too, and now she does not wish me to leave her side. You shall get used to it as well, little bug," he shot back.

Again, she took in air through her nose. "This means war, ogre prince."

"Ogre? Don't call him that!" I said to her.

"And you're the ogre's bride." She huffed, marching away.

"The mouth on her!" I stared in disbelief. "I have to tell Mama she is getting out of hand."

"Don't." Wilhelm chuckled, watching my sister stomp off. "It is refreshing. Your family is rather relaxing. Everyone else gets stiff, but they treat me as though I were any other gentleman. I enjoy it here. Even with your father's grimace."

I sighed. "I'm sorry—"

"You need not keep apologizing. It's fine. Besides, I have a method of my own to win over your parents."

"A method? What method?"

"I'm going to win all the hearts of their children. I already have you settled and secure."

I chuckled. "Is that so?"

"Yes, it is. And I've made plans with Damon later on this week, as well as gave Hector a book from the king's private collection."

"You did what? You stole one of the king's books?" I whispered as though it were treason. I think it might actually have *been* treason.

"I borrowed it and lent it to your brother yesterday afternoon. You should have seen your father's face as he tried not to seem interested."

"You mean to bribe my siblings onto your side? Is that not underhanded?"

He shrugged. "Did you not hear Abena? We are at war. All tactics must be deployed to ensure victory. Now, how am I to win over Devana? She rarely speaks."

Before I could reply, Verity called out, "Sorry to keep you waiting."

There were a few maids and footmen behind her, carrying several things to prepare for a picnic, though I thought we were only to go on a walk.

"Is there anything else you require, Your Highness?" Verity asked him.

I was sure he did not require that much.

"No, that is fine, Lady Verity." He nodded to her. He glanced at me from the corner of his eye, and I knew he very much did not require any of that.

"Let's be going. They can take their time to set up once we get to the park," I said, stepping out of the gates alongside Wilhelm. When I did, it was as if all the ton had been drawn to us.

Since arriving back in London, I had not had time to walk about in society. Every day, Wilhelm and the queen's coach were waiting for me. I was so distracted by him that I truly did not pay attention to much of the world beyond that. Then, in the palace, no one stared. It had been like that for so many days now that this experience was rather extraordinary. Every last person paused to watch us as if we were doing something astonishing, and not merely walking upon the footpaths.

"Good day, Your Highness," several men said to him, and what was more shocking was how they addressed me as *ma'am*, and not *my lady*.

Wilhelm just nodded back and gave them short smiles that, to me, looked clearly forced and tense. Was this why he had wanted to go back to the palace? He knew it would be like this, and why wouldn't it be? How often did royals simply walk about London with the rest of the gentry? Some people could live all their lives, lord or not, and never see a royal in the flesh. To me, it was just a walk. To them, it was royalty among men.

"Are you all right?" he asked me.

I nodded. "Yes, I just didn't realize it would be like this; how naïve of me. Are you all right?"

"Honestly, I must say I am rather surprised by this, too. It has been a while since I have had such attention. No one in England recognized who I was before, so I could walk around unnoticed. But since they all know you, Lady Hathor Du Bell, they can guess who I am."

"Should we go back?"

"Your friend is here. Speak with her, you both seem close. I will speak with her husband. Does he have any interests?"

"He's a doctor."

"A duke's daughter married a doctor?"

"It is a long story." I grinned, and then paused, causing Verity and Theodore to quickly stop, too. "Sir Darrington, Prince Wilhelm is curious about your profession and how you came to be married to Lady Verity. Will you inform him while Verity and I gossip for a moment?"

His eyes widened, and he froze for a moment before nodding and stepping forward. "Of course."

He and I switched places, allowing me to link arms with Verity. "Could you two not be so tense? You are making it awkward."

"Have we done something to offend him?" she questioned worriedly.

I groaned, pointing at her face. "This, your face, that is what is offensive. You are so overly cautious. Wilhelm is a very affable person."

"He's a prince, Hathor. There is no such thing as an affable prince," she whispered back. "And with the rumors around him, I do not know how you can describe him so."

"Rumors? Which ones?"

"Far too many to count. But everyone is speaking of him. The wild prince of Malrovia who broke hearts all throughout Europe, nearly beat Lord Covington to death at your family castle, and, of course, how he tried to steal his father's throne—"

"What?" I gasped. "Those are gross exaggerations and mischaracterizations, and the last is simply a lie. Who is saying this?"

"Everyone, Hathor. Why do you think I had to come and see you myself?" she replied. "The way everyone is talking, it was as if some horrible beast had fallen in love with you, and you with him."

I frowned at that, staring at his back. "He is not at all like that. Sadly, he doesn't seem to care to fix his reputation either. But I am so shocked that so many are speaking of him at all. Did we not win a war? Troops are returning; Napoleon has abdicated. You would think they'd have their fill of gossip elsewhere."

"All of that is happening rather far away, and it is hard to understand what exactly is happening throughout Europe right now. Everyone says it's a mess. A banished prince and famed lady of standing seeking to marry right here in front of our eyes is rather more interesting. I'm surprised I have to explain this to you of all people. You always know what is going on in society."

She was right. I usually had my ear to the wall, seeking to know as much as possible. But now: "He takes up a lot of my thoughts and time."

"Does he make you happy, though?"

I couldn't help but grin as I nodded. "Very much."

"Well, I guess in the end, that is all that matters."

"You do not think me vain, only desiring to marry him because he is a prince?"

She chuckled. "If I'm being honest, when I heard the news, for the briefest of seconds I thought it to be the case."

"Apparently I'm the one who needs to fix my reputation, if everyone thinks so lowly of me."

"It was only for a second." She squeezed my hand. "Then I

remembered who you really are, and how much love means to you. I am so happy for you, Hathor."

"I am very happy for me, too. But let's not talk only of me, what of you? Are you pregnant yet?"

"Hathor!"

"What? Is that not the logical next step for you both?"

"You should not know about—"

"Oh please, spare me that married act now. You've already told me far too much, and I've experienced enough."

"Have you? *Lady Hathor.*" She giggled, nudging me.

"Oh hush, and stop avoiding the question."

"Theodore and I are waiting."

"Waiting? On what?"

"When the idea does not scare me so much. I keep thinking of my own mother. Luckily, he understands, as he's seen many women die in childbirth. It is so tragic. I often wonder why."

"So, women can prevent themselves from getting pregnant?" I did not know such things were possible.

"He makes me a drink. It tastes awful, but so far it has worked. I think, in the next year or so, I shall be ready."

I had never heard of such a thing. And I had the mind to ask. But what did it matter? Wilhelm and I were to be married soon and I did not mind the thought of bearing his children.

"I hear we are about to be aunts," she added, taking me from my thoughts.

"Ah, right. Aphrodite is pregnant, I'd almost forgotten."

"Hathor!"

"What? I heard. I sent her a letter congratulating her, and she sent one back telling me to visit, but I have been busy, obviously."

"You at least told her of the engagement."

I did not reply.

"Hathor."

"Stop staying my name like that. No, I did not tell her. I was not sure how to write it. It felt as if it would be boastful."

"Do you not wish to boast? You have finally gotten your victory."

"That's the thing, Verity. He's more than some victory or tally to use against my sister. I don't want her to think I'm using him that way."

"Wow, you *are* changed. Love is truly powerful—"

"Theodore? Verity? Hathor?"

We all paused as none other than Henry Parwens called out to us from where he stood in the park. As always, he was loud and a towering figure of man, with broad shoulders and short hair.

"I did not realize you all were here," his voice boomed as he came up to us.

"Yes, we came to visit Lady Hathor and the rest of the Du Bells," Sir Darrington said as he stepped forward, taking his hand. "I did not think you were here either."

"Long story, my friend. Verity, how are you? And, Hathor, I need not ask, of course. Your name is all anyone can speak of at my house." He chuckled, looking at Wilhelm before bowing to him. "Hello, Your Highness, I am Henry Parwens. I am told you've met my family already."

Wilhelm glanced to me.

"This is Lady Amity's elder brother," I informed him.

"Ah, hello, sir." Wilhelm shook his hand.

"I apologize for whatever my sister may or may not have done."

"Apology not accepted." I huffed, crossing my arms. "Amity ought to apologize herself."

"So, she did do something?" Henry questioned.

"Honestly, I cannot recall, but nevertheless it is her responsibility, not yours, Henry. It is good to see you, though. You seemed to be hiding all year."

"Believe me, that is an even longer story." He groaned and smiled, shaking his head, when all of a sudden I felt Wilhelm very close to my side.

"You did not join your family at the Du Bells' estate. I take it you are not married, then, Mr. Parwens?" Wilhelm asked him randomly. And I was not sure what happened, but it was as if someone had snapped their fingers in Henry's face. His eyes widened for the briefest of seconds, before he stepped back and calmly shook his head.

"No, Your Highness. I am not yet married, and I could not imagine myself joining the Du Bells. Lady Hathor and the rest of those young ladies are more like my younger sisters."

"Henry, may I speak to you for a moment?" Sir Darrington said to him.

"Excuse me," he said to us before he, Verity, and Sir Darrington stepped to the side.

I looked up to Wilhelm. "What happened?"

"What do you mean?" Wilhelm asked dubiously.

My eyes narrowed. "I am not sure what I mean, but I feel as though something happened. Do you know what I mean?"

"Do not stress your mind by thinking on it." He looked down at me. "And do not stress me by so comfortably calling another man by their given name."

That was it. "You dislike me calling him Henry."

"And there you are, doing it again. Will you ever listen to me?"

"Are you jealous?"

"Do not be ridiculous. I merely remember proper manners, something you told me you were keen on following. Except with him, apparently."

A leisurely smile spread across my lips. "You are jealous."

"I am not."

"You are too."

"I simply . . ." He tried to think. "I simply am worried for your reputation."

I snorted so hard I held my hand to my nose. "Far too late for that, do you not think?"

"Believe whatever you like." He rolled his eyes and tried to walk away from me, but I grabbed his arm, linking it with mine.

"Henry—" He gave me a glare. "Mr. Parwens and I met a few years ago. His parents desperately wished to see us married. He is friends with Sir Darrington, so naturally we all spent time with one another. However, he made very clear to me that he was deeply in love with some mystery lady. He truly is like a brother, and due to his friendly nature, I did not think twice before using his given name. But if it bothers you so much, I shall be accommodating."

"Are you not benevolent?" His words dripped with sarcasm.

"I do not make a scene about all the ladies who hover around you at the palace, do I? And I know a lot about Lady Gallagher."

His whole face and demeanor changed. He looked ready to quickly explain, when all of a sudden something drew his attention behind me. When I turned to see what it was, all I felt was his hand on me, pulling me harshly, and all I heard was someone scream.

"Down with the house of Mürttewberg!"

Bang!

24

Wilhelm

I never expected to die at twenty-four.

I did not think I'd live to a very old age, but I had been sure I would be older than this.

That, in and of itself, was a sign of my own hubris. How could I have been sure? How could anyone be sure which day would be their last? All we could do was make sure we did not have regrets. Had you asked me a year ago, a month ago, I would have told you I had none. Even if I had died young, at least I had lived as I desired in the end. A year ago, a month ago, I would not have had regrets.

Today, I did.

I had one regret, and it was her.

I regretted putting her in this danger.

And making her suffer this pain.

The look on her face above me was so tortured that I regretted ever coming into her life, making her feel this way.

"Wilhelm!" She screamed so loudly and sobbed hysterically, holding on to my face, while I was so worried about the blood on hers. I hoped she wasn't injured and ignoring her pain to focus on me. "Help him! Help him now!"

My love, do not strain your throat so, I wished to say to her.

There was too much commotion, too many people around us, and she was yelling at all of them, not looking at me any longer.

"H . . . a . . . thor." She could not hear me, so I mustered as much strength as I could. "Ha . . . thor!"

When she looked to me, her eyes wide and full of tears, I smiled.

"I . . . love . . . you."

25

Hathor

I was covered in blood.

His blood.

I'd never seen so much blood before.

That was not good. Blood was not meant to be seen. It was to be covered by skin, and skin was covered by clothes. Blood was never supposed to be upon our clothes, and yet it was upon mine. How? Why? I did not understand. Everything was fine. The day was splendid. We were teasing each other in the park . . . then blood.

It didn't make sense.

"Hathor! Sweetheart!" My head rose, and there was my mother, holding on to my face, tears and panic in her eyes. She knelt before me. "Sweetheart, are you injured? Are you all right?"

How was my mother here?

Where was I?

I glanced around and realized I was at the palace. I did not remember coming here.

"Hathor, sweetheart, talk to me." She brushed my curls from my face gently.

"Godmother, she's in shock," Verity said beside me. Had she always been there?

"What happened? Was she hurt? No one is telling me. All I know is that there was a gun."

"Some madman fired toward Prince Wilhelm. He threw himself on top of her and was hit, Godmother. Theodore and the other doctors are in with him now. Theodore told us to go home, but she refused and came with him. Then she just sank to the floor here when they would not let her in."

I did not remember that.

I tried to think but all I saw in my head was blood. I stared down at my hands again. My gloves were gone, but my hands were stained with it.

"Hathor, my dear, let's go home and have you cleaned up," Mama said to me, rubbing my shoulders. I looked at her and shook my head. "Sweetheart, there is nothing you can do here. Let's get you home, and then we can come back."

Again, I shook my head, finally able to speak. "No, Mama."

"Hathor."

"Mama, I'm not leaving until Wilhelm tells me to leave."

"He is injured—"

"Why are you not listening to me!" I screamed at her. Shaking, I pushed her away and forced myself off the floor. "I am not leaving this palace until he can leave, too. I am not going anywhere. Stop asking me. Stop it! Please!"

"If that is what you desire, fine. But at the very least, have the good manners not to track dirt within my walls," the queen said at the other end of the hall. Her face was stern, her head held high. "Lady Crane, see to it she is cleaned and dressed properly."

"I am not leaving until—"

"Lady Hathor, this is my palace, and within the single blink of an eye, you can be dragged out and never allowed entrance again. Would you like that?"

I shook my head. "No, Your Majesty."

"I thought so. Follow Lady Crane, and be dressed properly if you wish to remain here."

I nodded, walking forward, when I felt someone grab my hand. When I looked, it was my mother. Her eyes begged me again to come with her, but I pulled my hand back and walked toward Lady Crane.

"Marchioness, you are free to come and visit your daughter as you please. However, I suggest you go inform your family she is all right," I heard the queen say to her. I turned the corner and did not look back.

I thought we'd have far to go but the room was right at the corner of the hall. When I stepped in, there were maids already preparing a bath in a bronze tub, and a new dress was lying on the bed.

"Girls, come and help her." Lady Crane's voice was much softer than I had ever heard it before. Or maybe my ears were still ringing.

It did not matter; the maids circled me, one by one, helping me out of the layers of my clothes. When I was stripped down naked, they carefully brought me over to the tub and helped me inside. The moment I sat down, they began working to fix the tangled mess of my hair. I saw blades of grass and dirt fall out, and instantly I remembered how my body slammed onto the earth. How tightly he'd held me. He'd put his hand on the back of my head to protect it, even in that moment. Then he slumped off me.

I looked down, and . . .

"I . . . love . . . you."

My lips quivered as I remembered. He told me he loved me, and that was the last thing he said before his eyes closed.

"It is all right to cry, Lady Hathor," Lady Crane said as she washed my hands herself. "When something like this happens, *everyone* is allowed to cry."

So I did. In the tub, I sobbed and wailed as if my soul were leaving my body. Everything was fine. It was a good day, and then it was horrid. All of this was so horrid. But as much as I feared I'd never truly recover from it, my deepest fear was that *he* wouldn't. That those were the last words I'd ever hear from him.

Verity

"Deanna? Hathor?" the marquess yelled from the front of his house, he and his son Damon running toward us before the carriage even came to a stop. He nearly pushed the footmen out of the way as he yanked the door open. He looked to his wife, my godmother, who had not said a single word since we left the palace, and then to me, confused. "Deanna? Where is Hathor?"

Gently, both he and Damon helped her down from the carriage.

"She refused to come." Godmother's voice was so quiet. If we had not been close, I was sure we would not have heard her at all.

"What do you mean she would not come? Is she all right? Is she injured?" the marquess pressed, staring down at her as Damon helped me out as well.

"I do not know," Godmother answered.

"What do you mean you do not know?"

"I mean I do not know!" she screamed back at him, causing my eyes to widen, as well as his and Damon's. "I do not know, Charles! She would not talk to me. She pushed me away. And she refused to come home. I do not know anything more than that she is alive. And—and she was covered in blood, Charles." Her voice broke and it was as though all the strength left her, forcing him to grab on to her. "She was hunched in a ball, covered in blood."

Her hands covered her mouth as she tried to push down a sob.

"Come, you must rest" was all he said as he held her, bringing her back into the house. I moved to follow them but Damon stepped in front of me. His head was down and his back was to the house. He did not look me in the eye, but his fists were clenched.

"Tell me what you know, Verity. I need to know before I face them."

I didn't understand whom he was speaking about, as his parents were already dealing with the matter. Then I noticed the rest of the Du Bells—Devana, Hector, and Abena—watching us from the window above, their faces pressed up to the glass, searching for their sister. That's when I understood, and so I told him about what happened at the park, the madman who had fired the gun.

"Hathor was not harmed?" he questioned, finally lifting his head to look me in the eye.

"Physically, no, but as you can imagine, she was traumatized: screaming and sobbing. She eventually became so overwhelmed by the shock that she collapsed by the door to the room in the palace where the doctors were treating him. Your mother tried to bring her home, but she refused, so the queen let her stay."

He inhaled deeply, slowly nodding. "And Prince Wilhelm? What of him, where was he hit?"

"I am not sure." I shook my head. "It was too bloody and chaotic for me to see clearly. I was trying to calm Hathor so Theodore could tend to him. However . . ."

"However?"

"It was a lot of blood, Damon. I heard the doctors at the palace whispering, saying they do not believe he will make it through the night."

"Where doctors fail, God prevails," he replied gently. "My grandmother used to say that."

"I hope she was right."

"Come, you need to rest, too, and change. There is blood on the hem of your dress." He placed his hand on my shoulder, stepping aside to allow me to go in.

Never had I heard the Du Bell house so quiet, and never had it felt so eerie.

"Your parents are in the drawing room," Silva said as she came toward us. "I'm so glad you are here, Verity; your room is already prepared. Why don't you follow Bernice and go get cleaned up?"

"Thank you," I replied. I saw Bernice already waiting at the bottom of the steps with the most ghostly look on her face. Walking up to her, I took her hand and offered a small smile. "She's all right. Hathor is all right."

She nodded. "This way, my lady."

As we walked up the stairs, I glanced back to see Silva's hands upon Damon's chest as they spoke. I had made it only halfway up before I came face-to-face with the trio of Du Bell children. None of them said anything. They all just stared at me, like they were scared to ask. Even Abena.

"Hathor is fine," I repeated, though I was getting the feeling none of them would truly relax until they saw her with their own eyes.

"If she is fine, why is she not here?" Abena questioned. "Why did Mama look as though she was crying? She never does that. Are you lying?"

"Abena, do not be rude," Devana scolded her.

"It is not rude. It is an important question," Hector stated sternly. "Why is Hathor not here, if she is fine?"

I sighed, going up farther. "Because Hathor wants to be with Prince Wilhelm. He is hurt very badly, and she wants to be there for him. Forgive her for making you worry. Hopefully, she will be home soon."

"Is Prince Wilhelm really that badly injured?" Devana asked me.

I nodded. "Very badly, that's why Hathor would not come home."

"All of you give Verity a moment. I am sure she is very tired," Damon called from the bottom of the stairs.

They looked as though they still had so many more questions, but they let me go up. Only when I reached their guest room did the exhaustion catch up to me. I moved over to the bed and took deep breaths.

"I shall call for tea," Bernice stated, and I just nodded.

My mind went to Hathor, the horror on her face. The way she screamed would haunt me forever. I could not imagine such grief. It made me shudder to even think of. My biggest worry was what would become of her if the doctors were right.

If Prince Wilhelm did not make it until the morning . . .

So I did what Damon said. I prayed.

God, please, I know all the world cannot always be happy, that all families suffer some misery. But please, spare the Du Bells, spare Hathor, if only to give hope to the rest of us that true love can prevail. That some families can truly be blessed with unending joy.

Please.

Hathor

When I finally stepped back out into the hall, it was full of maids, footmen, and the royal family. Not just the queen, but all of her children, including the prince regent, who stood beside her at the door. It must have been obvious that I belonged neither to the servants nor to the royal family, because everyone turned to stare at me.

I walked just as Lady Crane and I had practiced, toward where the queen and prince regent stood, before curtsying deeply to them both.

"You are my cousin's fiancée?" the prince regent questioned.

"Yes, Your Highness."

"They say you were with him at that cursed moment."

"Yes, Your Highness."

"And you have not returned to your family?"

I frowned at that. "He is my family, Your Highness."

"Lady Hathor—"

"He would want her here, so she is here," the queen stated matter-of-factly. No one else said another word.

I turned to the door, waiting, wanting to know if there had been any further news. But I was not sure whom or when to ask. Nor did I wish to push my luck and be forced to leave. So I stood there quietly for all of ten more minutes. Just as I was getting restless, the door opened, and out came a short man with a thin nose and white styled wig. He immediately stepped to the queen and shook his head.

"We stopped the bleeding and have done all we can for him, Your Majesty, but it is not likely he shall see the morning."

I understood his words, but I did not really feel them. Like he was speaking of another person.

"This will not be good for us politically." The prince regent sighed, then looked to his mother.

What did that mean?

Why were politics in this?

Why were people leaving the hall?

I did not understand any of them.

"Can he have visitors?" the queen asked the doctor.

"Yes, it might give him some comfort in these final moments."

"Hathor, go to him," the queen replied, turning to leave as well.

Why were they all leaving him? But again, I did not want to be excused from their home as well.

"This way, my lady," the short man said, and I followed him. When I entered the room, the first thing I noticed was how many doctors were inside: seven, not including Sir Darrington, who stood off to the side for some reason that was not as important as Wilhelm. He was upon the bed, his skin so pale he already looked dead. He was shirtless, with a large bloody bandage around his waist, breathing so very slowly.

They all moved away, allowing me to move beside his bed. I sat down, staring at this . . . person, who looked like Wilhelm, but could not possibly be him. Wilhelm was full of energy and life. He was not sickly. Reaching up, I laid my hand on his forehead, and then took his hands into mine.

Leaning over, I kissed his cheek before whispering in his ear, "Just so you know, I abhor tragedy, and so forbid you to make my life one." I bit back the tears trying to fall again. "You are not dying. Stop being silly. You're not allowed to die. I will not allow you to die."

Because if he died, I died, and I very much wanted to live.

26

Hathor

They were arguing.

Sir Darrington and one of the royal doctors.

I could not hear what the nature of their argument was, but it was stern, and the gestures toward Wilhelm clearly showed it was about him. Sir Darrington looked completely frustrated, while the other man looked annoyed.

"Are you sane? This is not some street dweller for your experiments. He is the prince of Malrovia, we cannot do something so—obscene!" the royal doctor snapped at him.

"Sir, at this point—"

"No. That is my final answer. Be grateful you are here at all. If not for your connection to the Lady Hathor and being first on the scene, I would have had you thrown out—"

"What is going on?" I asked now, right beside them both, though they did not immediately notice.

Startled, they both stared at me in silence. "Someone answer me: Why are you fighting at his bedside?"

"Forgive me, my lady, it is nothing," the royal doctor said.

"It does not seem like nothing." I looked to Sir Darrington. "What is going on?"

He made a face, his lips thin, but he still did not answer.

"Sir Darrington, I will not ask you again. Either you tell me, or I'll have you both sent from the room."

"I do believe there is some way to help him," Sir Darrington finally said.

"No, what you believe is fantasy and magic, not science, not reason. Lady Hathor, please excuse this man, he is—"

"He is the husband of my dear friend, the brother-in-law of the Duke of Everely, and a man knighted by Her Majesty. I will not excuse him. What is it that you wish to do?"

"I believe he has lost a lot of blood and needs more."

My eyes widened in shock. "What?"

"It is madness," the royal doctor muttered. "Utter madness."

"How do you plan to give him blood? From what?"

"Not what—*whom*. Is there any possible way you could get me an audience with the queen? I shall explain it all with her permission."

"The queen will never allow such foolishness. You are wasting your time and disturbing the young lady. Excuse me, while I actually check on my patient," the royal doctor replied, stepping around him and moving to Wilhelm's bedside, where he checked his pulse. Truthfully, that was all I had seen him do so far. No one was doing anything but checking to see if he was dead yet.

"I know it sounds insane, but I must speak with the queen about it," he whispered low.

"Can you save him?"

"I do not know, but we ought to try, oughtn't we?"

I looked him over for a moment before nodding. "Follow me."

I was not aware what his plan was, but if he needed the queen, then I'd get him to the queen. Though I did not entirely know how. It was so late in the evening that I was sure almost everyone had gone to bed. Nevertheless, I had to try. Out in the hall, I found a footman resting against the wall, asleep. He was the only one there. I looked to Sir Darrington, who stepped forward and tapped the man on the shoulder. Startled, he jumped up and looked at me, bowing his head.

"My lady, forgive me. Her Majesty told me to wait here for news."

"Has she gone to bed?"

"I am not sure, my lady. I do not believe so, as I saw Lady Crane call for tea to be brought into the blue room a few moments ago."

"Thank you," I said, turning to go myself.

"Is there any news, my lady?" he called after me, but I did not answer. Instead, I looked to Sir Darrington, who was staring at the décor, his hands behind his back as he followed me one step behind.

"I trust that whatever you have to say to her, Sir Darrington, will be of a pressing nature, especially considering the fact that I am no longer in the room with Wilhelm."

"Yes, my lady. I assure you, I do not mean to waste your time or hers. I truly seek to help him."

I believed him, because of Verity. I believed him because I had nothing else to believe in. So when we reached the doors and I saw two footmen standing outside of them, I was grateful: that meant she was still up. I stepped toward the doors, but the footmen stepped in my way.

"Her Majesty asks not to be disturbed," one said.

"I need to speak to her."

They continued to block my way, shaking their heads.

"Fine." I stepped back and inhaled through my nose before yelling at the top of my lungs, "Your Majesty, may I please have an audience?"

Silence.

"Your Majesty, the matter is pressing!"

Lady Crane opened the door. The queen was sitting beside the fireplace, dressed in a large blue dressing gown, her hair down. Several furry dogs slept all around her.

"Is he dead?" she asked me calmly.

"No, Your Majesty," I said quickly.

"Then whatever could be so pressing?"

"One of his doctors wishes to speak with you," I said, moving aside so Sir Darrington could step forward.

"Who are you?" the queen asked.

"Sir Theodore Darrington, Your Majesty." He bowed to her.

"He was the one who first treated Prince Wilhelm in the park and brought him here, with the help of a few other gentlemen," Lady Crane informed her as she offered the queen tea. "He is the husband of Lady Verity, formerly Eagleman."

"Ah, right. What is it, Sir Darrington?" the queen asked.

"I wish your permission for a course of treatment—"

"Dr. Alderton is there, is he not? Why have you not spoken to him on the matter?" she questioned.

"He disagrees with the treatment, ma'am."

"What is this treatment?"

"To give him blood."

She nearly dropped her teacup. She stared at him with the same look I was sure I had worn just moments earlier.

"Did you say blood? Give him? Or do you mean you seek to *bleed* him?"

"Your Majesty, in 1665 an English physician by the name of Richard Lower successfully managed to transfer blood from a healthy dog to a wounded one, thus saving its life. Another test was done at the Royal Society, which confirmed the sharing of blood from one dog to another had saved its life."

The queen handed her cup back to Lady Crane and picked

up the nearest dog at her feet. "Sir Darrington, does this creature resemble my nephew?"

"No, Your Majesty—"

"Then why would you tell me such a horrifying story?"

"Because, Your Majesty, there is little that can be done for Prince Wilhelm at this point. He will die by daybreak if no one can think of something."

I inhaled sharply, my chest feeling tight.

"Do you know why people dislike doctors, Lady Hathor?"

"They do not want anyone to think them sick?" I answered.

"People do not like those who understand things they do not," she replied, her eyes drifting to Sir Darrington. "Doctors do not easily explain their methods, because they barely understand them either. I am sure that is why the Royal Society has not made this research known. They cannot explain it, because it is awful. Imagine the chaos that would be unleashed on the world if people hear or believe they can heal themselves by taking another person's blood. Such a horrid thing should never be accepted into society. Such a monstrous act should *never* be done, certainly not by any royal, ever."

My shoulders slumped. "Your Majesty—"

"My official answer is no."

My eyebrow rose as I looked over her face. Her "official" answer? Why say that?

"And the unofficial answer?" Sir Darrington questioned.

"Doctors must do whatever they must do to save their patients. However, should a certain gentleman wish to remain a doctor and not become a prisoner, he will not be caught, nor will he ever mention, doing such a procedure. For no one, not even the queen, would be able to save him."

I smiled. "Thank you, Your Majesty."

"I do not have any idea what you are thanking me for. In

fact, I am feeling rather ill. Lady Crane, fetch me the royal doctors."

"Yes, ma'am," Lady Crane said, walking over to the door. Sir Darrington and I ran after her.

Theodore

It was one thing to study something in theory; it was another to actually do it. I did not even know why it had come to mind. The papers had suggested the blood be taken from multiple men, so as to keep a continuous flow of blood without endangering the donor, as no more than a cup—maybe two—of blood could be given. And a cup was ten syringes full. How was I supposed to do this?

"How are you to do this?" Lady Hathor eyed me and the syringe in my hand.

"You draw from one person's arm, and place it in the other's as quickly as possible," I answered.

"All right, that is simple enough," she said, and outstretched her arm to me. "Begin."

The ease with which she offered herself up to something so utterly dangerous and unheard of was shocking to me. This was not at all the Lady Hathor I remembered, who was discontent sharing even a biscuit with her sister. "Do not be ridiculous, Lady Hathor. I cannot in good con—"

"It is either you or me, and we do not have much time before Dr. Alderton returns. And if you cannot rightly do this on yourself—"

"I shall take my own, as I do not know what could go wrong. You are a lady; it is not right. Besides, I do not know if the blood of a woman would have an adverse effect on him."

"But—"

"It must be me, or it will not be done at all."

She frowned but nodded. "Very well. Please tell me if there is anything I can do."

"I must ask you to leave."

"What?"

"It would be best for you not to see this. And I work best without the attention. Please, Lady Hathor."

She frowned but nodded. She moved to his bedside and kissed his forehead. "Everything is going to be all right."

For a brief moment, I was jealous. I wished my own wife were here to comfort me. Though knowing Verity, she'd be enraged by my impudence and hazardous choices. She was always telling me patients were important but so was I, and that as such, I could not be risking my own life to save them. Clearly, I did not listen well.

"I shall be outside."

I nodded, waiting for her to leave before I quickly rolled up my sleeve and moved the syringe to my arm.

Hopefully I did not kill the prince or myself.

Verity would have my head.

I felt sick. So sick I had to move over to the corner of the room, sitting on the chair there and trying to rest. I could have sworn I had only closed my eyes for two minutes or so, but when I reopened them, the sunlight was blinding. Worse than that, the room was now reoccupied by the royal doctors, a footman, a maid, Lady Hathor, and Lady Crane. Meanwhile, I was nearly falling out of the chair.

"Forgive me—"

"Well, Doctor? How is he?" Hathor asked, sitting at his bedside. I quickly glanced around the room and noticed all of my things had been cleaned up. Even the bloody napkins were gone.

Had she done this while I was asleep? How disoriented was I?

"I am unsure, but he is alive, and that in and of itself is a miracle," he answered, his eyes drifting to Wilhelm's arm, which was a bit red and bruised in the same area where I had injected him. "I shall continue to keep watch over him. Sir Darrington, may I speak to you outside?"

When he turned to me, his face was stern, his nostrils wide as he took in air.

Nodding, I followed him out of the room and closed the door. He then stepped toward me in a fury.

"What have you done?"

Hiding my hands behind my back, I calmly replied, "Whatever do you mean, sir?"

"Do not be coy with me. I am no fool, and I've inspected all of Prince Wilhelm: His arm was not like that yesterday."

"I have not yet seen his arm, and as such I do not know what you speak of—"

"He is a prince!" he snapped at me. "He is not some commoner on the street, for whom no one would question your science or methods. His blood is sacred, and—"

"Sir, be careful what you accuse me of in these halls," I said sternly, nodding toward the maids in the hallway. He paused, just then noticing them, too. "Prince Wilhelm was greatly wounded, and due to your skill, he is not yet dead. You should be pleased."

"And if he does die?"

"Who could blame you or me? For wasn't that always the possibility—no, the assumption? If he dies, he was always going to die. If he lives—"

"You shall wish to be made a lord?" he huffed. "I've heard

of you, Sir Darrington, and how you've used your connections and slight knowledge to enrich yourself. I assure you that I will not stand by and watch this."

"If Prince Wilhelm lives, would you accuse me of saving him with vile means, and in so doing make an enemy of him—and the queen, who occupied your time last night, did she not?"

At the mention of the queen, his eyes widened.

"Any miracle that happens here, sir, is due to *your* skill and God's mercy. Nothing else happened, for all of our sakes."

He and I shared a long look before he exhaled and shook his head. "His condition is not worsening, and so I will continue to watch him. I suggest you return to wherever it is you came from."

"Very well. Let me gather my things," I said, turning back to reenter the room.

"Lady Hathor, you must rest," Lady Crane said to her, but still Hathor had not moved from his side.

"I am fine."

"You are not fine—"

"Sir Darrington, where are you going?" Her tired eyes snapped to me, noticing me gathering my things. "Are you leaving?"

"Yes—"

"You cannot!" She jumped up now, rushing to me. "What if he still needs—"

"I've done everything in my power for him, Lady Hathor. The doctors here are much more knowledgeable than I."

"I doubt that," she frowned. "So I wish you to stay."

"Lady Hathor."

"Please." Her strong voice nearly cracked, her eyes begging me. In her hands was the same towel she'd been using all night, her hands pale and ash-colored from the continuous contact with water.

"All right. I shall return to your home and inform my wife, as well as your family, of the conditions here before I return. But only if you promise me you will rest."

"I am fine."

"You are not, and I cannot have two patients to worry about in this room. I won't return otherwise."

"Fine. I shall rest for an hour."

"Very well." I smiled, knowing she would most likely sleep beyond that—her body would see to it.

"He's not dead," she whispered, smiling to herself. "You all said he would not make it through the night, but he did, and he's going to make it through this morning. He's getting better."

Such hope . . . I could not break it.

The things we did and believed because of love, only heaven could understand.

27

Hathor

My one-hour nap ended up being nine hours. I had not realized how exhausted I was. But the moment I woke, I readied myself as quickly as I could to go see Wilhelm. Just as I reached his doors, a footman approached, telling me the queen wished to see me. And to be honest, even though I was in the palace, I had forgotten all about her. That was very foolish of me. I could stay only by her grace, and did not wish to be ungrateful. Everyone in the palace treated me as though I were part of the royal family already. The food given to me and the freedom I was allowed were all because of her. So before the footmen opened the door I took a deep breath to calm myself. I had not had a moment of calm since this whole ordeal began.

"Your Majesty, the Lady Hathor," the footman announced.

I stepped in, and curtsied before her. "Your Grace."

"Leave us," she ordered sharply. When I looked up, I saw she stood at the window, dressed in several layers of dark burgundy silk, a diamond necklace and crown upon her head. She held a glass of wine in one hand and a letter in the other.

The footman quickly made his escape.

"Come closer," she ordered. I did so, still keeping a good distance from her, which she apparently disapproved of. She said again, in a strained voice, "Closer, right beside me."

I stepped beside her, not sure I'd ever stood so close to her.

I could see every line and wrinkle, every divot of her skin under the powder she wore. Her face was so old; I knew she was old, but I had never thought of it until now.

"I did not ask you to inspect me, Lady Hathor, but to follow my gaze out the window."

"Forgive me," I said gently, and turned to look out the window with her.

"What do you see?"

I stared out into the distance, only to see the front gates. "The gates, ma'am."

"It's silly, is it not?"

"What is silly, Your Majesty?"

"The thought that that measly iron gate could protect us." She chuckled to herself. "It exists merely for show, nothing but an illusion of power. It's easy to forget that, when everyone else has so much belief in it."

"I do not understand," I said without thinking. I was not meant to talk, just listen.

"Of course you don't. You are a child—or *were* a child. Events such as these have a way of aging you quickly," she replied, her eyes still trained on the gates. "I'm afraid you will have to age even more, with this news."

She gave me the letter in her hands. It had no signature, nor was it addressed to anyone. It merely read: *"His Majesty King Wilhelm II of Malrovia has been assassinated while hunting."*

My eyes widened as I looked to her again. "This is Wilhelm's father? He's dead?"

"A group of disgruntled infantrymen were denied their full wages and compensation for their time in the war. They heard that King Wilhelm was lavishly spending their wages and those of fallen soldiers on his mistresses and children. They believed the whole monarchy to be greedy and evil, and wished to do away with him, as well as his heirs."

"That's why they attacked Wilhelm?" I asked angrily. "He knows nothing of his father's dealings—"

"August's father was a disgusting brute of a man: cruel, harsh, and self-righteous to an unbearable degree. However, he was a good king. Their wages were stolen by their commanding officers, but their commanders blamed the royal family, because the monarchy is so easy to blame. God's anointed, who live in splendor they cannot imagine." For the first time she turned to look at me. "None of them actually see us. They see our crowns and jewels, our vast estates and fine dress. But they do not see us, and you can easily make a villain out of someone you do not know. It is what makes rumors so powerful. What solution can be had?"

"You show yourself to the people."

"We cannot. Because if they know we are human, too—that we bleed, too—they will stop believing in the power they give to us. And when they stop believing we are special, that we were chosen by God, they will come over those gates."

My heart clenched tightly. Slowly, I gathered what she was saying. "The monarch is to be revered, but people do not give reverence to those who are the same as them. You must be different and distant. But because of that, people can go only by what they hear.

"With mere words, lies, men who swore to protect their country picked up arms to kill their king. And they will tell you it is justice, because they were swindled. The truth no longer matters more than their own suffering, their own desires for something different, something new. That was the case in France, they say, before they killed their king and queen. And ever since, Europe has been plagued by wars, all at the behest of one little man. When the people want someone to blame, they come over the gates for us. Then when it is over for us, they destroy themselves." She held her glass out in front of her and let it drop from her hands. I jumped back as the wine spilled out over the broken shards of glass.

"Your Majesty, step back—"

"Ever since I was a little girl, I wished to be queen." She chuckled as she stared at the glass. "I wanted to be special, and special I became. But this is how fragile *special* is, Hathor. I do not know what happens next, but I do know this: Should August live, should you wed him still, you will need to watch those gates, too. It is the price you pay for being married to royalty."

"I—"

"Leave me."

I curtsied and stepped back slowly, turning to leave as she ordered. It was only when the doors were closed behind me that I let go of the breath I had been holding. And as I was walking back to Wilhelm's room, I remembered what my mama had said only weeks ago, though it felt like years. *Royals are very . . . complex*, she had said. I did not understand her meaning then, but now I felt her words to be the greatest of understatements. How silly and naïve I had been, to not realize she was right. I wanted so badly to be a princess; I thought she was merely dashing my hopes. In reality, she, and I was sure my father, also, merely desired for me to live a life unlike this. A life free of assassinations, free from being forced to adhere to unparalleled authority all the time. Being close to the queen made me aware of how everyone within the palace lived around her—including me.

I now knew, with the greatest certainty, that I disliked this very much, and I did not want to be a princess any longer.

However . . . stepping inside Wilhelm's room and seeing his face, my heart twisted.

I did not want to be a princess—I just wanted to take the prince away from here. Hide him in my castle—well, it was my father's castle, but the sentiment was nevertheless the same.

"How is he?" I asked Sir Darrington, who sat in the corner. He had returned, as promised, though I knew the royal doctors were not pleased with it. But they were not in the room.

"He is well. See for yourself," Sir Darrington answered.

Walking over, I sat by his bedside. His complexion looked much better. Smiling, I reached up and touched his face.

"I told you all he'd get better." I smirked, brushing his hair gently. "He's too stubborn to die."

"You're more stubborn."

I jumped away, eyes wide, and pulled my hands back. I froze, not sure if my mind was playing tricks on me. But sure enough, his eyelids fluttered open, and his blue eyes stared back at me. He smiled, and I turned quickly to Sir Darrington, to make sure he was seeing this, too.

"He awoke while you were with the queen. She's being informed now," Sir Darrington said to me. My head whipped back to Wilhelm; he was still staring at me. I did not know what to say, but my eyes began to water, and my lips quivered.

"Sir Darrington . . . would you give us a moment, please?" His voice was so hoarse, and so incredibly good to hear. I waited until I heard the door close before letting out a sob, resting my forehead against his. "You are beautiful, even when you cry."

"I know. That is why I reserve my tears for the worthiest of moments." I sniffled, squeezing his hands. He squeezed back. "Let us make this sight a very rare one, please."

"I shall do my best, my love." He lifted my hand, bringing it to his lips to kiss as he lay back on the bed, closing his eyes.

"Thank you for living."

"Thank you for making living worth it."

Wilhelm

"Thankfully, God had the sense to keep you alive and take your father instead" was the first thing my aunt said to me as I lay weak upon the bed.

I lay there in shock, not understanding. "What? My father is dead?"

Before she could answer, Hathor stepped closer to her. "Your Majesty, please, let him recover—"

"If a bullet did not kill him, my words shall not either," she said to her, and looked back to me. "Your father is dead, your brother is king, and your mother is on her way here. Isn't it all so splendid?"

"What? My mother?" I tried to sit up, but the pain that sprang up in me made me groan.

"Stop moving!" Hathor rushed to my side to hold me down. "You are going to reopen your wounds!"

I ignored her, and the pain, to focus on the immediate danger before me. "Why is my mother coming here?"

"Your father is dead, August."

"Yes, Aunt, so you have said—three times now. That still does not explain why my mother is coming here. She hates England, remember?"

"No, she hates me," she said with a smirk. "So clearly, the only reason she is coming is for you. I suggest you prepare yourself for that, and all that it means, by hastily recovering your strength. You look horrid, and I shall not be accused of providing poor care." She looked to the doctors to the left of the bed. "Fix him quickly."

Just as quickly as she entered, she turned and left the room, everyone bowing to her as she went.

"I am glad you are all right. Get well quickly. You doctors, please take care of him," Hathor said with a small smile on her lips as she took my hand again. "That is what she means, of course, but she cannot say it so simply."

"You can interpret the queen's speech now?" I asked her.

"Yes, a strange talent that I have developed recently," she replied, sitting back down beside me. "Lady Crane has been a most excellent teacher."

"Your Highness," the short doctor with the very white wig called out to me. "Can you tell me about any pains or symptoms you're having?"

"The only symptom is aching, sir."

"Where? Is your arm all right?"

I looked to him, my brow furrowed in confusion. "My arm? Why would my arm ache? I was not wounded there."

He looked to Hathor and not me. She spoke up to dismiss them. "Gentlemen, will you leave us once more?"

The doctors nodded before walking out of the room. I glanced back at her. "What is the matter? Was my arm injured?"

I lifted both of them just fine. It was the rest of my body I was concerned about. She let out a breath before telling me the truth. Never had I heard of such a thing: sharing of blood. She tried to explain it, but she looked just as confused as I.

"It matters not. I am alive, that is what matters," I replied, my fingers intertwining with hers. It was in that moment that I remembered she had been here beside me since that day. She looked so tired; she had been through so much because of me. "I am so sorry you were left to deal with all of this alone. It must have been terribly frightening."

"I want to lie and say I do not frighten easily, but I do not have the energy to," she whispered. I could see that she looked unlike the free-spirited woman I had first met. I lifted my hand, placing it on her cheek.

"Then you and I will both need to recover ourselves." I smiled. "We still have a wedding to host, remember?"

She frowned, and her eyebrows furrowed together. "There can be no wedding now."

"What? Why? You do not—"

"Wilhelm . . . your father is dead," she whispered slowly, looking me over. "You are mourning."

I stared at her. For some reason, the concern and sorrow on her face made the words coming from her lips feel more real. The queen had said it three times, but only now did I feel it.

My father was dead.

I sat in silence, not sure what to do. Not sure what I was supposed to feel.

"Wilhelm?" She shifted closer, cupping my face as I had done hers. "Are you all right?"

"I hated him," I whispered. I loathed him for years and had dreamt of the day he would no longer be alive. I wondered if he would regret his life one day. "I did not expect to be sad to hear of his passing."

"Despite all his cruelty, he was your father. Being sad is normal."

"But that is the thing: I am not sad, as I expected, but I am not happy either. I am nothing. I feel nothing. My father is dead, and I feel nothing. It is as if I have been told a bird somewhere has fallen from the sky. Is that not odd?"

"Papa says you can only mourn what you love or loathe."

"I loathed, though."

"You might have, at some point; maybe now, you do not. Or maybe you are in shock. Either way, whatever you feel, you are not wrong."

This felt very similar to the day I fought Lukas at her estate. How she took my side, even when it was clear I did not deserve it—that I did not deserve her. Every time I looked upon her face, there was this pulling at my heart.

"Lie with me." The words slipped from my lips before I could contain them.

Her eyes widened. "What?"

I could have pretended to have misspoken, but it was not a mistake. I wanted her to lie with me.

"I am tired. Will you rest beside me?"

She stared. I was almost sure she was going to mention her reputation, but, without another word, she shifted and lay down upon the pillow beside me, though she did not go under the sheets. She did not look at me, choosing to stare up at the canopy above. I lay back down, staring up as well.

"Will your mother like me?" she asked softly.

"I am not even sure if my mother likes me."

"Hmm . . . then will your mother allow you to marry me, after your mourning?"

"I shall marry you no matter what. I am not mourning."

"Wilhelm—"

"Hathor, do not worry about anything else. You've worried enough for me. It is I who am meant to take care of you."

"We shall take care of each other."

"You've done your part already. Leave me to handle anything else."

She shifted onto her side now, looking at me. "Do not push yourself. You—"

I pinched her nose. "Do not be a worrywart; it ages you."

Her face bunched up angrily. "Have you seen yourself lately? You're nearly elderly-looking now. You should be grateful I still wish to marry you at all."

I scoffed. "I am ill, have mercy."

"No. That excuse only works for the king here." She huffed,

and I smiled. There she was: the woman I first met. I liked her most like this.

"When we are married, you must stop telling me no."

She giggled. "That is a condition that cannot be met. I love the word *no*; it is rather freeing to say."

"So, am I allowed to use it?"

"No."

She and I teased each other until she drifted to sleep at my side, her body turned toward me. I wanted to bring her closer, but I did not have the strength.

"Enter," I said gently when I heard a knock. When it opened, it was Sir Darrington, alone. His eyes shifted to Hathor, and then back to me.

"Shall I call to have someone take her to her room?"

"She is fine where she is," I answered. He opened his mouth, then closed it suddenly. "Yes, I know there will be rumors if anyone sees us, but I am sure there already are. There is no point pretending now."

"She has gone through a lot for you, Your Highness."

"I am aware. I shall not disappoint her. I am also aware of your efforts to save me. I thank you for them."

"It is my duty, sir."

"I shall not forget it. Should you need anything, simply ask. If it is in my power, I shall see it done."

"May I ask for that favor now?"

"What is it?"

"Lady Hathor refuses to go home, not wanting to leave your side, and her family is greatly worried for her. Will you please tell her to go see them?"

I did not want to do that. I did not want her out of my bed or my sight. This was what I meant when I said my heart pulled whenever I looked at her face. One side of me greedily wanted all of her time, her mind, her body—all of her, without a care for anyone else. The other part of me wanted her to be blissfully free.

It was strange how getting shot—nearly dying—didn't change anything about my life or feelings. I was exactly the same person, only with a stronger desire to live.

"I will tell her to go, but you are to make sure she returns, as she is vital to my good health."

28

Hathor

When the carriage came to a stop in front of my home, I felt strangely nervous. I did not know what to say to any of them. Especially not to my mama, not after how I'd yelled at her. I could only imagine how angry Papa would be. I'd broken a great many rules, and ignored my family entirely. The lecture I would surely get did not matter as much to me as the disappointment and embarrassment I was sure my behavior had caused them. It did not matter if Wilhelm was a prince, or that I was at the palace with the queen; I knew for certain that rumors of me would have reached the ton. How I often stayed alone with the prince at his bedside. Along with the other things that had happened before he was injured. I saw the maids whispering about all of it in the palace. So I did my best to ready myself. Stepping through the doors, I expected to find Mama and Papa waiting, and I was right—but it was not just them. It was everyone. Even Mini was in the foyer, looking at me from Damon's arms.

I opened my mouth to speak, but all of a sudden, I felt a force slam into my waist so hard I nearly stumbled.

"You're finally back!" Abena cried, hugging me tightly.

"My turn!" Devana called out as her arms wrapped around my neck.

"No, it is mine!" Hector said, also hugging me from my left side.

Suddenly, all three of them were hugging me at once, and very tightly.

I grinned. "Is this your way of saying you missed me, or of wishing me dead, as I am slowly being suffocated here?"

"It is far too soon for jokes of dying," Damon said as he came forward. "Especially considering how you currently look as though you have arisen from the dead."

"Even still, I look better than you. Is that gray hair on your head?" I shot back.

"Yes, that is how much stress you cause, troublemaker. I am quickly getting Father's hair color."

"Well, at least you take after him somewhat now," I teased, reaching out and poking Mini's cheek. "Not to worry. With any luck, you shall only take after your mama, Mini."

She giggled at me, and I made faces back at her.

"I wonder whom you take after," came the voice of my own mama, and just like that, all my siblings stepped away from me as though they were afraid, too. Mama's face was stern, but her brown eyes were soft. "It must be you, Charles. I never worried my mother so much."

"I must disagree, as I was not a troublesome child either, my dear. If she takes after neither of us, then she must have fallen from the sky. If so, she is a gift from heaven," my father replied, and then walked over to me. As if I were a little girl again, he pulled me into the tightest hug. "Welcome home, my dear girl."

"I'm sorry, Papa," I whispered, hugging him back. He kissed the side of my head before letting me go to face Mama.

"Well, you all may welcome her, but I shall—"

"Mama!" I ran to her and hugged her waist tightly. "Do not say anything you will regret. My heart is very fragile of late."

"Hmph!" She scoffed. "There is not a fragile bone in your body. You are made of brick and mortar."

"How mighty you are, for bearing me then?" I replied, and she glared at me. I merely smiled back, and soon enough, she chuckled and shook her head, hugging me back.

"You are still silly. I thought the palace would have dulled your tongue."

"They have tried, but I am the daughter of Lady Deanna Du Bell, and if you could not manage it, no one else can."

"You are buttering me up."

I nodded, laughing. "Is it working?"

"Barely." She reached up, touching my curls. "Welcome home, sweetheart."

"Thank you, Mama. Forgive me for being so troublesome."

"Not yet. You still have to receive your punishment."

"What?"

"Abena, show her to the pots!"

"Mama!" I gasped in horror as I quickly ran to my father and clung to him. "Papa, help! She means to destroy my pretty hands."

"Let's go!" Abena giggled and pulled on my dress.

I shook my head, holding on to Papa for dear life. "Absolutely not. Mama, can you not be reasonable? Papa, say something, please."

"Let us eat first, and *then* make her do the pots, my dear," Papa said to her.

I let go of him, aghast. "Papa, you would betray me so? If you all have missed me, why show me this much cruelty?"

"Consider it repayment for the stress you cause, trouble-maker," Damon snickered, making Mini laugh with him.

In fact, they were all laughing, and it felt good to laugh with them.

"Fine, I shall do the pots, and I shall do them excellently. But first, little bug . . ." I looked to Abena, because only she would know. "Is there any pie?"

She grinned, nodding. "I shall tell them to bring it!"

"Come, let us all eat. We've been waiting since we heard you would return this morning," Papa said, already walking forward. My mama stopped me, taking my hands into hers.

"Mama?"

"I wished to apologize to you, sweetheart."

"What?"

"You were right. I did do all I could for everyone else and their loves, but then came down harder on you. I am sorry."

"Mama, you don't have to—"

"I do. Parents should never be too proud to apologize to their children, especially when we hurt them so deeply. I see now that you truly love him, and I should support—*we* should support you in that, for love is the greatest of all things. And so, your father and I will. Whatever you need, we shall do."

I did not wish to cry, but my eyes teared up again and I moved to hug her. "Thank you, Mama."

"All I ask, my dear, is that you be safe and think of us before you act. You children are our greatest treasures, and I cannot bear to see any of you harmed."

"I will. Always."

No matter what happened in the future, I was so glad to have them all. I never realized how glad until now.

Wilhelm

She'd been gone for the last three days, and to say I was rather discontent would be putting it lightly. I'd improved slightly and wished to be up and about, but the doctors treated me as if I were glass. Apparently, I was very lucky the bullet had not hit any vital organs. When I tried to get up, I found my body too weak to move far, leaving me merely lying in bed, wondering when she'd return. Each time the door opened, I expected it to be her. Even now, I sat up hopefully as the door opened, only to be disappointed by the maid, who'd entered to air out the room.

"Your Highness, your food will get cold." Sir Darrington snickered. When my gaze shifted to him, my overseer with his book of notes on my condition in his hands, I knew exactly why he was snickering. I had grown that pitiful.

"Did I not charge you with the task of returning her?"

"Yes, but you did not tell me by which time she was to return," he replied.

"Would it not obviously be soon?"

"*Soon* is relative."

"Is it? Tell me then, is three days away from *your* wife a relatively short time?" He did not answer. "Exactly."

"Well, she is not yet your wife," he muttered.

Now I was silent. He was right, though. Sighing, I lay back on the pillow, lifting an apple to eat. "How long have you been married to Lady Verity?"

"Nearly two years now."

"And you both are still happy?"

"Happier, in fact." His snickering had now become a sly smile as he hung his head. It was good to know I was not the only pitiful one. "I owe the Du Bells greatly for my current fortunes."

"You are close with their family?"

"Verity is Lady Monthermer's goddaughter, though she is seen more as a daughter."

"Is she close to Hathor?"

"Quite, though they are both so different. Verity despises being the center of attention, where Lady Hathor seems to thrive on it. Verity says she's very good at making people like her, even when she is mocking them."

I grinned. "She does not mock people undeservingly. She is keenly aware of people's character. She is pompous to those who are pompous, kind to those who are kind, and ready to help them no matter how awkward the situation may be. And she . . ."

I would have carried on, had he not given me a look of amusement.

"And she?" he pressed.

"Why am I saying this to you? Your time would be better spent in going to bring her back now."

"You wish me to go to Lord Monthermer and tell him Prince Wilhelm misses his daughter doting on him hand and foot, and that she is to return at once?"

"Surely, you can think of better words than that, can you not? Tell them—tell them my condition is worsening."

"It is not."

"Obviously, but she'd return, which is the point."

"Lady Hathor was deeply affected emotionally when you were injured. She nearly pushed her mother to the ground, refusing to leave you, and you wish me to lie and put her in that state once more?"

"Well, when you say it that way, I feel immature and unkind—wait, she pushed her mother?"

"Yes. Verity said Lady Monthermer was hurt by it, and so I assume Lady Hathor is staying longer to make up for her actions."

There was something truly wrong with me, I was sure of it—but I was glad. I was happy she would go through so much, do so much, just to remain at my side.

"Tomorrow. Say what you must to bring her back tomorrow," I replied, taking another bite just as the door opened. Once more, I leaned toward it, hoping it was her. Instead, it was the very last person I wished to see in this moment.

She was dressed head to toe in black silk except for her white gloves, her brown hair was pinned into a curl on one side of her head, a row of diamonds across her neck. Her blue eyes looked over me calmly, then the food, then Sir Darrington, who now stood up and stared back at her. He bowed his head, but from his expression it was clear he was at a loss as to who she was.

"I presume you are the doctor?" she asked him.

"Yes, Lady—"

"Queen Augusta. His mother. What is his prognosis? Will there be any lingering damage to his person?"

"I am not the royal doctor—"

"Then why are you here?"

"He is here because he saved my life," I finally interrupted. "Good day to you, too, Mother. Worry not; I am well. And in time, I shall return to full health."

"Leave us," she said coldly to Sir Darrington, who merely nodded to her, taking his things before shutting the door behind him.

Her eyes examined every corner as if it were vile. "She placed you in the worst rooms, there is barely any light."

"If by *she*, you mean Aunt Charlotte, the Queen of England, I can assure you she's given far too much care to me."

"You are her nephew. There is no such thing as too much."

"Did you come here solely to inquire about my accommodations? What a pity. A letter would have sufficed."

"I am here because your father is dead."

"So I keep hearing. May he be judged accordingly by God."

"I am also here because I missed you, son," she replied as she came around the bed, dusting off the chair Sir Darrington had been sitting in with her handkerchief before taking a seat.

I chuckled. "How convenient that such an emotion came after his death."

"You are still angry with me. And here I thought you would have matured over the years, and come to understand my position—"

"Mother, I have always understood your position."

"Then why the anger, still?"

"Because I hate your position," I sneered, glaring at her, breathing through my nose as I felt my temper rising. "You always did your best as queen, and you have always been a good one. However, as a mother, you have failed me greatly. As such, I do not need you here, though I congratulate you on your recent widowhood."

She did not even flinch, she just removed her gloves. "Well, that was some welcome speech, after such a long journey. Does it make you feel better?"

I moved the tray, no longer hungry. "What do you want, Your Majesty?"

"For you to assume your duties, of course. It is what all mothers want."

"My duties? Which duties?"

"The ones to your brother and your nation."

"I beg your pardon?"

"It's time for you to come home, August. That is why I have come. To bring you home."

I laughed. Even though it hurt, I laughed. "It's your duty to banish me and your duty to retrieve me, is it?"

"Your brother needs you. You know he is not strong enough to shoulder all this alone. The parliament, the rebels, all of our enemies know he is sickly—"

"Frederick is no longer a sickly little boy, Mother. He's actually quite strong, in fact, considering he was able to withstand both you and father for so long."

"And he can be stronger with his brother at his side."

"Why should I live my life for Friedrick, or you, or a nation that did not care if I fell to the ends of the earth?"

"Then you will see us all hunted down?" she pressed. "Look what they have done to you. The war is over, but Europe is still in chaos. Yes, you have been treated unfairly, but such is everyone's life. You cannot be so childish and petty over it. You are a prince. Gather your wits, we leave in three days' time."

"I will not be going anywhere. If you wish to leave, you may."

"August, I have given you an—"

She paused as the door opened wide, and sure enough, Hathor entered. She had a large smile on her face, and quite a lot of art supplies in hand.

"You're awake! Good, have you missed me?" Because of the positioning of the door, she did not see who was sitting beside me. It was only when she took a few steps toward me that she noticed her. "Oh—hello! Forgive me, I did not see you." She curtsied slightly to her.

"And you are?" my mother asked.

"She is Lady Hathor Du Bell, my fiancée." And she truly had the worst timing in history. "Hathor, this is my mother, Queen Augusta."

Her eyes widened, and she sank into a much more pronounced and slower curtsy before her.

"Your Majesty—"

"What on earth do you mean by *fiancée*, August?" My mother's eyes whipped back to me, and she now spoke in German. "I am not in the mood for your jokes."

"I am not joking, Mother, and I thank Aunt Charlotte for making the introduction," I replied in English, looking at Hathor as she stared at my mother.

"My sister introduced you to this lowly girl?"

"While I am not a royal, I do not think I can be considered lowly, Your Majesty," Hathor spoke back to her in German. "Also, my parents have seen very well to my education, so if you would like to speak in a language I cannot understand, I would suggest Spanish."

I snorted a little bit, and had to bite down on my own lip at a look from my mother.

"How good of you to be so accomplished, Lady Hathor. However, it seems my sister has made a mistake. My son is a prince, and therefore he shall be wed to a princess."

"Mother—"

"Your Majesty, with all due respect, I believe no princess would marry him, due to your decision to banish him. And it must be said that *our* queen makes no mistakes. She chose me, as she believes me best suited for him, and I thank her most graciously."

All of a sudden, I was hungry again. I lifted my apple, leaning back on the pillow as my mother rose to her feet slowly.

"In the education your parents gave you, did they not see to it that you watched your manner of speaking, young lady?"

"Yes, they did, Your Majesty, and if I were in Malrovia, I would be greatly mindful. But this is *England*; this is the palace of Her Majesty Queen Charlotte, and we both are her guests. Who can be fearful, under her protection?"

My mother's nose flared. "How unfortunate that this is not Queen Charlotte's son, then, but mine. You are aware of that, correct?"

"Of course, Your Majesty," she said graciously. "I know the names of all our queen's dear children. I would not mistake them for anyone else's."

"Good, then you should also be aware it is *my* choice whom my son marries."

"Is it not by permission of the monarch?"

"I am *his* queen."

"Forgive me, I presumed by your blacks that you were now the queen *mother*. Is that not correct?" Hathor looked to me, as now even I was too shocked to move during her mighty battle. "Are the customs different in your country, Wilhelm? In England, the king must give his blessing for marriage, and if he is indisposed, it falls upon the queen?"

"Yes, that is the custom there, too. So, if we were in my country—and we are not—then we would need my brother's or my sister-in-law's blessing."

"Ah, so it is as I thought." She smiled, and shifted her gaze back to my mother. "Do you have any other questions for me, Your Majesty?"

The doors opened once more. It was as if we were in a play: The scene was now two queens, a sick prince, and a young noble lady in one room. Heaven help me.

"Augusta, you are here. How . . . timely," my aunt said with the most amused smirk on her face as she looked between my mother and Hathor. There was no possibility she was only now finding out my mother had arrived. Had she been listening? "I see you have met Lady Hathor. Is she not a great beauty?"

"We consider great beauties in Malrovia better seen than heard, yet I have heard quite the mouthful from this one. Where did you find such a provoking creature, Charlotte?"

"Monthermer. Her father is the marquess. Let us speak over tea, you must be exhausted. Come along, August needs his rest."

My mother glared at Hathor as she turned to exit the room. "Well done—"

"Oh, dear!" Hathor sank to the floor once they were gone, dropping everything. She took a deep breath, raising her hand over her heart, her hazel eyes wide in terror. "Why did no one tell me she was here?"

I laughed. "What happened to your courage all of a sudden? You stood unmoved toe to toe with her, and now you are terrified when she is gone?"

"Do not laugh at me! I had no choice, you know the words come out of me before I can truly stop myself. And I could not just ignore her, when I knew she was speaking of me. Then I could not simply stop speaking, or else it would have been worse. Papa says if you end up in a fight, you must see it through, if peace cannot prevail."

"Hathor, you are not breathing. Take a breath," I reminded her and she did so, still on the floor. "Good, now please come and sit beside me, since I cannot go to you."

"Wilhelm, what am I going to do? She hates me!" She frowned as she sat beside me. I took her hand.

"Did I not tell you before that it does not matter what she feels? Only what *I* feel, and I feel happy now that you are here."

"Well, that's good for you. But it is still important that your mother does not dislike me."

"Why?"

"Because she is your mother."

"I know, but she does not matter—"

"She does. Even if you despise her. She matters because she bore you. You would not exist without her. No person truly wants to be at odds with their parents. It hurts."

"What am I to do, if talking to her hurts as well?" I asked quietly, and she paused, her shoulders relaxing as our fingers played together. "Hathor, you are right: No person wishes to be at odds with their parents. But some simply are, as I am. She is strong-willed, and so am I. There is no remedy for it. You mustn't let it bother you."

She nodded to me. "Did she at least apologize to you? For all that happened."

"She did not, nor will she. Instead, she did as she is accustomed to doing: She gave orders. Queens apologize only to kings."

"So, what now?"

"Now you stay close to my side, so she does not poison you."

Her eyes widened and her mouth fell open. "Would she do such a thing? That is a bit drastic, do you not think?"

Again I laughed. She truly was the sun to me. All of my soul brightened at the sight of her.

29

Hathor

I was not allowed to stay the night at the palace as I had previously. Though I wanted to, especially when Wilhelm started to feel pain again and his doctors began to give him medicine. I stayed until he fell back asleep, as late as I could possibly stay, before taking my leave. However, before I could go, I was summoned by Queen Augusta, and I could feel the nerves racing to my heart once again. When I entered, she was seated across from my queen—which meant I now had two queens to face. I had barely gotten used to dealing with one.

"Your Majesties." I curtsied to them both again.

"Lady Hathor, I've been informed of your great care for my son. I thank you for that."

"Of course, Your Majesty," I said, waiting for the second part.

"You clearly have a strong and clear wit, and I'm willing to make use of such gifts," Queen Augusta said, but it made me wary, for I was sure she did not like me enough to concede so easily.

"Thank you, ma'am."

"Good. Now, as you know, my husband, the former king, is dead. Do you know what is to happen next?"

"A new king will be crowned."

"Yes, Wilhelm's brother; has he spoken of him?"

"He has," I said, glancing to Queen Charlotte, hoping she'd give me some clue. She merely sipped her tea slowly.

"Frederick was not born with the greatest strength, but he is very sharp in mind, and I have no doubt he shall make a great king. However, he is still very much in need of help, and the only person whom he can truly trust to aid him is his brother, Wilhelm. So, he will need to leave with me as soon as possible. Do you understand?"

"I fear I will need further clarity on what you want from me, Your Majesty."

"I want you to tell him to leave with me."

"He does not wish to."

"Of course not. He's had a great deal of fun throughout the years; youth is like that. But it's time he becomes the prince he was born to be. Since you care about him, you ought to want that as well."

"I want whatever Wilhelm wants."

"How sweet she is, sister." She smiled, though her eyes did not carry it. "And how naïve. Princes do not know what they want. It is a side effect of having so few choices since birth. They need to be told. And sadly, he will not listen to me—but he cares for you, and you care for him. You would not wish him to lose his inheritance and title and position, and protection—"

"Does that not all come from the king?" Oh no—I interrupted her.

"Ah, that comment again. Frederick is my son; he shall listen to me. And if I return, telling him that his brother has been misled and beguiled by some little noble girl after his title, then I am sure he too will see the necessity of cutting him off completely. Wilhelm thinks I abandoned him. He does not know that all these years it was my coin, my letters, that got him entrance throughout Europe. It was me who funded his life. My sister merely took credit—something she is very good at," she sneered, looking over to Queen Charlotte, who was still taking the longest sip of tea, unbothered by her.

"You are saying if I do not force Wilhelm to return with you, you will cut him off and leave him to fend for himself here? And the queen will allow it?"

"My sister's government would not like to make an enemy out of ours, now, would they? Princes are not just people; they are branches of a nation, sweet girl. And you would not wish him to suffer further humiliation and poverty because of your little dreams to be a princess, would you?"

"I assume he would have to return without me?"

"Yes. This engagement is not suitable. I understand my sister sought to help him settle in his ways, and it was difficult, considering his time away from our court. However, things will change now. He must return to his place, and you to yours. Your queen and I are not heartless, of course, and will see to it that you are married to the very best of society. No one will dare speak ill of you. So, Lady Hathor, I must ask you to *please* step aside and allow my son to finally be honored as he should have been."

I inhaled deeply, exhaled harshly, and said, "No."

"What?" she gasped out.

"I will not step aside, Your Majesty. Not unless Prince Wilhelm asks me to do so himself, and even then, I would have to challenge him to a duel for the sake of my reputation."

"Ha!" Queen Charlotte laughed so hard, she actually had to cover her lips with her hand.

"You claim to care about him, and yet you will see him ruined?" Queen Augusta snapped, sitting on the edge of the chair now. "You will see him stripped of all that is owed to him?"

"Yes. If the queen's hands are tied due to politics, I am quite sure my family will help him. Just as you care for your children, my family cares for me. So, my papa will most likely increase my dowry, so it is enough to live on, and we have other properties; I'm sure he'd give one to me. If we are shunned by society because of that, it is fine. My family will simply leave society. Luckily, I have a large enough family that I will not be bored. I do worry for my younger siblings' marriage prospects, but I am sure something can be worked out, as Father has a great many loyal friends that would not see us so truly ostracized—"

"Lady Hathor!"

I jumped at the sound of her voice. "Yes, Your Majesty?"

"Do I look as though I am joking with you?"

"No, Your Majesty, you seem very serious, as am I."

Her head whipped to her sister. "What is the matter with this girl? Did you not say she was reasonable?"

"Her reasoning is sound to me. I am surprised such a young girl can be so quick in wit, stubborn, and persevering. I wonder who taught her that," Queen Charlotte said, and I had to hang my head to hide my smile. Did she always know this would happen? Was that why she chose me? She knew I would be able to speak to her sister like this?

"Whoever her teacher was, they clearly lacked refinement," Queen Augusta said. "Have you ever been an enemy to a queen, Lady Hathor?"

"No, ma'am, I've only ever read about evil queens in storybooks. Fortunately, I have never met any in real life. I hope to remain so blessed."

"Evil queens?" she repeated, and then looked back at her sister. "Is she calling me evil?"

"No, sister, I believe she is talking about books she's read, not you; she would never. That would be rude, and no young lady under my care would be so ill-mannered."

"Lady Hathor, whom do you consider to be an evil queen? Surely not a mother looking out for her son?"

"Any queen who works against love and not for it, Your Majesty, is usually deemed evil in books."

"And you believe yourself in love with my son?"

"I do not believe. I know I am."

"And how do you know?"

"I do not know how to tell you what I feel. Or convince you of my heart. I love him and because of that I am working to hold my tongue before you."

"This is you holding your tongue?"

"Yes, Your Majesty."

"I cannot believe it. What would you say if you were allowed to speak freely? If I were not Prince Wilhelm's mother?"

I was silent.

"Oh, do not hold back now. Speak. That is an order."

I was insane, surely. I was mad. But I did so. "If you were not a queen, if you were not his mother, I would tell you to apologize."

"I beg your pardon. Apologize to whom?"

"To your son, for banishing him after he fought to protect you, for being so cold. Leaving money and calling in favors does not redeem that. My mama says we children should think more of our parents, and I try. I cannot imagine what a hard position you must have been in. How you must have suffered, torn between being a mother, a wife, and a queen. I have learned that being royal is unforgiving and suffocating. I know that women have little power against their husbands, and none at all against kings. I understand it all, but nevertheless, a mother should never be too proud to apologize. No matter how old we children are, we need to hear it. That is the only way we can forgive you. Wilhelm found out his father died, and he could not feel anything. My heart hurts for him. I cannot fathom how much pain it takes before you feel nothing, but it must be a lot. Each time he speaks of home, he is in pain. Why would anyone wish to return to that? Even if I were not here, he would not return. I am sure of it. Because you have not truly apologized to him. It seems so little, but it means so much." I realized my voice had gotten too high and that my words were a little too direct. So, I quickly added, "That is what I would say if I were not holding my tongue, Your Majesty."

She was silent.

So silent I could hear my own breathing.

"Lady Hathor, that is all. You may retire for the evening," Queen Charlotte said.

I curtsied and quickly left, before I lost my head.

Wilhelm

It was dark when I awoke, which is why the sight of my mother dressed in black, standing by the window, nearly caused my heart to sink in terror.

"Mother, it is evening. Must you wear black even now?" I grumbled, rubbing my eyes to adjust to the dim light coming in from the moon.

"What do you see in that girl?" she asked, still looking out the window. I had no idea why she and my aunt did this so often.

"Mother, I am in no mood to talk about this—"

"I do not care. Tell me, of all women, why have you chosen her? Were you not against marrying?"

"Who told you that? Were you spying on me?"

"Do not answer my questions with questions; it is vexing," she snapped. "Make me understand why her, or I will not leave."

"I cannot make you understand it. I barely understand it myself. For the first time I can ever remember, I am happy with someone. She frustrates me one moment and makes me laugh the next. She is very proudly and boldly herself. She takes my side, no matter how wrong I am; she does not care. Yet at the same time, she does not allow herself to be bullied by anyone, myself included."

"So, she is very much unlike me."

I frowned at that. "I merely meant she is like a whirlwind of life and fun. I cannot answer beyond that."

"I have a proposition."

"What are you talking about, and can it wait until the morning—"

"I am talking about your Lady Hathor."

"What about her?"

"If you promise to return home with me, I shall give my blessing to this marriage."

I rolled my eyes. "Mother, I am marrying her whether you give your blessing or not."

"And how shall you provide for her?" I did not answer, as I had no answer. "Exactly. Do you know she said she was willing to provide for you?"

"She what?"

"Apparently, she is so in love with you, she's willing to take as much as she can from her father in dowry. So, I guess your assessment is right. She is bold, daring, loyal, and a bit self-serving. I see why you both like her." She huffed, turning back to me. "But luckily, I know you to be proud, and your ego would not allow you to live off her dowry alone. You will want your inheritance."

"Not if it costs me my freedom."

"Do not be ridiculous. You have never had freedom, none of us have. Freedom is for peasants. We are bound by higher things. No matter how far you travel, you will need us, and we will need you. Your brother needs you. The moment your father died, everyone was bowing to him, and his very first order was for you to be escorted home safely. He was going to send an army if needed. That is how much he missed you."

"And yet I see you, and not an army," I said, though the truth was, I missed my brother too. We could never be close because of our father. But even when Father insulted and berated him, he never took it out on me. He never hated me.

"I missed you, August," she said and I frowned.

"Mother, please do not—"

"This is the only time you shall hear an apology from me. Do not interrupt me."

An apology? I did not believe it could happen. "Go on."

"I was cold to you and your brother because your father liked to break things I cared about or use them against me. I did it for so long that I did not know how to stop. He stole everything from me . . . even the love of my children. The day you stood up to him, I was so grateful—and so scared he'd punish you worse. So, I banished you, hoping to keep as much distance between you both as possible. It was my small way of protecting you, too. Do you know he never struck me again after that?"

"I did not know that." I hung my head.

"I think he feared you. No one had made him feel so small and weak before." She laughed. "He was sure I was hiding you somewhere close. He'd question me as to your whereabouts, and I'd pretend not to know or care. I worried he'd search for you himself, but he never did. I didn't know why, until the day he was shot. When he realized he was dying, he whispered into my ear, *Stop calling him August; Wilhelm is a good name, he'll use it better than I did. He's a good boy, that Wilhelm.* Those were his last words. You were his last thought. I'm not sure it brings much comfort, all things considered."

My throat ached.

"Mother, it's late and I wish to—"

"I am sorry, Wilhelm," she said. My lips cracked to the side. Covering my mouth with my hand, I took a deep breath. "I am so sorry that such a good boy as you ended up with such bad parents as us. I pray you do much better."

I hung my head as my eyes stung. What was the matter with me? Tears? At my age? Fuck.

"This proposition . . . do I have to go back permanently?"

"I would like that, but I doubt you will. So instead, I ask that you help your brother settle, and assure the government you are always ready to be called if needed."

"Hathor—"

"You will have to marry her before you leave."

"What? Did you not say you wished to leave in three days— now two?"

"Yes. However, it is not safe to be traveling in a large party, so she will have to remain here. And truthfully, I fear she will be a distraction. But I doubt either of you would like to wait until after you return to England. Your aunt will have you married secretly and quietly, since we are supposed to be in mourning. It will be done today. Will you be able to convince her?"

"Mother, she is a lady. She would want a grand wedding with—"

"Talk to her first. Convince her, if you need to. But we must hurry," was all she said before leaving.

I was sure that if I slept, I would wake up thinking it had all been a dream. So I did not sleep again. I sat up and waited . . . anxiously, for the first time.

It did not feel like it was such a long time. She came first thing in the morning. I knew it was her, because only she would think to knock.

"Enter."

The first thing she did was look around the corner for my mother.

I smirked. "She's not here."

"Thank goodness. I do not believe I am ready for another sparring session," she replied as she rushed over to me, nearly jumping onto the bed beside me. "Good morning, how are you? Did you sleep well?"

"Sort of. What about you? Did you sleep well?" I reached for her hand, and when she gave it, I kissed the back of it.

"Sort of," she mused back, and I was not sure what expression was on my face, but she seemed to perceive that something was amiss. Her tone became much more serious. "What is wrong?"

Again, I kissed her hand, this time on the inside of her palm. "Will you marry me?"

"Have I not already answered this question?"

"You have. But I am wondering if you will marry me today."

"What?"

"I must go tomorrow, with my mother. I will be back, I swear it. I would not dare leave you if it were not so important. There is much that needs to be done, and I cannot yet bring you with me—"

"All right."

I paused, confused. "What? All right?"

"Yes, all right, I shall marry you."

"Just like that?"

She giggled and nodded. "Again, I have already said yes before, so it is not hard to decide."

"Hathor, the wedding would happen today, as in *now*. Your family will not be there, and then I shall be forced to leave—"

"But you will return. If you wished to abandon me and planned never to return, you would not be seeking to marry me now, before you left. And I know you would not ask if it were not important." She lifted my hand and kissed it. "I trust you, because I love you."

"Will you forever shatter my mind and heart like this?" I whispered.

"It is only fair, since you chose to do the same to me."

Leaning in, I kissed her lips quickly. "Here is to a lifetime together, and the marriage of two of the most ridiculous people in England."

She grinned wide and nodded. "When the world finds out, they shall tell the most epic stories of Hathor and the prince."

"The prince and Lady Hathor?"

"I like my title better." She hopped up off the bed. "Now, where are we getting married?"

It did not matter where to me so long as the day ended with her as my wife.

30

Hathor

I used to have great expectations of my wedding day, of the type of dress I'd wear, the type of cake we would have. I did not expect my wedding to be in the palace, just after dawn—but that is when the royal carriage came for me, a servant saying the queen wished to see me immediately. I was wearing the most modest of dresses and no jewelry. I had left home as quickly as possible, thinking something was the matter with Wilhelm. Instead, I arrived to him asking me if we could get married now. I'm sure he did not expect to be so casual, in trousers, a clean nightshirt, and a long jacket. Meanwhile, we were in a chapel filled with sacred gold.

None of this was how I dreamt it, but it was altogether perfect. After all, who else could say they were married by the archbishop before two queens, and Queen Charlotte's fourth daughter (who was apparently good at keeping a secret), along with Sir Darrington as my witness.

"Do you, Lady Hathor Du Bell, take Prince Wilhelm Augustus Karl von Edward of Malrovia to be your lawfully wedded husband, before God, king, and country?" the archbishop said, keeping things brief, as he was ordered to.

"I do. As I love you," I said, staring at Wilhelm. He smiled.

"And do you, Prince Wilhelm Augustus Karl von Edward of Malrovia, take Lady Hathor Du Bell to be your lawfully wedded wife, before God, king, and country?"

"I do. As I love you," he replied, and I smiled back.

"Then with the power vested in me, I now pronounce you husband and wife. Your Highness, with a kiss, you seal this covenant."

"Gladly," Wilhelm said, moving slightly to me, making me giggle as his lips touched mine. He would have kept kissing me, if not for someone coughing. "We must continue later, wife."

"Very well, husband."

"I must advise against that," Sir Darrington said quickly, bringing the wheelchair over to him, but Wilhelm swatted it away with his cane.

"At least let us have today, all of you," he said, taking my hand. "My wife and I will be busy."

Each time he said *wife*, I grinned. "Come on, I shall take you away with the wheelchair."

"I do not want the chair," he frowned.

"A good husband listens to his wife," I reminded him, taking the chair from Sir Darrington. He gave me a pitiful look, and I gave him one back.

"Fine." He sighed, taking a seat.

"Where shall we go?" I said, already pushing him down the aisle.

"Anywhere but a church—I fear to speak freely here."

"And where can you speak freely?"

"Our bedroom, of course."

I laughed, and quickly pushed him there.

I could not believe it.

Just like that, I was married.

And I had not, and could not, tell my family. I could only imagine how angry they would feel. Damon was right: I really was a troublemaker, even when I wasn't trying to be. But I could not be sad. I was far too glad to finally be his wife.

"The only thing that would make this day more perfect would be both of us in bed, making love to each other," he said when we'd returned to his room. He lifted the back of my hand and kissed it. "I'm sorry it had to be done like this. When I return, we can make it a much bigger spectacle, I promise."

I placed my hands on either side of his face. "So long as you go and come back safely, I shall not care."

"You are too good to me," he said as I helped him sit back on the bed.

"It's only because you are injured. When you are recovered, I shall go back to behaving stubbornly against you."

"Is that so?" His hand reached around, grabbing my bottom. I jumped, surprised. "I am prepared to deal with that in various ways."

"Really?"

"Really," he said.

"What are these various ways?"

"If you undress, I shall show you one now."

"Wilhelm! The doctor said we are not to engage in such activities until you are completely well."

"I am well enough, I assure you. Can you not see?" he stated, and I glanced down to the bulge in his breeches.

"You will need to control yourself; you were greatly hurt," I replied, kneeling down before him to help him take off his boots.

"Your current position does not inspire control," he muttered.

"What?"

"Nothing." He sighed dramatically before lying back on the bed. "At the very least come lie next to me."

"That is the least a wife can do, I suppose."

"Would it be much of an imposition if I asked you to lie naked?"

"Wilhelm!"

He chuckled. "Surely you cannot blame me for asking, since I do not know how long it shall be before I am graced with the sight of your divine beauty again. Have pity on me. I am but a mere man at your mercy."

I tried not to laugh, and I could not help but do as he asked. Before him, I began to strip, layer by layer, until I stood before him utterly naked. I allowed him to look at me for only a minute before dashing quickly into the bed beside him, pulling the sheets up to my neck.

"Now you are shy?"

"I am not shy; it is merely unfair that I am the only one so . . . undressed."

"True, I shall rectify the situation at once," he replied, sitting up to take off his clothing as well. Though he needed some help to avoid reopening his wounds or undoing the dressing of his bandage. When he was comfortable against the pillows, he pulled me closer to him.

I wished to stay like this forever. I did not wish him to leave. But at least I knew for certain that we were together. We had won; our love story had won.

"Now, how am I supposed to bear you leaving?" I whispered gently.

"I wonder the same," he replied as he stroked his hand down my back. "I shall be back as soon as humanly possible."

"You must miss me horribly, but not so much that it ruins your health."

He chuckled and nodded. "Any other orders?"

I sat up and grabbed his face, forcing him to look at me. "No more drawing other women. From now on, the only lady's naked form you should ever see is mine."

"That is reasonable." He pinched my nipple, making me

jump and giggle, but he held me. "May I dare ask to draw this form?"

"You shall get your answer when you return."

"For that reason alone, I must discover a way to fly back." He kissed my neck, seeming to inhale the scent of me.

He kissed from my neck up the side of my face. "Wilhelm, we can't—"

His lips interrupted my words, his tongue already in my mouth, licking mine. That familiar heat spread through me. My eyes closed and my mouth opened wider for him. My body moved closer to him. All of me wanted him.

He took hold of my waist and pulled me as close to him as our bodies would allow. I could feel his manhood, standing tall, and brushing against me.

"Tell me to stay," he whispered when our lips parted, cupping the side of my face.

"I cannot," I whispered back, holding on to his hand. "I fear I cannot win another battle with your mother. She has accommodated us enough. You must go."

"Shall you not miss me terribly?" he teased, though he did not seem to realize the gutting feelings it stirred within me. And I did not desire to cry; I'd cried far too much this year as it was.

"I shall not think of it now when you are right before me," I replied, kissing his lips quickly.

"I love you, Hathor."

"As I love you, Wilhelm."

Neither of us slept. We spoke of nothing important. We laughed about nothing funny. We prayed time would slow, so we would never have to let each other go.

Epilogue

Hathor

"He takes after you," I whispered as I pinched the little brown cheeks of the baby boy before me in his basket. "Evander must be pleased."

"No matter what he looked like, Evander would have been pleased," Aphrodite said as she moved to lift him up. The boy clung to her happily. Since we'd arrived this morning, I had yet to hear him cry or fuss. Instead, he grew silent with all the new faces around him. Another thing he'd taken from his mother. "You should have heard the names he wanted to choose. You'd think he was naming a future king. I had to beg for something subtle."

"The name Antoninus Charles Maximilian Eagleman is subtle for a baby? Isn't Antoninus the name of one of the five good emperors?"

She sat carefully in the chair by the fire. "It's also the name of an ancient philosopher. And he can carry a nickname like Antony or Tony."

"Oh, dear God, not Tony. That is an awful name for a future duke," I replied, taking a seat across from her as she pulled out her breast from the top of her dress to feed him. Watching his little mouth latch on to her made me stiffen. "Does that hurt? You did not wish to get a wet nurse?"

She giggled. "Mama nursed us, and we turned out splendidly. As such, I shall do the same. But yes, it does hurt some-times."

"Why must everything with women hurt? It is unfair," I replied as I leaned back in the chair, grateful for the heat, as it was the coldest winter I had ever seen.

"What else has hurt you? Your monthly? You never had pains before."

I did not mean that, and I did not want to think of what I did mean, so I just offered a smile. "Never mind me, I am merely being silly."

Her head tilted to the side as she patted the bum of her son. "Everyone is right: You are very much changed."

"What do you mean? I have changed?"

"Yes, you."

"If anyone has changed, it is you. You are a mother—well, that is incorrect, I would not wish your daughter to hear me and feel affronted. You have given birth; that is a change. How does your daughter fare with her new sibling. Well, I hope?"

"Very well. She wishes to check on him any moment she can. And I will not let you escape from my conversation."

"I am not seeking to escape anything, I assure you."

"Hathor," she said softly with a sad smile, pity or sorrow in her eyes. "I know I have been very much absent in your life over the last few months. And so much has occurred for you in that time. But know I am here, if you wish to speak on it all. I do, unfortunately, have experience in these things."

I stared at her effort in both love and amusement. She, like everyone else, believed I had been abandoned, as it had been five months since Wilhelm left. There had been no letters, and no more summonses to the palace. Instead, there were only rumors—a great many rumors. It had become so bad in Lon-don that Papa and Mama quickly returned to the castle, no more than two days after. The staff had barely finished unpacking before we were leaving once again. But that still did not help—the rumors reached us in Monthermer. We received no Christmas ball invitations this year, since many believed I'd ruined myself with a prince. Aphrodite luckily had given birth, giving us a reason to go and spend Christmas with her. Verity and Sir Darrington would be arriving tonight as well.

"Hathor?"

"Hmm?"

"You are not saying anything, which is very strange for you. Mama and Papa are worried."

"Mama and Papa are always worried. They've always wished me to calm myself. And yet now, because I am not crying and throwing a fit, they are concerned still."

"Because crying would be normal. You have dealt with a lot."

"As have you, Aphrodite. It was not so long ago that all of society was talking about the chaos at Everely."

"You are changing the subject again. And you know that was different. I did not have to struggle with it alone, as I had . . ." Her voice trailed off.

"You had your husband?" I finished for her.

"Forgive me. I do not wish to pry—"

"Then don't, Aphrodite. It is all right. I am all right, and pleased to know you are well."

She pouted like a child. "It scares me when you speak like this. Where is my baby sister who would not give me a moment of peace and envied me greatly, wanting to know all my affairs?"

"She grew up, and realized your affairs are not my affairs. Young ladies cannot stay silly forever."

"But silliness is part of your charm."

I giggled. "It is, isn't it? Luckily, I was blessed with a great many other attributes. So, fear not, I shall think of something else to concern you all. Maybe I shall mock your horrid sewing skills, for what on earth is *that*?"

I pointed to the deformed doll on the ground with several poorly sewed arms.

"Do not make fun of my son's bear!"

"That is supposed to be a bear? In what land do bears look like that? It is all right not to be good at everything. You could have simply bought one for him, or had one made."

"Since you seem so knowledgeable, why don't you make one for him?"

"Me?"

She looked down at her son. "Sweetheart, your aunt Hathor is going to make you the most spectacular doll ever, with her own hands."

"No. No. No. Do not tell him that. He shall be expecting it, and I have no idea how to make a doll."

"Oh, but you can judge one."

"Yes, all that requires is my eyes, not my fingers."

She grinned. "You would disappoint him? Silva made him shoes on her own. Devana wrote him music and Abena brought him—well, she came with candy he can't eat."

"When were gifts given? I do not remember this."

"No, you have been lost in thought, like I once was after Evander left."

I sighed and had to shake my head. "You will not let this go, will you?"

"I am a wife, a mother, and a big sister. I am no longer allowed to let anything go."

"Mama would be proud."

"Were you two you speaking of me?"

We both jumped at the sight of our mother at the door, her brown eyes looking over us both skeptically.

"No, Mama," Aphrodite and I said in unison, which made her eyebrow rise. I quickly moved to get up.

"I shall leave you two alone while I go for a walk."

"A walk? It is snowing outside, Hathor!" Mama called out to me.

"Then I shall walk inside!" I did not wish to stand by as they both questioned me about my feelings. I barely had enough energy to face one of them alone. I knew they were worried, and I truly tried my best to keep up my spirits for their sake. The more I tried, the more exhausted it made me. The first day after he left was the hardest, because I had been so happy moments earlier. We had been married, we'd given ourselves to each other, and then he was gone. It was as if I'd been in winter ever since, seeking to stay in bed and sleep until spring came. But I could not do that; I had told my parents he promised to return, but when the weeks turned to months and there was not a single letter, I could tell they grew skeptical. But no one said anything. Instead, they awkwardly asked if I was all right, multiple times a day.

"Sweetheart?"

I turned back down the hall to see my father and Evander, dressed in their hunting attire, both of their hair wet and Father's nose and ears a bit red with cold. They walked side by side, their valets not far behind them.

"Welcome back, Papa. How was the hunt?"

"Splendid. Your father is an excellent shot. Is that not so, Evander?" He grinned and outstretched his hand for me.

"Yes, sir, I believe you to be the best in the county."

"Evander, you need not humor him so; you are already married to my sister." I smiled, walking over and linking arms with him. "Papa is known to be a horrible shot."

"I'll have you know I caught a massive fallow deer that shall feed us all for Christmas."

I gave him a look. "And Evander did not help in the slightest?"

"I was nothing but a spectator," Evander lied, grinning as he did.

"See how little faith you have in me?" Papa grinned. "We are going to see it weighed, would you like to come?"

I cringed, my nose bunching up. "No. I'd rather not see the creature before he's properly prepared for Christmas dinner."

He chuckled. "Very well. If you change your mind, we shall be down at the stables. You are all right, correct? Why are you alone?"

"Yes, Papa. I am walking indoors, since the snow prevents me from taking the fresh air. Enjoy your day," I said, heading back down the hall in the opposite direction.

When I heard them start walking as well, I turned back to see Papa and Evander talking, laughing as they went. It made me jealous. I was no longer of jealous of Aphrodite, but now covetous of all the moments denied to me by Wilhelm's absence. I wished to see Wilhelm also go on hunts with Papa, but I had no idea when such a thing would come to pass. I was merely walking around aimlessly until I grew tired, but I could not go to my room to lie down, either. The maids would tell Mama, and then Mama would come check on me, followed by all my sisters, Silva, and then Damon. No one in this family allowed me to sulk in peace. It would have been funny, if it did not happen so often.

"Hathor? Where are you going? Are you all right?"

I turned around to see . . . Silva and Damon behind me.

For the love of all heaven and earth!

"Yes, I am fine. Are you both on your way to see Father's fallow?" I asked, trying my best not to be annoyed.

"Father's what? He caught a fallow?" Damon looked at me skeptically.

"Yes, apparently, and he's quite proud. They've gone to see it weighed."

"Why don't we all go see it together?" Silva asked me.

"Thank you, but I am walking—"

"Walking to where? Outside?" Damon asked.

"No, inside. I am walking about the house."

"Like a ghost or the mad? That is eerie, Hathor." Damon frowned, making his wife smack his arm lightly. "What?"

"Would you like company?" Silva questioned, ignoring him.

"I would not. In fact, I would prefer if everyone did not so closely watch over me. I am truly fine." I was not, but I was not as greatly pitiful as they thought. "Enjoy your day."

I quickly left them, and figured the only place I would be left undisturbed was the study. I made my way toward the painting I'd started last night, but I could tell it had been tampered with. I normally covered my work as it was in progress and pinned the cloth down, but the pins had not been replaced correctly.

I let out a deep sigh. It could have been any one of them; they were all so nosy. Lifting the sheet up, I stared into a canvas painted in one color: blue. There was nothing else. I did not know what else to do. I had painted the color of his eyes, and that was all I could manage. I sat before it and stared, hoping and seeking to think, but nothing came to mind.

I did not know how long I sat there. Eventually, there was a knock at the door.

"Enter?"

Bernice entered. "I was told to inform you that Lady Verity and Sir Darrington have arrived."

I glanced to the window. Somehow, it had become dark already. Time was so odd in periods of melancholy; some days went by so slowly, and others, it was as if time sprinted forward.

"My lady?"

"I shall be down in a moment," I said gently, as I knew I would need time to build up my energy or be subjected to their onslaught of worry as well.

When the door closed, I took a few deep breaths and patted my own cheeks to bring life back into them. I tried smiling over and over again, but it didn't work. Repeatedly, my face fell.

"Come on, Hathor, come on. Gather yourself," I whispered, squeezing my own hand. "There is nothing to worry about. He's coming back. Everything will be well. I am sure of it. Have faith."

Nodding once to myself, I covered the painting and then brushed my hair back with my hands. Adjusting the pearls around my neck and dusting off my dress, I walked out with my head lifted.

It took me a few moments before I reached the grand stairs, where I heard muttering.

"Verity, I hope you have come with a magnificent gift for me or I . . ." When I turned the corner to go down the main stairs, my voice simply ceased. I could not speak, because I was not sure I was truly awake. I had to have fallen asleep in the study some time ago, and now I was dreaming. For he could not be there.

Wilhelm could not possibly be at the bottom of the stairs, dressed as finely as any man could be, in an embroidered coat of green and gold with three stars upon his epaulets, his brown hair slightly shorter than I remembered but his blue eyes even more piercing. He was all I could see, and his gaze never left me.

It was not possible.

When he opened his mouth to speak, I lifted the skirt of my dress, turned around, and ran as fast as I could. I ran right back into the study, slamming the door shut behind me, eyes wide as I tried to breathe.

Maybe Damon was right.

Maybe I had gone mad.

Help! Someone please help! I am too young to be mad.

Wilhelm

Seeing her run from me left me sick. I feared this. Truly, it was my greatest apprehension as the weeks turned to months and still I could not go to her. I could not even write to her, and so I wondered often of her feelings toward me. Now I had my answer. Even if she did not hate me, she clearly did not wish to see me. But nevertheless, I had to see her. She was, after all, my wife. Without a second thought, I stepped forward, only for my path to be blocked by little Lady Abena, behind her Damon and Hector. I was sure once the rest of the house was informed I'd arrived, they would all appear as well.

"Why are you back again?" Abena snapped at me.

I reached out my hand to the side, my friend handing me the box of chocolates. Bending down, I offered them to her. "Before you give me a hard time, Lady Abena, remember how you lost the last time."

Her eyes narrowed and so did mine.

"Du Bells don't take bribes," Hector stated, but his sister walked up to me and snatched the box. "Abena!"

"Everyone says it is a boy's duty to carry the family name. I am a girl. So, I shall leave it to you all, good luck!" She quickly ran off her with her chocolates, and I tried not to laugh.

"Traitor!" Hector yelled after her, and then his brown eyes were on mine. "That shall not work on me!"

"Yes, I know. Hathor told me you are the most like your father. Which is why I bring several books from my brother's library in Malrovia. One is a brand-new book on maps of the known world, along with several newly established cities," I stated.

His eyes widened.

"It would not be considered a bribe, of course, because you'd one day have to return them to my brother, the king, eventually," I added.

He looked to Damon, who had just entered, and offered a smile. "You're the first son, it's strictly your duty to handle this. So, I shall wait with Abena."

Damon only shook his head as the boy ran off. "Do you mean to play the role of Father Christmas, Your Highness? Should I ponder on what you have you gotten me?"

"I will be happy to tell you, after I speak with Hathor," I said, not liking how much time was passing.

"You believe you will just be allowed access to my daughter once more?" came the marquess's voice, along with one other gentleman beside him. Next coming into the foyer was his wife, who I could only assume was Aphrodite, based on her appearance.

"Prince Wilhelm?" the marchioness spoke, shocked, then looked to her daughter. "Were you aware he was coming?"

She shook her head. "I do not even know him, Mama."

"Verity, Theodore, did you bring him?" She turned to the couple who had arrived only minutes before me, and who now stood off to the side quietly.

"No, Godmother, he arrived right behind us. We are just as shocked as you."

They all began talking, trying to discern how I came to be here. And it was a very long story, but right now, the only one I wished to speak to was Hathor. I was growing more and more anxious that she had not returned.

"Does Hathor know he is here?"

"She came down and then left."

"Oh no, I shall check on her—" her mother said, and started up the stairs.

"Lady Monthermer!" I yelled out, causing them all to freeze. Walking past Damon and toward the stairs, I looked up at her. "If you would, I believe I shall see her alone first."

The duke stepped forward. "Sir, you have come uninvited. Prince or not, it is disrespectful. This is not your home—"

"You are correct, sir, it is not my home—but she is my wife."

Silence.

They all were silent as I walked over to her sister. "Lady Aphrodite, I presume? Will you be so kind as to escort me to where she is?"

"Wife? You married my sister?" she asked me.

"Yes, before my mother, Queen Augusta, and Queen Charlotte. Sir Darrington was her witness. I will explain later, but first I must make sure Hathor is all right. So, will you escort me, please?"

She glanced at her mother for a moment, who just slowly nodded. "This way. She is often in the study, I believe."

As I walked, there was only silence, which made the thundering of my heart grow louder. I did not even know what to say to her. I feared the expression she would make, or the words she would speak. But I was more afraid of never seeing her.

"Hathor, you have a visitor." Her sister knocked on the door, but there was no answer. So she knocked again. "Hathor?"

She opened it, and when she did, the very first thing I saw was Hathor on the floor. I nearly pushed Aphrodite out of the way to rush to her.

"Hathor!" I grabbed her arms to lift her up, checking to see where she was wounded, but she just gasped and stared back at me shocked. "Are you hurt?"

"Am I still dreaming?" she questioned.

"What?"

"You're here?" She reached up and poked my face, and then pulled my cheek. "You are really here?"

"Yes, I am really here, why are you on the *floor*?"

"Stop yelling at me!" she yelled. "I was resting!"

"Who rests on the floor?"

"Where else am I to rest? There is no bed in here."

"Why would you come in here to rest at all? Did you not see me?"

"I did see you. I thought I was going mad and ended up back here. Then the world was spinning, so I lay down on the floor to rest. Now you are here, yelling at me. In a tone I do not appreciate, by the way."

I exhaled the deep breath in my chest, speaking softer. "I was nervous you were hurt."

"Why would I be hurt?"

I reached up and brushed the curls from her face. "I do not know. I have not seen you in some time."

"It has been five months, not just some time," she muttered slowly.

"You are angry with me. Forgive me. I did not wish to be gone for so long. It took much more effort and time settling my brother than expected."

"It was not that long."

"Oh, so you did not miss me?"

She shrugged. "Only slightly."

"I see. Then I shall go, and return when you are aching for me," I replied, getting up, only for her to grab me back, hugging me tightly.

Grinning, I stood stiff. "This is a very intense embrace for 'only slightly.'"

"You know I missed you terribly. I missed you so much that I am scared to believe you are actually here."

I turned back toward her, wrapping my arms around her waist. "I am here, and I will not leave without you ever again."

Before I could kiss her, I heard Abena call from behind us.

"Verity told me to tell you to hurry and come down before Papa kills her husband!"

We both turned back to the girl, whose mouth was covered in chocolate.

"Why would Papa kill Sir Darrington?" Hathor asked her.

"Because he knew you got married. You're in trouble!" she giggled and then took another bite.

"You told them!" she yelled at me.

"It was the only way I could come see you. They were guarding the stairs like an army."

She placed her head on my chest. "That was the worst way to tell them. They are going to kill us. Well, mostly you. Mama will throw me into a cellar with pots to clean."

I smiled. "Do you want to escape and take your chances in the snow?"

She giggled, lifting her head to look at me. She said, "I am laughing, so you must really be here."

"Have you not laughed since I left?"

"Not truly."

"Nor have I," I whispered, kissing her forehead, and she closed her eyes, holding on to me.

"You're taking forever. What do I tell Verity?" Abena called again.

"Little bug, I will throw you out the window!" Hathor separated from me and snapped at her.

"Now, is that the demeanor of a princess?" Abena mocked her.

"You are right. Wilhelm, is it possible to get guards to throw her out the window?"

"I do have guards outside that will happily do as you ask, my love," I said, turning to face Abena as well.

"You two are perfect together: You're both monstrous."

"Shall I take my chocolate back?"

"Mama! Hathor and her prince are bullying me!" she yelled as she ran away.

"I shall show her a bully." Hathor laughed and looked back to me. "Are you prepared to face them?"

Reaching over, I brought her lips to mine.

God, it had been far too long. My tongue entered her mouth, and I did not wish to stop. But I had to. Resting my forehead on hers, I nodded.

"I love you. So long as you are with me, I can face anything, wife," I whispered in the space between our lips.

"I love you, husband." She lifted my hands and kissed them. "Into the midst of the storm we go . . ."

". . . fear not the waves, the thunder, the breaking of ships, or the creatures below, for I am with you, and thus you are always safe."

I swore it.

Now until the end of time I would dedicate my life not to kingdoms or even myself, but to her most magnificent smile.

For she was my sun, my sky, my air, my present and future.

She was everything.

She was Hathor.

Acknowledgments

To all the amazing people who helped me craft this series: Shauna, Natanya, Mae, Jordan, Molly, as well as every other editor and designer, thank you all for the remarkable care, support, and joy you put into the Du Bells. I am truly grateful to each and every last one of you. It has been so wonderful seeing this work come to life, and it would not be possible without you.

Also, to my fans: I see your messages, and I am honored by them. Thank you for loving Aphrodite, Verity, Hathor, and me so much.

COURTESY OF THE AUTHOR

J. J. McAvoy has written numerous independently published novels that have been translated into six languages and are international bestsellers. Her historical romance series featuring the Du Bells includes *Aphrodite and the Duke, Verity and the Forbidden Suitor,* and *Hathor and the Prince.* She is active and delightful on social media.

jjmcavoy.com
Twitter: @JJMcAvoy
Instagram: @jjmcavoy

About the Type

This book was set in Berling. Designed in 1951 by Karl-Erik Forsberg (1914–95) for the type foundry Berlingska Stilgjuteri AB in Lund, Sweden, it was released the same year in foundry type by H. Berthold AG. A classic old-face design, its generous proportions and inclined serifs make it highly legible.